The Eye

Cassandra Jones
Southwest Cougars Year 2, Age 13

Southwest Cougars Year 2: Age 13

The Extraordinarily Ordinary Life of Cassandra Jones

Tamara Hart Heiner

paperback edition
copyright 2018 Tamara Hart Heiner
cover art by Tamara Hart Heiner

Also by Tamara Hart Heiner:
Perilous (WiDo Publishing 2010)
Altercation (WiDo Publishing 2012)
Deliverer (Tamark Books 2014)
Priceless (WiDo Publishing 2016)

Goddess of Fate:
Inevitable (Tamark Books 2013)
Entranced (Tamark Books 2017)

Kellam High:
Lay Me Down (Tamark Books 2016)
Reaching Kylee (Tamark Books 2016)

The Extraordinarily Ordinary Life of Cassandra Jones:
Walker Wildcats Year 1: Age 10 (Tamark Books 2015)
Walker Wildcats Year 2: Age 11 (Tamark Books 2016)
Southwest Cougars Year 1: Age 12 (Tamark Books 2017)

Tornado Warning (Dancing Lemur Press 2014)

Print Edition, License Notes:
This book is licensed for your personal enjoyment only. This book may not be resold or given away to other people. If you would like to share this book with another person, please purchase an additional copy for each recipient. If you're reading this book and did not purchase it, or it was not purchased for your use only, then please purchase your own copy. Thank you for respecting the hard work of this author.

This is a work of fiction. Names, characters, businesses, places, events and incidents are either the products of the author's imagination or used in a fictitious manner. Any resemblance to actual persons, living or dead, or actual events is purely coincidental.

Table of Contents

Episode 1: A Fresh Start
- CHAPTER ONE - Tree Huggers — 1
- CHAPTER TWO - Competitive Edge — 10
- CHAPTER THREE - Hot Dishwashers — 19
- CHAPTER FOUR - Keeper of the Ashes — 27
- CHAPTER FIVE - Weakling — 36
- CHAPTER SIX - Upward Start — 45
- CHAPTER SEVEN - Keep the Old — 49

Episode 2: My Fair Lady
- CHAPTER EIGHT - Big Plans — 61
- CHAPTER NINE - Fortifying — 70
- CHAPTER TEN - Music Overload — 79
- CHAPTER ELEVEN - The Eyes Have It — 86
- CHAPTER TWELVE - Tricks and Treats — 95
- CHAPTER THIRTEEN - Little White Lies — 104

Episode 3: Falling Short
- CHAPTER FOURTEEN - Attitude Adjustment — 113
- CHAPTER FIFTEEN - Lunch Plans — 122
- CHAPTER SIXTEEN - Stood Up — 131
- CHAPTER SEVENTEEN - Discovering Truths — 141
- CHAPTER EIGHTEEN - Cold Start — 151
- CHAPTER NINETEEN - Emotional Overload — 160
- CHAPTER TWENTY - Forgotten — 169
- CHAPTER TWENTY-ONE - Christmas party — 176

Episode 4: Changing Game Plans
- CHAPTER TWENTY-TWO - Going Unsteady — 183
- CHAPTER TWENTY-THREE - Crossing the Line — 192
- CHAPTER TWENTY-FOUR - Too Much Stuffing — 200
- CHAPTER TWENTY-FIVE - Shown Up — 210
- CHAPTER TWENTY-SIX - Finding Light — 217
- CHAPTER TWENTY-SEVEN - Conspiracy — 227
- CHAPTER TWENTY-EIGHT - For the Love — 234
- CHAPTER TWENTY-NINE - Great Expectations — 242

Episode 5: Red Flags
- CHAPTER THIRTY - Worst Holiday Ever — 251
- CHAPTER THIRTY-ONE - Considering Promises — 261
- CHAPTER THIRTY-TWO - Birthday Blues — 270
- CHAPTER THIRTY-THREE - Fortunate Events — 278
- CHAPTER THIRTY-FOUR - Desperate Measures — 286
- CHAPTER THIRTY-FIVE - Grasping for Attention — 294
- CHAPTER THIRTY-SIX - Burglar — 304

Episode 6: Someone Special
- CHAPTER THIRTY-SEVEN - Dance Off ... 316
- CHAPTER THIRTY-EIGHT - Divisions and Splits ... 324
- CHAPTER THIRTY-NINE - Glances and Blushes ... 333
- CHAPTER FORTY - Popularity Calls ... 346
- CHAPTER FORTY-ONE - Free Pass ... 356
- CHAPTER FORTY-TWO - Casting Lots ... 367

Episode 1: A Fresh Start

CHAPTER ONE
Tree Huggers

The End.

Cassandra Jones settled back at the kitchen table, still gripping the pencil as tightly as she had while she wrote the last words to her book, feeling immensely pleased with herself. Done. This little book was finally done.

Little, ha. By the time she'd finished writing it, squishing her words onto the lined paper she'd folded in half to imitate a real book, she had over three hundred pages. While she had to admit there were times the plot wandered in her fictional adventure about four kidnapped girls, overall, it was a solid story.

"I'm done!" she shouted out into the living room for anyone to hear.

There was no answer, but she hadn't really expected any. School had been out for the summer only one week, and her siblings still gathered in front of the television downstairs every day until noon.

Cassie gathered the pages of her book in her hands and pushed away from the table. She ran to her mom's room, knocking on the door before bursting inside.

"What is it, Cassie?"

Mrs. Jones was awake, though deep shadows ringed her eyes and her hair was in disarray. She still had on her work uniform even though she'd come home half an hour ago from the breakfast shift at Wendy's. The buttery scent of biscuits and pancake syrup sifted about the room.

"I finished my book." Cassie waved it at her mom, feeling a bit guilty that her mom wasn't in bed sleeping. But that wasn't Cassie's fault, she reminded herself.

Mrs. Jones' face wreathed in a tired smile. "Good job, honey. Can I read it?"

She extended a hand, and Cassie pulled back. "Later. I'm going to finish typing it up and then I need to revise a bit. It's still a rough draft, you know." Cassie knew these terms from her seventh grade English class. Rough draft first, but then revise, revise, revise, proofread, and finally it would be a finished novel.

Mrs. Jones nodded. "Good idea." She gestured to the bed. "I'm going to take a nap. Will you get lunch for everyone?"

"Sure." Cassie would have without being asked. Her dad was at the soccer store after having done his morning paper route. She was the oldest of the four kids, and she knew it was her job to keep the household together while her parents tried to provide money for them.

She meandered out of the room, closing the doors behind her. Maybe she could get a few pages typed before everyone asked for lunch.

The computer was downstairs, in a room next to the den. Cassie sat down and turned it on, then pulled up the word document she'd been adding to little by little. She had about ten chapters typed up. Ten of thirty. She stretched her arms over her head and wiggled her fingers. She wasn't the fastest keyboarder, but she managed to hammer out two chapters before her youngest sister, Annette, wandered in almost an hour later.

"Cassie, I'm hungry," Annette said. Like a miniature Cassandra, she had brown eyes and straight brown hair, though both her hair and her skin were lighter than Cassandra's, who took after the her mother's darker-toned line. At seven, Annette was precocious and talkative and affectionate. She turned her eyes to the computer.

"Can you get me some lunch?" she asked, still looking at the screen.

"Yes." Cassie pushed out of the chair. "Ramen?"

Annette nodded, and Cassie went into the den. She leaned over the couch where her other siblings lounged, eyes glued to the television.

"I'm going to make ramen for lunch, okay?"

They didn't even glance at her. Cassie bounded up the stairs. Her fingers itched to get back to the computer and continue typing, but she forced herself through the routine of filling the pot with water and waiting for it to boil.

While she waited, she surveyed the kitchen. With a groan, she realized it needed cleaning. Loading the dishes was her job, not sweeping and mopping and wiping down the counters and sink. But she lacked the authority to rally her siblings into a cleaning brigade. And she knew she couldn't expect her mom or dad to do it, not when they both worked so hard just to try and keep food on the table. With a grumble, she grabbed a rag.

Twenty minutes later, she and her siblings gathered around the kitchen table to eat ramen and crackers. Even Emily and Scott had torn themselves away from the television long enough to fill their bellies.

"Emily, clear the table when you finish," Cassie said, putting her own bowl in the sink. "I'm heading back downstairs." She didn't wait for Emily's answer, just took the steps two at a time back to the computer room.

The screen had gone dark in the time she'd been gone. Cassie settled into the big computer chair and wiggled the mouse. The screen flickered and then came to life, the bright white image of a word processing document filling the frame. Cassie waited another moment for the words to appear, but they didn't. She moved the mouse curser over to the up arrow and scrolled the page to get to the last thing she'd typed.

Except, no matter how much she scrolled, nothing appeared. Her heart pounded a little harder. Trying not to panic, she hit the Home button, going all the way to the first page.

Nothing. There were no words, no title page with her author name beneath, no bold header proclaiming "Chapter One."

Gone, gone, it was all gone! "No!" she shrieked.

In an instant, she knew what had happened. She'd left Annette alone in the computer room, and her little sister, illiterate and curious, had touched something. Done something. Whatever she had done had deleted every word, and Cassie didn't know enough about computers to fix it. Her dad might, but he wasn't here.

Hot liquid burned behind Cassie's eyes, and she jumped up, running from the room before anyone could see her cry. Anger battled with the discouragement, and she slammed her bedroom door as hard as she could, only remembering afterward that her mom was sleeping. Cassie stomped to her bed and threw the books onto the ground, then tossed herself on top of the blankets. All her hard work for the past few months, gone.

☙❦❧

Mrs. Jones knocked on the bedroom door a few hours later and poked her head in. Cassie lay on her bed reading, though her body felt stiff from not moving. She simply lacked the motivation to get up and do anything else.

"Is everyone still watching TV?" Mrs. Jones asked, a note of disapproval in her voice.

Cassie shrugged. "I don't know. I haven't been downstairs in a few hours."

Her mom frowned at her. "You need to pack for camp. We leave on Sunday."

Camp Splendor! Her dismal mood had taken over her thoughts, and she'd forgotten she would be at camp in two days. "Thanks."

That gave her something to occupy her mind, at least. She

pulled her duffel bag out from under the bed and stuffed enough clothes for one week inside. But no, this year she was going for two weeks! She grabbed her phone and texted Riley. She still didn't know if she considered Riley a best friend, but Cassie didn't have anyone else. And Riley had been going to church with her for months, so they saw each other all the time.

Excited for camp? She sent off the text and put the phone down to search out her swimsuit.

It chimed two seconds later, and Cassie sat on her bed to read the response.

Can't wait!

Well, that was a good sign. Sometimes Riley acted morose and moody. So much better when she was chipper. Cassie texted back and forth with her, her mood lightening with each word.

By the time Mr. Jones got home from work, Cassie had managed to conquer her disappointment. It would take some time, but she hadn't lost the handwritten book. She could type it up again.

Mrs. Jones placed a simple dinner of rice and canned green beans on the table. "Everyone hold hands so we can bless the food."

Cassie reached out and took her brother's hand on one side and her mom's hand on the other. After the blessing, Mr. Jones grabbed the bowl of rice and spooned some onto his plate.

"Thanks, honey, this looks great."

"Thanks, Mom," Emily said, and Cassie chimed in with her own appreciation.

"How was your day, Annette?" Mr. Jones asked.

Annette began a lengthy and excited rendition of her activities for the day. Cassie noted, somewhat bitterly, that she didn't mention touching the computer and destroying Cassie's book.

"And you, Cassie?" Mr. Jones finally turned his attention to her. "How was your day?"

"It had its ups and downs," Cassie said, casting a quick glance at Annette. "Someone touched my computer file and deleted the whole thing."

Annette's mouth froze mid-chew, and her eyes grew wide.

"Oh no!" Mrs. Jones said. "Can you save anything?"

Cassie shook her head. "The whole document is blank. I think I'll have to start over."

Mr. Jones frowned at her, his jaw working on a bite of green beans. Pausing to take a swig of water, he put his cup down and focused his blue eyes on Cassie, peering at her through his glasses. "Did you try to open the last version you saved?"

"Um, no." She hadn't thought of that.

"Unless you saved the empty document, you should be able to access your old document before the changes happened. Even if you did save, we can probably pull up a backup copy somewhere."

Cassie's heart gave a little thump of hope. If all she had to do was redo this morning's work, it would be so much easier than starting over. She scooted her chair back and stood. "I'll be right back."

Nobody stopped her as she bolted down the stairs to the computer room. Taking a deep breath, she hit the Close button on the word document. A little gray box popped up.

"Do you want to save the current changes?"

"No!" Cassie said, hitting the button emphatically with her mouse. A moment later the screen went gray. Heart pounding in her throat, shaky with anticipation, Cassie opened up her book document again.

Little black type on a white background flooded the computer screen. Cassie let out a whoosh of air and collapsed into the chair. It wasn't gone! All of it was right here! She scrolled down to the bottom, a little laugh bubbling up in her throat. Sure, she'd lost the work she'd done that morning. But compared to thinking she'd lost the whole thing, that was nothing.

Smiling to herself, she saved the document before closing it. She would spend tomorrow at the soccer store helping her dad. There wouldn't be time to work on this until after camp. But she knew it would be here waiting when she got home.

⊙~⋆~⊙

Riley greeted Cassie as soon as she opened the car door in the church parking lot.

"Ready?" she asked Cassie.

"Ready," Cassie said. She patted the pillow and duffel bag on the car floor beside her. "Camp Splendor right after church."

"You're going to love it. Two weeks is so much more fun than one."

Cassie pushed aside the stab of jealousy that Riley had gone to camp for two weeks last summer. It hadn't worked out for her last year, and if it weren't for the Girls Club scholarship money, it wouldn't have worked out this year. But she didn't say that. Her dad didn't like them to talk about how they struggled with money.

"Let's get inside, girls!" Mrs. Jones said.

Riley leaned in close to Cassie as they headed across the parking lot. "I already saw Tyler. He's looking sooo hot."

"Hmm," was Cassie's noncommittal reply. She was quite familiar with Tyler, the cute boy her age who went to the other junior high in town. His good looks did nothing to make up for his arrogant attitude. She'd rather talk to his older brother Jason, who always had a smile and a kind word. But she had already figured out that Riley had a crush on Tyler. She looked for him every time they came to church and talked about him nonstop.

Never mind that Tyler had never spoken a word to her.

This Sunday wasn't any different. Cassie sat through the sermon with Riley next to her, both of them fidgeting and writing back and forth to each other on a piece of paper.

"Remember," Mrs. Jones said to them when the sermon finished, "we're leaving right after Sunday School. Riley, did you put your things in the car already?"

"Yes," Riley said, straightening.

"Riley's riding with us?" Emily said, standing next to Cassie.

Cassie glanced at her younger sister. At first, she'd resented that they'd be at camp together again, but then her mom told her Emily would be staying with a different group. Besides that, how could Cassie forget the way her sister looked after her last time? Maybe she should be more concerned that her sister wouldn't be with her.

"Yes, I told Mrs. Isabel that we could take Riley. Not much sense in both of us driving out there."

Riley shot Cassie a grin, and Cassie returned it.

"Come on, let's get to class," Riley said, grabbing Cassie's hand and tugging her down the hall.

"What's your hurry?" Cassie said, but she already knew the answer.

They stepped into their Sunday School class. Riley scanned the room and deflated when she spotted Tyler sitting next to Sue. They spent every Sunday flirting together, even though Sue was a year older, the same age as Jason. Cassie had always wondered if Sue liked Tyler.

"Let's sit here," Riley said, falling into place beside Sam, a younger boy.

Sam's brown eyes lit up. "Hi," he said, scooting over to make room.

Cassie gave him a smile, then pulled out her scriptures and paid attention to the instructor. Sue and Tyler whispered through the whole class, earning several glares from the instructor, Sister Meredith. Sister Meredith was an older, plump woman with fluffy dark hair.

Riley poked Cassie, trying to get her attention, but Cassie kept her eyes on the teacher. She and Riley would have plenty of time to chat later.

As soon as class let out and they were heading to the car, Riley said, "Why didn't you look at me? I was trying to tell you something."

"I wanted to pay attention," Cassie replied. "I didn't want to be rude to Sister Meredith."

"So you were rude to me instead?" Riley scowled.

Cassie kept quiet. She knew Riley well enough to know when she was becoming moody. She wanted to enjoy these two weeks together at camp, and keeping Riley distracted and happy was the best way to do that. "I finished my book," she said instead, changing the subject.

"Good for you," Riley grumped.

Figured. Cassie opened her purse and pulled out her phone. "I better text Farrah and let her know. She was really anxious to read it." Farrah had moved away last year, but she always cared what Cassie was doing.

They reached the van and stood beside it while Mrs. Jones got the other kids in. Riley stayed silent as Cassie sent the text message. Finally she said, "Did Farrah respond?"

"Not yet. But I'm sure she'll want to read it. I'll send it to her as soon as I have another copy."

"Do you have it with you?" Riley sounded completely put out that she had to ask.

"Of course," Cassie said. She climbed into the car, claiming the chair behind the driver's side. "Why?" She knew why. But she wanted to hear Riley say it.

"No reason," Riley replied. She sat in the other captain's chair behind the passenger and turned her head to the window, not looking at Cassie.

Cassie rolled her eyes. Seriously? But that was fine. She pulled out a book and read for the next hour as Mrs. Jones drove them to Camp Splendor.

CHAPTER TWO
Competitive Edge

Mrs. Jones dropped Emily off with her unit first, and Cassie put her book away to breathe in the familiar surroundings of platform tents tucked into the wooded area. She watched her mom talk to the counselors while Emily hauled her bag away to her tent. Someone already had a small fire going in the campfire ring, and several girls stood near the logs surrounding it. Never mind that it had to be nearly ninety degrees outside. So far this June was proving to be hotter than most.

But not as hot as Texas. It had been three years since the Jones family moved to Arkansas from Texas, but Cassie still remembered the heat. She had never wanted to play outside unless it involved swimming.

Mrs. Jones got back in and backed away from the campsite. "Ready, girls?" she called back.

"Ready," Cassie said, leaning forward in excitement.

"Yes," Riley said, sounding only slightly less disgruntled than earlier.

They drove down a bumpy dirt road and around a bend before a second campsite came into view. Just like the one where Mrs. Jones had left Emily, a dozen platform tents sat in a semi-circle around a small campfire. Cassie opened the van door just as it came to a stop, not waiting for Riley as she bolted toward the leaders standing at the pavilion.

"Hi!" she said, dragging her duffel bag and pillow behind her. "I'm Cassandra Jones."

"I remember you, Cassie," one of the leaders said. Cassie focused on her and realized she'd met her two years earlier, but she didn't remember her name. "I'm Skippy," the counselor added with a smile.

"Oh, hi!" Cassie exclaimed. She wondered what her counselor's real name was. They kept their names a secret until camp was over.

Another counselor stepped up, her blond hair pulled back by a bandanna. "Cassie! Hey! I'm Rainbow. I was your counselor a few years ago!"

Rainbow hadn't been as nice to Cassie last time. She'd acted annoyed that she had to help Cassie, since Cassie was on crutches after a week in the hospital from a serious snake bite. But maybe Rainbow had changed.

"We picked your tent, I hope that's okay," Rainbow said. She consulted a clipboard in her hand. "You have a friend, right? Where's Riley?"

Cassie turned around, almost disappointed Riley was coming. "There," she said, pointing as Riley trudged up the path behind her.

"You girls are both in tent three. Do you need help with your things?"

"I got it." Cassie shouldered her bag. One, two, three. She stopped at Tent Three and took a deep whiff of the air. The latrine had to be close by.

"Right next to the latrine?" Riley joined her, her forehead wrinkled in a familiar scowl.

"I didn't pick it," Cassie said, refusing to let Riley spoil her mood. She pulled her duffel bag in and set it on the cot nearest the door. "Hi," she greeted the girl in the tent. "I'm Cassie and this is Riley."

The girl sat cross-legged on her sleeping bag, writing on a sheet of stationary. She looked up and smiled. "I'm Brittany! Nice to meet you."

Riley plopped her things down on the cot behind Cassie's. "Who's the last girl?"

"Tiffany. She's by the fire ring."

Tiffany. Cassie remembered a Tiffany from a few years back. Could it possibly be the same person? She left her bags and went out to the fire ring.

"Tiffany!" she exclaimed when she spotted the girl. Though she had gotten taller and filled out a bit, Cassie would recognize the blond hair and freckles anywhere.

Tiffany turned around, her eyes widening at the sight of Cassie. "Cassie! Wow, you've grown up!"

Was that a compliment? Cassie glanced down at her T-shirt and jeans, feeling self-conscious. Last year she'd more than grown up—she'd grown out. She'd spent months trying to get the extra weight off her frame. This would be a good week for it, since she'd be outside so much and walking everywhere. If she could resist dessert, even better.

"You, too," she said, bringing the conversation back to Tiffany. "Great to see you."

Tiffany gave her a hug and then turned her around to see people. "This is Tina, Ashley, Sara . . ." She rattled off several more names, and Cassie smiled and nodded, unable to keep track of everyone.

"And this is Cassie," Tiffany finished. "She's the funnest, nicest camper you'll ever meet. She was bit by a snake once. And she can sing!"

Cassie's face flushed, but she beamed under the praise. The other girls crowded around, greeting her excitedly as if she were someone special.

Yep. Cassie loved Camp Splendor.

After dinner, the counselors gathered all the girls into the pavilion.

"The camp leader has asked us to nominate one girl from each unit to be on the camp council," Skippy said. "That girl is in charge of making sure her campsite is clean and her campmates are well."

Cassie raised an eyebrow. This was new. Last year she'd only gone to camp for one week, and there hadn't been a camp council.

"Raise your hand if you want to nominate someone," Skippy continued. "This girl should be friendly, kind, and a true Girls Club girl in everything she does."

Oh, how Cassie hoped she was that kind of girl.

"How are we supposed to know?" a girl with red pigtails said. "We just got here. We don't know anyone."

"You've met each other. Maybe you came with a friend or know someone from a previous year. If you can't nominate someone, don't worry about it."

Tiffany raised her hand, and Skippy pointed to her. "Yes?"

"I nominate Cassie," she said.

Cassie's face warmed. She glanced at Riley to see what she thought, but Riley had her hand in the air.

"I nominate Brittany," she said the moment Skippy pointed at her.

Cassie bit back a gasp and tried not to feel betrayed. How could Riley pit someone against her?

"Thanks, Riley," Brittany said, beaming at her.

"I second for Cassie," a girl she didn't know said.

"Me, too," another chorused.

"Great, two nominations," Skippy said. "Let's put it to a vote. Raise your hand if you vote for Brittany."

Was Cassie supposed to vote for herself? Was that considered rude? She kept her hand down and surveyed the other girls, hoping no one thought she was horrible for not voting for Brittany. About seven girls had their hands up, including Brittany and Riley.

"And for Cassie?"

The rest of the hands went up, voting Cassie in by a landslide.

"Congratulations, Cassandra," Skippy said. "You're on the camp council."

Her first council meeting would be in the morning, and she would help plan the Thursday night social. Tiffany chattered nonstop about it, just as excited as Cassie that she'd been voted in. But when they reached the tent with Riley and Brittany inside, Cassie waved at Tiffany to hush.

Tiffany looked at them climbing into their sleeping bags. "You guys aren't jealous, are you?"

"No, it's totally fine," Brittany said. "I mean, everyone seems to know you. I didn't really stand a chance. I'm new here."

"But if everyone knew you, they would have voted for you," Riley said. She rolled over on her cot and opened a box of cookies. "After just a few hours of knowing Brittany, I know she's a much nicer person than Cassie."

Tiffany's mouth dropped open, and she gaped at Riley. "How can you say that? I thought you were her friend!"

Cassie waved Tiffany off, totally not even caring. "She always treats me this way. It makes her feel better."

"Better about what?" Tiffany looked back and forth between the two of them, blinking her confusion.

Better about the fact that everyone likes me more than her. Cassie bit back the words. They weren't kind or the kind of words someone on the camp council would say. What could she say instead? "Better about new places. She's a little shy." That was probably true, anyway.

Tiffany tilted her head, seeming to consider that. "You'll make friends here too, Riley," she said.

"I know I will. And I'm not shy." She glared at both Tiffany and Cassie, and Cassie knew even though she'd tried to be nice, her words hadn't appeased Riley.

She also found she didn't much care.

Monday morning after breakfast, Cassie stayed at the mess hall for the camp council meeting. Tiffany sat outside with the other buddies who had to walk their camp councilor back to the unit when it was over.

"Welcome, camp council!" Zelda, the camp leader, said. She wore a spirally tie-dye shirt, her poofy blond hair cascading around her head in a mess of bouncy curls. "Before we plan the Thursday night activity, I would like a report on your units and how things are going."

Cassie listened to the other girls and formulated her own answer. When it was her turn, she said, "Things are going well. Everyone's pulling their weight at the campsite, keeping it clean. We do seem to have a division in the group. One girl seems particularly upset that her friend didn't make it on the council and has been a bit angry about it. We're all doing our best to be kind to her and help her feel included."

"Excellent. Make sure the girls feel like they all have a voice, and hopefully they won't be upset for long." Zelda pointed to a board on the wall behind her. "You see here the weekly duties. Help your counselors remember when it's your turn for cleaning up."

Cassie found her unit on the board and wished she'd brought something to write with. She hoped she wouldn't forget.

"What about dish duty? I don't see that on there," an older girl from another unit said.

"We have hired staff this year to do the dishes," Zelda said, and the girl nodded.

"On our last Thursday night," Zelda continued, "we'll have our big luau party. All the girls are encouraged to be creative and wear flowery shirts and leis. We'll have prizes for the best dressed."

Dressing up. Cassie hated this part. Other than writing, she had no creative bone in her body. Unless someone laid the clothes out for her, her costume would be the worst one. But she dutifully memorized everything Zelda said so she could take it back to her campsite.

"And for those of you who don't know, at the end of the camp session, we have an ending night bonfire. It's a special time with memories, skits, and songs. As a council, I expect you to come up with a skit to put on."

"And Keeper of the Ashes?" another girl said, squirming a bit in her chair. "Do we have any input on that?"

Keeper of the Ashes, Keeper of the Ashes. Cassie wracked her brain, trying to remember that from the last time she'd come.

"No," Zelda said. "Only the counselors have a say. But all of you are just as eligible as any other girl."

Cassie felt a spark of interest. Keeper of the Ashes sounded important. And Cassie was also eligible.

"How was it?" Tiffany asked when Cassie finally emerged from the mess hall. They began the trek down the path back to the campsite. "What did you talk about?"

"The big luau party and when we'll be cleaning, that sort of thing."

"Sounds exciting."

"Not really." But Cassie didn't mind. She felt honored to be on the council at all. "What's Keeper of the Ashes?"

"Oh, you don't know?" Tiffany picked up a rock and chucked in into the leaf-covered ravine to their right. "During the session, the counselors pay attention to the girl who helps the most and is kind and embodies the true Girls Club spirit. She's announced as the Keeper of the Ashes at the bonfire, and some of the ashes are put into a jar for her to take home. She's supposed to bring the jar back to camp the next year and pour the ashes into the fire."

"Oh, wow." A kind, helpful, spiritual girl. Cassie was that

kind of person.

As if reading her mind, Tiffany said, "I bet you'll get it. You're the perfect example."

"Oh, I'm sure there are others who deserve it," Cassie said, though she wasn't sure at all.

Tiffany turned around and walked backward for a moment, shooting Cassie a mischievous grin. "Did Zelda talk about the dishwasher at all?"

Cassie blinked, a little confused why this would be intriguing. "The dishwasher?"

"You know, the one she hired." Tiffany lowered her voice, even though they were the only ones in the forest. "He's supposed to be really hot."

"Oh. Oh!" Cassie raised both eyebrows. "She mentioned they hired someone, but she didn't say it was a cute boy."

"No, of course not!" Tiffany laughed and faced forward, almost taking out a low-hanging tree branch. "Watch for him at meal time."

☙ ⁂ ❧

Cassie did watch for the new dishwasher. She tried to catch a glimpse of the face connected to the hands appearing out of the little window, accepting their dirty dishes, but she couldn't even tell if the hands were male or female. Besides, as they gathered around the hearth for singing time, she had other things to worry about.

Like Riley.

If she thought things would improve the rest of the week between her and Riley, she was sorely mistaken. Every mealtime, Riley made a huge campaign effort to get people to line up behind Brittany, as if she wanted to prove Brittany was the true leader. At swimming time, she clung to Brittany like a life jacket, calling attention to the tall girl as she went off the diving board and swam laps.

Cassie did catch sight of the dishwasher during swimming time. He and another man were swimming when the girls arrived, but they quickly got out of the pool. Cassie stood next to Tiffany with a towel wrapped around her body, waiting their turn to get into the water. His eyes, a light blue, traveled over her and Tiffany, lingering on her friend, before he walked out with the man.

"That's the dishwasher!" Tiffany squealed, grabbing Cassie's hand.

"How do you know?" She'd never seen him before.

"I saw him in the kitchen once when we walked in to get something for the cookout. That man's his dad. He's the caretaker of Camp Splendor. They live here."

Cassie turned with Tiffany, both of them leaning against the chain-linked fence and watching the boy and his dad get into a truck. "What's his name?"

"Ben." Tiffany sighed. "He smiled at me once. He's so cute."

He looked pale and skinny to Cassie, but she didn't say that.

CHAPTER THREE
Hot Dishwashers

At the next camp council meeting, the girls planned the Friday night bonfire. Goosebumps of anticipation flooded Cassie's skin as she considered the bonfire and everything it represented. She'd been the best camper, the best example, the friendliest, and most helpful. Her counselors adored her, the girls all wanted to be around her. She had to be the Keeper.

The council practiced their skit, silly and simple, something to make the girls laugh before the talks and memories began and drove them all to tears.

Cassie didn't see Ben again, though she supposed the hands handing out food and taking the dirty dishes were his. She noticed Tiffany lingering by the kitchen window sometimes, but every time Cassie asked her if she'd gotten to talk to him, she shook her head.

During the second week when they did the ropes course, Brittany and Cassie were both chosen as team leaders, and Riley loudly declared that she would not be on Cassie's team.

"Brittany has the Girls Club spirit," Riley said. "I bet she gets Keeper of the Ashes."

Prickles ran up Cassie's spine, and she held her breath, forcing herself not to turn around and stare at them. Nobody was nicer or more helpful than Cassie. The one thing she wanted more than anything else was to be the Keeper. Brittany hadn't done anything to be worthy of Keeper. Cassie put the discouraging thought from her mind.

The hike up the mountain to the rope course was labor intensive but not too strenuous. But by the time the girls climbed the rope ladder and locked themselves into harnesses for the rappelling, they were red-faced and panting.

"Drink water, guys," Cassie said to her team, making sure they all had their water bottles out. She knew from her experience in soccer and summer camp last year that being hydrated was essential to good health.

They rappelled down the tree, some of the girls whining a bit and requiring coaxing. Cassie was getting tired and hot as well, but she forced herself to be generous and encouraging until each girl from her team had reached the bottom.

The next part wasn't as strenuous but required balance. Each girl had to tiptoe across two ropes from one platform to the other. Luckily the platforms were only two feet off the ground, so if someone fell, they didn't have far to go. Still, Cassie walked beside the girls, ready to catch one if they needed her. When her team finished, they sat again on the platform and drank more water while they watched the other team.

The counselors went first, laughing and squealing as they nearly fell off the ropes.

"Oh, let me help you!" Brittany said.

Brittany, who stood a full head taller than Cassie, held the leaders' hands and led them around. Then she followed them to the next section of the course, leaving her team of girls behind.

"We could use her help," Tina said, nearly falling off the course. "This is hard."

"I'm sorry," Cassie said, stepping over to Tina. She offered her hand, but at just barely taller than five foot, she wasn't much help.

"You're doing great," Tiffany said. "We're lucky we have such a nice team leader." She shot a nasty look after Brittany.

Brittany's team grumbled along with Cassie's help, and then they stayed with her team. Up ahead, Brittany and the counselors laughed and joked as they went through the course ahead of them. Had the counselors even noticed Brittany left her team behind? That had to count in Cassie's favor.

She instantly felt bad for thinking that way. But surely if anyone deserved to be Keeper of the Ashes, it was her.

⸻

Thursday night after dinner, the girls hurried back to their cabins to get ready for the luau.

"I'm not sure what the point is, since there won't be any boys there," Ashley grumbled, walking in sync with Cassie down the trail.

"There's one boy," Tiffany said, a twinkle in her eyes.

"Hey," Rainbow said, stepping closer. Tiffany jumped and looked guilty; none of them had realized how close their counselor was. "No talking about boys. This is Girls Club camp."

Tiffany lowered her head, her expression meek. But as soon as Rainbow walked away, she whispered, "I hope he's at the luau."

"What boy?" Ashley asked, stepping closer.

Tiffany glanced around to make sure no one else was listening and said, "The dishwasher. He's just a kid like us. He's thirteen."

Thirteen? Cassie hadn't realized he was their age.

No more was said about a possible boy being at the party. Cassie rummaged through her duffel bag, wishing she'd brought something flowery. The closest she had was a purple shirt with a yellow sun on it. Oh well. Shrugging her shoulders, she slipped it on. She looked over at Brittany and felt a flash of envy. Not only did she have a Hawaiian-themed flower shirt, she'd made herself a daisy chain. And she'd made one for Riley, too, which made her ridiculous tie-dyed shirt look almost tropical.

Riley noticed her looking and lifted her nose in the air. "Sorry we don't have anymore leis. Maybe you have time to make one." She and Brittany walked out of the tent.

"Who needs leis?" Tiffany said. She opened a pocket on her suitcase and pulled out a necklace with a sparkly pink flower on the end. "We've got necklaces."

"You brought necklaces to camp?" Cassie said, totally impressed as she took a cord from Tiffany with a nearly identical flower on it.

"They do this every year," Tiffany said. "And I always bring one extra for my favorite tentmate."

"Thank you," Cassie said, putting the necklace around her neck.

"And," Tiffany said, lowering her voice, "I'll share Ben with you."

Cassie couldn't help laughing.

The mess hall had been cutely decorated with plastic palm trees and coconuts on the tables. Fun, peppy music played as the girls danced around the room, stopping at the long tables to eat snacks of dried fruit and nuts. Cassie swayed and bobbed to the music, but she had to admit, Tiffany had her insanely curious. Where was Ben? Would he make an appearance?

"Limbo time!" Skippy shouted, brandishing a long stick. Another counselor joined her, and together they held the stick at eye level. A cheer ran up from the girls, who formed a line.

Cassie joined them, then looked around for Tiffany. She gave a start when she saw her—standing next to the food dispensing window, talking to a boy.

Ben! He was here!

Intrigued, Cassie left the line and wandered over to them. He was the same height as Tiffany, with dark brown hair, light blue eyes, and long, long lashes. He and Tiffany chatted, and then he looked over at Cassie. His gaze held hers, and for a moment the music, the laughter, and all the rest of the room disappeared.

"Cassie," Tiffany said, taking Ben's hand and turning him to face Cassie, as if he weren't already. "This is Ben. His dad was hired to fix up the campsites this year, so Ben gets to work in the kitchen."

Something cool and tingly shivered down her spine when she met his eyes. "Hi," she said.

"Hi," he replied. He looked back at Tiffany. "I can't ask you to dance. I'm not supposed to mingle with the girls."

"That's okay. I just wanted to meet you." She raised her eyes to Cassie's. "Aren't you going to do the limbo?"

"Yeah." Cassie nodded. "I was just headed that way." She cast another look at the two of them, her eyes lingering on Ben, before turning and joining the long line of girls. She limboed a few times, and every time she went to the back of the line, Ben and Tiffany were still talking. And then one time she finished and he was gone, and only Tiffany stood there against the wall.

Cassie got out of line and went and stood by her. "Well? Was he everything you hoped?"

"He's wonderful," Tiffany said dreamily. "He asked me to go with him."

"Go with him? Go with him where?"

Tiffany shoved Cassie's shoulder with her own. "Nowhere, you goof. Just to be his girlfriend."

Cassie had encountered this scenario before, and it made as little sense to her now as it had in sixth grade when her best friend got a boyfriend. "You're at camp. How can you go out?"

"It's just knowing that we belong to each other, silly. Come on, let's limbo."

Cassie followed her friend back to the line, just as

bewildered as she'd been a minute ago. Was it possible for two thirteen years olds to like each other enough to be boyfriend and girlfriend? What did it mean to be a couple?

And why hadn't Ben asked her? It wasn't a question formed out of jealousy so much as of curiosity. If she were prettier, with blond hair and no glasses, a little bit skinnier, would Ben have been interested in her? The thought of having a boy like her, want to be her boyfriend, fired up a fervent longing in her heart. Whatever it was she needed to do to have that, she was going to do it.

All thoughts of Ben vanished by Friday night. Cassie got more anxious all through dinner. She saw the other girls getting emotional through singing time, some of them already crying as they imagined the departure they'd have the next morning. Cassie's throat was tight, also, and she knew she'd miss her friends: Tiffany and Ashley and Tina and the other girls she'd gotten close to. But that wasn't what was really on her mind.

That evening in the campsite, Rainbow told them to pack their bags and get ready to leave the next day. Then, as darkness descended upon them, she approached each tent and told them to get their flashlights and meet at the trail head.

They gathered in silence, a poignant, expectant air around them. Skippy and Rainbow took up the front and back of the line, and they started down the path, only the lights of their flashlights bobbing ahead of them. None of them spoke, nobody sang. They were breathless with the anticipation of goodbye, of the heartache from parting for a year. Or more.

They reached the mess hall and kept going, hiking down to the meadow and over to the amphitheater. A bonfire already raged, and the soft singing of the units already at the amphitheater reached Cassie's ears. She scanned the group and spotted her sister. They'd seen each other from time to time but stuck with their own units, content in the security they'd found with their new friends.

Cassie sat in the back row, sandwiched between Tiffany and Skippy. They joined in the song, singing the soft melody about learning and trusting and working hard. Everything that being in Girls Club represented. And Cassie felt she'd embodied those attributes well.

Zelda stood up and silenced them all. "Welcome to closing ceremonies, campers! Session two is drawing to an end. We've all had a wonderful time and hope you've enjoyed every moment! We want you to come back next year! To begin our program tonight, we have our camp council. Everyone give them a hand while they start our entertainment!"

The campers clapped and cheered, and Cassie stepped down, following the other council members to the front. They went through a silly skit about an invisible bench, but Cassie hardly heard the laughter and applause when they finished. Her mind buzzed with nerves and anxiety. She tried to pay attention as the counselors of each unit ran through skits also, but she just wanted them to get on with it.

Zelda stood up next and led them through some of their favorite camp songs, bringing up memories of the pool and the luau and campfires. Girls began to cry, reaching out and holding each other's hands. Tears came to Cassie's eyes as well, and she knew she would miss being here and being around these people. Girls Club camp was one of her favorite places. It was a place she felt accepted and admired and special.

"We're now going to present the ashes to the Keeper," Zelda said, drawing silence from the girls. "Since the girl is in Skippy's unit, Skippy, would you do the honors?"

In Skippy's unit. That was Cassie's unit. She straightened, her heart pounding a little bit harder until it almost drowned out Skippy's words.

"This special young lady has been a delight in our camp." Skippy held a ceramic box in her hands and smiled around the amphitheater. "She's always there when we need someone. She's the first to volunteer for clean up and service. Every girl in our camp loves her, and there is no doubt that she embodies the Girls Club spirit."

It's me, Cassie thought, heart thumping like a drum beat with each word. Skippy had just described exactly how she tried to be, exactly how she acted.

Skippy turned her face to the girls in her unit, her eyes moving over their faces. "It is with great pleasure that we announce the Keeper of the Ashes to be—Brittany."

CHAPTER FOUR
Keeper of the Ashes

Brittany! Cassie gasped out loud as something akin to a dagger pierced her heart. Nobody heard her, not with the clapping and cheering, but Cassie felt her chest tighten and shrink in on itself like she was being crushed. Disappointment and confusion and anger welled up inside her. Brittany stepped down and accepted the box, and Skippy hugged her.

"Thank you for being so wonderful," she said.

Skippy led the girls in another song, but Cassie dropped her head into her hands, unable to keep singing. She sobbed, not even bothering to muffle the sounds of her crying. Tiffany reached over and put an arm around her, and Cassie bawled against her shoulder.

"Is she okay?" Cassie heard someone ask, and Tiffany answered.

"She's really going to miss everyone."

The singing continued, but Cassie just cried her heart out.

The girls sniffled all the way back to camp, flashlights bobbing on the dark trail. Cassie's face felt stiff, her throat tight. She didn't speak to anyone as she dressed for bed and climbed into her sleeping bag. She turned her back on her tentmates and closed her eyes, pretending to be asleep. But the tears still trickled past her lids and down her cheek.

Saturday morning was a quiet affair. The girls ate breakfast with sad expressions on their faces, though most, including Cassie, had gotten their tears out the night before. She hugged a few more campers, feeling distanced and disillusioned from the whole experience.

"Goodbye," she said over and over. "See you next year."

Back at the campsite they gathered their bags up to the pavilion and waited for the parents to come take them home. It was only when Mrs. Jones pulled up in the blue van and called Cassie and Riley that she realized they'd be in the car together.

She turned to Tiffany and gave her a big hug. "I'll miss you."

"Don't forget me," Tiffany said. "You're the best. I wish we went to school together. You'd be my best friend."

Cassie sure wished she could have Tiffany's friendship year round. "Good luck with Ben. I'll see you next year."

"Same time, same place!"

Cassie lugged her things into the van and waved goodbye once more before settling in the middle row next to Emily. "Riley can sit up front," she told her mom.

"That's very nice of you, Cassie," her mom said.

"That's because I'm very nice," Cassie replied, the words stinging in her throat.

Being nice might be overrated.

༺ ⚜ ༻

Cassie had a little over a week to recover from Girls Club camp before she left for church camp.

"Do I really have to go?" Cassie sighed Monday night as she packed for camp. "I don't know anyone."

"You know Riley."

Cassie gave her mom the evil eye. "You know she's one of the reasons I don't want to go." Cassie had told her mom everything that happened at camp.

"You can't be mad at her forever."

Cassie folded a shirt and added it to the duffel bag. "I'm not mad at her. I'm just not going to be friends with someone who treats me that way."

"Fair enough," her mom said. "I don't want you to be near someone who treats you badly either."

Cassie pressed onward, hoping to sway her mom's opinion. "It's not just Riley. It's Sue and Michelle and Jessica. None of them like me. They're not my friends."

"Who are your friends?"

I don't have any. She bit back the words.

"Don't you have friends from Rogers?" her mom continued.

"Yes," Cassie admitted. She thought about Elise and Tesia, the two girls who had become like sisters to her last year at church camp. "I haven't talked to them in a year, though. I don't know if we're still friends." She felt bad about that, but once school got in full swing, it had become really hard to make time for anything extra, including her out-of-town friends.

"You won't know if you don't go."

Cassie heaved a sigh and added another T-shirt to the bag. "They better be there."

They weren't at the same place this year, as Cassie quickly saw when they pulled into a wooded area dotted with cinder-block cabins. Last year they had been in tents around a pavilion. Cassie perked up.

"Air-conditioning!"

"What do you need air-conditioning for?" her mom teased. "You're an all-natural girl."

All-natural, indeed. Cassie lifted the sleeve of her shirt and sniffed it self-consciously. At some point in the past year she'd had to start wearing deodorant, but she still found it didn't work as well as it should. "I hate being hot and sweaty."

"It's good for you." Mrs. Jones shot her a worried look. "Make sure you eat enough. I'm not sure they fed you at

Camp Splendor."

Cassie opened the car door and hauled her things into the cabin marked "Second years." Her mom followed her inside.

"There's no one here," Cassie said.

"This is nice, though," Mrs. Jones said. "You won't even be with Springdale girls, see? You'll be with girls your age."

"Yeah," Cassie said. Riley would still be in her group, but it didn't look like she'd arrived yet.

The door shoved open again, and a familiar girl with dark hair and freckles walked inside. Her limbs were even lankier than the year before.

"Tesia!" Cassie squealed, opening her arms.

"Cassie!" Tesia dropped her bags and fell into Cassie's waiting embrace. They hugged, and Cassie felt the weight of isolation lift from her shoulders. She'd be fine.

"Well, I guess I'm out of here, Cassie," her mom said.

"Bye," Cassie said, barely glancing at her. She turned all of her attention on Tesia. "Where's Elise?" The year before, Cassie's first year at camp, would have been unbearable if not for Tesia and Elise, the two girls who befriended her and saved her from spending the week by herself.

Tesia's face fell slightly. "She's not coming."

Something in the way Tesia formed the words had Cassie taking a step back and studying her friend. "Why?"

"She's—struggling with a few things."

"With church?" Cassie couldn't believe that.

"Yes. Church. And a few other things."

"Like what?"

Tesia shrugged. "She doesn't talk to me as much anymore. So I don't really know."

Cassie swallowed against a lump in her throat. She hated to think of her friend going through any sort of difficulty. If only they lived close enough to be a part of each other's lives. "But you're taking care of her, right?"

Tesia nodded. "Yes. And praying for her. Every day."

Me too, Cassie thought.

⊙⌒※⌒⊙

The other second-year girls arrived over the course of the next hour. Some of them Cassie had seen the year before. Cynthia was a pretty Native American with wide cheekbones from Oklahoma. Marcelle and Tori were also from Oklahoma, and they were very friendly and goofy. Ana Julia lived closer in Eureka Springs, but she was so quiet that Cassie didn't get much else from her.

And of course there was Riley, who arrived as the other girls were introducing themselves, so Cassie didn't have to say hello. She didn't greet Riley or introduce her, leaving that instead to Riley, who sat on her bunk and did nothing.

Cassie turned to Tesia. "Want to explore the campsite?"

"Sounds fab."

They went outside and headed over to the meadow where the opening and closing devotionals of each day would be held.

"I'm so sad Elise didn't come," Cassie said.

"Yeah," Tesia sighed. "I couldn't believe it. I thought she'd come for sure, if for no other reason than to see you."

But Cassie hadn't been enough to lure her here. The guilt pricked her conscience. "I haven't been a good friend to her."

"It's hard when we're so far away."

"Elise tried," Cassie admitted. "She called me sometimes. Wanted me to come over. It almost worked out a time or two, but we never managed to get together."

"You can't blame yourself. Elise has to be stronger."

Wasn't that the truth? Nobody could be carried through life. They each had to find their own two feet and stand on them.

Guitar music down by the pavilion attracted their attention, and both of them meandered that direction. A man with thick dark hair in a T-shirt and jeans sat on one of the benches, strumming his guitar and playing an old folk song.

"That's nice," Cassie said.

"Yeah," Tesia agreed.

They stood around with several other girls for a few minutes before the oppressive heat began to get the better of her. Cassie turned around. "Let's head back to the cabin."

By the time they got there, the second-year leader had arrived.

"I'm Sister Tenney, and I'm in charge of you ladies this week. Devotional starts in ten minutes, girls! We'll do some morning orientation before we head to the mess hall for lunch. Everyone unpack your things by your bunk and make your beds!"

"What about a swim test?" Marcelle or Tory asked. Cassie couldn't remember who was who.

"Well, there's no pool." Sister Tenney offered a smile, brushing a lock of curly brown hair away from her face. "So no swim test."

"There's no pool?" the girl said.

There had been no pool last year, either, but they'd been in a lovely location with a nice creek and a cistern to cool off in. "How about a creek or something?" Cassie asked.

Sister Tenney shook her head. "Nope, none of those, either. Sorry, girls. You're just going to have to tough it out."

A murmur of complaint rose in her chest. Cassie turned back to her bed before she said anything negative. The other girls were already voicing her thoughts, anyway. She began to unload her bag on the bunk under Tesia's. She spotted Riley glancing around and then choosing a bunk with Cynthia, the pretty dark-haired girl from Oklahoma. Cassie's conscience pinged, but it wasn't like she was going to kick Tesia off the top bed so Riley could be there.

Using those words to ease her conscience, Cassie unrolled her sleeping bag and placed her pillow at the head of the bed.

༺❀༻

The next few days passed in misery as the oppressive heat beat down on the girls whenever they were outside. They weren't supposed to spend any time in their cabins except to sleep. But they all found excuses to go in there and get things, and Cassie found herself, as well as the other girls, lingering longer than necessary in the forced air-conditioning of the cabin.

"I hate arts and crafts," Tesia complained on Wednesday as they sat at the pavilion and dumped out a bag of paper crafts.

"Me too," Cassie agreed. "I'm so not good at this stuff."

Tesia groaned and fanned her face. Sweat beaded along her forehead and upper lip. "It's so hot!"

Cassie glanced over at Ana Julia, who had a small paper cut out and was making a pattern on her cardstock. With long dark hair, dark eyes, and a creamy complexion, Ana Julia was one of the prettiest people Cassie had ever seen. But she didn't talk hardly at all.

Cassie scooted over to her bench. "What are you making?"

Ana Julia lifted her eyes to Cassie before lowering them again. "A card for my brother," she said in soft, accented words.

Cassie leaned closer, intrigued. "It's beautiful. Where's your brother?"

"He is doing service work in Chile. He won't be home for another year."

"That's so awesome!" Cassie picked up another card Ana Julia had already completed. The paper cutouts she'd added to the stiff paper gave the card a professional, store-bought appearance. So much nicer than anything Cassie could do. "I want to do a service trip when I'm older also." The church provided opportunities for young adults to go on service missions to different states and countries, doing volunteer work for anywhere from six months to two years. Her dad had gone to South America when he was younger, and Cassie had grown up hearing about the life-changing experiences he had working with the native people. She looked forward to doing something similar.

"Maybe I will too," Ana Julia said, shooting another shy glance at Cassie.

The girl had hardly spoken ten words, but Cassie knew already she liked her. She touched Ana Julia's hand and stood up to grab her own paper. "You'll have to teach me how to do this." Not that she cared about card marking. She just wanted to hear Ana Julia speak again.

⁂

That night in their cabins, Sister Tenney said, "Don't forget we go on our hike tomorrow. Ana Julia's dad will lead you girls."

Hike. Cassie shot a worried look at Tesia, remembering their failed experience last year. "Maybe I shouldn't go."

Sister Tenney waved her off. "You'll be fine. It's not too strenuous and just on the other side of the campsite."

"No poison ivy?" Tesia asked, and Cassie resisted the urge to giggle. Last year Tesia had accidentally laid Cassie in poison ivy when she got sick on the hike. It hadn't affected Cassie, but Tesia, it turned out, was highly allergic.

"It's nature." Sister Tenney frowned at them. "Of course there's poison ivy. Just don't touch it."

"Or lay in it," Cassie said, and both girls gave in to the giggles.

"That would be stupid," Riley said, interrupting them with an evil glare. "No one would do that."

Cassie fell silent without comment, and she saw the way Tesia furrowed her brow in confusion. Almost every time one of them said something, Riley had a snide comment to echo it. Cassie had tried to explain to Tesia, but Tesia still didn't get how someone she didn't know could dislike her so much. At least she followed Cassie's example and didn't bait her.

Sister Tenney eyed Riley as well as if waiting for more, but when none was forthcoming, she said, "Get some rest. We'll head out early so we beat the heat of the day."

"Beat the heat," Tory groaned as she collapsed on her

bottom bunk. "It's so hot."

They murmured their agreement as they lay on top of their sleeping bags. Cassie stared at the top bunk, listening to the whir of the manufactured cool air as it swirled through the cabin. She blinked heavily and rolled over on the lush sleep sack, then closed her eyes.

CHAPTER FIVE
Weakling

Morning came too early, as it had every day at camp.

"Up, girls!" Sister Tenney said, turning on the light and flooding the cabin with a yellow glare. "Dress quickly and don't forget your water!"

The girls woke groggily, stumbling one by one into the bathroom and then emerging again. Cassie changed her clothes, huddling into the corner of her bunk where the shadows mostly hid her from view. Anytime she lifted her eyes, she saw the other girls in similarly modest huddles, each trying to change without being seen.

The girls made their way to the pavilion, leaning groggily against the pillars and each other. A man joined them, his dark hair thick on his head, face dark and tanned from days in the sun. Cassie recognized him as the guitar player. Every night after devotional, he set up by the pavilion and sang and played songs for any of the campers who were still up and wandering around.

"Good morning, girls," he said, his voice even more heavily accented than Ana Julia's. "I'm Brother Moda. Are we ready for some hiking?"

Cassie supposed so. She pushed away from her column and

followed Tesia down the trail.

The morning was breezy and pleasant, but Cassie knew that very soon it would get hot. They headed into the forest, and soon the darkness of the tree canopy enveloped them. They hiked up a path to a stone formation, and from there they climbed to a small waterfall. Cassie's heart rate rose with each step, and by the time she reached the top, she held a hand to her chest.

"Have I ever mentioned I hate exercising?" she murmured to Tesia.

"Surprising, really," Tesia said, leaning her arm on Cassie's shoulder. "You look like you work out."

Cassie straightened up and tried to control her breathing when they started hiking again.

"Just a few more ridges and we'll be at the top," Brother Moda said. "The view is incredible! You will love it."

"Hasn't he ever seen the top of a mountain before?" Marcelle grumbled.

Ana Julia turned her head and gave Marcelle a hurt look before facing forward. Cassie noticed and fell into step with her.

"Your dad really likes nature?"

"Yes. Me too. It's so beautiful. And quiet. Where we can actually think."

What was it about nature that Ana Julia liked? Cassie couldn't seem to see past the bugs and sweat and humidity.

The next hilltop was steeper and rockier, and the girls had to use both hands to find good support.

"Ouch." Cassie cut her palm on a sharp rock and scowled at it.

"Are you okay?" Tesia asked, stepping over.

"Fine." She wiped the blood on her shorts, searching for the tranquility Ana Julia claimed was here. But all she found was a sharp stinging in her hand.

Some of the girls stopped to pull out their water bottles at the top, but Brother Moda urged them onward. "Almost there! We'll stop for a few minutes at the top of the next one!"

The sun had crested over the edge of the earth now and was making its lazy ascent into the crisp blue sky, dotted here and there by a translucent white cloud. With the tree cover gone, the rays beat down on Cassie's face. She swallowed against the dryness in her throat. She both felt and heard her heartbeat pounding in her ears, and her breathing came a little too fast.

"I need a break," she whispered to Tesia.

"Almost there," Tesia replied. "Are you okay?"

Cassie refused to be the weakling who collapsed under the heat like last year. "Fine. Just thirsty."

The next ridge was easier to climb but very steep. The heat made Cassie sluggish, and she had a hard time lifting each leg up the steep, narrow trail weaving its way between rock outcroppings.

"Here we are!" Brother Moda said, reaching the top first. He turned around and grinned at all of them, then held out a hand and helped each girl the last few feet to the summit.

Cassie panted from exertion and couldn't wait to take a drink of water. But as her eyes focused on the horizon, she almost forgot to breathe.

Hills covered in leafy green trees rolled away from her as far as she could see, covering the expanse of the earth. They rose and fell in little peaks, like waves bobbing in the ocean after a tugboat slips by. The different shades of green radiated in the sunlight, vibrant and opaque, and they contrasted sharply with the brilliant blue of the sky. A hawk shrieked overhead and glided across the view, breaking up the sky for a moment before disappearing into the trees.

How had she never noticed this before? "It's majestic," she whispered.

Ana Julia stepped up beside her. "Grand," she agreed.

A few girls pulled out their cameras and snapped pictures, but Cassie remembered her thirst. She found a rock to sit on and swiveled her backpack over to her belly so she could open it and get her water. She dug her hand into the large pocket and fished around. Where was her water? She frowned and widened the opening, then peered inside. Camp manual, bandanna, trail mix . . . no water.

Cassie closed her backpack and stared at the horizon in front of her. Sister Tenney had specifically reminded them to grab their water bottles. She remembered picking it up and setting in on her bed with the trail mix. And then—then what? She'd moved her sleeping bag around looking for a pen. Cassie groaned, realizing she must have covered the water bottle up and left it there.

What now? She cradled her head in her hands, feeling how her pulse throbbed in her temples. Here she was, the stupid little girl who once again screwed up the hike.

"All right, girls, let's start back down," Brother Moda said cheerfully, corralling them with one arm back down the trail.

Cassie straightened up and shouldered her backpack. They would be in the tree cover soon. She could handle this and no one would even need to know she forgot her water.

The way down from the summit was somehow even harder than the way up. The steep, narrow trail beneath her feet took all her concentration, and Cassie focused on each footstep down, trying not to look at the bottom and imagine what a tumble would do. She heard Riley and Marcelle chatting behind her, and Tesia was singing softly in front of her. Coming up with coherent words and speaking would take too much energy, though, so Cassie kept quiet and concentrated on walking. Place the foot, test for sliding, put her weight on it. Grip the rock wall in front of her if need be. Move the next foot forward. Repeat.

A few pebbles slid out from her foot, and Cassie nearly fell on her face before she threw herself sideways into the rock next to her. Her shoulder smarted from the impact, and adrenaline surged through her from the close call, but she hadn't fallen.

"You okay, Cassie?" Marcelle asked, helping her straighten up.

"Fine," Cassie mumbled. The word felt thick and cumbersome in her mouth.

They paused for a moment before the next ridge and Cassie leaned her head against a cool rock under a shaded ledge. She closed her eyes and fought her body's urge to lay down in the dirt and go to sleep.

"No stopping, let's keep going down!" Brother Moda said cheerfully.

Was he trying to make her life miserable? A stab of resentment poked her, and she glared at him as she followed everyone.

As soon as she saw the girls gingerly climbing down the edge of a rock face, using both hands for support, she remembered this section. Her stomach flipped over. It had been hard enough going up. Now she was struggling to form coherent words and keep her eyes open. How would she be able to do this? Her hands shook as she faced the rock wall and let her feet guide her down. It wasn't a straight wall, but too steep to walk standing up. Her foot found one foothold, then another, and she pushed onward, hoping the bottom would greet her very soon. She rested her head against the rocks and took several deep breaths. Closing her eyes, she let her heart rate slow. But the pounding in her head did not diminish.

"Keep going!" Brother Moda yelled, and Cassie jerked her head up. That meant her.

A few more steps, and she had reached the bottom. Her legs decided they were done and gave out beneath her, thrusting Cassie gracefully to her knees.

"What are you doing?" Tory asked, giving Cassie an odd look as if she thought she'd chosen this position.

Cassie sucked in deep, gulping breaths of air, fighting the

desire to cry. "I can't keep going," she said.

"Is something wrong?" Brother Moda appeared in front of them. He knelt to Cassie's level. "Are you okay?"

She wanted to nod and say yes, but the lie wouldn't come. Instead she shook her head from one side to the other, wincing at the pounding pressure. "No."

"Where's your water? You need to drink some."

Now would be the moment when she had to admit her stupidity. "I forgot it."

"Here. Use mine." He handed her an insulated water bottle, concern etched on his face.

Cassie didn't hesitate. She opened the bottle and slurped down the water.

"Slow down," he crooned, one hand on her back to support her. "Hold the water in your mouth to help cool you down."

"Do you have your bandanna?" Tesia went through Cassie's backpack without waiting for a response. "Here, let's wet this." She poured water from her own bottle on it and then wrapped it around Cassie's head. Cassie shuddered at the sudden coolness.

"Can you keep going? Let's get you into the trees."

She bobbed a head and allowed Brother Moda and Tesia to guide her to her feet. The other girls whispered around them, but Cassie's eyes struggled to stay open, and their words didn't register.

The temperature dropped rapidly within the tree coverage, and Cassie wilted in relief, sagging against Tesia.

"All right, we are going to rest here a bit," Brother Moda called to everyone. "Ana Julia, come sit with her, please."

Ana Julia sat down next to Cassie. Her straight almost black hair was pulled into a pony tail, and a wisp of soft hairs curled around her face. Her expression was solemn and concerned. She took Cassie's hand and studied her.

The girls spoke above Cassie.

"Should we go back for help?"

"No, we'll just give her a moment to rest. She'll be able to make it back."

"Didn't she get sick last year?"

Cassie didn't know who said it and she couldn't tell if the question was meant to be answered or not, but a familiar voice spoke up.

"She just wants attention. She's fine."

If she'd had the energy, she'd have sat up and glared at Riley. As it was, her heart gave a little leap of indignation, but Cassie could do nothing else.

Riley kept on talking. "One year at Girls Club camp she expected the nurse to drive her everywhere and wouldn't use the bathroom with the rest of us. She expected special treatment."

I'd been bit by a snake! Cassie screamed in her head.

"I just remember she got sick on the trail last year," Tory said.

"I was there," Tesia said. "She got overheated. We had to carry her down the hill because she couldn't walk."

"Overheated like this?" Marcelle asked.

"Just like this," Tesia said, her tone defensive.

"I didn't know she had this issue," Brother Moda said. "Maybe she should not have come. Definitely not without her water."

Cassie heard all their words and wished she could speak up for herself, but her eyes wouldn't open. Her head ached like someone had spiked her temples. So she just huddled there.

She didn't exactly sleep, but she wasn't awake, either. Voices floated in and out of her consciousness and sometimes she felt the pressure of a hand on her face or back. Finally a firm hand landed on her shoulder.

"Can you get up?" Brother Moda asked.

She had to, right? Cassie pried her eyes open, blinking against the gummy scratchiness. She fought the urge to vomit as Tesia helped her to her feet.

"Nice and slow," Brother Moda said. "Let's get you back to camp."

Somehow, one step at at time, Cassie made it with the other girls. They guided her back to the cabin, where Brother Moda left Cassie on her cot and gave his daughter strict orders to stay with her. Cassie rolled over on her sleeping bag and closed her eyes. She didn't even hear him leave.

When she woke up hours later, she could tell from the one window in the cabin that it was late. Ana Julia sat in a chair beside the cot, her scriptures open in her lap as she read them. Cassie's head raged, and she let out a little whimper. Ana Julia looked up.

"Here," she said, helping Cassie sit up and giving her water. "Drink. You'll feel better."

Cassie took several gulps and lay back down. "Thanks. Have you been here this whole time?"

"I left for lunch." Ana Julia gave her a smile. "I didn't mind. It's nice and cool in here. Are you hungry?"

Normally Cassie had to pretend to not feel the gurgling, burning hunger pains in her stomach. Not today. "No."

"Maybe if you ate more, you wouldn't get sick."

"Ha." Cassie grunted. "Last year I ate tons and I still got sick."

"Oh, well." Ana Julia shrugged. "Who knows, then."

Indeed. They sat in silence until Cassie said, "Thanks for staying."

"You're welcome." Ana Julia's brown eyes crinkled as she grinned.

⊙~⁂~⊙

Cassie made it to dinner and the evening devotional, and by the time night came around, she felt more like herself. Many of the girls expressed concern for her and wanted to know how she was, but the whole incident embarrassed Cassie, and she preferred not to talk about it.

By Friday morning, everyone had forgotten. The girls

hugged each other goodbye as parents arrived to escort them home.

"Until next year," Tesia said to Cassie, wrapping her up in a big squeeze.

"Yes," Cassie said. "Take care of Elise. Get her out here again."

"I will, I'll make sure she's okay."

Tesia left, and Cassie turned to Ana Julia. She took her hands in her own.

"I'm so glad I met you and your father this year. I hope I'll see you next year."

"You will," Ana Julia said, lips curving upward. "But I think you should skip the hike."

Together they laughed, and Cassie gave her a hug. She saw her mom's van pull up outside and shouldered her bag, giving quick goodbyes to the other second-year girls.

She hesitated before saying Riley's name. But no matter how rude Riley was, Cassie refused to fall to her level. "Bye, Riley."

All the girls looked at Riley to see if she'd respond. The feud between them definitely hadn't escaped their notice. But Riley didn't answer; didn't even look at Cassie.

Cassie raised an eyebrow and shrugged. Maybe they'd make up before school started next month, but at this rate, probably not.

CHAPTER SIX
Upward Start

Even though this was her second year at Southwest Junior High, nothing managed to drive down the butterflies banging around in her stomach as Cassie walked up the sidewalk toward the orange awning.

She kept her eyes on the front doors and tried not to make eye contact with the students milling around. The only real friend she had was Riley, and she hadn't spoken to Riley since they'd had a fight at Camp Splendor over the summer. Their friendship had been touch and go for a few years, so it wasn't a surprise. But still, it didn't help the twisting in her stomach to know she was about to start her school year with no best friend—again.

She caught sight of her reflection in the four glass doors as she approached the school. Her long dark hair hung over one shoulder, only a slight curl remaining even though she'd slept in curlers all night. Her wire-frame glasses reflected the morning sunlight. Her lip bent in a scowl, and she jerked the door open before she could dwell anymore on her appearance.

She made a right turn at the office and headed for the eighth-grade locker hall. Ha. She smirked at the seventh graders scrambling to the farthest hallways, smug that she no longer sat at the bottom of the totem pole. There was her locker, a top one, luckily. She spun the combination, reciting the numbers in her head.

"Cassie? Cassandra Jones?"

The voice that spoke behind her sounded familiar and yet not. She turned around and saw her friend Emmett. Only he'd earned braces over the summer, and they didn't quite fit his mouth. His brown hair had lightened and sported reddish highlights.

"It is you!" he said, his voice squeaking on the last word. It couldn't seem to decide if it wanted to swing high or low.

"Emmett!" Cassie tossed aside her backpack and threw her arms around him. "How are you? How was your summer?" She backed away, grinning at him.

Emmett looked her up and down. "Great, great. Spent a lot of time outside. You too, apparently."

Cassie glanced at her arms, dark from endless days in the sun. "Yeah, tons. Church camp and Girls Club camp. Both of them were outside." She peered around Emmett, hoping to catch a glimpse of his friend Miles. Nobody tagged behind him, though, and she wasn't brave enough to ask.

"Cassie, hey!"

Cassie turned her head as Jaclyn, a friend from art class, sidled up to her.

"Jaclyn!" Cassie gave her the expected hug. "You got taller." Skinnier than ever, Jaclyn stood a few inches taller than Cassie, her dimples showing in both cheeks when she smiled.

"You got skinny," Jaclyn said, pinching Cassie's arm.

"But not taller." Cassie brushed off the comment, annoyed with the ugly black hole it opened in her chest. She didn't want to be just skinny; she wanted to be beautiful and popular and well-liked.

A few other kids crowded around them, greeting Emmett and Jaclyn and Cassie. Cassie smiled and said hello to Luke and Nicole, two good friends from last year. She tried not to look for them, but she couldn't help scanning the group for Riley and Miles.

And though she told herself she didn't care anymore, she knew deep down she was hoping to see Andrea, the girl who had been her best friend for two years before becoming too cool for Cassie. Would Andrea finally think Cassie was good enough to be her friend again?

The warning bell rang, and Cassie shifted her books from her bag to her locker.

"Where's your first class?" Jaclyn asked.

"P.E." Cassie made a face. The one thing she hated doing was physical activity.

"I'm going to math."

"That's the same building." Cassie closed her locker and fell into step beside Jaclyn. They exited the main building and walked across the sidewalk to the building housing the gym, math wing, and music wing. "Do you have P.E.?"

"For now. I'm trying out for the basketball team. If I make it, I can drop P.E."

"Oh." Cassie stole another glance at her friend. Not only was Jaclyn tall and beautiful and slender, but now she could do basketball? And Cassie could do what? Braid hair?

"Maybe we'll have a class together." Jaclyn waved. "See you."

Cassie waved back, heaving a sigh as she turned to the gym.

One woman who Cassie assumed was the P.E. coach stood in the middle of the gym wearing a white shirt, a whistle, and green shorts. She had her hands on her hips. "Here for P.E.?" she barked at Cassie.

"Yes," Cassie replied, hoping she didn't sound as reluctant as she felt.

"Go to the changing room." The woman pointed to her left. "I'll be right in."

Changing room? Cassie blanched.

She walked into the room, her eyes sweeping over the blue

tiles and the open lockers, freezing on the exposed shower heads pushed against the wall. Whose idea was that? What girl in her right mind would want to shower in front of everyone?

"Cassie!"

The high-pitched female squeal cut off the quiet chatter from the other girls, and Cassie didn't dare move. She knew that voice. She would know it anywhere.

A hand landed on her arm and spun her around, and Cassie found herself face-to-face with a pair of blue eyes and a big, toothy grin.

Andrea Wall.

CHAPTER SEVEN
Keep the Old

"Andrea!" Cassie gasped out, amazed to be having a conversation with her former best friend. "Are you in this class?"

"Yes!" Andrea clasped her hands and pumped them together, beaming. "Can you believe it? We finally have a class together!"

Cassie couldn't believe it. It didn't seem real. After how Andrea had spurned her last year, now she was excited to see her?

"All right, girls!" The P.E. coach stepped into the locker room, her brown hair permed in an old-fashioned halo around her head. "I'm Coach Peters, and I'm your instructor this year. Let's go over the basics. First—"

"Are we going to have to shower in here?" a girl interrupted.

Cassie leaned forward, peering around Andrea to see the speaker. She recognized Sierra, a girl who had been in Girls Club in elementary school. It was the question on her mind, too, but she was glad someone else asked.

"No, you don't have to shower, but I highly recommend it," Coach Peters said. "You will have to change clothes every day, though. So tomorrow bring a T-shirt or tank top, sports bra, and shorts. And tennis shoes and socks."

Sports bra. Cassie looked down at her flat chest and resisted an eyeroll.

"Can't we just wear those clothes to school?" another girl asked.

Coach Peters eyed her as if leery of a troublemaker. "No. You are required to change."

The class broke into murmurs and whispers, but Coach Peters kept on talking. "I'm handing out a liability form that I'll need you to take home and get signed before class tomorrow."

Andrea leaned toward Cassie, her wavy brown hair brushing Cassie's face. A whiff of floral perfume floated in the air around her. "You look great, Cassie. What did you do this summer?"

"Just hung out outside." For some reason she felt a bit embarrassed to mention the camps she'd gone to. Would Andrea think they were cool enough? Would she laugh at Cassie and think she was childish?

"Well, whatever you're doing, it's working. I wish I looked like you."

The words went straight to Cassie's heart, lighting her up like a strobe light on glitter. "But you're beautiful just the way you are."

Andrea squeezed her hand. "You've always been such a nice friend."

Cassie didn't hear anything else Coach Peters said. All she could think about was Andrea, sitting next to her, complimenting her, and being her friend.

☙ ❦ ❧

The bell rang after first hour, and Andrea waved goodbye as they stepped out.

"I'll see you tomorrow, Cassie!"

"Tomorrow," Cassie echoed. She practically skipped down

the hall to her science class. She stepped inside, pleased to see Mr. Adams, her favorite teacher, at the blackboard. She'd requested him as her teacher, but that hadn't been a guarantee.

"Cassie, sit here!" Nicole Bass waved to Cassie and gestured to the desk in front of her.

Cassie slid in beside her, giving a quick glance around at the other students. No Miles.

Mr. Adams started the expected introductions, but Nicole distracted Cassie.

"How's your book coming? Did you write anymore over the summer?"

A smile pressed itself to Cassie's lips, and she turned in her desk to give Nicole her full attention. "I finished it! Now I'm just working on getting it all typed up."

"That's awesome! I can't wait to read it."

"Cassandra, you need to face forward," Mr. Adams boomed, his gray mustache wiggling over his mouth.

Cassie dutifully faced the front, clasping her hands in front of her like a model student. She knew Mr. Adams was all bark and no bite. But she paid attention, not giving him further reason to chastise her.

After science she had math, and she saw more familiar faces, including Emmett and Leigh Ann. But no Miles. She heaved a sigh and sat at the table with Emmett.

"Did you hear from Farrah all summer?" he asked.

Cassie nodded. Farrah had been another friend of theirs last year, one who sat with them at lunch and told funny stories and held them all together when Cassie herself was falling apart. "Yeah. We texted a lot. And talked on the phone a few times."

"But you didn't see each other?"

"No." Cassie twiddled her pencil between her fingers. She and Farrah had planned several times to get together, but now that she lived in Conway, over an hour away from Springdale, it wasn't so easy to make that happen. It wasn't like she or

Farrah could drive. They relied entirely on the good nature of their parents.

"Oh."

The conversation nearly died there, but Cassie saw her chance to find out what she wanted to know. "What about you?" she asked nonchalantly, putting the pencil down and picking it up again. "Did you see any friends this summer? Miles?"

Emmett's lip twitched like he wanted to say something but didn't. He bobbed his head. "Sure, of course. We hang out a lot."

"Oh," was Cassie's reply, echoing his own word. What else was she supposed to say? She couldn't hammer him for details, or he'd suspect her never-ending crush on his friend. But she hadn't even seen Miles since last year.

They fell into silence as Mr. Adams began discussing the upcoming projects, including dissections and science fair in the spring. Cassie shuddered. No way was she doing dissections. The very thought made her queasy.

"See you at lunch," Cassie said to Emmett when class ended.

"Are you going there now?" he asked.

She double-checked her schedule. "No. Now I have English."

He furrowed his brow. "Then we won't have lunch together. I have A lunch."

Crapola. That familiar surge of panic powered through Cassie. "I have B lunch," she said, as if that weren't obvious.

"Maybe Riley does too."

She didn't want to sit with Riley. She managed a fake smile and a nod, wondering who on earth she'd sit with this year.

She did her best not to get too nervous about the upcoming lunch. She was not going to sit with Riley, even if they had the same lunch. If only Farrah hadn't moved!

"Hello, students!" Ms. Talo said.

Cassie welcomed the familiar face. Ms. Talo taught the advanced English classes, and Cassie had her the year before. She knew from experience this would be a hard, demanding class, but Ms. Talo was also very encouraging and fair.

"Hope you all had a great summer," she said, putting a stack of papers on each desk. "Here's your class syllabus and your homework for the week. You'll see the first assignment is due tomorrow."

So much for starting out easy. Cassie picked up her packet of papers and thumbed through them.

"You'll also see that we are having Market Fair in the fall this year instead of the spring." Ms. Talo reached the front of the classroom and turned around to beam at them. "You're all totally experienced now. Should be easy for you."

Right. There was nothing easy about Market Fair. It was supposed to represent a craft fair or something similar, with each student creating an attractive product and booth to sell to their fellow students. Cassie looked around and made eye contact with Nicole, who stuck out her tongue and crossed her eyes. Cassie giggled. They'd survived Market Fair the previous year by working together, but it hadn't been a super successful venture.

"You can work with partners or you can do it by yourself. But start thinking. I want a hypothetical business plan turned in to me in one week."

Cassie approached Nicole as class ended. "Want to be partners again?"

"Oh, I'd love to." Nicole looked a little guilty. "I have an idea I want to try by myself though. Is that okay?"

Cassie heard what Nicole didn't say: she'd have more success without Cassie.

"Of course," Cassie said, plastering her fake smile firmly in place. "I have something I want to try also, so that will work—great."

"I knew you'd understand." Nicole stood and gave her a

hug before shouldering her bag.

Cassie followed her out of the room and toward the cafeteria, realizing they would have lunch together. "Everyone's different."

"Yeah, you're right."

They entered the bustling cafeteria, and Nicole turned to her. "Where are you sitting? Are you getting a tray?"

"Just an apple."

"Cool. Want to sit together? There's Leigh Ann and Jimmy." Nicole pointed to a few other people from their English class.

"Sounds great." Relieved, Cassie got in line to buy her apple. At least she had a place to sit now.

She looked around the cafeteria, trying to see what other friends were there. She spotted Luke but no one else. Must be a totally different crowd. She waved at Luke, and he headed toward her table.

She stiffened when she spotted Andrea sliding into a table on the other side of the cafeteria. She was there with all her friends, Amity, Cara, Janice, Maureen. She watched them, annoyed with herself for the little green dragon of envy that sprouted in her chest and breathed down her throat. She paid for her apple and sat down to wait for Nicole.

"Hi, Leigh Ann, Jimmy," Cassie said, and took a bite of her apple.

"Hi, Cassie!" Leigh Ann greeted her enthusiastically. "Did you have a wonderful summer? How's your book?"

"Great!" Cassie had forgotten that Leigh Ann, as well as half the girls in Girls Club, were reading her book. "I finished it! Now I'm working on typing it up!"

"Oh!" Leigh Ann squealed. "I can't wait to read it! Do you have it?"

"Not with me. I'll bring some pages tomorrow."

Nicole slid into the spot beside them, carrying a blue tray with an assortment of food on it. "Love your apple, Cassie," she teased. "Looks so yummy."

"Hey, guys!"

Cassie swiveled along with the others at the table and nearly dropped her apple when she saw Miles standing at the head of the table. She forced her jaw to keep chewing so her mouth didn't drop open. How had he gotten so much cuter? She had not thought it possible! He still wore wire-rimmed glasses, but his brown hair was longer, not spiked in the front but falling casually across his forehead. And where before he'd carried the customary round face of a pre-adolescent, his face had thinned, matching the slight increase in height.

"Miles!" Nicole jumped up and hugged him, and Cassie felt a spasm of jealousy. Why couldn't she do that? "How are you? Sit down and eat!"

"I'm great!" He beamed at them all, a tray of food in his hands. "Hey, Cassie!"

"Hey, Miles," she managed to choke out, grateful she didn't squeak.

"I can't stay," Miles went on, "I already told some friends I'd sit with them. Maybe tomorrow, though!"

"Anytime!" Nicole waved him off and opened her carton of milk.

"I think you like him," Jimmy said, sounding slightly disgruntled.

"Oh, no, he's so sweet, but he's just a friend," Nicole said.

Cassie turned her head, watching Miles walk away. She could not say the same thing. Miles was not just a friend, not in her heart.

And the reality was, he wasn't even a friend. They'd barely spoken two sentences to each other all last year. What made her think this year would be different?

Because she would make it different.

Her eyes narrowed as Miles meandered his way around tables, finally stopping at one with a handful of giggly girls.

Andrea's table.

Cassie spent the next two classes plotting how she could convince Andrea to let her eat lunch with her. Sitting at that lunch table would solve so many problems. She'd immediately have a network of friends, and popular girls, no less. That was sure to launch Cassie into the stardom of popularity as well.

But also, and perhaps even more importantly, she'd be able to sit with Miles.

She wasn't even sure how to rank these things in importance, but one thing was very sure: she had to sit at that table.

She got excited for seventh hour, when she had the select choir, Unison. Only the best singers in the school got to be in Unison, and she couldn't wait to be a part of it.

She stepped into the classroom, and Ms. Berry gave her a smile.

"Afternoon, Cassie, great to see you. Go find a spot in first soprano, please."

Cassie did so, lifting her chin proudly. Here, she was recognized for how high she could sing. Ms. Vanderwood, the director of the children's choir Cassie went to twice a week, didn't place Cassie in such esteem, relegating her instead to the second soprano section. That fact burned Cassie.

She scanned the girls in the soprano section, seeing a few familiar faces. Her eyes landed on Maureen, a friend from Girls Club.

"Hey, Maureen," Cassie said, sitting down in the chair beside her.

Maureen wore her long, light brown hair in a braid down her back. She was busy on her phone, which wasn't a flip phone like Cassie's, but a new smart phone. She glanced at Cassie once before turning back to it. "Hey."

Well, that was the end of that conversation. Apparently they were only friends outside of school. Her eyes wandered around the classroom as more girls came in, settling themselves in the proper section. One eyebrow quirked up when she saw Riley come in. She'd forgotten they'd both made Unison. She watched Riley enter the room and held her breath, hoping she wouldn't sit near the first sopranos.

Nope. Riley was an alto. She moved to the other side of the room and found a seat next to Kendra, a pretty Latina with dark skin and black hair.

"Don't you want to go talk to her?" Maureen asked, drawing Cassie's attention back to her.

"Talk to who?" Cassie asked, narrowing her eyes.

Maureen bobbed her chin across the room. "Riley. Isn't she like your best friend?"

Cassie's face warmed at the condescending tone in Maureen's voice. "Not since fifth grade."

"I thought you guys hung out all the time."

An image flashed through Cassie's mind: Maureen sitting at the table with Andrea and Miles. She straightened, realizing this was yet another avenue to her planned popularity. And Riley was not a part of that plan. "No way. She's really immature and a total jerk. She just follows me around a lot."

Guilt rushed Cassie's belly at the words, and she flinched, knowing she shouldn't talk that way about someone. But Maureen laughed.

"Yeah, I remember her being that way." She put her phone away and studied Cassie. "You look different. Did you cut your hair?"

"I wish." Cassie fingered the ends of her super long brown hair, now barely showing any evidence of the curl she'd labored to put in it that morning.

"New glasses?"

Cassie shook her head.

"I know," Maureen said, and her eyes lit up. "You lost weight. A lot of it. How did you do that?"

This topic made Cassie uncomfortable, and she did not want to talk about it with her peers. "Just a little bit. I still have more to lose."

The conversation cut off when Ms. Berry went to the front of the room and began talking to them with a huge, earnest smile on her face. But Maureen shifted her body in the chair just enough that Cassie felt included, somehow.

"We're not going to waste any time in here," Ms. Berry said, "because there is none to waste. First thing you need to know is we have all-region tryouts coming up in October."

The ninth-graders, probably already familiar with the terminology, whispered and huddled together. But the rest of the eighth-graders looked just as confused as Cassie felt.

Kendra's hand flew into the air, and she called out, "What's all-region?"

Ms. Berry pointed at her. "Great question! All-region is a special choir made up of only the very best singers in this, well, region. Every singer has the chance to try out for the choir. Those who make all-region get to spend a day under the tutelage of a professional director and then put on a concert that evening. It's a very prestigious honor, and one that very few people will get."

Crapola. Cassie knew from the way her palms grew hot and her heart rate sped up that making this choir was not optional. She simply had to.

"So now I'm going to hand out your music and we're going to run through it. Starting next week, I'll be available after school for anyone who wants to stay and practice."

Cassie wouldn't be able to stay often. Between her activities and her parents' schedules, maybe she could make it work once a week . . .

Maureen accepted the sheet music from Cassie as it came down the row, and then she said, "We should get together and practice. Maybe at my house."

"That's a great idea," Cassie said, unable to believe her luck. "I'm going to need the practice."

"And you're a great singer. You'll be able to help me."

Cassie's heart warmed as she basked in the praise. "Of

course."

It looked like eighth grade was off to a good start. P.E. with Andrea, choir with Maureen, and both of them showed signs of wanting to be friends.

This was her year, Cassie just knew it. This was the year she'd become popular.

Episode 2: My Fair Lady

CHAPTER EIGHT

Big Plans

The first week of school would be a little easier and slower than the rest of the school year.

Or so Cassandra had hoped.

No such luck. By Tuesday all of her teachers were handing out assignments and giving pages in the text books to read.

And then she had community choir, also.

She walked through the doors of the community center and headed for the choir room along with several other kids, trying to ignore the prickling of dread building under her skin. Lately she hadn't enjoyed this choir so much as before. She didn't have any good friends here; in fact, there were some people she really didn't like. Ms. Vanderwood didn't consider Cassie one of her star singers and rarely played her to her full potential.

Worst of all, last year during the school performances, Cassie had made a fool of herself by spreading a false rumor about someone.

She took a deep breath and walked inside.

"Come in, come in, come in!" Ms. Vanderwood sang, clapping her hands as each student came through the door. Her reddish blond hair was up on top of her head, small kinky curls escaping around her face and softening her angular cheeks and nose. She waved at Cassie. "You know your position, just like last year!"

Cassie climbed the tiered steps and found a chair in the second soprano section. She smiled and nodded at a few people, but the familiar stirring of unrest cropped up in her chest. She could be doing something else right now. She didn't want to be here anymore.

The other kids all whispered and laughed together, replaying their summer adventures. Cassie reached into her backpack and pulled out a book. At least she'd had a chance to get to the library at school and check out the new selections.

"Now that we're all here. . . ." Ms. Vanderwood's eyes sparkled with barely contained excitement. "I hope you've had a great first two days of school. I need everyone's full attention, please, I have a big announcement."

Cassie supposed that meant she should put her book down. She did so, looking at Ms. Vanderwood expectantly.

"I met with a few choir directors from other states over the summer at a conference for choir directors. We talked about putting on a huge joint choir performance with our combined choirs."

Cassie just watched Ms. Vanderwood, unable to drum up the same level of anticipation her director obviously had. She preferred solos to large groups, feeling the pure, authentic sound was lost when too many voices joined the music. The bigger the choir, the worse the cohesive sound.

"But we need somewhere huge for all of our choirs to perform, right? Well." She took a deep breath, her toes lifting back and forth on the linoleum flooring. "We pulled some strings and managed to reserve Carnegie Hall!"

Cassie had no idea where that was, but judging from the gasps and shrieks in the room, some people did.

"Where is that?" Chris, a redhead boy in seventh grade, asked.

"New York City, of course," RyAnne said, her snotty,

condescending tone filling the room.

Cassie winced, especially glad now she hadn't asked. She and RyAnne had a long standing disagreement between them, both barely standing the other. She cast the thought aside and focused on the immediate present. New York! They were going to sing in New York! Cassie had been to New York state, but the last time she'd been to the actual city, she'd only been seven years old. This would be awesome! A trip with her choir and not her parents, even better!

Ms. Vanderwood kept talking. "It's going to be an expensive trip. So I've set up some fundraising opportunities for you guys throughout the year to help pay your way. Here are the dates we'll be gone." She turned around and wrote on the white board behind her, *June 10-14*.

Cassie pulled her backpack over and found the calendar where she wrote school assignments and projects due. She flipped to the very back, to the month of June. A little wave of euphoria rushed over her as she realized by the time she got to June, she would be done with eighth grade. The finish line was in sight.

Using her pencil, she wrote down, *choir trip to New York* on Tuesday, June 10. She drew the line across the dates until she reached the 14th, and then she wrote, *perform at Carnegie Hall*. Lifting her pencil, her eye caught the day written above the calendar square.

Sunday.

A hard knot tightened in Cassie's chest. Her family had very strict rules about how they spent their Sundays, which they held sacred as a day of rest. Most of the time Cassie found this a very convenient commandment, as it gave her an excuse to relax and not do any homework. But sometimes it was a sacrifice, when there were fun parties or events she didn't go to because they would not allow her to keep an attitude of worship. Her parents always allowed her to make her own decision, but after many years of debating whether she should go to birthday parties or an outing on Sunday, only one option left her in peace.

While everyone chatted excitedly around her, Cassie closed her calendar and put it back in her binder. She found a book and opened it, but she couldn't concentrate on the words. They ran circles and circles around her, and she knew her mind was elsewhere imagining the fun, jubilant trip everyone would have except her.

Ms. Vanderwood clapped her hands. "I know it's a lot to think about, but let's discuss it later. I have flyers for you to take home to your parents, and we will have many discussions and planning meetings over the next few months. For now, let's take a look at our new music!"

Cassie opened her music folder and tried to ignore the sour taste in the back of her mouth.

When practice finished, she didn't join in with the friendly conversations going on around her. She put her music folder into her backpack and stood up, eyes focused on the door.

"Cassie." Ms. Vanderwood stopped Cassie as she stepped off the risers. "Come over here for a second." She gestured to the small space between the chalkboard and the piano.

Cassie glanced over her shoulder as if she expected one of the other singers to say something, but nobody was paying any attention to them. Hesitant, Cassie made her way over.

Ms. Vanderwood give her a pleasant smile. "Cassie, I know you probably saw that the performance is on Sunday."

Cassie's throat closed up, and the emotions that she had managed to keep at bay all during the practice suddenly rose to the surface. She nodded, not trusting herself to speak for fear she would cry.

Ms. Vanderwood continued looking at her kindly. "I've already thought about your situation. I wanted to let you know, and you can tell your mother, if you would like to come on the trip, we can arrange for a chaperone to stay with you at the hotel on Sunday."

Was it really possible? They would let her come even if she wasn't going to sing with them? All she could do was nod, though her fingers gripped the straps of her backpack tighter and her toes did a little tap dance in her shoes, eager to get out the door and discuss this with her mother.

"You would still be required to practice with us every day and go through the routine as if you were singing with the choir. Then we would make other arrangements for you on Sunday. Think about it and let me know."

Finally Cassie found her voice. "Thank you. I'll talk to my mom."

Again she turned to leave, but again Ms. Vanderwood's voice called her back.

"Cassie? You probably shouldn't lose any more weight. You're looking kind of skinny."

Cassie tried to look humble and contrite, but the bubble of pride bursting up in her chest made her feel as if she were glowing. Last year nobody would have called her skinny.

She hurried out the door before anyone else could stop her, eager to tell her mom about this new development in choir.

Then something else occurred to her as she skipped toward the exit doors, and her steps slowed, the joy sucking right out of her. Even if Ms. Vanderwood said she could go, her parents had no money to send her. Her dad still didn't have a job, and the money situation had not gotten any easier over the summer. Frustration stung her eyes, and she wished, not for the first time, that she could be living a different life. One where she was beautiful and popular and rich.

Cassie didn't say anything about the trip to New York to her mother in the car. She desperately wanted her family to be able to afford for her to go, but she was afraid the answer would be no, and she wasn't ready to hear that.

She poked around at her dinner food, eating the green beans but not touching the rice and chicken. Chicken . . . a hundred and twenty calories per cup, without butter. She knew her mother had put butter in the chicken. Rice. She couldn't remember the calories. The only thing that she knew for sure was good for her was the green beans. So she ate them.

She was helping her younger sister Emily clear the table when her mom's phone rang.

"Hello?" Mrs. Jones answered. "Oh, hi, Ms. Vanderwood!" Her eyes darted over to Cassie, and Cassie knew her stalling time was over. "No, Cassie didn't mention it yet, but we just barely finished eating dinner. I'm sure she was going to."

Cassie pressed her hands on the back of the chair and leaned forward, neither confirming nor denying her mom's words.

"Wow, that sounds like quite an opportunity." Mrs. Jones wandered into the kitchen and turned her back on Cassie, looking out the dining room windows instead.

Cassie tried to read between the lines as she listened to her mother's end of the conversation. Her mother wasn't giving anything away. Her voice sounded neutral, not excited or discouraged.

"Oh. Oh really?"

Only with those words did Cassie detect a slight change in her mother's tone. And Mrs. Jones shot a quick look at Cassie over her shoulder. "Well, yes, I've noticed, but I didn't think— okay. Thanks for letting me know."

Mrs. Jones turned off the phone and turned around to face Cassie, her expression unreadable.

Cassie squirmed. "Well? Did she tell you about the trip to New York?"

"Yes, she did. And that's very interesting and we can talk about that more later. I'm more concerned with what else she brought to my attention."

Cassie frowned, wondering what she could have done to upset her mom.

"She said you've lost a lot of weight," Mrs. Jones said, her expression morphing into something of a glare. "She said she's concerned that you're too skinny."

"No, I'm not!" Cassie protested, though she still couldn't understand why this should be something negative. She tried to look innocent and indignant. "I'm perfectly normal."

Mrs. Jones's eyes were assessing Cassie differently now than they had before. "What did you eat for dinner?"

Cassie made a noise in the back of her throat, irritated by this interrogation. "The same thing you ate."

"You have lost lots of weight. Are you trying to?"

"Not really. I've just been trying to eat healthier and get in better shape." It was a white lie. Yes, she had been trying to, but she also wanted to be healthy, so they went together.

"I think you've lost too much. You need to stop."

Cassie felt the first twinge of panic, but she beat it down. "Stop what?"

"Stop dieting or eating healthy or whatever it is you're calling it. You need to gain some weight."

She forced a short laugh, all the while fighting down the urge to hyperventilate. "Mom. You're overreacting. I'm not on a diet, I'm just not eating everything I see. You don't want me to be fat, do you?"

Her mother's expression was torn as she chewed on her lower lip. "I'm going to be watching you. If you don't gain weight, I'm taking you to the doctor."

Cassie shrugged. "Fine." But what was the doctor going to say? There was nothing wrong with her.

She wanted to ask her mom about New York, but she sensed that somehow this wasn't the right moment. Turning around, she walked to her room, hoping she didn't look too defensive.

⁂

Cassie had never been excited about P.E. before. But now every day she got to see Andrea, who greeted her excitedly, hugging her and fawning over her as if they were long-lost best friends. Which, in Cassie's mind, they were.

"My mom said she's going to start watching what I eat," Cassie complained.

"What are you going to do?" Andrea asked. "You look so fantastic, you don't want to gain the weight back."

"I don't know. I'm really happy with how I look."

"Except maybe your hair," Andrea said.

Cassie looked at her in surprise as she switched into her tennis shoes. Andrea had never criticized her hair before. But even Cassie knew her hair could use a trim or style or something. It fell long and straight to her lower back, with no layers or even bangs. She'd worn her hair the same way as long as she could remember.

"I asked my mom to cut it but she wouldn't. I guess she likes it long."

Andrea sucked in an excited breath. "I know. I'll bring some scissors tomorrow and cut your hair for you."

Cassie gave her a skeptical look. "You know how to cut hair?

She waved off the question breezily. "Oh sure, it's easy. I cut all my friends' hair."

Excitement stirred in Cassie's chest. What could go wrong, anyway? "Okay, yeah. Let's do it!"

Coach Peters called them all to order and sent them outside for some tag football. While Cassie hated getting sweaty and forcing her body to move, she told herself it was just another way to burn calories.

She didn't say a word to her mom about her upcoming haircut at dinner. Instead, she focused on the cream sauce surrounding the eggs and toast, pushing her fork into the sauce so it bubbled around the tines and then putting her fork in her mouth to suck off the cream as if she were taking a full bite. She felt her mother's eyes on her, watching her, and in truth she was hungry, since she hadn't eaten anything at lunch. *It's probably okay to eat something*, she justified to herself. *I'm not going to suddenly get fat if I eat a little bit of dinner.* But she didn't like the way her mom was watching her as if she might step in at any moment and take control of Cassie's eating. Cassie cut the bread to tiny pieces with her fork. With each bite she took, she also swallowed a gulp of water.

The dog, Pioneer, sniffed around under the table like he did at every meal time. When Mrs. Jones turned to say something to Scott, Cassie loaded up half of a piece of bread with eggs and cream and slipped it to the dog. She finished the rest of her food herself, shooting her mom a smile as she cleared her plate. Mrs. Jones looked satisfied and didn't bring it up.

It wasn't until Cassie was putting away her math assignment before bed that she remembered to ask about New York. Her mom had just finished clearing the counters and was wiping them down.

"So about New York," Cassie said. "What do you think?"

Her mom straightened up to face Cassie. "It sounds like so much fun. And it's so nice of Ms. Vanderwood to think of you and provide an option so you can still go and not participate on Sunday. "

"But?" Cassie prodded.

"No buts, honey. Let's see what we can do, okay? Your dad is applying for jobs, and maybe something will work out."

As Cassie had suspected. It all boiled down to finances. She folded up her homework assignment and slipped it into her binder and put her binder by her backpack so she would have no difficulties finding it in the morning. She didn't say anything else about the trip to New York, but she cursed the soccer store and the financial difficulty it had placed upon them.

CHAPTER NINE
Fortifying

Cassie met Andrea as soon as she got to P.E. the next morning. "Did you bring the scissors?" she asked.

Andrea blinked at her with a look of mild confusion. "What scissors?"

Cassie just stared at her. "You're kidding, right? You're going to cut my hair today!" She didn't care what it took to get rid of this hair.

"Oh, right!" Andrea's eyes grew large. "I completely forgot! So sorry, Cassie! I'll bring them tomorrow, I promise!"

Somehow Cassie doubted Andrea had forgotten. More like, she hadn't taken it serious to begin with.

She didn't have much time to dwell on her disappointment, however, as they quickly moved out to the gym to practice—of all things—football.

"Why are we learning this?" Cassie said as they tossed the ball back and forth. "Girls don't play football!"

"I heard they have a girl on the team at Central!" Andrea replied, throwing the oval ball back to Cassie.

Central was the rival junior high. "Really?" Cassie caught the ball and tried to picture a girl dressed in padded gear and a helmet.

"Yeah. I guess she's real big and manly." Andrea giggled like this was hilarious, but Cassie still couldn't imagine it. She threw the ball back to Andrea, trying to put some curve in it.

"Nice spiral! Catch this one." Andrea pulled her arm back and chucked the ball at Cassie.

Cassie leaped for it, her arm stretching out. Almost, almost —

The ball hit her fingers with a slap, and Cassie shrieked as sudden pain jolted through her hand. She pulled her fist into her chest and bent over, sucking in deep breaths.

"Cassie? Are you okay?" Andrea hurried over, her eyebrows etched upward in concern.

"Uh-uh," Cassie grunted, blinking back tears. Her fingers throbbed, and she wasn't sure if she'd answered in the affirmative or negative.

The other girls had crowded around now, and Coach Peters pushed her way through.

"Okay, what happened?"

"I just threw the ball and Cassie caught it, but she got hurt!" Andrea said, looking close to tears herself.

The teacher gave Cassie an annoyed look. "Didn't I tell you to never catch the ball with your fingers?"

Had she said that? Cassie had to admit she hadn't paid so much attention. But if not with her fingers, how was she supposed to catch the ball?

"Let me see." The teacher took Cassie's hand none too gently and pried her fingers open.

"Ow!" Cassie cried. The tears slipped from her eyes, falling unbidden down to the hardwood floor.

Coach Peters released her with a sigh. "Let's call your parents and hope it's not broken."

The girls trailed behind, giving Cassie sympathetic looks.

"I'm so sorry," Andrea said, one arm around Cassie's shoulder as they walked. She released her at the teacher's office and watched as Coach Peters wrote a note for Cassie.

"Take this to the office," she said. "Wait there for someone to come get you."

"Should I go with her?" Andrea asked, but the teacher shook her head.

"Excitement's over, girls. Everyone head back to the gym. And catch the ball with your whole hand, not your fingers!"

⸙

By the time Mrs. Jones arrived at the school, Cassie's middle finger and ring finger had swelled up and turned purple. The nurse and office assistants had clucked over Cassie like mother hens, offering her ice and soda and candy. The sight of the chocolate made her stomach growl, but Cassie held strong and declined all but the water.

Mrs. Jones did not look thrilled as she walked into the office.

"What happened?" she asked, taking Cassie's hand and examining her finger.

Cassie winced at the slight pressure. "We were playing football. I thought I was doing pretty good. But I guess I caught the ball wrong."

Her mom sighed, then let go of Cassie's hand and sighed again. "All right. Let's get you checked out."

The medical clinic had an emergency room attached to it, so Mrs. Jones filled out paperwork while Cassie sat and waited. She pulled out a textbook and read ahead.

Mrs. Jones finally returned, sitting herself next to Cassie with a huff. "It could be awhile to get you back for an x-ray. In the meantime, I mentioned that I was concerned about your weight, and the doctor's going to give you a physical."

"What?" Cassie's alarm-o-meter went into high gear. "Why?" She thought they'd moved past this.

"Just to make sure, Cassie. Sometimes if someone loses a lot of weight on accident, they could have a hormonal imbalance or a thyroid issue." She cast a sideways glance at Cassie. "Unless your weight loss hasn't been accidental?"

Cassie didn't know what to say, so she lifted a shoulder in a shrug and turned back to her textbook, trying to pretend none of this mattered.

They finally called her back for the x-ray, and her fingers didn't even hurt anymore. She wished she hadn't called her mom.

"The x-ray will be ready in a minute," the nurse said to her mom when it was over. "And then the radiologist will come and talk to you about it. In the meantime, the doctor ordered a urine sample and a blood test."

A blood test? Cassie's heart rate increased. How long could she carry on this charade? There was nothing wrong with her. But she couldn't voice her objections without causing suspicions, so she gritted her teeth and bit her tongue while the nurse took her blood. Then, like a good girl, she went into the bathroom and peed in a cup.

The radiologist was waiting when she returned. "Good news!" he said, laying black and white photos on a projector. "No broken fingers. Definitely jammed, though. You can see that from the swelling in the tissue. We've got a little finger splint here, but you'll probably only need it for a week."

Cassie just nodded while he helped her put it on, her thoughts brooding on what the doctor was going to say about her weight. If only she hadn't jammed her stupid fingers!

"How're your fingers, honey?" Mrs. Jones asked, stepping close and brushing her hand over Cassie's head.

Cassie cocked her head, pulling out of reach. "They're not hurting anymore."

"Well, I'm glad they're not broken."

Cassie wished they were. At least then she'd have a real reason for being here.

The door opened again, and another nurse poked her head in. "We're going to move you across the hall to the regular clinic rooms, Cassie. But first, let's get your height and weight."

Cassie kept her eyes down as they led her to the scale. Why

was her mother hovering over her shoulder?

The nurse moved the scales and then wrote down the number. Cassie lifted her eyes and stole a glance, and relief flooded her. The number was two pounds less than the last time she'd weighed herself. Pleased, she followed the nurse to the ruler and let them get her height.

Mrs. Jones moved to the nurse's side and examined the clipboard. "Where is she on the weight chart?"

"Let's sit in a room and I'll show you." The nurse moved them to an empty room and pulled up a screen on the computer. "Cassie's definitely underweight, though not extremely. The biggest concern is that since we saw her last summer, she's lost almost twenty pounds."

Last summer. With an effort, Cassie remembered the summer before seventh grade. She'd done soccer camp and church camp, and that was when she'd first become aware of how much larger she was than her peers. "But I'm not unhealthy. I was then. Now I'm normal."

The nurse and Mrs. Jones turned to look at her, and then the nurse flashed her mom a smile. "I'll tell the doctor you're ready." She left the room.

Cassie and her mom sat in silence. Cassie wasn't sure what to say. She had the feeling anything she said could be used against her.

The doctor came in, breaking the awkward tension. "Hi, Cassie." He shook her hand and wiggled the mouse to wake the computer screen. "You've been having fun with a football, I hear."

"Yeah," Cassie grunted with an eye roll.

He sat on a rolling stool and scooted in front of the bed she sat on. "So tell me how you're feeling. Your mom's worried about your weight loss."

"I feel fine. Great, actually, better than ever." She gestured at the computer. "You can see from my chart that I used to be overweight. I haven't done anything crazy. I just wanted to get healthy."

"So this is intentional. Good to know." He made a few notes on his pad. "How have you gone about being 'healthier'?"

She shrugged. "Watched what I ate. Exercised more. Cut out sweets."

"These are good things in moderation, Cassie. But I have to tell you from your urine sample, you're cutting out too much. We found protein in your urine."

She wrinkled her nose. "Wouldn't that mean I'm getting too much meat?"

"Actually what it means is that you're getting so little protein, your body has started to metabolize your muscles. You're losing muscle mass and getting weaker."

Cassie gulped, a cold chill washing over her. "I didn't know that."

He turned to Mrs. Jones. "Make sure she eats lots of protein. And Cassie." He faced her again. "You don't need to be dieting anymore. You've reached a healthy place and can even afford to gain some weight."

She nodded at his words but again felt a rush of pleasure. Who would have guessed last summer that she would be thin?

"She's fine otherwise," he said to Mrs. Jones. "Just keep mothering her and asking the hard questions." He gave them both a genuine smile and left the room.

"Well," Mrs. Jones said, her grin a little weak, "what do you think?"

Cassie exhaled. "I feel good. I like how I look. I want to be healthy." *And pretty, and popular, and well liked.* But she didn't add that last part.

"You are. So let's not lose anymore weight, okay? You don't want to take it too far."

Too far. Apparently there was such a thing. She didn't want her body eating its own muscles, so she gave a nod. "Sure. I'm good."

They stopped at Wendy's to get lunch, since her mom got

the employee discount.

"Want a hamburger?" Mrs. Jones asked. "Lots of meat."

The thought didn't sit right. She couldn't eat that. She mentally calculated the seven hundred plus calories involved in a hamburger. "How about some chili? Beans and meat. That's protein."

"Sounds great." Her mother ordered, and Cassie took tiny bites of the food, convincing herself the entire time that the calories going in were not going to hurt her.

⚜

Ms. Malcolm's perfectly coiffed hair didn't even move as she nodded a greeting at Cassie when she walked into voice lessons later that evening. "Come on in, Cassandra. Put your bags down, and let's do a scale to warm up."

Cassie obediently placed her music books next to the piano. She situated herself in front of the mirror and placed her feet hip-width apart, as she'd been taught.

They went through the warm-up, and then Ms. Malcolm told her to pull out her book. Cassie did so, dreading the moment when she would have to try to sing the song she hadn't practiced at all.

"Go ahead and turn to the song I gave you last week," Ms. Malcolm said, her tone pleasant.

Cassie opened her book and turned to the correct page.

"Now I want you to start memorizing the words. Are you having any difficulties with the music?"

"Um, no. Well, it's been a little harder than I thought. But I'm getting there."

"Let's sing through it and see where your trouble spots are."

Ms. Malcolm stopped only eight measures into it. She rested her fingers on top of the piano keys and met Cassie's eyes in the mirror. "You're having a difficult time with the rhythm. Did you practice with the voice recording I made?"

"A few times," Cassie fibbed. "Not as often as I could have."

Ms. Malcolm lifted her chin. "I know this is a challenging

piece, Cassie, but I really think it shows off the flexibility of your vocal chords. I need you to practice a little harder."

"Sure," Cassie said. She needed to practice more. If there was one person who believed in her, it was Ms. Malcolm.

⊙⌒⚬⌒⊙

The next morning in P.E., the girls gathered around Cassie to examine her fingers, solidified in their splint.

"I guess you're done with football," Coach Peters said, looking none too pleased about it. "But you can still run, so why don't you do laps while we play?"

Crapola. Cassie would rather jam all her fingers than run. But since that wasn't an option, she dutifully changed into her running shoes and started jogging around the gym while the other girls threw the football around. About five minutes in, she got too tired to continue and excused herself to the water fountain. Then she hung out around the fountain, dawdling as much as she could.

Andrea came out and found her. "How's your hand? I'm so sorry."

"Oh, it's fine." Cassie waved the splint. "I wish I hadn't gone. My mom asked the doctor about my weight, and now I have to eat more."

Andrea looked suitably alarmed. "Do you think you'll gain weight?"

"A little weight is okay, I guess. The doctor said I'm too skinny."

"I think you look beautiful." The admiration was clear in Andrea's voice as her eyes roved over Cassie.

"Thanks." Cassie followed her back into the gym.

"Oh, I almost forgot!" Andrea spun back to Cassie and grabbed her arm, a big smile splitting her face. "I brought the scissors!"

Cassie had forgotten, with all the other excitement. Now a thrill went through her chest. "Fantastic!"

While the other girls changed, Andrea sat Cassie down on

the bench closest to the showers. The lockers blocked them from view, but still Andrea didn't waste any time. Cassie faced the lockers and tried to watch for approaching shadows, any indication that someone might be about to walk in on them. Particularly, a teacher.

The scissors made an odd sighing sound with each snip, and strands of dark brown hair floated to the ground.

"Almost done," Andrea said, breathing loudly through her mouth as she concentrated. "This side's too long—ugh, no, now this side's too long."

Cassie shifted anxiously on the bench, aware that time was slipping past them. The other voices in the locker room had drifted away, and she suspected they were the only ones not on their way to class. "How short is it?"

"Just below your shoulder blades—right here." Andrea's hand brushed Cassie's shirt in the back.

The warning bell rang, and Cassie jumped up, not about to get a tardy. "That's good enough." She glanced over her shoulder but realized she couldn't even see it. "How does it look?"

"Great, great, it looks great!" Andrea's cheeks were flushed, and she gave a big smile.

"Thank you!" Cassie gave her a quick hug, holding her hand out to avoid any more unintentional damage, then hurried from the locker room, not even bothering to change her clothes. She could do that before lunch.

CHAPTER TEN
Music Overload

"Cassie, you cut your hair!"
"Cassie! I love your hair!"
"OMG, I thought you would never cut it!"

Throughout the rest of her morning classes, nearly every person Cassie talked to had a comment about her hair. No one could believe she'd cut it, and everyone loved it. Cassie still hadn't seen it, but their compliments made her beam with pride. If only she could get rid of these wretched glasses. She was on her way to becoming pretty.

She finally had the chance to stop at a mirror before lunch. She hurried into the bathroom and changed into regular clothes, and then stopped to examine her reflection. Straight on, she couldn't tell her hair was different, but when she turned slightly and looked in the mirror, she saw the hair stopped about halfway down her back.

She frowned. The edges didn't look very straight. Maybe it was the way she was standing. She turned around and tried looking over the other shoulder, but that didn't help.

Oh well. What could she do? At least she'd gotten it cut.

"Love the hair, Cassie," Nicole said at lunch. "I noticed it in class but didn't get the chance to say anything."

"What's different?" Luke asked. He peered around Cassie's back. "Hey, you got it cut!"

Cassie nodded. "Finally. It was like all the way down my back. I hated it." She spotted Miles walking into the cafeteria with a couple of other guys, and her eyes trailed him as he went to the table next to the hot lunch pick up. Amity and Cara scooted over, making room for him to drop in next to them. She exhaled and opened her carton of milk. How much longer before Andrea considered her popular and pretty enough to sit at their table?

Cassie didn't go home straight after school, since she had community choir. She received more attention there than she ever had before, kids who she didn't know stopping to compliment her hair. Who knew chopping off a few inches would make such a difference?

It took all of ten seconds after Cassie got into her mom's van for Mrs. Jones to notice.

"Cassandra. What happened to your hair?"

Crapola. Cassie had turned her back to her mom while she slammed the door, not even thinking. Oh well. She couldn't hide it forever. "Well." Her mind whirled, trying to come up with a plausible solution. "I got some gum in my hair at school and couldn't get it out, so we cut it."

Her mom's eyes narrowed. "Who's we?"

"Just some friends who happened to have scissors." Cassie didn't want to tell it was Andrea. Her mom still wasn't too happy with Andrea for ditching Cassie last year, and she might become suspicious that it had been planned.

"Well, your friends did a horrible job." Her mom pushed on the gas and moved the car away from the community center. "I'm going to have to fix it tonight."

Cassie's heart soared. Yes! That's what she'd been asking for this whole time! This might not be how she'd planned it to happen, but that hardly mattered. She was getting her hair cut.

Friday Cassie walked into the school building sporting her new shorter hair. Her mom had complained about the horrible job Andrea had done the whole time, and finally only stopped cutting when the hair was just barely below Cassie shoulders.

"I'm sorry it's so short," her mom lamented. "The more I tried to get it even, the shorter it got."

"I love it," Cassie said, swishing her head from side to side and watching the hair dance across each shoulder. She felt lighter, older. Prettier.

"Oh well," Mrs. Jones said. "I guess I couldn't keep you young forever."

Cassie scowled, irritated that her mom had been trying.

But now the ordeal was behind her, and she was at school looking different than anyone had ever seen her. For the first time ever, she appreciated her straight dark hair, which shone brilliantly with each flash of her head as if she were modeling in a shampoo commercial.

People stopped talking as she walked by, and heads followed her to her locker. She preened a little bit as she pulled out her books, feeling, for the first time, beautiful.

Even in P.E., people stared at her. Andrea's eyes widened as Cassie came in.

"Cassie! You look beautiful!"

Cassie smiled and felt a flutter of hope that today would be the day Andrea invited her to eat lunch with her and her friends. But by the end of class no invitation was forthcoming, and Cassie battled off the disappointment.

She got the same reaction the rest of the school day, and she knew getting her hair cut had been the best decision ever.

She found her mom in the kitchen after school, prepping for dinner, as usual.

"Everyone loved my hair," Cassie said, leaning on the counter and picking up an apple. She examined the shiny green peel and thought better of it. Eighty calories. She'd eaten lunch, so she better skip the apple. "Thanks for cutting it for me."

Mrs. Jones looked up from the onion. "I didn't want to do it, but I have to admit it looks really good. Suddenly you're so grown up."

Cassie smiled back, a surge of happiness rushing through her. Maybe the apple wouldn't hurt her. She picked it up again and took a bite before she could change her mind. "I was thinking about my glasses."

Her mom gave her a searching look, then focused on the onion again.

Cassie gathered courage from the response. At least she hadn't been shot down. "I would really like to get contacts. I'm thirteen now. I'm mature enough to take care of them. I wash my face every day, I brush my teeth, and I shower without being told. I'm not a little girl anymore, Mom."

Her mom didn't say anything for a solid minute. Cassie counted the seconds as she chewed her apple.

"You have your annual eye doctor appointment next week," Mrs. Jones said finally. "We can look into it."

Yes! Cassie contained her jubilation and nodded calmly. "Thanks, Mom. I appreciate that."

Her mom exhaled. "Now go do your chores and practice your music."

"Sure." She hopped off the stool and headed for the laundry room, elated. She would do whatever her mom wanted if she could just get contacts.

On Tuesday, Cassie waited after the children's choir practice to talk to Ms. Vanderwood. As the last kid cleared out, she stepped up to the piano and cleared her throat.

Ms. Vanderwood stuffed the last binder into her plastic crate and looked up. "Hi, Cassie. I was about to ask you what you guys decided."

Cassie beamed. "My mom said I can go on the trip. She said it's really nice of you to let me come along even though I won't be performing."

"Fantastic. You're a part of this choir, and we want you involved." Ms. Vanderwood hesitated. "Did you discuss the costs?"

"No." Cassie frowned. "My mom didn't say anything about that at all."

"Well, I talked about it with her a little bit, but let her know we'll be doing fundraisers as a choir and trying to raise money. Plus it's nine months away. Maybe you can see what opportunities you have to earn money."

"Oh. Oh, right." Cassie hadn't even thought about herself earning the money. How? The only people that paid her were her parents, either for babysitting or working in the soccer store, and they didn't pay her very much, at that. "Sure, yeah, I'll work on that."

"Your hair looks great, by the way," Ms. Vanderwood said. "I really like it."

"Thanks," Cassie said. She thought about saying how her weight was none of Ms. Vanderwood's concern, that the doctor said she was fine. She decided not to. It might not have been Ms. Vanderwood's place to be so nosy, but Cassie knew her director just wanted to help. And she didn't want to get on her bad side when they were planning this trip to New York. She shouldered her bag and walked out the door.

On Thursday Ms. Berry handed out the music for all-region, and Cassie felt her head spin. So much music. She had promised Ms. Malcolm she would memorize that song, and Ms. Vanderwood already had them practicing Christmas music. Now she had to put this together too? While she loved music and was glad it got to be such a big part of her life, she wondered if there could be too much of a good thing. She didn't want to become burned out or annoyed with all of her musical activities.

"When are you going to practice for all-region?" Maureen

asked her. "Are you staying after school tomorrow?"

"I'll have to ask my mom," Cassie said. She hadn't planned to stay after school on Friday, but she really should practice. And maybe if she became better friends with Maureen, Andrea would start to think she was cool, also.

"Did you say you're staying tomorrow?" Kendra, another girl in the choir, asked.

"I have to talk to my mom first," Cassie said, but Kendra didn't seem to care about the response so much.

"I'm sure you're going to make it, you're one of the best singers in here. If you're staying to practice, I should too."

Cassie didn't have the chance to say again that she didn't know if she would be able to. Maureen spoke up, saying, "I'll be staying too. Cassie knows the music, and she'll be able to lead us."

Cassie turned her head in surprise, but nobody else had a chance to say anything before Ms. Berry clapped her hands.

"Let's go over the songs. I know it's the first time you guys are seeing it, but let's practice."

"Not Cassie," Maureen whispered. "She already knows the music."

Cassie's face burned. She didn't know the music, and she didn't like being set up for false expectations.

Somehow Cassie convinced her mom to let her stay after school on Friday. Luckily she didn't find the song too hard, and after they'd gone over it in class twice, she felt pretty comfortable.

"Watch those high notes, ladies," Ms. Berry said, holding her hand above her head and pointing her finger toward the far wall. "Stand on your tippy toes if you need to, but get on top of that note. Let's try it again."

Cassie stood around the piano with five other girls who also had stayed after school to practice. Today was just the sopranos. On Monday the altos would get a chance, and second sopranos on Tuesday. Cassie doubted she'd be able to stay every Friday, but at least she could today.

They ran through the measure again, and Ms. Berry stopped them.

"Nice job, Cassie!" She smiled at Cassie. "Follow her lead, ladies, she's got that high note."

The other girls looked at her.

The rest of the practice, Cassie did her very best to hit each note right on target. She couldn't help being hyper aware of the other girls, leaning closer to her and trying to match pitches with her.

Maureen walked outside with Cassie when practice was over.

"We should get together next week and practice," she said.

"Sure," Cassie said. "I'd love to."

"Are you still in Girls Club?" Maureen asked.

Before junior high, Maureen had been in Girls Club with Cassie, and they'd been friendly. But Maureen had quit going last year. "Yeah, I'm still in it," Cassie said, a bit sensitively. Would Maureen think she was childish?

"Cool," was all she said. Maureen pushed her bangs back from her face, and they fluttered in waves by her temples.

Cassie pointed to the blue van as it pulled up to the school. "There's my mom. I'll see you Monday."

"See ya," Maureen said.

Cassie climbed into the car and couldn't help feeling excited. Things were looking up. Finally.

CHAPTER ELEVEN
The Eyes Have It

Cassie spent the weekend typing up her book and was pleased when she got nearly thirty pages done. She also practiced her song, certain that this time when she walked into music lessons, she wouldn't disappoint Ms. Malcolm.

Monday after school, Mrs. Jones took Cassie to the eye doctor. Cassie sat in a chair by the window, filling out paperwork and trying not to get too excited. Or nervous. Contacts! She couldn't wait to try them. It had been so long since she'd seen her face without glasses, she wasn't even sure what she looked like!

"Cassandra Jones," a woman in scrubs said, stepping into the waiting room and scanning the crowd.

"Here," Cassie said, standing, her mother beside her.

She tolerated the preliminaries, sitting down in the seat and finding the hot air balloon in the view finder, and moments later enduring a puff of air to her eye from that same view finder. Only when they'd entered the examination room did she blurt out, "I want to get contacts." Then she remembered her mother and added, "If that's okay."

"Your mom already talked to us," the woman said, using an alcohol wipe to clean the chin rest. "We'll get you fitted for them today."

"Ha!" Cassie couldn't help the laugh that escaped her lips. She tried to wipe the grin from her face.

"But Cassie," her mom said, "we're getting the ones that you don't throw away. They're cheaper than disposables in the long run. But if you rip one, you have to buy a new one with your own money."

"So I keep them forever?" Cassie asked. She didn't really know the difference between disposables and not. Was that a big deal?

"Until your prescription changes," the assistant said. "We'll show you how to clean them. And you soak them in enzymes once a week."

"Okay." Sounded great to Cassie.

The doctor came in and adjusted the device in front of her eyes, instructing her to read different lines of text to him. "Everything looks good," he said, turning to Mrs. Jones. "Her myopia has gotten a little worse, but that's typical for this age. I'll update her prescription and let my assistant get her fitted for contacts."

"Are you sure this is what you want?" Mrs. Jones asked as she led Cassie to the next room. "I had contacts for years and hated them."

Cassie glanced at her mom and tried to imagine her without the frames around her eyes. "I want this more than anything."

"Let's do it, then," Mrs. Jones said, gesturing at the chair.

"Okay," the assistant said cheerfully, pulling a few boxes from shelves on the wall. "First time for contacts?"

"Yes," Cassie said, wiggling her feet.

"Well, let me tell you, there's a bit of a learning curve to putting them in."

This was the part that most scared Cassie. She hated anything that had to do with even looking at the eyeball, let alone touching them. And she strongly suspected that to get the contacts into her eyes, she'd have to touch them.

"So here we go." The woman opened a small foil container and removed a flimsy transparent circle, about the diameter of a dime, with her finger. "You have to make sure your fingers are clean before you touch these. Sit very still and open your eyes wide."

Cassie sucked in a breath and widened her eyes. She stared as hard as she could at the wall in front of her, but as the woman came near with the little lens, Cassie's fingers dug into the armrests on either side of her chair.

"Keep your eyes open," the woman said, her finger coming closer.

"Epee!" Cassie squealed, barely moving her mouth. Her heart pounded harder, harder, and her eyelids trembled, trying desperately to close.

"Come on, honey, eyes open."

Cassie forced them open, and suddenly the little circle pressed upon her eye.

She's going to poke my eye out! Cassie thought, but before the woman had even touched her, she took a step back.

"There. That one's in."

It was in? Cassie blinked and noticed the sensation of an object directly beneath her eyelid. "It feels weird."

"It always does at first. You'll get used to it. Now." She picked up the other foil case. "Let's do the other."

Uh-oh. Not again. Cassie's breathing quickened, and she tensed up even quicker this time. She gripped the armrests and squeezed her eyes shut.

"I can't get it in with your eyes closed. Open up."

Whimpering, Cassie pried her eyes open and blinked several times.

The finger came closer—closer—

Cassie gasped and closed her eyes.

"Ma'am, look at this," the woman said, and then she and Mrs. Jones started laughing.

"Cassie, take a look at yourself," Mrs. Jones said.

Cassie peeked one eye open to see what they were laughing at. To her surprise, both of her legs were extended straight out in front of her. She'd been aware that she was gripping the armrest super tight, but she hadn't realized the tension had spread to her legs.

Cassie started laughing as well, and they all giggled for a bit before the nurse said, "I can keep trying with this, or you can put it in yourself."

Cassie let out a slow exhale. "I think I would rather try it. How do I do it?"

"First you clean your fingers. Then you check and make sure the lens is turned the right way, like this." She showed Cassie how to read the numbers on the flimsy sphere so she knew it was the right way. "And you need to hold your eye open. Most people do this with the other hand. Then with the lens on your index finger, gently place it on your eye."

She made it sound so easy, but Cassie was already taking several deep breaths at the thought of nearly touching her eye. She wanted this. She wanted contacts. She would do this.

Cassie washed her hands and dried her trembling fingers on the paper towel the nurse placed in front of her. Then she dipped her finger into the foil package with the contact lens and removed the little half-sphere. She held it up to the light and examined it for the letters to indicate she had it correct. So far, so good.

The nurse placed a mirror in front of her, and Cassie stared at her reflection. She grabbed the skin around one eye and held it open while she used her other finger to bring it up close to her eye. Closer, closer, closer.

Plop. She stuck it on her eye, surprised at how quickly the lens pulled away from her finger. She blinked several times, trying to get used to the sensation of a foreign object under her eyelid.

"Great job," the nurse said. "How does that feel?"

"It's all right," Cassie said. "It doesn't hurt, at least."

"Make sure you dry your fingers before you touch it. If your finger is wetter than your eye, the contact will stick to your finger instead."

"Look at me, Cassie," Mrs. Jones said.

Cassie turned her face toward her mother, still blinking at the sensation of something in her eyes.

"I'll get the doctor," the assistant said. "He's going to want to look and see how those fit."

"What do you think?" her mom asked.

Cassie turned back to the mirror in front of her and examined her reflection. She could see herself, really see herself, no glasses to block the view. And she liked what she saw. "I love them. They look amazing."

The eye doctor came in, and he shined a light into Cassie's eyes, checking how the lenses looked. "These look great. Let's try them out. I only want you to wear them for two hours a day for the first two days, then four hours a day for two days, then six hours a day. Go ahead and work up to ten hours a day, but don't wear them for longer than that. If you have any issues, please call. I want to see you in two weeks, and we'll make sure everything looks good."

Cassie nodded, beaming. She could hardly wait to go to school.

Cassie stepped onto the bus in the morning, trying not to glance around at everyone, fully expecting that most people wouldn't notice she no longer wore glasses. Still, she couldn't help being disappointed when nobody, not even the bus driver, said anything. She sat down and pulled out her science vocabulary sheet, using the last few minutes before school started to study.

By the time she got to the eighth-grade locker hall, Cassie had almost forgotten anything had changed. She turned the dial at her locker and put away her science book. She had just retrieved her tennis shoes when Nicole slid over, giggling hysterically.

"Cassie, you're never going to believe this, guess who—" Nicole's eyes narrowed. "Did you get contacts?"

A sheepish grin spread its way across Cassie's face, and she nodded.

"Oh, wow, you look great!"

It was like Nicole had never seen her before. Cassie put her tennis shoes in her backpack and said, "Really?"

"Yeah, you look so different!"

Cassie's heart squeezed hopefully. Maybe a certain boy would think she looked really great also.

"How're the fingers?" Coach Peters said cheerfully when Cassie walked in.

Cassie wiggled her bandaged fingers at her. "Just a few more days and I get this off."

"Excellent. Go ahead and dress out, you can run laps."

"Yay," Cassie muttered to herself.

Andrea plopped down beside her on the bench as Cassie tied her shoes.

"Hi, sweetie, how are you?" Andrea said, giving Cassie a shoulder hug.

Cassie lifted her head. "Great! I—"

She never got the chance to say what it was she had, because Andrea was already squealing, "You got contacts!"

"Yes." Cassie grinned at her.

"Oh Cassie! I can't believe how beautiful you are!" Andrea launched into song. "You are so beautiful . . ."

Cassie laughed and shushed her, but her heart warmed under the attention. Maybe today would be the day she would be invited to eat lunch with Andrea.

☙❦❧

Cassie had just squirmed into the seat next to Nicole and across from Luke at lunch when someone tapped her on the shoulder. She turned around to see Andrea standing there.

"Andrea!" Cassie exclaimed, vaulting to her feet.

"Hi, Cassie," Andrea said. "I didn't mean to bother you, but I want to see if you want to eat lunch with me."

Cassie's heart leaped into her throat. This was what she had been hoping for. "With you?" she said, just to clarify. "Like, here? In the cafeteria?"

Andrea gave a head-bob. "Well, me and my friends." She gestured toward the table behind her, but Cassie didn't even need to look. She knew all of Andrea's new friends were there. And Miles.

"I'd love to! That would be great! Let me just get my things." She turned around and swept up her phone, as well as the apple and sandwich she had purchased for lunch.

"Are you leaving us?" Luke asked.

Did Cassie detect a note of accusation in his voice? She put on a big smile and flashed it at him and Nicole. "I'm just going to go eat with some other friends today. I'll see you guys later."

Luke still didn't look too thrilled, but Nicole just gave a wave. "I'll have to tell you my news later then."

Cassie nodded. "Right. Okay, I'll catch you in class!" She felt a twinge of guilt as she followed Andrea to the other table, feeling Luke's eyes on her. But she pushed it down quickly as Andrea introduced her.

"Guys, this is Cassie. Cassie, that's Amity, I think you know Cara, Janice, and Maureen. Oh, and." Andrea gave her a little shove with a twinkle in her eye. "That's Andrew and Jacob and maybe you know Miles?"

There was no mistaking the teasing in her voice, but Cassie refused to look at Miles even as she felt the heat rush to her cheeks. "Hi, everyone," she said. Where was Kitty? Kitty was the one who most intimidated Cassie. She had been Andrea's best friend before Cassie, but then she moved away and Andrea and Cassie became best friends. It was when Kitty moved back that Andrea underwent her swan-like transformation and didn't want to be friends with Cassie anymore.

"Hi, Cassie," Janice said, giving her a smile. They already knew each other from Girls Club.

"Oh, I'm glad you're eating with us," Maureen said. "Now we can plan when to get together and practice our music."

Cara smiled and gave a little wave. Only Amity seemed disinterested, casting a glance at Cassie before turning back to an animated conversation with Jacob.

Cassie settled in next to Andrea, silently observing Amity on her right side. Everything she knew about Amity was from observation. Amity was loud and giggly and very flirtatious. And she didn't have a preteen figure like Cassie did, but had already filled out enough that Cassie was certain she wore a real bra. How was that possible? She looked at Jacob, the object of Amity's attention. His face was bright red as he attempted to eat his lunch, though he seemed to be having a hard time focusing in between Amity's giggles and pokes.

"I really like your hair, Cassie," Miles said.

Her heart skipped another beat, and Cassie stared down at the table for a moment before lifting her face to his. She'd been waiting for this moment. But now that he'd spoken to her, she didn't know what to say.

She met his eyes across the table and had to smile at his own friendly expression. Unlike her and Andrea, Miles still wore glasses. It didn't matter; he was as cute as ever. Cuter, even, because he was losing that little boy look and looking taller, thinner, and a little bulkier.

"Thank you," she said, her face warming again.

Amity swiveled slightly in her chair and turned her attention on Miles. Immediately she started teasing him, chucking bits of her lunch at him and stealing the entire conversation.

Cassie tried to go quietly back to her apple, but inside she fumed. Even more than being upset with Amity, though, she wondered why she couldn't just have a conversation with him. Why couldn't she act normal around Miles and talk to him the way she talked to Luke or Emmett?

"Oh, I'm so hungry," Andrea said beside her.

Cassie raised an eyebrow. "We're at lunch. Eat something."

Andrea shook her head. "I'm on a diet. I'm trying to be skinny like you."

Cassie guffawed loudly. "You're already skinny. You're perfect."

"Yeah, but I want to be skinnier." She sighed loudly, her eyes on Cassie's sandwich.

Cassie noticed. She tore it in half and offered some to Andrea. "Here. Just take half. A little won't hurt you."

Andrea took the bread hesitantly. "Are you going to eat yours?"

Cassie had been wondering that herself. She knew her mom wanted her to gain weight, but every time she stepped on the scale and saw that she had, it made her feel gross. And that grossness followed her around all day.

Still, if she didn't, Andrea wouldn't either.

"Yeah." To prove her point, Cassie took a bite.

"Okay, then." Andrea took a bite as well.

"We're done and going outside," Andrew said, standing up. Miles and Jacob joined him. "You girls coming?"

"We're still eating," Maureen said.

"I'm done," Amity said.

"No, you're not," Cara said, grabbing Amity's wrist as she stood. "Bye, guys!"

"Why couldn't I go with them?" Amity grumbled as the boys walked off.

"You have a boyfriend," Janice hissed.

"And you're here to be with us," Cara said. "Don't forget that. Girlfriends before boyfriends."

Cassie put her sandwich down and instead worked on her apple.

CHAPTER TWELVE
Tricks and Treats

Cassie's dad picked her up from music and drove her to church, so there was no opportunity to explain the difficult situation she'd created to her mother.

She stepped into the classroom for the teenage girls and was surprised to see Riley there. Riley hadn't come to church since over the summer. Now Riley caught her eye and gave a little wave, but Cassie turned away. It would take more than that to apologize.

Sister Cindy stood up to get their attention, particularly Sue and Michele, who didn't stop talking until Sister Cindy called them by name. Cassie rolled her eyes. Typical. Those two girls thought they were something special.

"We're having a Halloween dance the last week of October," Sister Cindy said. "We're combining with the Fayetteville and Rogers units, so we'll have a good crowd."

That just made Cassie think of her Rogers friends, Elise and Tesla. How she missed them.

"As usual, the dance is only for ages fourteen and up," Sister Cindy said.

This announcement was met with groans and sighs of dismay. Cassie kept quiet, but she wondered what the dances were like.

"But don't worry," Sister Cindy said, "for those of you not old enough to go to the dance, we're putting on a Halloween carnival for the families. We get to help with that!"

Now Cassie groaned. Like helping with the carnival was supposed to make it better? That did not sound like something she would enjoy.

The older girls got started on a different activity while Sister Cindy gathered the younger girls into a smaller room.

"I need you girls to think of fun activities that the children would enjoy. Like fishing for candy, or a haunted hallway. I'll be back in a moment to see what you've come up with."

"This sounds so boring," Jessica, a short girl with blond hair, said, looking perfectly annoyed.

Cassie couldn't agree more, but because Jessica thought it also, she wanted to object. "We're in charge of the Halloween party. Whether it's lame or not depends on us."

"Nothing we do will make this fun," Jessica said.

"I agree with Cassie," Riley said. "At least we can brainstorm some cool activities."

"Have at it," Jessica said, crossing her arms over her chest.

Cassie looked at Riley and gave an exaggerated eyeroll, inclining her head slightly toward Jessica. Riley snorted, and then they both fell into a fit of giggles.

And just like that, the resentment she'd harbored toward Riley for the past two months melted away. She scooted closer to her, and they began planning the Halloween carnival.

"Bye, Cassie!" Riley said, waving when her mom picked her up from church. "I'll try to come on Sunday so we can hang out!"

Cassie had to admit it felt nice not to be mad anymore. But if Riley thought Cassie was ready to be her best friend again, though, she was wrong.

"Okay. See you later."

As Cassie got into the Jones' van, she immediately thought

how much fun it would be if Andrea came to the Halloween party.

⁂

Cassie had a hard time getting Andrea's attention Thursday morning. Though she'd eaten lunch with Andrea's friends, she didn't think of them as her friends. They must have felt the same, because none of them looked at her or talked to her at the benches before school. Not even Andrea noticed Cassie standing to the side, waiting for a chance to speak.

The warning bell rang and Cassie went inside, fully irritated. When would the other girls think she was one of them?

She went to P.E. and dressed out. For the first time in a week, she had no splint on her fingers, and the bruising had faded to a weak yellow. She glanced up as Andrea bounced in.

"Hi, Cassie!" she said cheerfully, her light brown hair curled and parted on one side and falling in her face.

Cassie's indignation over earlier faded away. "Hey, Andrea." She pulled her dark hair into a pony tail. "My church is having a Halloween carnival next Friday. Want to come?"

"Oh, sure, that sounds like tons of fun!" Andrea said, changing her shorts and pulling her own hair up.

She'd been a little afraid Andrea would laugh at her and tell her she didn't celebrate Halloween anymore. "Oh, awesome. You know what would be so fun? You could spend the night after!"

"That sounds great! Why don't I just come over right after school?"

"Okay!" Cassie said, hardly believing her luck. What she'd wanted for the past year was actually coming true. She and Andrea were becoming friends again.

⁂

"Our first choir concert is the week after All-Region tryouts," Ms. Berry said in seventh hour. "We'll sing the All-

Region songs for your parents, since that's what we'll be working on for the next month."

"A choir concert. How fun," Maureen said.

Cassie nodded.

"So we need choir dresses," Ms. Berry said. "I'm going to call you out into the hall one by one and measure you for your dresses. Most of them are in stock, so we might even have them by tomorrow."

Cassie had seen the green dresses the select choir wore. They were floor-length and layered, tight around the waist and flaring at the hips. She loved them and couldn't wait for her own.

As Ms. Berry began calling the students, Cassie turned to Maureen.

"I'm staying for practice tomorrow after school. Are you?"

Maureen squinched up her nose. "I can't. I'm spending the night with Amity. She's still sad she didn't make Unison, and I don't want to make it worse."

"Oh, of course." Cassie nodded, though she hadn't realized Amity tried out for Unison. How would she know? Amity didn't even look at her at lunch. But that made her think of something else. "Where's Kitty? Does she have a different lunch?"

Maureen's lips turned downward. "Kitty moved at the end of last year. She doesn't live here anymore."

"Oh, I'm sorry," Cassie said, while inside her heart churned. Kitty moved. Kitty had moved! No wonder Andrea was being so nice. She didn't have a best friend anymore.

Cassie ought to feel used, but all she felt was elated that Kitty was gone, leaving room once again for Cassie to be the best friend. This time, she was determined to keep the role.

※

"I want to remind you guys," Ms. Talo said in English class on Friday, "that we have the Market Fair in November this year. That might seem forever away, but it's only a month out.

It's time to be brainstorming."

"Are you sure you'll be okay without a partner?" Nicole asked Cassie as they packed up their bags after class.

Cassie had no idea. But she knew Nicole didn't want to be her partner this year. "Oh, yeah."

Jimmy came over to them and shocked Cassie when he put an arm around Nicole and rested his chin on her shoulder.

Nicole flashed a grin at him. "Hi."

"Hi," he replied, then took a step back from her. "See you at lunch."

Cassie gaped. "Are you guys—?"

"Going out," Nicole replied, a smile splitting her face from ear to ear. "That's what I kept trying to tell you. He asked me out a few days ago."

"Wow," Cassie said, flabbergasted. "Do you like him?"

A deep rosy color crept up Nicole's cheeks. "I've liked him since last year, but don't tell him that. I couldn't believe it when he finally asked me out."

"Well, I'm happy for you." She followed Nicole out of the classroom, trying to wrap her mind around this development.

"Are you eating lunch with us? Jimmy sits at our table now too."

"Oh, thanks." Cassie shook her head. "I've been eating with Andrea and her friends."

"Ditched us, did you?" Nicole said, but she didn't sound annoyed.

Cassie's face warmed. "I'm sorry. I didn't mean to."

"No worries," Nicole said. "I know why you did it."

Cassie just blinked at her. "You know why? What do you mean?"

Nicole smirked. "Everyone knows you've had a crush on Miles for years. I don't blame you at all for taking the chance to sit with him at lunch."

Cassie wanted to sink into the floor, fade into the wall. "What do you mean, everyone knows?" Did Miles know?

"I bet he likes you too, Cassie."

This conversation was unbelievable. How did they all know? Was she so obvious? Suddenly she dreaded going to lunch and sitting at the table with him.

But Nicole continued shepherding her toward the cafeteria, completely unaware of the turmoil she'd caused in Cassie's head.

Once inside, Nicole abandoned her for her own table, leaving Cassie standing there, breathing hard and trying to calm herself.

Nothing's changed, she reminded herself. *Just walk over and sit down like normal. Miles doesn't know.* There was no way he could know.

She tried to comfort herself with these words as she went to the table and sat down. Andrea hadn't arrived yet, and while Janice said hello, nobody else glanced at her. Cassie pulled out her lunch of cheese and crackers and waited for Andrea to join them. The boys weren't even there, much to Cassie's relief—and disappointment.

She listened to the conversations around her and took a nibble of her apple. How could she feel so lonely when she was surrounded by people?

The table jostled slightly as the boys arrived, and her heart took a nose-dive. Great.

"Hi, Cassie."

She uttered a small gasp and almost dropped her apple. Miles had sat across from her! "Hi," she said, forcing her lips into a smile. Her fingers fumbled, and this time her apple did roll away from her.

He nodded at it. "Might want to grab that."

"You could—grab—" Her voice choked up. She'd meant to tease him, say something flirty, but instead she sounded whiny and confused. She lunged forward and wrapped her hands around the apple.

"Hey!" Maureen exclaimed, speaking to Cassie for the first

time. "You made me spill my soda!"

"Sorry," Cassie said, and her face burned. She took a big bite of her apple and stared at it.

"I'm here, I'm here!" Andrea fell into the seat beside Cassie, and Cassie exhaled. She turned slightly to face Andrea, completely blocking Miles from view.

"I'm so glad you're here," she breathed.

"Oh, yeah?" Andrea flashed her a smile, and finally Cassie had someone to talk to.

Maureen was all chatty in seventh hour, as if she hadn't ignored Cassie all through lunch—except for when her soda spilled, of course. Cassie didn't feel like chatting. She pasted on a smile and nodded politely to everything Maureen said. Finally Ms. Berry started class.

"I've got great news, girls!" Ms. Berry said. "They actually had all the dresses in inventory that I need for you. I want you to take your dress and try it on in the band room. If it doesn't fit, now is the time to make changes."

Immediately the choir room lit up with excited chatter. Cassie felt a shiver of anticipation. What if the dress didn't fit her the way she imagined it would? She got up and joined everyone else in the hallway, getting their dresses, still in the plastic sleeve, off the rack. The band room sat just behind the choir room, and one of the only times it wasn't blasting loud music was during seventh hour.

Cassandra Jones. Cassie found the dress with her name pinned to the plastic. A little self-conscious, she did her best to hide behind it as she followed the mass of girls into the other room to change. She kept her eyes on the ground as she stripped out of the jeans and T-shirt and pulled the dress over her head.

It flowed over her shoulders and settled around her hips, none of it bunching up or pinching. She looked down at herself and spread her fingers down her torso. Where was a mirror when she needed one? She turned around and spotted

Riley, just getting her green dress down to her waist and shimmying to drop the layers.

"Does it look all right?" Cassie asked.

Riley nodded, her eyes brightening. "It looks perfect! It's like it was made for you."

The words encouraged Cassie, but she didn't know if she could trust Riley's judgment. She spotted Maureen, a frown creasing her forehead as she tried to smooth the dress out around her waist.

"How does the dress fit me?" Cassie asked.

Maureen spared her a glance. "It looks great, Cassie. But of course it does. You're so skinny."

Cassie pulled the dress off and put it back in the plastic, trying to keep the smug smile off her face.

⁂

"Don't forget our Girls Club meeting on Saturday," Riley said as the bell rang after choir on Friday.

"There's a meeting Saturday?" Cassie said, furrowing her nose. She'd hoped to have the day to herself, for once.

"Yeah. We're going to learn to crochet, so it might take a few hours."

Cassie could only assume she didn't know any of this because she hadn't paid attention the last time they met. Maybe she'd missed a meeting.

"I quit this year," Maureen said. "My mom's not the leader anymore."

"She's not?" Cassie said, surprised.

"Jaiden's mom's in charge now," Riley said, watching Cassie closely.

For good reason. Cassie and Jaiden's mom had a fight years ago, and even though it hadn't ever been brought up again, Cassie never forgot. She didn't care for the woman and always preferred to spend her time with Maureen's mom. "Maybe I won't be in it anymore, either," Cassie said.

"Yeah," Maureen said. She stepped closer to Cassie. "It's

kind of childish now." She hooked an arm through Cassie's and stepped closer. "Aren't you going to miss your bus, Riley?"

Riley looked back and forth between the two of them. "You're not coming, Cassie?"

"Not today," Maureen answered for Cassie, a haughty note entering her voice. "She's staying for All-Region practice."

"Oh. See you tomorrow, Cassie." Riley turned around and walked toward the buses.

Cassie slipped her arm away from Maureen and faced her. "I thought you weren't staying?"

Maureen shrugged. "Amity had something come up, so she's not spending the night. I can stay now."

Was Cassie the backup friend? Amity wasn't spending the night and now Maureen was being friendlier?

She told herself not to think about it too much and just be grateful for the friendship.

CHAPTER THIRTEEN
Little White Lies

"Get ready to go, Cassie, you've got Girls Club in an hour," Mrs. Jones said, walking through the front door on Saturday afternoon.

Cassie had just finished making sandwiches for her younger sister and brother and was chopping carrots for herself.

Mrs. Jones cast a weary look around the kitchen, which Cassie had taken the time to clean up before making food. "Thank you for your help, Cassie."

"Daddy's at the store?" Cassie asked, crunching into a carrot.

"Yes. Are you ready to leave?"

Cassie chewed slowly as she considered her next words. She swallowed and took a swig of water before speaking. "I don't want to go."

Mrs. Jones sighed. "Let's not go over this again. We signed up for the year, so you need to go."

"Maureen's mom quit," Cassie said, playing her trump card. "I don't want to be in it without her."

Mrs. Jones fell silent, and Cassie knew she was thinking about the implications. "Okay," she said finally, "you can quit. After today. But you have to go to this one. I told Mrs. Isabel we'd give Riley a ride, so you're going."

Cassie had lost. Her mom wouldn't take Riley without Cassie. "Fine." She took another carrot bite and spoke around the shards in her mouth. "I'll be ready when it's time."

They picked Riley up and arrived at Jaiden's house. Cassie took a quick head count as they entered the dimly lit living room. No new faces, but a few people were missing. Most notably were Maureen and Janice, two girls who had been in Girls Club since Cassie moved to Arkansas.

They also happened to sit at the table with Andrea.

That did it. Girls Club was officially uncool.

Leigh Ann smiled and waved her over, and Cassie left Riley's side to sit with her. Jaiden stood next to her mother, organizing skeins of yarn.

Trisha, Jaiden's mom, looked around at theml. "This is a lot of fun, and I know you girls are going to enjoy it. First, come pick your colors and type of yarn."

Cassie examined the different types of yarn and had to admit she was a bit impressed by all the varieties. She picked a multicolored one with a dark brown prominent throughout, reminding her very much of autumn. Strands feathered out away from the skein, making it appear thicker than it was.

"That one might be hard to work with, Cassie," Trisha said.

Trisha always seemed eager to discourage her. "I'll give it a try," Cassie said.

Trisha shrugged. "All right, girls, now that you have your yarn, everyone needs one of these hooks!" She brandished a metallic wand with a little nub inverted on the end. "Everyone have one? Good. Now, wrap your yarn like this."

Cassie followed the instructions, looping the yarn around the hook and pulling it through, then making another loop and doing it again. And again. What she expected to feel monotonous and boring became intriguing with each loop as she watched a semblance of a shape take form.

"When you reach the end of your row, this is what you do

to turn it around." Jaiden's mom demonstrated again.

Cassie reached the end of her row, a little excited. She turned the hook and started going back the other way.

"What are you making?" Leigh Ann asked.

"Nothing yet," Cassie said. "Just experimenting." But as she continued to weave the yarn back-and-forth, she thought it was starting to look like a scarf.

The next thing she knew, the doorbell was ringing as parents arrived to take the girls home.

"Let's see what everyone made!" Trisha said. She walked around and looked at their crocheted items.

"I'm making a pot holder," Leigh Ann said, showing off her oddly shaped hot pad. It wasn't quite square or circular, but somewhere in between.

"Very nice," Trisha said. She stopped by Cassie. "Did you get anything done, Cassie?"

Cassie tried not to bristle under the finely veiled insult she heard in the words. "Yeah, I got a lot done. I've got the good beginnings to a scarf here."

"Oh, that would make a lovely scarf!" Leigh Ann said.

Trisha raised one eyebrow and surveyed the rows of stitching skeptically. "The edges are not straight enough to be a scarf. You'll definitely want to keep practicing."

"Well, that's the idea, right, I'm just learning," Cassie responded, in spite of her better judgment. She knew she should not engage Trisha, but why did she always have to put Cassie down? Yet another reason to be done with Girls Club.

Jaiden's mom had no response to that, but after she walked away, Leigh Ann gave Cassie a wink.

⚜

Cassie couldn't wait to show her mom the scarf. While Riley thought it was cool, Mrs. Jones fawned over it like it came out of an expensive boutique.

"So you had fun?" her mom said, stealing glances at Cassie as she drove, an almost giddy expression on her face.

"Yes," Cassie said grudgingly, knowing where the conversation was going.

"And you didn't think you would? You thought it would be boring."

"Yes," Cassie granted.

"To think, you might've missed out on an experience you loved."

Cassie didn't respond. It would involve launching into a lengthy discussion she didn't want to have in front of Riley. Yes, she had enjoyed learning to crochet, but she had not enjoyed Girls Club. And she still fully intended that to be her last meeting.

After they got home, Cassie rummaged through her mom's crafting supplies until she found a crochet hook. Of course Mrs. Jones had one; Mrs. Jones had tried just about every craft out there, and was pretty good at most of them. Cassie turned on a movie and holed up on the living room couch, watching TV while she crocheted. Mrs. Jones found her that way.

"I can't believe you're still doing this. I thought you would've gotten tired by now."

Cassie held up what she had done of her scarf so far. "Look, it's beautiful."

"It sure is. And that's very fancy yarn. Beginners have a hard time getting it around the hook."

"Sometimes it gives me trouble," Cassie admitted. "But for the most part I'm managing."

"I love it. Don't forget to do your chores."

"Yes, Mom," she replied, simply because she knew that was the expected response.

She took the scarf to school on Monday and worked on it during the bus ride. She couldn't wait to show people.

"That's so cool," Nicole said when Cassie showed her at the lockers before school.

"It's a little crooked, don't you think?" Jimmy said, giving his opinion without being asked.

Nicole swatted his arm, though she didn't seem the least bit upset with him. "No, it's not. It's lovely."

"Look what I learned to do over the weekend." Cassie brandished the partially completed scarf to Andrea in P.E.

Andrea was busy adding more powder on her nose, though it was already whiter than the rest of her face. She turned with a smile, and then her eyes landed on the scarf, and her smile turn into a perplexed frown. "What is it?"

Feeling slightly let down that she had to explain, Cassie said, "It's a scarf. I learned how to crochet."

"Oh, that's nice."

It wasn't the excited affirmation Cassie had hoped for. She rolled the scarf up and put it in her backpack.

It got brought up again at lunchtime, when Maureen said, her tone teasing, "How was Girls Club, Cassie?"

Since nobody ever spoke to Cassie except Andrea and sometimes Janice, Maureen's comment attracted attention. Amity swiveled in her seat, her light hazel eyes giving Cassie a once-over before looking at Maureen.

"What's Girls Club?"

Maureen took a swig of her chocolate milk and tossed her long ponytail behind her. "It's this club a bunch of us were in in elementary school. Cassie's still in it."

Cassie's face warmed, and she felt the need to defend herself. Before she could, Janice spoke up.

"It's actually really fun. I would've stayed in it this year except my mom didn't want to take me anymore."

Cassie shot Janice a grateful look, and Cara said, "What do you do in it?"

All eyes were on Cassie, and this was the first time most of these girls had spoken to her. Cassie gathered her courage and answered. "We do lots of things. Like learn how to put on make-up or tour restaurants. This weekend we learned how to crochet."

Maureen snorted. "Sounds like something my granny

would do." She lay back in her seat and propped her arms up so everyone could see her hands and imitated knitting needles. She opened her mouth and made a snorting sound. "What's that, honey, I can't hear you!" she said in a gravelly old lady voice.

The table rocked with laughter, and Cassie felt foolish for having been singled out.

"What did you crochet, Cassie?" Janice asked, and Cassie could tell she was trying to redirect the conversation to a positive light.

"A scarf," Andrea answered for her. "She's making a scarf."

"Really, you can do that?" Amity lifted an eyebrow. "Can I see?"

"I didn't bring it to lunch," Cassie said, unsure if Amity's interest was genuine or not. "I can bring it tomorrow if you'd like."

"Yeah, I'd like to see it," Amity said.

"Me too," Janice said. "I bet it's really nice."

Cassie gave Janice a smile. She was always a kind person.

Cassie finished off the scarf while she worked at her dad's soccer store that evening. She could hardly wait to get home and show her mom.

"This is lovely, Cassie," Mrs. Jones said. "Your rows are a little uneven here, did you notice?"

Cassie shrugged. "Yeah, but I don't think anyone else will."

"Well, if you want to straighten the edges on the next scarf you make, you just need to count as you go across, and then make sure you do the same number each time."

That was simple enough. Cassie could do that.

She stuffed her finished scarf into her backpack before school, excited to show her friends. She found Nicole first as she went to her locker after the bus. Nicole was standing next to Jimmy, the two of them staring at each other as if they were having a conversation with their eyes. Cassie wondered if they'd run out of things to say to each other.

"Look, I finished it," Cassie said, brandishing the scarf.

"It's beautiful!" exclaimed Nicole, fingering the material. "What are you going to do with it?"

"Now that I know how to make these, I'll make some for people for Christmas."

Nicole clutched the scarf tightly in her fingers. "Can I have this one?"

Cassie blinked in surprise. "This one was my trial one. The rows are crooked." She saw Jimmy grin out of the corner of her eye.

Nicole pulled the scarf up to her chin. "I don't care. I love this material. Please? Can I have it?"

Cassie hesitated, but she didn't see why not. "Okay. It can be your Christmas present."

Nicole stuck out her bottom lip. "I can't have it now?"

"No." Cassie took it back from her. "You have to wait until Christmas. Or it won't be a Christmas present!"

"Fine." Nicole slipped her hand into Jimmy's. "But I won't forget."

⊙~✤~⊙

Mr. Jones had his suitcase out when Cassie and her mom got home from the children's choir Thursday evening.

"Where are you going?" Cassie asked.

"I have a job interview in a different state," Mr. Jones said. "I'll be gone tomorrow."

Cassie turned to look at her mom. "A job interview in a different state?" she repeated. "But what happens if he gets that job?"

Mrs. Jones gave a shrug. "We'll cross that bridge when it happens."

"But that means we would have to move," Cassie said, not about to let it drop. "We can't move, not now that I'm actually making friends!"

Mr. Jones chuckled, and Mrs. Jones held up her hand to quiet Cassie. "I said let's wait and see, Cassie. None of us know what's going to happen."

Cassie went back to her room, disgruntled. The last thing she wanted to do was move.

Friday evening was quieter without her dad around, and when she heard him in the kitchen making breakfast Saturday morning, she jumped out of bed and ran to greet him.

"You're home!"

"Yes, this is where I live."

Cassie bypassed the pancakes and settled for slicing an apple instead. She had to admit, she was getting tired of all these fruits and vegetables, but at least she hadn't gained weight. Much. "Did you find a good job?"

"I had interviews, that's all."

She kept it to herself how much she hoped they wouldn't work out.

Cassie wasn't quite as excited to see her dad when he woke her up at three a.m. Sunday morning to help with the paper route. This was a task she dreaded. She splashed water on her face and went out to the car in her soccer sweats.

"Doesn't Mom bring in enough money working at Wendy's for us to quit this paper route?" she asked her dad.

"I'm afraid not. The house is expensive, and we spend a lot of money on you kids. We'll only be able to quit the paper route when I get another job."

Cassie concentrated on putting the inserts into the paper and rolling them up before rubberbanding them. "Why can't you just find a job in Arkansas?"

"Don't you think I've tried? We love our house. I don't want to have to leave it."

Cassie's fingers trembled as she handed the next roll of paper to him, and it wasn't because she was cold.

There had to be a better solution. Moving again was not an option.

Episode 3: Falling Short

CHAPTER FOURTEEN
Attitude Adjustment

She had reached the point of desperation.

Cassandra Jones hated mornings. She hated the cold. And most of all, she hated her monthly turn helping her dad on his paper route, bending and rolling and wrapping rubber bands so he could toss them out the window onto the driveway and grass of the still-sleeping customers.

Today was no different. One hour into the delivery route, it started to rain. Cassie groaned. The addition of rain to the papers was a much more grueling exercise. Now not only did she have to wrap rubber bands around the papers, but she had to stuff them into plastic baggies.

"Work faster, Cassie, I need more papers!" Mr. Jones said.

She grumbled under her breath. Like she wasn't already going as fast as she could? Did he think she in some way enjoyed this? Her fingers stumbled over each other as she shoved the papers into the plastic. The water came down harder, managing to filter through the open driver side window and to the middle row where she sat. She tried to keep her fingers dry, because if they got wet, the paper would stick to them and would smear the ink, still hot from the printing.

There was absolutely no part of this that was fun. How

many more times could she suffer this if it meant they didn't have to move away from Arkansas?

"What if I got a job back in Texas?" her dad asked.

Cassie paused. Her family had moved from Texas a few years ago, and for the longest time, all Cassie had wanted was to move back. She thought of her best friend in Texas, who she hadn't spoken to in three years.

"I don't know," she said. "Maybe that would be okay."

"Well, we'll see. Nothing's happened yet." Her dad reached his hand onto the console for more bags of papers, but there were none. "Cassie! More papers!"

"I know!" she snapped, forcing herself to focus on the task at hand.

The sun had just started to rise when Cassie and Mr. Jones arrived back home. Streaks of orange and pink filled the sky, but Cassie's eyes no longer wanted to stay open. She stopped in the bathroom long enough to wash the majority of the black ink from her fingers and face, where it seemed to gather whenever she brushed her hand to her skin. And then she stumble to her bedroom and fell on her bed, dreams of sleepy mornings and moving to a new town flooding her mind.

꧁ ✦ ꧂

It seemed Cassie had barely shut her eyes before her sister Emily was shaking her shoulders and telling her to get up.

"Wake up. It's time to get ready for church."

It couldn't be. She had barely fallen into bed. But Cassie rolled over toward the window and saw the sun rising in the sky. She felt like she could sleep another five hours.

Her sister had already left the room, but Cassie managed to pull herself out of bed. Her stomach rumbled. Cassie paused in her closet to choose a dress before going to the kitchen for breakfast. She picked the black dress with white polkadots and pulled it on over her frame. It fell loosely around her hips and she tied the sash, turning backward and forward and looking over her shoulder to see how it fit. It looked pretty good. The positive thought energized her enough to go to the master bathroom and examine her reflection in the mirror.

She put in her contacts first. Her dark brown eyes, unhindered by frames and glasses, stared back at her. The hair fell just past her shoulders, straight and without even a hint of curl. She plugged in the curling iron to try to rectify the situation and admired the way the dress hung loosely on her slender shoulders.

Her mom's scale was tucked behind the toilet, and Cassie pulled it out, curious. She wasn't supposed to obsess over her weight or weigh herself very often, but she couldn't help herself sometimes. She stepped on it and waited for it to turn on. When the numbers flashed, she felt a surge of panic. Two pounds? She had gained two pounds? It didn't seem possible. She looked skinnier than ever; even her cheekbones were silhouetted nicely on her face. It must be a mistake. She stepped off the scale, waited for it to go blank, and then stepped on again.

The same numbers flashed as before.

There was nothing she could do about it. Cassie went to the living room and sat on the couch, grabbing a set of scriptures to read and trying to ignore the tightness in her chest.

"Look who's here," Mr. Jones said as he parked the car in front of the church building.

"Well, isn't that nice," Mrs. Jones said. "We haven't seen him in awhile."

Cassie crossed her arms over her belly and looked toward the church entrance. Elek, the young man who had lived with her family for a few weeks last year, stood resting against the brick building. Some of the anguish she felt over her weight gain diminished when she saw him. Elek was like the older brother she'd never had.

"Elek!" Emily said. She and the younger kids bounded out of the car ahead of Cassie and ran to give him hugs.

"Hello, everyone," Elek said in his crisp Greek accent. His family had immigrated to the area when he was a teenager, but he still spoke English a little awkwardly.

Cassie reached him and gave him a hug as well. "Great to see you here."

He nodded, looking a bit sheepish. "I've been busy."

"How's the soccer going?" Mr. Jones asked, shaking Elek's hand when he reached him.

"Good, good. I'm refereeing games all day on Saturdays. It's really good."

"Come by the store sometime, and I'll help with any equipment you need."

Knowing her dad, he'd probably give it at a steep discount, as well. No wonder the store didn't make much money. Not that Cassie blamed him; Elek was practically family.

"And dinner tonight," Mrs. Jones added. "We always have room at the table for you."

"Sure, sure," Elek said, his dark-toned skin flushing pink. He pulled his arms free from Annette and Scott as they hung on him. "I would love to."

Emily nudged Cassie. "There's Riley."

Cassie glanced over and spotted her friend by her van, talking with Jason and Tyler. Jason, the older brother, was always polite, but Tyler had acted superior to Cassie for years, even though they were in the same grade. Cassie gave a grunt but headed toward Riley.

"Let's go in, Riley," Cassie said, hooking an arm through hers. "Church is going to start soon."

"Hi, Cassie," Jason said.

"Hi," Cassie replied. Using her hold on Riley, she turned both of them away from the car.

"No hi for me?" Tyler said. "That's rude."

Cassie swiveled back. She didn't remember the last time Tyler had spoken nicely to her. Well, that had been sort-of nice. "Hi." She faced the chapel again and continued walking, her arm hooked to Riley, until they got through the double doors and Riley started to giggle.

"What?" Cassie asked, letting go of her and glaring.

"I think he likes you."

"Tyler?" Cassie let out a derisive snort and rolled her eyes. "He's a total jerk." She'd never forget how he'd mocked her two years ago when she dropped the ball in basketball.

"Maybe he's nicer now."

"Hm." She bit back her words. But she replayed the conversation in her head. He'd smirked at her—or had it been a friendly grin? She couldn't be sure. And he was cute, with his dark blond hair and blue eyes.

But no. She couldn't think that way. Tyler was an arrogant, conceited boy. Besides— "I thought you liked him."

"Who says we can't both like him?" Riley's grin was devilish, and Cassie laughed, her chest lightening slightly.

☙ ❈ ❧

Monday morning rolled around, and Cassie didn't feel any more rested than she had Friday night. She blamed the stupid paper route. At least she'd gotten all of her homework done early Saturday.

She studied a few flashcards for science on the bus, then leaned her head against the window. The fifth-grade boys in front of her were making fun of Jeremy, the kid who sat by himself a few rows up. Cassie wasn't sure what was different about Jeremy, but she knew he had some sort of disability from the way he spoke.

"He smells like pee again," one boy said.

"He pees his pants every day," the other chortled.

"He should try changing them." And they both laughed like it was insanely funny.

"Shut up, both of you," Cassie said, irritated. "You're so stupid."

They shut up, but probably only because she was an eighth grader and they weren't.

She kept yawning as she walked into school and hoped she didn't look as tired as she felt.

She woke up a bit more when she walked into the locker room for P.E. She changed her shoes and clothes, glancing at the door every few seconds to see if Andrea had walked in yet. But Andrea didn't until after the warning bell rang.

"Whew!" she exhaled, shaking her head. "Almost didn't make it." She spotted Cassie as she started to dress out. "You look positively cadiving."

"Cadiving?" Cassie shot her a questioning look. "What does that mean?"

"Like death," Andrea giggled.

Flattering. So she did look as tired as she felt. "Thanks."

"Let me fix you after class."

Fix her? But Cassie didn't get a chance to find out what that meant, because the bell rang and their teacher came in.

Only after they'd gone through another sweaty game of flag football, push ups, and running laps did they return to the locker room.

"Everyone take a shower!" the teacher said.

The girls looked at the shower heads jetting out of the wall, no barrier or even a curtain between them and the lockers. None of them said a word as the teacher left the room, but Cassie knew no one would shower.

"Quick, Cassie!" Andrea said, fully dressed again and retrieving her purse from her locker. "To the mirror!"

Cassie followed Andrea to the mirror stretched above a wall of sinks, not quite sure why they were going there unless it was to admire Cassie's death look. But as soon as they got there, Andrea pulled a giant bag of powders and brushes out of her backpack and began applying them to Cassie's face.

"What are you doing?" Cassie asked, flinching slightly and pulling back.

"Fixing you," Andrea said in a no-nonsense type voice.

Cassie started to pull away again, but Andrea grabbed her

chin and held her, still putting blush on her cheeks. Makeup! What would her mom say?

"Close your eyes," Andrea said.

Cassie did so, and Andrea swept her brush over the closed lids. Cassie started to open them, but Andrea exclaimed, "No, no, keep them closed!" And then something wet and sticky rolled through Cassie's eyelashes.

"Now look up," Andrea commanded.

Cassie opened her eyes and look toward the ceiling, catching a glimpse of the mascara wand as Andrea pulled it over her eyelashes again.

"There. You're finished."

Cassie focused on her reflection and widened her eyes in surprise. She was obviously the same girl, but the effect of the makeup, particularly the concealer underneath her eyes and the black mascara on her eyelashes, had changed her appearance from that of a child to . . . well, something older. Not a woman, but closer.

Andrea pressed her cheek against Cassie's and looked in the mirror with her. "You're beautiful. You should let me do your makeup more often."

Those words brought Cassie back to reality. While this looked nice, she had to get it off before she went home. Her mom would not approve.

✦

Cassie stepped into second hour and took her seat in the back of the classroom. She said hello to a few people and then pulled out her vocabulary words for her quiz in science later. The morning announcements turned on, but Cassie pretty much ignored them.

"And now for the student of the week."

She didn't lift her eyes from her paper, not wanting anyone to think she paid attention to this part of the announcements, but she couldn't help the way her heart rate increased and her head pulsed. Each week a student was recognized for outstanding work ethic and good behavior, and every week she held her breath, hoping it was her.

"This week's student is . . . Cassandra Jones!"

All of the breath went out of her in a whoosh, and her classmates turned around to stare. Some cheered and others said, "Good job, Cassie!"

Her face warmed and she lowered her eyes, but she basked in the praise, a delicious feeling bubbling up in her chest. And suddenly she really appreciated that Andrea had put makeup on her.

By the time she walked down the main hallway to get to fourth hour, her school picture had been put in the display case with pretty cut out signs saying "star student" and "student of the week." The attention she received was a little overwhelming, but at the same time incredibly flattering.

It was all anyone wanted to talk about at lunch, and suddenly Cassie found herself the center of attention.

"Cassie, sit by me," Amity said, scooting over to make room beside her.

"You know you're not even in choir with us," Maureen said. "Cassie and I have to talk about our music."

"You guys hardly even know Cassie," Andrea scoffed. "She's been my best friends since sixth grade."

Before Cassie could even relish those words, Amity reminded them all of reality. "Since sixth grade?" she jeered. "Where was Cassie all last year then?"

Andrea shrugged like Amity's disbelief was irrelevant. "We had different lunch schedules. And no classes together. Now that we do, we can hang out again."

Amity look mildly pacified, but Cassie knew there was a whole lot more to it than that. And it had to do with her new haircut, her contacts, and her makeup. And her weight. It had never been so obvious to her that appearances mattered.

But even enjoying the limelight like she was, Cassie made

sure to stop at the bathroom and wipe off the makeup before she got on the bus.

CHAPTER FIFTEEN
Lunch Plans

The excitement over Cassie being Student of the Week didn't die down after Monday. On Wednesday an office helper delivered a candy bar and soda to her desk in fourth hour with a note on it that said, "Congrats, Student of the Week!"

Cassie promptly put both under her desk and tried to ignore them.

"Aren't you going to drink your soda, Cassie?" Jimmy asked.

"Not in class," Cassie said, her face beginning to burn.

"You can, Cassie, it's your privilege," Ms. Talo said. "Go ahead."

What could Cassie do now? With all of her classmates staring, she pushed the soda tab until the satisfying pop and hiss filled the room. Then she lifted the can to her lips and took a sip, staring straight at the white board while she did.

"Don't forget the candy bar," Nicole said, and Cassie had only to glance at her to know Nicole was enjoying Cassie's embarrassment.

"Right." Even her ears burned as she fumbled with the noisy wrapper and opened the chocolate.

Normally she avoided candy, but she couldn't get around this one. Steeling herself, she took a bite.

As the milky chocolate melted on her tongue, Cassie forgot everyone stared at her. She forgot that candy wasn't on her diet. For a moment, she disappeared into the goodness of sugar and cocoa and milk. She closed her eyes, relishing the taste.

"Okay, everyone look at me," Ms. Talo said, redirecting the class. "As if you've never seen someone eat chocolate before."

"I don't think anyone's ever enjoyed it that much," Jimmy muttered, and those around him chuckled.

Crapola. Cassie's eyes shot open. Had people actually noticed her reaction? She tucked the candy bar into her lap and tore off tiny pieces, letting them dissolve on her tongue in between sips of soda.

In church that evening, they made final preparations for the Halloween carnival on Friday, and Cassie remembered she hadn't brought it up with Andrea in days. Before she could forget again, she pulled out her phone and sent her a quick text.

Still on for the Halloween party at my church this Friday?

Of course! came the instant reply. Maybe I can spend the night after?

Ah, that would be wonderful. I'll ask my mom, Cassie responded.

Could this week go any better? Cassie was floating on air.

She walked with Riley out to the parking lot after church, their parents already waiting. "See you tomorrow," Cassie said.

"Yep," Riley replied.

"See you tomorrow," a boy voice mimicked.

Cassie turned around to see Tyler grinning at them as he and Jason walked to their car. At first Cassie thought he was making fun of them, but then he waved, and it appeared totally friendly.

"Right," Cassie said, shooting Riley a cockeyed glance.

Riley shrugged. "Beats me."

✦

"Andrea's coming to the Halloween party," Cassie said on the drive home from church.

"Really?" Her mom sounded a little suspicious. "Why?"

Cassie shifted in her seat, annoyed by the question. "Because she's my best friend and she wants to."

"She's your best friend again?"

"Yes."

"The same girl who quit hanging out with you or talking to you last year just because you had different classes?"

Cassie refused to go down that path. "She wants to know if she can spend the night after. Can she?"

Mrs. Jones remained silent a moment, and Cassie grew more desperate. "Please, Mom? It's the first time in nearly a year. We're just starting to get close again. Please? Please please?"

"Okay," Mrs. Jones said finally. "I'll talk to your dad about Emily helping him with the store on Saturday."

"He doesn't need help, the store's dead on Saturdays," Cassie grumped.

"What?"

"Nothing." She already felt guilty for saying it. Soccer season had ended, so of course the store was slow. But even when soccer had been in season, things hadn't been going well. "Thank you. Thank you so much." She pulled out her phone and quickly let Andrea know the good news.

✦

The morning ritual of putting makeup on Cassie had migrated from the P.E. bathroom to the hall bathroom before school. Cassie met Andrea there and let her color her face and fix her eyes.

"I'm so excited you're spending the night tomorrow!" Cassie said, trying not to squirm with childlike glee. Just like old times.

"Yeah, so fun," Andrea agreed. "What are you dressing up as?"

Cassie shrugged. "I think I'll just paint my face and wear something pretty. Then I can be a fairy princess or something." That made her think of Farrah, the closest person Cassie had to a best friend last year. Farrah had wanted to go Trick or Treating together as fairies, though Farrah's costume idea was a little different than Cassie's. Still, if it hadn't been for Farrah, seventh grade would have been unbearable. Cassie felt a pang of guilt that she hadn't contacted Farrah in weeks. In her defense, neither had Farrah. Hopefully she was busy with school and new friends.

A ninth grade girl stepped into the bathroom wearing long, rainbow-colored fake eyelashes. Cassie stared at her, looking away only when the girl glanced her direction. The girl checked her reflection, fluffed her hair, and walked out.

"I need eyelashes like that," Cassie breathed.

"They were wicked awesome," Andrea agreed.

Cassie pulled out her phone and texted her dad, describing the eyelashes in detail and asking him to find some for her for Halloween. He responded that he would look for some, and she put the phone away, smug in her mental image of her costume.

In second hour, Cassie's math teacher handed out their tests from the previous week. She dropped Cassie's test face down on the desk and said, "Which teachers are you inviting to lunch with you tomorrow?"

"I don't know," Cassie said. She'd completely forgotten the highlight event of Student of the Week: going to lunch with two teachers on Friday. She could pick any two teachers and any restaurant. The idea excited and unnerved her all at the same time. "I'm still deciding."

"Well, if you don't know, I'm always up for a good lunch," her teacher said with a wink.

Cassie gave her a smile but offered no promises. She hadn't gotten the vibe that her math teacher liked her, and Cassie wasn't all that great at math anyway. Her two favorite teachers were Ms. Talo and Mr. Adams. She imagined they would be who she chose. But as for where to go? So many options.

In seventh hour Cassie received a note to go to the office. She did so, fighting down the paranoid feeling that she was in trouble.

"Hi, I was told to come in here? I'm Cassandra Jones," she said to the woman behind the desk.

"Just a moment," the lady said. She disappeared down a hall and reappeared with the principal.

"Hi, Cassandra!" he boomed. "I'm delighted to meet you. Congrats on being student of the week! Your teachers have all said such nice things about you."

"Oh, thank you," Cassie said, knowing from the heat on her face that she was blushing.

"Let's get a picture for our hall," he said, handing a camera to the secretary. Cassie pasted a smile on her face just in time for the camera to flash.

"There," he said, stepping away and beaming at her. "Tomorrow you get to go to lunch with two teachers. Just let me know where you're going and which teachers and I'll get it all arranged." He pulled a pad of paper and a pen from his jacket.

"Okay," Cassie said.

He remained standing there, watching her, and she realized he wanted an answer now. "Oh. Okay. I want Mr. Adams and Ms. Talo. And we'll go to . . ." Her mind landed on a restaurant she'd gone to with her dad last year for her birthday. "Roadkill Cafe."

"Fantastic! Tomorrow for lunch come to the office and the teachers will be waiting for you. Oh, and take home this permission slip so that you're allowed to ride with them."

"Thank you," Cassie said, her head spinning slightly.

Cassie didn't see her mom until after the children's choir practice. She slammed the car door as she slid into the passenger seat and pulled the permission slip from her backpack. "Can you sign this for me?"

"What is this?" her mom asked, barely glancing at it as she pulled away from the building.

"A permission slip so I can go to lunch with my teachers. You know, because I'm student of the week."

"Oh, that's right," Mrs. Jones said, this time stealing a look at Cassie's face. She faced the road, then squinted at Cassie again. "Are you wearing makeup?"

"Makeup?" Had she forgotten to take it off before leaving school? "No, of course not!"

"Turn on the light."

Caught. No choice now but to fess up. Cassie turned on the cabin light and let her mom examine her face.

"Cassie. Why did you lie to me?"

Cassie shrugged, not sure what to say. "I didn't want you to get mad at me."

"Lying sure doesn't make that happen. Let's try again, Are you wearing makeup?"

"Yes," Cassie said. "Just a little."

"Where are you putting it on?"

Cassie sighed. "The school bathroom."

"You need to stop until we've talked to your dad about it. You're too young for makeup."

I'm thirteen! she wanted to shout. But she knew it wouldn't make a difference. Her mom knew her age. "Okay."

Not that she had any intention of stopping. She just needed to be better at taking it off.

"Where's your overnight stuff?" Cassie asked Andrea in the bathroom the next morning. She didn't mention a word of her mom's mandates as Andrea put makeup all over her face.

"Oh, I'll just meet you at the church tonight. I've got some things to do after school."

Cassie frowned, not thrilled with the change in plans. "I thought you were riding the bus home with me."

"Sorry." Andrea flashed a bright smile. "I'll see you when the carnival starts, though."

"Okay," Cassie said, relenting. What choice did she have?

Footsteps sounded on the tile, and Amity came in, followed by Maureen. The girls had taken to gathering in the bathroom instead og in front by the benches, now that it was getting chilly outside in the mornings.

"You're so pretty, Cassie," Amity said with a sigh, and then she turned to the mirror and pouted at her reflection.

"You too," Cassie said, wishing she had Amity's developing figure. So far Cassie's bra hadn't gotten past the A stage. "All the boys like you."

"They'd like you too if you talked to them," Amity replied, changing her pout for a perky smile.

The conversation turned to other things, and Cassie tried not to worry about Andrea's lack of overnight gear. It was all planned for her to spend the night. It would work out.

After fourth hour, Cassie made her way to the office.

"Not going to lunch today, Cassie?" Nicole asked as she and Jimmy walked by, holding hands.

"Today I'm going to lunch with my teachers," Cassie said, hoping she didn't sound like she was bragging. Even as she spoke, Ms. Talo stepped our of the classroom and closed the door, locking it.

"Ready, Cassie?" Ms. Talo asked.

"Just waiting for Mr. Adams."

"Have fun!" Nicole called out over her shoulder as she and Jimmy continued down the hall.

Mr. Adams' heavyset frame came around the corner, his trademark suspenders dark against the light shirt. He nodded a greeting at Ms. Talo and turned twinkling blue eyes to

Cassie. "Ready for this?"

"I think so," Cassie said, pleating her fingers and trying not to feel nervous. These were her favorite teachers, the people she felt most comfortable with at school, even over her friends.

"All right if I drive?" Ms. Talo asked.

"Be my guest," Mr. Adams said.

They piled into Ms. Talo's small blue sedan and drove the three minutes to the restaurant. Cassie tried to think of something to say, but nothing came to mind.

They parked and walked inside, and only after they were seated with their menus did Cassie relax a bit. The waiter deposited a bucket of peanuts on the table, and Cassie said, "You eat the peanuts and throw the shells on the ground."

"On the ground?" Ms. Talo repeated.

"Yes, it's really fun!" Cassie demonstrated, and her teachers laughed.

"Now we see her playful side," Ms. Talo said to Mr. Adams.

"I knew she had one," he replied.

Cassie tried not to be embarrassed as her teachers laughed at her. Why was she so serious all the time? She needed to lighten up.

Mr. Adams exclaimed over feeling guilty, throwing his peanut shells on the ground, and Ms. Talo couldn't decide what to order, since everything on the menu was named after roadkill and dead animals. They made Cassie giggle, and the conversation was light and fun. She ordered some chili with crackers, and she didn't even feel guilty eating it.

☙ ❧

"Are you staying for All-Region practice?" Maureen asked in seventh hour.

Cassie frowned. "I hadn't planned on it. I was taking Andrea home, but now she's not coming with me."

"Oh, right." Maureen nodded sagely. "Since she'd spending the night at Amity's house."

"What?" Little pricks of heat ran over Cassie's skin, and she straightened. "No, she's not. She's coming to my church Halloween party and then to my house."

Maureen arched an eyebrow. "Amity said she's spending the night at her house."

"No, she's not," Cassie repeated, trying not to shout. Her skin felt clammy and her breathing came hard. Andrea had said quite clearly she was going with Cassie. No way would she ditch her.

Ms. Berry called the class to order, but Cassie couldn't concentrate. She needed class to end—now—so she could track Andrea down and find out what was gong on.

Maureen kept trying to talk to her and ask questions throughout class, but Cassie ignored her.

As soon as seventh hour ended, she hurried to the main building to track down Andrea. She located her by the vending machine—with Amity, she saw with a flash of jealousy—talking to a bunch of boys.

"Andrea." Cassie snagged her sleeve and pulled her away.

"Ow." Andrea looked annoyed as she yanked back her arm. "What is it, Cassie?"

Cassie exhaled. Her heart pounded with nerves and the need to rush. "Are you spending the night at Amity's house?"

"No." Andrea straightened her shoulders. "I'm just going over after school. And then I'll see you at your church. I'm spending the night with you, remember?"

Of course. Cassie relaxed. Maureen had gotten the information wrong. "Yeah. Yeah, see you later."

"Bye, Cassie," Amity said with a wave.

Cassie waved back and then ran to the bus stop.

CHAPTER SIXTEEN
Stood Up

Cassie's hands trembled as she attempted to paint a glittery butterfly on her face. She scowled at the instructions in front of her and glowered at her reflection. No matter how she tried, she couldn't get her drawing to look anything like the image.

"I'll do it for you," Emily offered. Two years younger but incredibly skilled with art, Emily's own paint job looked as if professionally air brushed.

"Fine," Cassie said with a sigh. She leaned back against the mirror and let her sister work her magic.

"Just needs some glitter," Emily said. She dumped a bit into the palm of her hand and sprinkled it on Cassie's face. "There."

Cassie turned to examine the effect. "It looks seriously amazing," she admitted. "Thanks."

Emily smiled, her brown eyes and hair just a few shades lighter than Cassie's. "You're welcome."

Now she just needed the rainbow eyelashes from her dad to complete the look.

As if on cue, the front door opened.

"Daddy!" Annette squealed, her little footsteps pounding through the kitchen to the front door.

"Hey, little one!" he greeted. Cassie wandered toward the entryway and watched as Mr. Jones whirled Annette around.

"Not much longer and I won't be able to do that," he said with a sigh. "My big second grader."

"I'll always let you," she said congenially.

He spotted Cassie over Annette's head. "Oh, yes. I have something for you."

Cassie beamed at him. "Thank you so much! You remembered! How much?"

"Five dollars."

Cassie pulled the package from the plastic bag and froze. The eyelashes staring back at her were not full and rainbow colored, but stiff-looking, plastic red things. Like red claws poking out in a semi-circle. "These are not what I asked for."

Mr. Jones shrugged. "That's all they had. It looked pretty close."

"No," Cassie bit out, blinking back tears. "They are not pretty close!" She couldn't cry now, it would ruin the paint job her sister had so masterfully done. But she couldn't wear these, either. She put them back in the bag and threw them at her dad. "Just take them back! They're awful!"

"Cassie!" Mrs. Jones appeared in the hallway, her eyes wide with alarm and disapproval. "Don't you talk to your dad that way."

"But he bought the wrong thing!" The burning tears were making a run for it, in spite of her best efforts. "The whole look is ruined!"

"You're lucky you got them at all!"

"I'm not lucky! I don't want them! I'm not paying for them!" She turned around and ran to her room, shutting the door loudly—but not slamming it—behind her.

⁂

Cassie dried her tears and fixed her makeup before they left for the church. Last thing she wanted was for Andrea to see her crying. Or worse, Tyler.

She wasn't even sure why she cared what Tyler thought. She didn't want him to make fun of her. That was all.

"You're not going to wear those eyelashes your dad bought you?" Mrs. Jones asked, eyeing Cassie as she went out the door.

"No," Cassie said. She offered no further comment.

Festivities were already in motion at the church, and Cassie put on a smile so nobody would guess at the tantrum she'd thrown. All would be fine in a a moment. She wandered the building looking for Andrea but didn't see her. What was Andrea dressed as? Had she ever said? Cassie glanced down at her own tie-dye shirt and hoped it went well with her butterfly makeup. If only she'd had the eyelashes . . .

Enough of that. She pulled out her phone and sent a text to Andrea.

Are you at the church already? What are you dressed as?

She didn't get to wait for a reply before Sister Cindy found her and hauled her off to do the fishing booth.

"Hi," Riley greeted her, already sitting behind the divider. She used a paper clip to stick a piece of candy to the laminated fish on a string some child had just thrown over. "I like your makeup."

"Thanks," Cassie said, barely paying attention. She had to find Andrea. Likely Andrea wouldn't want to wander around by herself and would feel out of place. She checked her phone, but there was no response yet. "I'm going to get a drink of water. Be right back, okay?"

"Sure," Riley said. "It's not hard. I've been doing it fine by myself."

"Oh, good," Cassie said, and she rushed away.

A quick perusal of the gymnasium didn't reveal Andrea. Cassie slipped into the hallway and wandered all the way down to the chapel, though she couldn't figure out why Andrea would be out here instead of with all the people.

The door to the boys' bathroom opened as Cassie passed it, and Tyler came out.

"Hey, Cassie," he said. "What are you doing out here?"

Dressed as some kind of mummy with a bloody Axe coming out of his head, Tyler made an impressive dead man. Only his head was wrapped, leaving his blue eyes exposed, though wrappings draped off his hands, reminding Cassie of when her sister was attacked by a dog the previous spring.

"Looking for a friend," she said. She thought to ask him what he was doing, but seeing as he'd just left the bathroom, it was a little obvious.

"Riley's inside the gym."

Cassie bristled, annoyed that everyone seemed to think Riley was her only friend. "She's not who I'm looking for. I invited Andrea from school. She's spending the night."

"Oh. Well, if I see her, I'll tell her."

"Do you even know her?"

"No," Tyler said, giving an easy grin. "But I know everyone else, so that means the person I don't know must be her."

"Yeah, okay. Thanks." Cassie gave him a befuddled look, not quite sure what to make of his behavior. She never knew if he was being nice or sarcastic. "Guess I'll go back in."

She checked her phone one more time before rejoining Riley at the booth. Still no response from Andrea. A cold, hard knot of dread formed in her chest. Andrea wouldn't leave Cassie hanging.

Would she?

By the time the carnival ended a few hours later, Cassie was having a hard time keeping her tears at bay. There was no sign of Andrea. She wasn't answering her phone, not calls or texts. There was simply nothing.

"Can we stop by her house?" Cassie begged her mom as they walked to the car. "Please?"

Mrs. Jones hesitated, and Cassie could tell she was torn

between wanting to help and wanting to go home. "Honey, if she's not here, she probably can't come over."

"But she said she could! She promised!" Cassie's throat tightened, the tell-tale ache warning her that the water works were not far behind.

"Let's just go home. These kids need to get to bed," Mr. Jones said.

"Please?" Cassie said, putting on her sweetest voice. "I'm really sorry for the way I acted earlier. I was just so nervous for tonight, it meant a lot to me, and I really want her to come over."

"I'll just drive by real quick," Mrs. Jones said, relenting.

Cassie wiped at the stray tear that had escaped down her cheek, hope flourishing inside her. "Thank you, thank you!"

It would all be fine now. Andrea would be home, and she would come over. Maybe her parents hadn't been able to take her to the church. Whatever the reason, it didn't matter. All that mattered was that she come now.

Ten minutes later Mrs. Jones pulled up to the curb outside Andrea's house, and Cassie hopped out. She ran to the door and rang the bell, bouncing on the balls of her feet anxiously.

Mrs. Wall opened the door, and a flicker of surprise crossed her face. "Cassie! What can I do for you?"

"I'm just here for Andrea," Cassie said with a bright smile, mustering all her confidence. "She's supposed to spend the night tonight."

"Oh?" Mrs. Wall's smile faded to a frown. "She didn't tell me. She's spending the night at Amity's."

Cassie took a step back as if someone had punched her in the gut. No. It couldn't be. "But she said . . ." Cassie whispered.

Mrs. Wall's expression morphed to one of sympathy. "I'll tell her you came by. I'm sorry for the confusion."

Cassie nodded, trying to maintain a little dignity. She turned around and hurried to the car with her head down, not bothering to stop the tears now.

"Is she coming?" Mrs. Jones asked when Cassie climbed in.

"No." Cassie turned her face to the window. Maureen had been right. Was this what Andrea had planned all along? A stab of anger pierced her heart, and Cassie realized she couldn't trust Andrea. Too much had changed over the past year.

Mrs. Jones knocked on the bedroom door after the girls had gone to bed. Emily opened it for her, then sat back and watched as Mrs. Jones walked over to Cassie.

"I'm sorry tonight didn't work out, honey," Mrs. Jones said, brushing the hair from Cassie's forehead.

A knot welled up in her throat again, and a part of her wished her mom wouldn't show sympathy. "It was a rotten night," she said.

"I know. I feel bad. I have an idea. Why don't we go to the costume shop tomorrow and pick out a fun costume for you to rent? Anything you want. Since Halloween is next Friday, we haven't missed anything."

The idea was appealing, though it didn't quite take away the sting of tonight's disappointment. She gave a small nod, knowing her mom was trying and knowing also she didn't really deserve it. She'd been a pill tonight. "Okay."

"Great." Mrs. Jones stood up.

"What about me?" Emily asked. "Can I rent a costume also?"

"Of course. We'll all go."

Emily squealed and Cassie smiled, feeling a bit better.

⁕

Cassie told herself not to say anything to Andrea about it at school. She told herself it didn't matter, that Andrea could be a flake, and it wouldn't affect Cassie. She could act indifferent.

She skipped the bathroom routine and hung out at her locker with Nicole and Jimmy, avoiding any chance of running into Andrea.

But then she had P.E. She kept her face impassive while she dressed out, practicing for when Andrea arrived.

Andrea arrived in a flurry, giggling and laughing on her phone as she made her way to the locker room. Cassie pulled open a book and sat on her bench, saying nothing. Andrea dropped the phone into her backpack and fell onto the bench beside Cassie.

"Hey, Cassie!" She put an arm around Cassie's shoulder and squeezed her. "How was your weekend?"

Why did she have to be so nice? Cassie pulled away, trying to hold on to her anger. "It was fine."

"Oh, good." Andrea began dressing out, and Cassie realized Andrea wasn't going to apologize.

She put her book away and stood up, keeping her chin lifted. "I thought you were coming to my house."

"Oh." Andrea turned around, twirling her hand and rolling her eyes. "Yeah, sorry. Amity was going through a crisis and needed me to stay. She like begged me. I told her I had to go, but she was so insistent. I couldn't leave her." Andrea met Cassie's eyes. "You're not mad, are you?"

Of course she was. Cassie was furious. And she didn't believe a word Andrea said. She'd probably planned that lie the whole time. But she shrugged. "No. I don't care."

The teacher blew her whistle, and Cassie pushed her way to the front of the line with the other kids, completely ignoring Andrea.

⁕

"Don't forget, Market Fair is this Thursday!" Ms. Talo reminded everyone in fourth hour.

Cassie wasn't concerned. This year, she had it in the bag. Literally. She was simplifying and taking advantage of the myriad of paper bags in her mom's laundry room, turning them into cutely decorated trick-or-treating bags. Since Halloween was on Friday, she figured it would be a big draw.

She was also taking a note from Nicole's book. Last year,

Nicole's brownies went like hot cakes. So this year, Cassie was making spider cookies out of Oreos. They were sure to be well received. And she'd have everything done by Wednesday night.

She considered not sitting with Andrea at lunch time, but thought that might send the message that she actually cared what Andrea had done. Instead she plunked herself down beside Cara and Maureen, the opposite side of the table of Andrea and Amity. She gritted her teeth, as angry at Amity as she was at Andrea. She took apart her sandwich, eating the bread but ignoring the cheese and meat.

"Cassie's mad at me because I spent the night at your house," Andrea said, quite loudly.

The whole table turned toward Cassie, and she glowered at Andrea, annoyed she'd brought their disagreement to everyone's attention.

"Oh, Cassie!" Amity's large hazel eyes focused on Cassie, looking wounded and vulnerable. "It wasn't Andrea's fault. I really needed her. Don't be mad at her."

Cassie turned her attention to Amity. She felt vaguely manipulated but couldn't pinpoint how. "I'm not mad at her. She can spend the night wherever she wants."

"If I'd known she was supposed to spend the night at your house—" Amity began, but she cut off shortly when Andrea elbowed her. "Next time I'll invite you over also," Amity said hurriedly. "We can have a slumber party."

A slumber party at Amity's house? The idea was appealing. And now that Cassie knew Amity hadn't been in on a plot against her, Cassie's anger toward her relinquished. Still, she had to keep her cool.

"Sure," she said with a shrug. "That might be fun sometime."

Thursday morning, Cassie's mom drove her to school so she wouldn't have to take her bags and cookies on the bus. She was one of the last ones to arrive and had to get a table next to a few seventh graders. Cassie ignored them and set up her Halloween bags and the tray of spider cookies. Then she sat behind her table and pulled out a book. This would be easy.

"These look nice, Cassandra," Ms. Talo said, stopping by and making notes on a notepad. "What are you selling them for?"

"The cookies are a dollar and the bags are five bucks," Cassie said.

Ms. Talo nodded. "How's your book coming along?"

"Oh." Cassie straightened up, excited by the topic. "Finished it awhile ago, and I've gotten it all typed up. Soon I'll start writing the sequel."

"Fantastic, that's great news! I still want to read it. What do you plan next for it?"

"Well." Cassie hesitated. "I'd really like to get it published, but I'm not sure how."

"That's definitely something to look into. I'll see what I can find out." She tapped Cassie's table. "Good luck today!"

"Thanks."

The first group of kids shuffled in an hour later. They glanced at Cassie's table and walked on by. Cassie wasn't worried. There were lots of kids to come, and they might circle back.

But an hour later when the second group had left the gym and Cassie hadn't sold a thing, she began to worry. She stood in front of her table and surveyed it. What could she do to make it more enticing? She rearranged the bags around the spider cookies. When the next group came in, she stood in front of the table and shouted at them, "Free cookie with the purchase of a bag!"

That worked minimally, and she relieved herself of two bags. Still, by the end of the second hour, she'd only sold three bags. Three bags! That was only fifteen dollars for two hours! Feeling a bit more desperate, she began offering two cookies for each bag sold. Finally, with only half an hour left, she offered a free bag with each cookie.

The last group filed out, and Cassie studied what was left. At least it hadn't been hard to turn a profit, with only a few art supplies and the Oreos costing her money. But she'd only sold seven bags out of the twenty she'd brought, and two of those she'd sold for a dollar when someone bought cookies.

She uttered a long sigh and packed up what was left, giving the four remaining Oreo cookies to the seventh graders next to her. Huge bummer. Apparently she wasn't that great of a business woman.

CHAPTER SEVENTEEN
Discovering Truths

"Cassie!" Andrea greeted Cassie at lunch with a huge hug and an equally huge squeal, throwing her arms around her in front of the cafeteria. "I missed you at P.E.!"

Andrea's theatrics had only gotten louder this week, as if she were trying to show how sincere her friendship was.

"I'm sure you were fine without me," Cassie said, patting her arm and pulling out of the grip.

Andrea latched an arm through hers. "So listen, I was thinking, since it didn't work out for me to spend the night last week, why don't you spend the night tomorrow?"

The offer caught Cassie by surprise, and she swiveled to face Andrea. "Spend the night at your house?" When was the last time she'd received such an invitation?

"Yes!" Andrea smiled.

"It's Halloween. I'll have to ask my mom."

"Sure, but Halloween makes it even more fun! We'll dress up together and go trick-or-treating!" Andrea clasped both of Cassie's hands and squeezed them.

It did sound really fun. "I'll ask my mom and let you know."

"Can't wait." Andrea hooked an arm through hers and led

them into the cafeteria.

To Cassie's surprise, Mrs. Jones said yes, and Andrea told her to bring her stuff to school and then come over after.

"I'm staying for All-Region practice," Cassie told Andrea. "I'll just have my mom bring me."

"Sounds perfect!" Andrea said with her usual excitement.

By the time Cassie got to school Friday morning, she'd decided she wasn't mad at Andrea anymore. She went to their usual bathroom and found Andrea and Cara already there, laughing at some video on Cara's phone.

"Cassie! Long time no see!" Andrea said, moving away from the phone and directing Cassie in front of the mirror. "Let's see what we can do with you today."

"What are we dressing up as for Halloween?" Cassie asked.

Cara slipped closer to them, her blond hair pulled into a ponytail at the nape of her neck. Easily the prettiest of them all with her brown eyes and blond hair, tiny waist and full chest, Cara remained an enigma to Cassie. She smiled a lot but didn't speak hardly at all. Cassie couldn't tell if Cara just didn't like her or if she didn't want to talk to her.

"Are you going trick-or-treating together?" Cara asked, one of the only sentences she had ever directed at Cassie. Well, toward her, anyway.

Cassie waited for Andrea to answer, but she appeared very focused on the mascara wand. "Yes," Cassie said. "I'm spending the night with Andrea."

Cara looked at Andrea for confirmation, and Andrea shrugged. "Well, maybe. I have to call my mom first."

What? Cassie pulled away from the approaching mascara and faced Andrea. This was the first she was hearing of a maybe. "I brought all my stuff, just like you told me. My mom said she'd bring my costume to your house. You haven't even asked your mom?"

Andrea appeared nonplussed. "Calm down, I'm sure she'll say yes. I'll call her at lunch."

She went for Cassie's face again, but Cassie reared back, trying to contain her anger. Why was it so hard to get a straight answer? "I need a drink of water."

Cassie grabbed her bag and stepped out of the bathroom, nearly running into Amity as she approached.

"Hi, Cassie!" Amity said.

"Hi," Cassie returned. She started for the water fountain and then froze. What would they say without her in there? She stepped up to the bathroom opening and stood close to it. She heard Amity and Andrea's voices, something about, "all set for tonight," and "don't tell Cassie."

"Why?" Amity asked.

Cassie didn't hear the response, but she moved away, glad she'd brought her backpack with her. Her emotions battled between rage and hurt, and the mixture churned within her, not sure which would win.

There was no avoiding Andrea at P.E., so Cassie did her best to act normal. But she already knew when her mom picked up after choir practice, she was going home.

⊙⤙⚜⤚⊙

Cassie's teacher looked up from her desk as Cassie set her math assignment on top, face down with all the other assignments.

"Cassie," Ms. Theler said, "you didn't invite me to eat lunch with you." She sounded a little wounded, a bit confused.

Cassie's hand hovered over the desk, surprised. "Eat lunch with me?"

"When you were Student of the Week and got to pick two teachers." Her teacher smiled, but it didn't reach her eyes.

"I'm sorry," Cassie said, not sure why her teacher was bringing this up. "I could only invite two teachers."

"So who did you pick?"

Increasingly uneasy with this line of questioning, Cassie said, "Mr. Adams and Ms. Talo."

"But you know I'm the one who nominated you for Student

of the Week, right?"

Actually Cassie hadn't known. No one had told her. As she wasn't the brightest math student, this teacher honestly hadn't even crossed her mind. But now guilt flashed hot and liquid through her chest, and her face warmed. "I didn't know. I'm so sorry. Thanks for nominating me."

Not sure what else to say, she returned to her desk. But she mulled over the teacher's words. If she'd known who nominated her, would she have chosen differently? Quite possibly. But not by choice. By obligation. And she didn't know Ms. Theler as well and wasn't as comfortable with her. She was glad she'd gone to lunch with Mr. Adams and Ms. Talo, her two favorite teachers. So even though she felt bad for Ms. Theler, she also realized it was a good thing she hadn't known.

Still, she decided to make a better effort in class and be super kind to this teacher.

Cassie sat next to Cara again at lunch.

"Hi, Cassie," Cara said, giving her a smile and scooting over to make more room.

"Hi," Cassie said, wishing Cara hadn't overheard the conversation in the bathroom that morning. Was she laughing at Cassie behind her back also?

Andrea entered the cafeteria with Amity and Maureen, then went around the table to talk to Cassie.

"So I called my mom," she said, "and she said you can come over after school, but you can't spend the night. That's okay, right? We can still hang out, but then you can go trick-or-treating with your family and not miss a family event."

Like Andrea cared. "That's all right. I'll just go home after my choir practice. My mom won't want to drop me off and then come back into town a few hours later."

"Are you sure?" Andrea asked, but she didn't look too concerned.

"Yep."

Cara was watching Cassie, and Cassie met her gaze with an eye roll, which elicited a small smile from her.

"Okay, then, maybe next time!" Andrea skipped back over to her side of the table and sat with Amity.

Cassie swallowed hard and focused on picking the sticker off her apple.

"Want some fries?" Cara asked, pushing them toward Cassie.

Cassie looked at her in surprise. Cara got fries and a soda for lunch every day, but she'd never offered to share before.

"I'll have one," Cassie said.

Cara leaned closer and whispered, "She does that all the time. I think she likes feeling like everyone wants to come over. You played it well."

Cassie mulled over that statement as she took slow bites of the fry. Was it just a personality quirk? But the Andrea Cassie knew would never do that.

She needed to get to know this new Andrea better.

⊙~ ⚘ ~⊙

The choir room was tense after school as a larger than usual group of girls huddled around the piano.

"Today's your last chance," Ms. Berry said. "I know everyone's going to eat lots of candy tonight, but tomorrow I expect you to show up here with voices warmed up and ready to sing."

Try-outs were the next day. The knowledge cemented itself in Cassie's brain like a brick, thickening her throat and jelling her blood. Her head pounded as if she were at the try-outs. She'd practiced and practiced and knew these songs. She had to make it.

"Okay, let's run through it!" Ms. Berry said.

Maureen stuck close to Cassie, leaning into her whenever they hit a tricky spot in the music.

"Stop, let's go over measure thirty-two again!" Ms. Berry

said, breaking them off. "Make sure you get on top of that note, ladies!"

"I'm just following Cassie," Maureen said. "She knows the song."

"Yes, but she won't be in the tryout room with you," Ms. Berry said. "So stand on your own two feet."

No one wanted practice to end. It appeared Cassie wasn't the only one nervous.

"You're such a good singer," Kendra said, her long black hair cascading down her back as always. "I wish I could sing like you."

"Thanks," Cassie said, tapping the pads of her fingers against her palm. "I'm so nervous."

"You'll do great, Cassie," Ms. Berry said. "You don't need to worry."

Cassie smiled and exhaled, relaxing a little bit under her teacher's vote of confidence.

"Have fun tonight, and no one get sick!" Ms. Berry called out.

It did look wet and cold out. But Cassie had the beautiful gown her mom had rented, and she knew her remaining years of trick-or-treating were limited.

With nothing else to do, Cassie sat down in front of the family computer and pulled up her book. She'd finished typing it a few weeks ago but hadn't looked at it since. Before she could send it to a publisher, she needed to revise and proofread.

"Well," she murmured, hitting the Print button on the screen, "let's get started." She stared, somewhat in awe, as page after page began spitting from the printer. Three hundred pages later, she gathered the still-warm manuscript into her arms and hurried to her room. Time to read.

"Let's get ready to go, guys!" Mrs. Jones yelled down the hall. "I've got the costumes in my room!"

Oh, her costume. Cassie tossed the manuscript aside and

hurried to her parents' room.

There it was. The long blue gown, complete with the giant hoop skirt to wear underneath. Cassie gave a little squeal. This year she wouldn't be at all embarrassed to go trick-or-treating in Andrea's neighborhood. She kind of hoped people she knew would see her.

Emily needed help getting into her banana costume, so Cassie wrestled with her skirt and dressed herself while her mom helped Emily. Cassie spun in front of the mirror in her mom's room, loving how it looked. And she didn't even need a corset. She was skinny enough to look good without it.

"Hair," she said to her mom, who laughed.

"All right. How do you want it?"

"In a bun." Cassie swept up the mid-shoulder-length strands and piled them on top of her head. "With just a few strands falling around my face that we can curl into ringlets." It was a style she'd seen a dozen times in photographs from the nineteenth century.

"Easy enough."

"And makeup? Can we put on makeup?"

"Of course. It's Halloween."

Cassie had never felt so glamorous as when they were done. She turned her body left and right to admire her reflection and decided she didn't care that she hadn't spent the night with Andrea.

⁕

Cassie knew before she even opened her eyes Saturday morning that something was wrong. She lay in bed and swallowed, drawing up moisture in her mouth to ease the ache. Then she swallowed again and winced at the sensation of sharp knives scraping down her throat.

She sat up, blinking to wake up and coughing. "I can't be sick," she whispered, alarm growing at the raspiness to her voice. Today was all-region tryouts! She could not be sick!

She thrust her legs over the side of the bed and shivered,

chills running down her spine. The night had been wet and cold while they trick-or-treated, but she'd taken care to change as soon as she'd gotten home, warming her feet in toasty socks. But as she stood up and a wave of dizziness washed over her, she knew the precautions had not been enough.

She went into the kitchen and gurgled warm salt water, trying to loosen up her throat like Ms. Malcolm had taught her. There was no make-up day for tryouts. It was now or never, and Cassie had to do her best no matter what.

"Mom?" she said, stepping into the bedroom and expecting she'd have to wake her.

But Mrs. Jones was already up, pulling on a pair of shoes. "You ready?"

Cassie's stomach knotted up again, twisting around like hands pulling taffy. "Almost."

She pressed a hand to the wall to help her keep her balance and returned to her room. The room spun, and she sat down for a moment before getting dressed, humming through the songs to warm up her voice and get the melody in her head. A mild buzzing filled her ears, and her humming sounded distant, like it came from a tunnel.

You've got this, she told herself. She'd practice and practiced and knew the music backward and forward.

It was still dark outside as Mrs. Jones backed the van out of the driveway. Cassie poked a finger in her ear so she could hear herself better and sang through the songs, flipping the pages in her binder.

She croaked on the high notes, and Cassie paused, clearing her throat and making little sigh noises. She tried again, and even though the note squeaked out, it didn't sound clear and pure.

Her mom arrived at the junior high and parked the car. "You sound fantastic, sweetie. You're going to do great."

"Uh-huh." Cassie bobbed her head, heart racing.

Mrs. Jones gave her a quick hug. "Call me when you're done

and I'll come get you."

"Okay." Cassie climbed out of the car, taking deep breaths. The choir kids were gathered in the cafeteria, finding their names and order of tryout on a sheet of paper by the door. Cassie avoided making eye contact with anyone and instead searched for her name, her finger scrolling down the paper.

"You're right here," a boy said, and Cassie turned to see Miles as he bumped her shoulder with his. "You go in an hour."

For a moment the room seemed to move sideways, but then she caught her balance. She tried to smile at him but feared it fell short. "When do you go?"

"In forty minutes." He returned to a long table and straddled the bench so he faced her. She followed, sitting next to him.

"Are you nervous?" she asked.

"A little," he admitted, running a hand over his hair. "It's the first time I've tried out for something. You?"

"Petrified," Cassie said.

He gave her a grin and tapped her hand. "You're the best singer in the school. You'll do great."

Her face warmed. She started to avert her eyes, but then she held his gaze instead. "How do you know? You're not in choir with me."

"I've heard you sing. We went to the same elementary school, remember?"

Like she could forget.

"And everyone says it. Everyone talks about you."

"They do?" Cassie pulled a leg up on the bench and wrapped her arm around her knee, resting her chin on it. "What do they say?"

He lifted a shoulder. "That you're a great singer, you're super nice, really friendly."

And pretty. Did they say she was pretty? But he didn't say that, and she certainly wasn't going to ask.

"Cassie, there you are." Maureen appeared beside the table, breathless, her bangs windblown and curling upward like a halo. Amity popped up behind her, eyes anxious. "We need to practice. Can you run us through our parts?"

"Oh, sure." Cassie stood up. She'd forgotten Amity was also in choir. She hadn't made the select choir, but she was in the girls' choir. So was Janice, but she sang alto. "Right here?"

"They have rooms set up for practicing." Maureen grabbed her arm and hauled her out of the cafeteria.

Cassie allowed her to, somewhat reluctantly. Though she wanted to practice, it was the first time she'd been able to talk to Miles by herself in a very long time. She glanced back at him, but he was already talking to another guy, and she knew the moment had passed.

CHAPTER EIGHTEEN
Cold Start

A music player was already set up in the classroom, and Maureen selected the track that had their songs on it. The musical accompaniment began, and Cassie tapped her fingers along the side of her jeans, counting out the measures. One, two, three, and—she started to sing, but Maureen and Amity jumped in a half second after her.

Cassie paused the music. "Guys, you have to count it in. You'll miss your entrance otherwise."

Amity nodded, her lips puckered, looking close to tears.

"Let's try again," Maureen sighed.

They went through it three more times, and by the third time they were coming in together. But when they hit measure thirty-two, someone was overshooting the note, and Cassie winced as the sharp rang through the air. She paused the music again.

"The piano doesn't play our note," she said. "You have to know it. Take a deep breath going in to it, or you won't get on top of it."

She started the music again, but no matter how many times they went through it, the sharp sound remained.

Cassie gave up and led them through the next two songs.

The tryout only consisted of a few measures of each song, but she didn't know which measures it would be yet. They would find out when they went to sing for the judges.

"Are we doing okay?" Amity asked, looking at Cassie with hopeful eyes.

"Yeah, you're doing great," Cassie said.

Maureen nodded. "You sound great. Just don't go sharp." She whacked Amity on the back of the head, and immediately Amity walloped her back.

"I'm not the one going sharp! You sound like a banshee!"

Maureen opened her mouth and let out a screeching wail. Then she spread her arms wide and flew at Amity.

Amity yelped and covered her face, then ran from the room laughing.

How could they play at a time like this? Cassie reset the tracks and started over, practicing by herself this time. But practicing with them had given her something else: confidence. She knew the music.

Her throat still hurt, and she had to sing softer on the high note than usual, but she hit it. And it sounded good.

Cassie returned to the cafeteria and found a quiet spot. She pulled out a few of her typed up pages and tried to edit, but her nerves were still too bundled up to let her concentrate.

"Hi, Cassie." Riley plopped down beside her. "What time is your tryout?"

Cassie glanced at the clock above the doors, and her heart did a little jump. "In about half an hour."

"Mine too. Are you nervous?"

"Yeah." Cassie sighed and put her manuscript away. "I hate auditioning."

Riley shrugged. "I don't really care. I'm sure I won't make it."

"You never know," Cassie protested. But in a way, she envied Riley. If Cassie thought she wouldn't make it, she wouldn't be so uptight right now.

But she believed she could make it. She just wasn't sure if she would.

A runner finally came in and called out Cassie's block of numbers, and she stood.

"Good luck," Riley said, pulling on her earlobe.

"Thanks," Cassie said. She gripped her music under her arm and followed the other sopranos down the hall. They paused outside a classroom, where Cassie could just hear another singer finishing up.

Great. Everyone would be able to hear her.

The door opened and the girl came out, her face flushed.

"Go on in," the runner, a kindly faced woman who had to be Kendra's mom said to the first person in line. "Announce your number and wait for the music to start."

Cassie could hardly breathe, she was so nervous. How would she hear the music over the pounding of her heart? The girls seemed to take forever during their tryouts. Finally the one in front of her went into the room, and Cassie hauled out her music. She poured over it, mouthing the words in time to the sounds coming through the door. She listened to the other singer, hearing where she got off rhythm, where her notes weren't quite on key.

I can do better than that. She squared her shoulders and braced herself.

The other girl didn't even meet Cassie's eyes when she came out, just hunched her shoulders and hurried away.

Cassie stepped in, surprised that she could see the judges sitting behind three desks at the front of the room.

"Number, please?" one of them asked.

Cassie's hand trembled as she moved her music around and found her number. "Two-fourteen."

"Thank you."

The judges rearranged their paperwork, and the first one lifted her head.

"Are you ready?"

Cassie nodded, not trusting herself to speak.

The woman pressed a button on a machine, and the music began.

Cassie heard the opening notes and began to count, tapping her finger against her thigh. One, two, three, four—no! She'd missed her entry! Sucking in a gasp, Cassie opened her mouth and began singing, hurrying the beginning lines to catch up to the music. All the time, her mind raced. How had she missed that? She'd practiced it so many times! It should have come together like clockwork!

The track changed, and a voice announced the next song and the measure. Cassie scrambled to keep up. She shifted her music to the right place and tried to hear the intro, but everything sounded a bit warbled, as if she were listening underwater. She thought she heard her cue and jumped in, only to find she was off half a beat. She fixed it at the end of the measure and sang the rest of the stanza flawlessly. Her courage grew as the track moved to the final piece, and this time she came in strong and steady.

It finished on the high note, and Cassie struggled to hold it strong. She couldn't hear herself so well, and her vocal chords felt tight, straining with the note.

The music finished and she closed her binder, blinking back hot moisture. She swallowed, trying to moisten her aching throat. She'd come in weak, but finished strong. Would it be enough to sway the judges?

The judges' pencils raced across their papers, and then the first one lifted her face again.

"Thank you. You may go."

That was it, then. Cassie nodded and walked out, the adrenaline slowly eeping out of her. Only time would tell now.

Cassie waited outside with several other kids who had finished their tryout. They all laughed and joked, relieved it was over. Nobody talked about how they'd done. The results would be up in a few hours, and Cassie knew she'd be back to see. She saw Amity and Maureen but didn't join them. No sign of Miles.

"How did it go?" her mom asked as soon as Cassie got into the car.

Cassie had anticipated this question but still wasn't sure how to answer it. "I don't know. My head and throat have hurt all morning, and I messed up at first. But then I got back with the music and did really good. So." She shrugged and pleated her fingers, trying to appear calm but anxiously jumping inside. "I don't know."

"Well, we'll find out in a few hours," her mom said, reaching over and squeezing her hands.

Cassie let her mom keep her hand there for a minute, and then she pulled free. She didn't want to be babied.

She managed to get herself involved with revising her manuscript, with her thoughts only going to All-Region tryouts every few minutes instead of ever second. Riley texted and asked how she'd done, and Cassie told her she'd let her know as soon as she knew something.

Finally, at five o'clock, she bounded downstairs to her dad's office.

"Can we drive to the school and see the results?" she breathed out. She knew her dad would be going to bed soon so he could get up early for the paper route. It was now or wait till Monday.

He finished up what he was typing and rolled his chair away from the computer. "Let's go."

The delicious aroma of sauteing onions and sausage drifted through the living room, but Cassie wouldn't be able to eat until she knew the results.

It seemed like Mr. Jones drove especially slow on the twisty, windy roads from their house in the country back into town. Cassie tumbled her fingers over and over around each other, more nervous now than when she tried out. She wished her dad would say something, and then she was glad he didn't because she didn't know what she would say back.

Finally he brought the van to a stop and parked behind the gym. Even from the car, Cassie could see the two sheets of paper taped to the door. Her heart rate sped up, and her breathing came in little gasps. Her fate was on that paper.

"Shall we?" Mr. Jones said, opening the door.

She climbed out after him, staying behind as he approached the school.

"I can't look," she said, halting. "You tell me." She took a few steps backward, staying well away from the papers.

"Okay." Mr. Jones stepped forward and read the names.

He stood there a minute, two minutes, three minutes. Then he turned to her, a gentle smile on his face, and said, "Come read the names of your friends so you know who to congratulate."

He put an arm around her shoulders, and Cassie's heart stopped. She hadn't made it. She crumpled against him, covering her face with her hands and turning into her dad's chest. She sobbed, the disappointment gushing out of her. How could she not have made it? She was the best singer in the class! How? How had she failed?

Cassie's sobs died down before they got home, but she sat dismally in the car, staring out the window at the black sky. Failure. The one thing she was really good at, she'd failed.

Her phone rang, and she looked down to see it sitting in her hand. Cassie didn't recognize the number, and she answered it without thinking. "Hello?"

"Hi, is this Cassie?"

"Yes," she answered.

"This is Kendra. Did you make it?"

Kendra had never called her before. Cassie hadn't even known she had her number.

"No. I didn't."

"Really? I can't believe it! My mom checked the list for me, she said I made it, I was so excited, but I thought for sure you would be on there too!"

Kendra had made it? Had Maureen? Had everyone except Cassie? The knot returned to her throat, and suddenly she dreaded going to school on Monday.

"Congrats, Kendra."

"Oh, I just can't believe it. I thought we could practice together—you always know the music so well."

"Yeah. Well, I hope it goes well for you." Cassie needed to get off the phone before she cried again.

"Thanks. I'll see you Monday."

Cassie hung up just as her phone rang again. Riley. She sighed and silenced the call. She didn't feel like talking to anyone else.

❦

Cassie had to endure Sue and Michelle's sympathetic noises all day at church when they found out she hadn't made All-Region. Sue and Michelle were also in choir as ninth graders, but neither of them had made All-Region. Riley hadn't either, and she actually seemed sad about it.

Not as sad as Cassie. She had to go to the bathroom in between classes and cry again.

She steeled herself as she got on the bus Monday morning. Now was not the time to be weepy.

She was so lost in her own world that it took several minutes before she noticed the boys in front of her laughing and ducking down below the seat. They bobbed their heads up again, then laughed and ducked. She furrowed her brow and straightened. What were they doing?

Both of them rolled up wads of paper, stuck them in their mouths, and spit them forward, then laughed and ducked. Jeremy, just a few seats up, turned around and yelled in his nasally voice, "Quit that!"

They roared with laughter as if it were the funniest thing.

Cassie'd had enough. She knew Rhonda, the bus driver, kept Jeremy in the seat close to her to protect him, but how could she help him while she was driving? If she knew what was going on, she was powerless to do anything. Cassie stood up, gripping the backs of the vinyl seats to keep from falling as the bus went around the curves.

"Hi, Jeremy," she said, falling into the seat beside him. "You're going to come sit with me, okay?" The stupid seventh-graders would leave him alone if he sat with her.

The bus stopped to let a few more kids on, and Cassie bounded up.

"Rhonda, can Jeremy come and sit with me from now on?"

Rhonda turned to her in surprise, curly blond hair nearly obscuring her features. "You want him to sit with you?"

"Yes." Cassie nodded.

"Sure, that's fine."

Cassie returned to his seat. "Come on." She led him down the aisle, giving death glares to the boys as they passed their seat. They both hunkered down in their chair, glowering at her but lacking the courage to do anything else.

"How are you, Jeremy?" she asked as he sat down beside her. He did smell like his pants had been peed on and not washed in days. But that was hardly his fault.

"I'm fine," he said. He settled into his seat. "Can I sit by the window?"

"Of course."

They made small talk all the way to the elementary school, and then Jeremy, who was only a fifth grader, got off. Cassie stayed on for the ride to the junior high.

"Hope you're proud of yourselves, making fun of a fifth grader like that," Cassie hissed, just loud enough for the boys to hear. They didn't respond.

The bus stopped at the junior high, and Cassie waited her turn to get off.

"That was a very nice thing you did, Cassie," Rhonda said,

stopping her before she went down the steps.

Cassie paused. She wasn't trying to be nice. "It's no big deal. I don't mind sitting by him."

"You're a nice person," the bus driver said.

Cassie stepped onto the sidewalk in front of the junior high and tried to rally herself up. She was a nice person, even if she hadn't made All-Region.

CHAPTER NINETEEN
Emotional Overload

All of Cassie's classmates, even those not in choir, wanted to know if she'd made All-Region. Each innocent question threatened to make the tears fall again, especially when Cassie saw Kendra and the others who had made it. Maureen and Amity hadn't, and the three of them commiserated over their lunch trays.

"I don't think it was fair," Amity said. "The judges picked who they wanted."

"Yeah," Maureen agreed. "They could see us. They only picked the older girls."

Cassie knew that wasn't true. "I came in wrong. And my throat hurt."

They both looked at her sympathetically.

"You should have made it," Amity said.

Cassie gave a weak smile.

She thought she just about had her feelings under control when sixth hour ended, and with a jolt of alarm, she realized what came next.

Seventh hour. Choir.

She put her books in her locker and gathered what she needed so she could go straight to the bus after school. How would she face her peers? Maybe she could pretend to be sick and skip class.

But no, she couldn't do that either. With a sigh, Cassie shut her locker and went outside, following the sidewalk to the building that housed the math classes, the gym, and the music classes.

Inside was a chaotic mad-house. Students clustered in groups, hugging, congratulating, a few looking sour or disheartened. Cassie made her way to her usual chair and sat down, trying her very best to look indifferent.

Ms. Berry came in after the bell rang and called them all to silence.

Oh, please don't make us sing, Cassie begged silently. What would they do, go over the same songs they'd been practicing for weeks for All-Region? She wouldn't be able to bear it.

"I want to tell you all how proud I am of you for trying out for All-Region," Ms. Berry said, a pleased smile crinkling her eyes. "I couldn't be happier for those of you who made it. You worked hard, and you deserved it."

Like daggers to the heart.

"We'll take a break for the first twenty minutes, but after that we need to practice for our choir concert this Friday. Now, I have here everyone's score sheet with what the judges said. I'm going to hand them to you."

Oh, no. Cassie stared at the little yellow and pink squares in Ms. Berry's hands. She didn't want her sheet. It would make her cry, right here in front of everyone.

But there was no way around it. Ms. Berry was already making the rounds in the classroom, scanning for faces and clambering around students to deliver the sheets. The conversation resumed, the normal gossip and chatter taking the place of the mournful tone from those who hadn't made it.

Cassie didn't talk to anyone. Instead she watched Ms. Berry as she handed out each form, speaking briefly with the student before moving on. Her eyes landed on Cassie, and Cassie's chest tightened as Ms. Berry made her way over.

"Cassie, honey, I know you're disappointed you didn't make it," Ms. Berry said, holding the forms out to her. "But I think you'll be proud of your chair and their comments. You did good, sweetie."

Cassie could only nod, swallowing hard against the painful knot in her throat. She wanted to shove the forms in her backpack and ignore them, but her willpower wasn't strong enough. With shaking hands, she brought them up to her face. The number "55" had been written in bright red ink and circled with pen.

Fifty-five. Chair fifty-five! That was horrible! Only the first thirteen chairs made it into All-Region. She hadn't been anywhere close! In spite of what Ms. Berry had said, she only felt worse. She took several deep breaths before reading through the comments.

Bit of a rough start—watch that high note. Pretty voice. Breath support. Stay with the music. Watch the rhythm. Count yourself in. Deep breaths to stay on pitch. Keep singing!

She put the judging forms in her backpack and focused on a spot across the room, staring at it as she took measured breaths. She had just proved to the entire school that she wasn't as good a singer as they all thought.

༺ ༻

By the time the choir concert came around on Friday evening, most everyone had forgotten about All-Region and its lucky recipients. Cassie told herself she was over it, though something wound tightly around her heart every time it was mentioned.

She stood in her bathroom and turned sideways to see how her new choir dress fell across her torso. She faced forward again and dug her hands into her hair, hiking it to the top of her head. The dress looked fantastic on her. She looked like a princess.

Mr. Jones whistled when Cassie stepped out of the bathroom, and her face flushed.

"Don't, Dad!" she said, pushing him away when he tried to hug her.

"You look beautiful," Mrs. Jones said, beaming at her. "Let's go get Grandma."

Cassie met Emily's eyes and made a face. Grandma lived by herself in Fayetteville and joined the family from time to time for holidays and family events, when she felt like it. Which wasn't often, and Cassie didn't mind. Grandma wasn't always very nice. She'd suffered a stroke in her early twenties, and ever since then she acted very immature.

The nitpicking started as soon as Grandma got in the car.

"That dress is so green. Wouldn't black be more appropriate?"

"Hmm," Cassie replied, biting her tongue.

"Maybe if you wore makeup it wouldn't be so bold. Your face looks washed out."

"Mom," Mr. Jones said, "leave Cassie alone."

Thank you! Cassie thought, and that silenced Grandma.

Cassie found Maureen in the hallway before the performance, but Maureen talked mostly to Amity, who stayed by her side until Ms. Berry made her go stand with her own choir. Then Maureen looked at Cassie.

"The dress looks good on you. I hate mine. It's so stiff and clingy."

It didn't fall as nicely on Maureen. But Cassie didn't say that. "You look nice also."

"Thanks." Maureen favored her with a smile.

The concert went off without a hitch, and when it was over Cassie hurried back to her family in the audience.

"You did wonderful up there," Mrs. Jones said, pulling her close. "You look so grown up."

"What was wrong with your face?" Grandma said. "It looked like you were trying to shoo a fly off your nose."

Cassie stared at her for a moment, not even sure how to respond. "What do you mean?"

"Your eyebrows kept going up and down like this." Grandma wiggled her nose and mouth garishly with her eyebrows.

Cassie turned to her mom.

"No, Grandma," Mrs. Jones said patiently, "Cassie was being expressive. That's how she sings. She tells a story with her face."

"It looked funny up there. Nobody else was doing it."

"It's how Ms. Malcolm wants me to sing," Cassie said, miffed.

"You should look more professional, like all the other singers."

"You mean bored out of my mind?"

"Cassie," Mrs. Jones said, a warning note in her voice.

Right. No sassing Grandma.

"Let's get out of here," Cassie muttered, moving past them into the aisle.

Mrs. Jones had a surprise for Cassie and Emily over Thanksgiving break: they were moving rooms. At first Cassie complained about having to pack up all her things, but when she and Emily stepped into the room previously the guest suite, she realized how much nicer it would be for them.

The room was as big as her parents' room, with a giant walk-in closet and a bathroom. Mr. Jones had already moved the beds into the room, and Cassie dumped her box of books and toys on the bed.

Toys? She didn't need toys anymore. She pulled them out of the box and put them in a plastic bag. Time for a donation run.

"You have so much space now!" Mrs. Jones said, coming in with her arms full of clothes. "All of yours and Emily's clothes fit in one closet!"

"And no more bunk beds," Emily said. The bunk beds had been apart for at least a year, but the two twin beds took up all the space in their former bedroom.

"Now you girls won't constantly be in each other's way."

"I doubt that," Cassie muttered. Besides, she knew the real reason for the move was so Annette and Scott could have their own rooms. The two were finally getting too big to share.

"We don't fight," Emily said, and Mrs. Jones laughed.

"I want you to get everything moved over and unpacked this week," Mrs. Jones said. "Just remember I expect you to keep this room clean!"

Yes. Clean. Cassie looked around at the bare walls, the visible carpet, and hoped they would be able to. She liked it better this way.

※

By the time school resumed after Thanksgiving break, choir and All-Region were pretty much forgotten. Her teachers were singing a different song: Finals. They invited all the students to join in the melody, and Cassie obliged.

"I didn't know why you worry so much," Amity said at lunch, popping open a soda can while Cassie wrote vocabulary words on note cards. "You have straight As. You're like the smartest person I've ever met."

Cassie doubted Amity had met many smart people. "That's why I worry so much. I'm a horrible test taker. And if I bomb one of these, it could destroy my GPA."

"GPA," Maureen snorted, spewing French fry pieces across the table. "Who even knows what that is?"

"Ew, you got food everywhere!" Andrea cried, and the attention was redirected from Cassie to Maureen, as usual.

Which suited Cassie fine. The past month, she'd gotten friendlier with the other girls who sat at the table, but they still tended to talk and joke around her rather than with her.

Miles and his friends had started sitting at a different table, but they stopped by the girls' table every day to say hi. Cassie always smiled at Miles, but she couldn't compete with Amity's loud flirting.

"What's everyone doing for Christmas break?" Janice asked after the laughter died down from Maureen's food mess. "Who's traveling?"

"We might go to my grandma's, she lives close by," Andrea said.

"My grandma comes to my house," Cassie said. "We never go anywhere."

"We're doing a Christmas party at your house, right, Cara?" Maureen said.

"I don't know," Cara said. "I haven't talked to my mom about it."

Christmas party! Would Cassie be invited? She thought of the scarves she had nearly finished. One for Janice and one for Amity. She would love to do one for all the girls, but she didn't think she'd have time.

"Oh, we have to do the Christmas party!" Amity exclaimed. "It was so much fun last year!"

"But it won't be the same without Kitty," Maureen said with a pout.

All the girls lowered their heads as if in a moment of silence, and then Cara said, "I'll talk to my mom and let you guys know."

The bell rang and they stood quickly, gathering their trash. Cassie looked at the half-eaten muffin in her hand. The rest of it called to her, tempting her to finish it. Cassie dumped it into the trash and hurried out of the cafeteria.

☙ ❧

Cassie walked with Maureen to choir, though she only half paid attention to what she said, nodding and trying to look interested.

And then Maureen elbowed her and hissed, "Look at Riley."

Cassie lifted her eyes in the direction Maureen indicated. Riley had just sat down in her chair, facing forward, but her face was flushed, nose and eyes pink in the tell-tale signs of crying.

Uh-oh. Cassie's heart twisted in sympathy. "I'll go see what's wrong."

Maureen didn't say anything, and Cassie took that as permission. She got up and walked over to the alto section, whispering her apologies as she climbed over toes and chair legs. There were no empty seats by Riley, so instead she crouched beside her.

"Riley. What's wrong?"

Riley sniffed and stared straight ahead, blinking her green eyes. "What do you care? You're busy hanging out with all your new friends."

For a moment, Cassie took pride in the fact that someone had noticed her new friends. Then she remembered Riley, and she said, "That doesn't mean I don't have time for my old friends."

"We're not friends."

The sentence hurt, and Cassie brushed it back. "Of course we are. We hang out at church, and you've come over to my house lots of times."

"But you don't talk to me at school. Only when we're alone."

"I'm talking to you now."

Riley finally looked at her. "Only because I'm crying."

There was more truth to Riley's words than Cassie wanted to admit. "Call me later. Maybe you can spend the night tonight."

Riley just bobbed her head and faced the front again, and Cassie inched her way back to her spot as Ms. Berry called the choir to order.

"What's wrong with her?" Maureen murmured.

"I don't know. But I invited her to spend the night tonight."

"On a Thursday? Will your mom let you?"

Cassie shrugged. "I'll ask. I have to make sure Riley's okay."

"You're such a nice person," Maureen said.

It was an odd compliment. Almost like she thought Cassie only invited Riley over to be nice, not because she was her friend.

CHAPTER TWENTY
Forgotten

Riley's mom approved the slumber party, but not until Saturday. Riley came over before dinner. Mr. Jones teased her when she cut her chicken up funny, and Cassie laughed so hard she spit rice across the table. By the time the girls retired to the bedroom, they were all giggly and goofy. Cassie's little sister Emily situated herself on her bed with headphones and a book in her hands, and Cassie and Riley sat on the floor against the other bed, out of sight and hopefully out of hearing range.

"So what was wrong?" Cassie asked her. She and Riley flipped through their elementary school yearbooks, looking at pictures of themselves and kids they'd known before junior high. "Why were you crying in choir?"

"I just got sad," Riley said. "Nobody really likes me."

"Of course they do. You have friends."

"Like who?"

"Well, Farrah. Emmett."

"Farrah moved away. Emmett doesn't sit with me. They were only my friend because you were."

"Me, then."

Riley rolled her eyes. "You're only nice to me sometimes."

There was a time not too long ago when it was Riley who was mean to Cassie. Now Cassie felt the burn of shame creep up her neck and over her ears. When had she become the mean person? "I'm sorry, Riley. I don't mean to be. Sometimes I'm just not paying attention."

"Sometimes it seems you don't like me."

"Maybe," Cassie said, thinking hard, "sometimes I kind of hold a grudge. Because of how you acted when we were younger."

Riley stared at her. "But we were just kids."

"It was just a few months ago. And you really hurt my feelings." The tears came to Cassie's eyes without meaning to. She remembered all the mean things Riley had said to her, the mean notes, the boycotting of her birthday party.

"I'm sorry," Riley said, and she began to cry again.

Cassie reached over and hugged her. "It's okay. You're right. We were just kids."

"So it's not that you think you're too cool for me?" Riley pulled back and wiped her eyes.

Amity and Maureen and Andrea certainly thought so. And the way they made fun of Riley made Cassie not want to be around her, either. She'd just barely entered this hierarchy and was still searching for her place. "Definitely not," she lied. "I love you like a sister."

"Me too. You're my best friend."

Cassie turned her attention back to the yearbook in front of her. Their sixth grade pages were open, Riley in one class and Cassie in another.

"Ew," Cassie said, pointing to the picture of herself. "Remember when I wore glasses and was fat?"

"You've changed a lot," Riley said. "You're really pretty now." She touched the picture of Miles, circled in red marker by Cassie several years earlier. "You still like him?"

Cassie shrugged. "Yes. But it's different. We're friends and it would be, well, weird." A trace of sadness rippled through her at the words. She jumped up, letting the book fall off her lap and hit the floor. "Come on! I have an idea."

"I know there's a curling iron in here somewhere," Cassie said, sifting through her mom's collection of electronic hair appliances. "I've used it before, though it's been a while."

Riley pulled on a few strands of Cassie's straight dark hair. "You should try again. I bet your hair is so pretty curly."

"Yeah, it looks really good, but it doesn't stay." She despised having straight hair. She always admired the way Amity, Andrea, and Maureen could put waves or even curls in their hair whenever they feel like it, but Cassie's stick hair absolutely refused unless she put in so much hairspray that it couldn't move.

"What's this?" Riley pulled out a device with a long cord on it.

Instead of having a round barrel like a curling iron, the outside was rectangle. Cassie took it from her and opened it. The metal plates inside were diagonal-shaped, with mountains and valleys to make ridges on the plates.

"I have no idea. Let me ask my mom."

Riley and Cassie walked back into the living room with the strange device in their hands.

"What is this, Mom?" Cassie asked.

Mrs. Jones had cuddled up in a corner of the couch, her knees tucked up to her chest, a book in her hands. Cassie suspected this was one of the only quiet moments her mom got and felt a little guilty interrupting her.

"It's a crimper," Mrs. Jones said.

"A what?" Cassie asked.

"Oh, I've seen crimped hairstyles!" Riley said. "They used to be really popular like thirty years ago."

Mrs. Jones laughed. "Yes, I suppose it gives away my age. They're a lot of fun."

A crimper. Cassie looked at the device with curiosity. "Let's try it."

Riley shrugged. "I'm game."

"Don't forget, girls," Mrs. Jones said, "we have church tomorrow. You should probably get to bed."

"Yeah, we will soon," Cassie said. She led Riley back into the big bedroom at the back of the house. "Let's do this fast."

"Not me, are you crazy?" Riley said. "Have you seen how short my hair is? If I crimp it, it will stick straight out like an Afro!"

Cassie giggled at the idea. She didn't really know what a crimped hairstyle looked like, so it hadn't occurred to her that it wouldn't work on short hair. "Is my hair long enough?"

"Definitely. Your hair goes past your shoulders."

"OK." Cassie plugged in the device. "Let's put our pajamas on and brush our teeth, and maybe it will be ready after that."

As soon as their pajamas were on, the girls gathered in the bathroom around the crimper. Even Emily hovered in the doorway, curious about their actions.

"Should I do it or do you want to do it for me?" Cassie asked Riley.

"You do it. If your hair burns and falls out, I don't want you to blame me."

"Is that even a possibility?" Cassie said with a little squeal.

"I don't know, but I'm not taking any chances!"

Taking a deep breath, Cassie separated sections of hair from her head and stuck them between the two blades. She counted to ten, like she did with the curling iron, then opened the blades, releasing the hair, and moved it down two more spaces. She did it one more time until the entire section of hair had been crimped.

"Wow!" she said, running her fingers over the ridges on her hair. The texture felt so strange compared to the soft straightness she was used to. "It looks really different!"

"Yeah, that's pretty cool," Riley agreed. "It looks like you put your hair in tiny braids and then took it out."

That was exactly what it looked like. Cassie remembered as a little girl how she had enjoyed when her mom would braid her hair because when they took it out, her hair had form. "Let's do all of it," she said.

Riley's eyes grew large. "Your hair will be huge!"

"I can't wait to see it!" Emily giggled.

"My mom said we can have the Christmas party this Friday," Cara said at lunch Monday. "We'll do a gift exchange and then just hang out all night. It'll be a blast."

The other girls squealed with excitement, and Cassie kept her eagerness to herself. She'd never been to Cara's house, but the others all acted like getting invited was one of the coolest things ever. And she had several scarves ready. But would that be the right kind of gift?

"I've got everyone's name in this jar," Cara said, placing it on the table. "Pass it around and draw one out."

Cassie watched as the jar came closer to her, her heart pounding anxiously. Who would get her name? More importantly, who would she draw? These were the cool girls. They required more than a pair of soccer shorts from her dad's store. What on earth would she get them?

The jar stopped at Janice, who sat beside Cassie. She drew out a slip of paper and paused. She looked at Cassie uncertainly.

And then Cassie realized why. There were no more papers in the jar.

Oh! She hadn't been invited to the party after all. It was just for Andrea and her group of cool girls, which Cassie was not a part of. She blinked, feeling the heat rush to her face, and prepared her best fake smile.

"Cassie!" Cara exclaimed. "We forgot Cassie!" She used "we" as if someone besides her had filled that jar. Cara grabbed it and passed the jar under everyone's noses. "Put your papers back, quick! We have to do it again!"

A slow warmth filled Cassie's chest, replacing her earlier humiliation. Sure, she'd been forgotten. But it wasn't intentional. They wanted her there. She smiled as Cara wrote her name on a slip of paper and added it to the jar.

Cassie drew Andrea's name.

⊙～⋆～⊙

Cassie made a special point to talk to Riley in choir. But after the hellos, Cassie always returned to Maureen, fully conscious of Maureen's eyes on her back from the moment she walked away.

"Why are you chatty with Riley all of the sudden?" Maureen asked on Wednesday.

Cassie shrugged. "She's been sad and lonely. I'm trying to be her friend."

"She's kind of dorky. And she's not usually very nice."

Neither was Maureen, if anyone wanted Cassie's honest opinion. But because Maureen was funny, everyone considered her meanness okay. Cassie certainly wouldn't say anything about it.

"Who are you riding with to Cara's party?"

"I was just going to have my mom bring me over. Cara lives out in Tontitown, just like I do." The rural parts of the school zone technically weren't in the city of Springdale. They were in the outlying countryside, in the long rolling hills and green farmland straddled between Fayetteville and Springdale.

"But we all kind of get together first and arrive in groups. You should ride with Janice or Andrea."

Maureen didn't offer to give her a ride, Cassie noticed. "Okay. I'll check with them."

She hesitated to ask Andrea. Their track record wasn't great. Andrea had a tendency to bail on her. But as much as she liked Janice, she hadn't ever been to her house and felt a bit timid asking. So she asked Andrea Thursday morning in P.E.

"Can I ride with you to Cara's Christmas party?"

"Um." Andrea considered it. "I already have Amity coming

over. But I'll ask my mom if you can come too. Call me tonight, okay?"

"Okay," Cassie said, once again a flutter with nerves. While Amity was friendlier and friendlier to her, they never talked on the phone or hung out.

She told herself not to fret it. Andrea would probably say Cassie couldn't come.

But she didn't. When Cassie called her Thursday night, Andrea said, "Yeah, it's perfect! I already asked my mom. Bring your stuff to school and ride home with me."

"Okay!" Cassie said, breathless with excitement.

It was all the girls could talk about on Friday. Cara had rented a few movies, and her parents were ordering pizza.

"Are we going to stay up all night like last year?" Amity asked.

"You were asleep before eight o'clock!" Maureen said, smacking Amity's leg.

"I was not!" Amity returned the smack.

"I'm not staying up," Janice said. "I'm opening my present and snuggling in my blankets and ignoring you all."

"I bet Cassie will bring a book to read," Maureen said with a giggle.

"Will you, Cassie?" Amity said, rounding on her. "Are you going to tune us out for your imaginary world?"

"You could bring the one you wrote," Janice said. "That would be cool."

"You could write one about us," Cara said.

All the attention had Cassie's head spinning. One second they were making fun of her, and the next second they were encouraging her. She could never make heads or tails of these girls.

The bell rang, and they gathered up their trash and hurried into the school hallway, heading to their lockers.

"See you guys tonight!" Cara said, her face flushed.

"After school, Cassie!" Andrea said with a wave.

CHAPTER TWENTY-ONE
Christmas party

Being at Andrea's house with Amity was eye-opening. When Cassie stayed with Andrea, they would watch a movie, maybe do their hair and makeup and jump on the trampoline.

Not with Amity. Immediately Amity was going through Andrea's phone, listing names as she went. "We're not calling James. Connor?"

"Not Connor!" Andrea exclaimed.

"You still have a crush on him?" Cassie said, surprised.

"You still have a crush on Miles!" Andrea returned.

Cassie's eyes widened. She couldn't believe Andrea had said that out loud.

Amity gawked. "I knew it! I knew there was something odd about the way you two act around each other!"

Cassie glared at Andrea. "It's an old crush."

"Let's call him." Amity scrolled through Andrea's phone.

"No, no!" Cassie cried, putting her hand on Amity's. "We're just friends."

"But he likes you, too, Cassie!" Amity said. "Can't you tell from the way he looks at you? The way he talks to you?"

Cassie blinked at her. Was it true? Did Amity see something Cassie didn't? "But he's never asked me out."

Amity's hand came down on Cassie's thigh, giving her a resounding slap.

"Ow," Cassie said, moving her leg away, surprised by how much that hurt. But Amity didn't seem to notice.

"Because he's shy, duh! You haven't really given him any reason to think you like him! I'm calling him."

"No!" Cassie reached forward and jerked the phone from Amity's hands. Or tried. Amity squawked like a chicken and held on tight.

"Help me, Andrea!" she shrieked.

A tug-of-war ensued, and Andrea got between them, yelling and referring. Cassie almost forgot what they were fighting about as the act of taking the phone away became a game. She got it and Amity tackled her, whacking her like a kitten after a mouse. By the time Cassie relinquished the phone, she was laughing so hard she couldn't breathe.

"Give me that, you crazies," Andrea said, snatching the phone back. "I'll decide who we call."

Cassie settled back, grinning, the rush of pleasure coursing through her having nothing to do with Miles and everything to do with friendship.

Cassie managed to convince the girls not to call Miles, and two hours later, Mrs. Wall drove them out to Tontitown. Cara lived even farther out than Cassie, and her house was situated at the end of a very long driveway. The house reminded Cassie of an old European cottage, with a triangular roof and brown shutters around all the windows.

Mrs. Wall parked the car, and the girls clambered out. Cassie slipped her arm through the soccer bag she was using as an overnight bag, wanting to pinch herself to make sure this was real. She, Cassandra Jones, was at a Christmas party at Cara Barnes' house.

"Hi, hi!" Cara greeted them with hugs as they came in, smelling like flowers and soap, her perfect blond hair halfway up with a red ribbon. "Take your bags upstairs to the loft. Show Cassie, Andrea."

"This way," Andrea said. She led the way up the stairs that wound over the kitchen to a loft that overlooked the living room. A tall Christmas tree had been set up near a picture window, adorned only in white ornaments and white lights. Four beds were in the loft, and Andrea dumped her stuff on one of them. Cassie did the same to another.

"Oh, you guys made it." Maureen came out of a bathroom connected to the loft. "I rode with Cara. Looks like we're just waiting on Janice. Too bad she didn't have someone to ride with."

Maureen's tone held a note of smugness, and Cassie saw the way she brushed Janice to the outskirts of their group, the only one who hadn't been able to find a friend to hang out with first. At least it wasn't her.

The doorbell rang, and a moment later they heard Cara greeting Janice.

"Everyone put your gifts beneath the tree!" Cara called up to the loft.

"I already did," Maureen said. "Since I got here first."

Andrea looked at Cassie and rolled her eyes. She removed her gift from her bag, and Cassie did the same.

"Come on, let's go down," Andrea said.

Janice sat on a window seat by the Christmas tree, looking out over the grassy hill and the bare trees beyond. "Look, guys. It's snowing."

"Oo." The girls gathered around her, watching the soft white flakes flutter to the ground in the growing darkness.

It didn't snow often in Arkansas, so the sight of the fresh, fluffy whiteness filled Cassie with a sense of wonder and peace. She leaned her head on Andrea's shoulder, and Andrea let her head fall on Cassie's.

"It's so beautiful."

They sat in silence for a few minutes until the doorbell rang.

The girls swiveled on the window seat and watched Mrs. Barnes answer it.

"Pizza's here, girls!"

Mrs. Barnes placed the pizza on the counter, and a dark trepidation crept up in Cassie's heart. She loved pizza with a passion, but she rarely allowed herself to indulge in the big slices of gooey cheese and greasy meat. Would her friends notice if she skipped it?

Cassie grabbed a glass of water while everyone else attacked the pizza, then she hung back while they ate. Amity noticed her and beckoned to the barstool beside her.

"Come on, Cass," she said. "Eat with us."

Cassie joined them before she became the center of attention. She loaded a thin slice of pizza on her plate, then took a bite of the tip under the watchful gaze of the other girls. By her second bite, the attention had swung off her, and she put the pizza down in relief.

But those two bites had tasted delightful, tangy and warm and flavorful. She lifted the pizza and took another nibble, then another. When she looked again, she'd consumed half of it.

"Now presents," Maureen said, grinning widely. She grabbed Amity's arm and dragged her back to the tree.

"Let me see, I have the list here," Cara said. She opened a notebook and brought it over to the tree. "We'll start with Maureen. Maureen, your Christmas person is—Amity!"

"Here you go," Maureen said, hauling a giant box out from under the tree. "Just for you, Amity."

"Geez, girl," Amity said. "You bought me a house?"

"It's to make up for your seventh-grader boyfriend," Maureen said.

"Ha ha," Amity said, glowering while the other girls laughed. "Adam's too immature anyway. I'm going to break up with him."

"Of course you are," Andrea said.

"Just open the present." Maureen giggled.

Amity ripped off the paper, then opened the box. Cassie leaned forward, eager to see what it was. Amity pulled out another wrapped box.

"Oh-kay," she said, drawing out the word and giving Maureen a curious look. Maureen grinned and tossed her waist-length brown hair behind her.

When Amity opened that box, she pulled out another, smaller wrapped box. Now she smiled. "I get it. Is there even a present in here?"

"Guess you'll find out!" Maureen crowed.

Cassie lost interest watching Amity unwrap all the boxes, though everyone else seemed to think it was funny. Finally Amity pulled the actual present out of the box.

"A book? I think this was for Cassie."

"It's a Magic Eye book, you goof!"

While Maureen explained the book to Amity, Cara said, "Amity has Janice."

Janice squealed over the teddy bear Amity gave her, then Cara said, "Janice has Cassie."

Cassie straightened up. It was her turn! Janice smiled at her and handed her a long box.

"Merry Christmas, Cassie."

"Thank you," Cassie said, tickled beyond words. She opened the box to find a cute pink shirt with flowers around the bottom. "Oh, it's so pretty!" And it would be nice to have something to wear besides soccer jerseys. She reached over and hugged Janice.

"Cassie has Andrea," Cara said, still reading down her list.

Cassie retrieved the small box for Andrea, suddenly worried she wouldn't like it. But Andrea opened it up and gasped at the makeup. "I love this blue color! And the orange! So pretty! Let's put it on!"

Cassie let Andrea drag her to the bathroom.

She missed the rest of the presents while Andrea decorated

her face, but she didn't care. Cassie had her very best friends here with her, pretty and popular girls who actually liked her, and she could ask for nothing better for Christmas.

Episode 4: Changing Game Plans

CHAPTER TWENTY-TWO
Going Unsteady

"Cassie," Ms. Talo called out.

Cassandra Jones was just about to leave her fourth hour English class for lunch, but she paused when her teacher called out her name.

"Can you stay behind, please?" Ms. Talo continued.

Cassie's friend Nicole glanced back at her, and Cassie shrugged. She didn't know what her teacher wanted, but she doubted she was in trouble. She did her very best not to put one toe over the line.

"You can go to lunch without me," she said to Nicole. "I'll see you later." The two girls didn't eat lunch together, but they walked to the cafeteria after class every day.

Second semester of eighth grade had started just a few days prior. Cassie didn't have P.E. anymore, and she'd switched around a few classes so she could be with her friends. She and her best friend, Andrea, were now teacher helpers for Mr. Adams' seventh grade class, but English had stayed the same. She hung back while her teacher talked to a few other kids. Then, finally, the short lady with dark hair turned a smile toward Cassie.

"I've been meaning to ask you about your book. We haven't talked about it since last semester."

"Oh." Cassie couldn't help the pride that rippled through her. Last year she'd written a book about four girls who got kidnapped. "It's finished. I spent all summer editing it and typing it up."

"I'd love to see it," Ms. Talo said. "That's quite an accomplishment. Not very many kids your age have written a book."

"Sure," Cassie said. "Want me to bring you a printed copy?"

"That would be lovely. What are your plans now? What are you going to do with it?"

"I'm considering a sequel," Cassie said, shifting her binder to the other hip.

"But what about the first one? Are you going to find a publisher?"

"I want to," she said, "but I don't know how. I don't even know where to look first."

Ms. Talo smiled. "There's a writer's conference for kids coming up next month. I'm supposed to select two students to come, and you're the first person I thought of. They'll talk about the publication process and how to get started. Is that something you'd be interested in?"

"Yes!" Cassie exclaimed, and then she tempered her reaction. "I mean, it would be great. But how much is it? I need to ask my parents." Though her parents had a paper route for extra money and her mom worked at Wendy's, Mr. Jones' soccer store continued to be their primary source of income. Or in this case, the primary source of sucking up their income. Cassie couldn't be selfish in her wants, no matter how great it sounded.

Ms. Talo beamed at her. "That's the best part. The conference is during the school day, so it will be a field trip. And the school will pay for your admission."

If Cassie hadn't been holding her binder in her hands, she would have clapped. "That sounds perfect!"

"Great. I'll submit your name. Now go on to lunch before

it's over."

The happy feelings over Ms. Talo's praise and the expectations for the future of her book faded as Cassie walked into the cafeteria. The aromas of food quickly infiltrated her nostrils, raising up the hungry dragon in her stomach, who cried and roared and clawed at her insides.

But she couldn't eat. She'd struggled all through Christmas vacation, trying not to indulge in the rich cheese balls and chocolate candies. To no avail. When she'd stepped on the scale at the end of the break, she'd gained three pounds.

Her head pounded at the thought of being near all this food, sitting by her friends who seemed to be watching her more closely these days. Last year she'd ended up escaping to the library so she could skip lunch and not have anyone notice. But her new status with Andrea and the group of cool girls made her reluctant to leave. What if they forgot her in her absence?

Telling herself to hold strong, she made her way to their lunch table and sat by Janice. Janice held a hamburger in her hands and talked with Cara about a project they were doing in history. Cassie's eyes focused on that burger, on the greasy liquid that dripped onto the tray.

Janice had left three pickles behind. Pickles had no calories. They were empty food. Cassie could eat them.

She couldn't take her gaze off them.

"Guys!" Amity appeared at the end of the table, her face red and splotchy, straight brown hair brushing against her shoulders. A great sob burst from her. "Adam broke up with me!"

Cassie had never met Adam, though she'd heard a lot about him from the others, who teased Amity endlessly about her seventh-grade boyfriend. But now was not the time for teasing, and every girl stood from the table and went to Amity's side, wrapping her up in a big group hug and comforting her.

All except Cassie, who shifted in her seat enough to grab Janice's pickles. She stuffed them in her mouth in one smooth motion before adding herself to the tangle of arms around Amity.

<hr />

Amity cried all through lunch, and when Cassie saw her after fifth hour by the lockers, she was still crying.

Andrea looked annoyed as Cara and Maureen rubbed Amity's arms and brushed her hair back from her face. "She's just going on and on for attention."

Cassie gave Andrea a surprised glanced. "Why do you say that?"

Andrea leaned against Cassie's locker while Cassie switched out her books. "Remember at Christmas she said she was going to break up with him? She totally likes someone else."

"That's because she likes everyone," Cassie said. Even though Amity knew about Cassie's crush on Miles, she didn't stop flirting with him every time he walked over to their table.

Andrea smirked. "Exactly." She grabbed Cassie's arm when Cassie straightened up. "Hey. Let's dress alike tomorrow."

Usually Andrea and Amity dressed alike. Cassie had wondered with envy if they often went shopping together and got the same clothes. "I don't have anything that matches you."

"I have some doubles. I'll bring the clothes tomorrow and you can change before school."

"Yeah, sure," Cassie said. All of Andrea's clothes were super cute and stylish. "Sounds like fun."

"Great." Andrea let go of her and winked. "See you later."

"Is Amity okay?" Cassie asked Maureen in choir. Maureen was late arriving, and Cassie imagined she'd been comforting Amity again.

"Oh, yeah," Maureen said. "She and Adam break up and get back together all the time. And it's always like this."

Cassie could almost hear her mom's voice in her head:

"They're too young to be going out. They aren't mature enough to handle a relationship." Cassie wholeheartedly agreed, but she knew saying so would not go over well. "I hope she'll be okay."

Maureen waved a hand. "Give her a few days. They'll be back together."

༺༻

Cassie didn't worry about her clothes the next morning. Andrea would be bringing something else for her to wear.

Just in case Andrea might forget, Cassie sent her a quick text reminder.

Got it all right here, Andrea replied. See you soon.

Cassie grabbed up her backpack and yelled down the hall, "Time to go, guys! The bus will be here soon!" She gathered her siblings to the front door and threw it open.

A thick blanket of fog rolled in off the porch, thick enough that when Cassie peered outside, she couldn't see past the large oak tree in the front yard.

Annette, the youngest at age seven, said, "Oh no! We can't go out like this! We'll never find the bus!"

"It'll be in the same place it always is," Cassie said. Just to be sure, she opened the hall closet and grabbed a flashlight. "Come on. The bus won't wait."

The four of them hurried outside. Cassie shown her light in front of them, but it was so densely foggy that only the faintest beam penetrated the misty particles. They made it up the street to the top of the hill, and Cassie made them all stand back in the grass. If they couldn't see the road, the bus probably couldn't see them.

The bus lights appeared only moments before the long yellow vehicle curved its way to the stop. The doors opened, and Cassie ushered her siblings onto the bus.

"It's really foggy out there," she said to Rhonda, the bus driver.

"I know," Rhonda said. "I can hardly see anything."

Cassie found her seat beside Jeremy, a mentally handicapped boy. Today he didn't smell like pee.

"Hi, Jeremy," she said. "How are you?"

"I'm good," he said in his nasally, high-pitched voice. "Look at these drawings I made."

Though only a few years younger than her, Jeremy had the mentality of a child Annette's age. Cassie treated him like she would her little sister, acting pleased and amazed by his drawings.

The bus finally reached the school, and she hurried off to the bathroom to wait for Andrea. She tapped her foot impatiently, though she knew the buses always arrived before her friends did.

"Cassie?" Andrea burst into the bathroom.

"I'm here," Cassie said.

"I brought them!" Andrea wore a tight blue baby tee with a white skirt. She held out a similar pair for Cassie, though they weren't exactly the same.

Cassie had a brief moment of panic. Why hadn't Andrea mentioned it would be a skirt? When was the last time she shaved her legs? "Thanks," Cassie said, grabbing the clothes and stepping into a stall. She dropped her pants and let out a breath of relief. She must've shaved just a few days ago. She slipped into Andrea's clothes and then came out to examine herself in the mirror. The shirt looked good, though Cassie was a little flat-chested. She pushed against her breasts, wishing they were bigger.

"That skirt's going to fall right off you," Andrea said, stepping back and giving the clothes a critical eye.

Cassie's eyes went to the skirt now, hitting just above the knee and contrasting nicely with her darker skin tone. She tugged at the waist. Though it was loose, it was in no danger of falling. "It fits great."

"It's supposed to be snug. You're too skinny." Andrea

pinched her arm. "There's no fat on you."

"Hi, guys!" Cara said, coming into the bathroom, and Amity came in next, ending the conversation.

"Oh, you look so cute!" Cara said, smashing them together and beaming at them. "I've got to take a picture!"

Cassie and Andrea smiled for Cara's phone, though Amity didn't look quite so pleased.

"We can dress alike tomorrow," she said to Andrea.

"Maybe next week," Andrea said. "I don't want to wear the same thing as someone else every day."

"How are you, Amity?" Cara asked, and Amity immediately transformed her expression into one of sorrow.

"I'm okay," she said, tears welling up in her eyes. "I just want to talk to Adam. But he wouldn't answer the phone last night."

Andrea heaved a sigh and hooked her arm through Cassie's. She tugged Cassie out the door, sidestepping Amity. They walked together to the locker hall, where they separated.

"I'll see you in first hour, Cassie," Andrea said.

Since they no longer had P.E. together, Andrea and Cassie had asked Mr. Adams, who was their science teacher, if they could be his teacher helpers for his seventh grade math class. To their surprise, he'd said yes. They hadn't had to do much and often spent the whole hour giggling out in the hall, but Cassie was glad not to lose their time together. She knew if they didn't have a class together, their friendship would drift apart.

"See you in a bit," Cassie said, slipping away from Andrea and heading to her locker to put her clothes away.

She got to first period before Andrea. Mr. Adams handed her a stack of papers and asked her to start grading. Cassie sat at the table in the back and waited for Andrea.

Just as Andrea walked in, the lights went out. Several of the students screamed.

"It's just a power outage, calm down!" Mr. Adams said.

Cassie poked her head into the hall. "Looks like it's out all over this wing, at least."

"I guess we're done with class," one of the kids said.

"We could tell ghost stories," another boy said, and several gave nervous giggles.

Suddenly Cassie remembered her flashlight. "I have an idea!" She fumbled under the table for her purse. She found the flashlight she'd used that morning to light the way through the fog. "Here, Mr. Adams!" She turned it on and made her way up an aisle of desks, following the narrow beam of light.

"Thank you," he said, his white mustache turning upward as he smiled. "All right, class," he said, shining the light on his mouth, "now we can tell ghost stories."

⁘

Cassie had both a math and science test to study for and found it hard to focus on the children's choir after school. But it was their first day back since Christmas break, and Ms. Vanderwood was excited.

"Where are we going this summer, guys?" she asked, smiling as she handed out binders.

Cassie had almost forgotten. Now a new breathless excitement fluttered in her chest. "New York!" she shouted with the other kids, though a few said "Carnegie Hall" instead.

"That's right." Ms. Vanderwood's smile threatened to crack her face. "And I've got our music! We'll still be doing our end of school performances, so we'll start practicing both. Such an exciting year for us!"

It was, but Cassie heaved a quiet sigh as she accepted her binder of music. She hadn't thought it would be possible to get tired of singing. The children's choir had become less exciting with her demotion to second soprano.

She scanned over the part, heaviness replacing the excited

flutter. She glanced over the notes above hers, the first soprano line. They got all the pretty harmony while she got the dissonant notes that fleshed out the chord without actually sounding nice. She forced herself to sit up straighter and sing, even though her heart wasn't in it.

"I've got a lot of studying to do tonight," Cassie said after choir when her mom picked her up. "I'll just eat dinner real quick and then go to my room."

She hoped that would be enough to get her out of meal time, but Mrs. Jones turned an evil eye on her. "You'll sit at the table until your food is gone."

"Because I'm like what, five?" Cassie said, annoyed by the commanding attitude.

"Because I'm your mother and that's what I said you'll do."

Cassie huffed and crossed her arms over her chest. She'd see about that.

CHAPTER TWENTY-THREE
Crossing the Line

Cassie dragged her text books to the table and studied while her mom finished cooking, hoping that would be enough to convince her Mom that Cassie was serious about the homework. Her brother Scott set the table around her.

"Mom, Cassie's books are in the way," he said.

"Put everything away, Cassie. It's time to eat."

"I need to finish this chapter. I'll eat later."

"Now!"

Cassie slammed her books shut with a glare and dropped them off on the couch. By then Mrs. Jones had called everyone to dinner, and they filed into their seats.

Spaghetti. Her mom plonked the pot of noodles on the table as well as the red meat sauce.

They grasped hands and blessed the food, then began to pass the noodles. Cassie took the tiniest helping she could manage with the tongs.

"Let me help you, Cassie," her mom said, standing up.

"I've got it," Cassie said. Why was her mom suddenly so involved in her food?

Mrs. Jones didn't even bother answering. She just dumped a huge helping of spaghetti on her plate. Then she grabbed a ladle of sauce.

"No sauce!" Cassie cried, but it was too late. Her mom had drowned the noodles in it.

"Parmesan cheese?" she asked, grabbing the canister, and Cassie swore she saw an evil glint in her mom's eye.

"No." She practically covered her plate with her hands.

"Fine." Mrs. Jones sat down heavily in her seat while the rest of the family stared at them both. "After you eat all that, you can study."

Crapola. What was wrong with her mom today? She used her fork to cut the noodles into tiny pieces and swished them around her plate. Then she ate one and swished some more. Where was the dog?

"You're not leaving until you clean your plate," Mrs. Jones said.

"Uh-huh," Cassie said. Her mom's eyes were on her, and she had no choice but to shovel a few more noodles into her mouth. As soon as Mrs. Jones turned her attention to her own plate, Cassie dumped several on the floor. Then she ate the rest.

"There," Cassie said, glaring at her mom as she brandished her empty plate. "Is that good enough?"

"Yes," her mother said, barely glancing at the plate. "Put it in the sink, please."

What was that about? Cassie burned with indignation. Why had her mom treated her like a little kid?

☙❧

"You should spend the night tonight."

Cassie stood next to Andrea in the bathroom close to Mr. Adams' class. He didn't have anything for them to do today, so they crowded in front of the mirror, applying more mascara and lipstick.

"I don't think my mom will let me," Cassie said. "It's a school night. And I have voice lessons."

Andrea made a face at her in the mirror, her blue eyes

crinkling. "You always have something going on. My mom can take you to school, you know. Amity and Maureen stay over all the time on school nights."

That little prickle of envy Cassie had become familiar with tickled her heart. If only she didn't live so far out in the country. "My mom doesn't think I should do sleepovers on a school night."

"Fine," Andrea said with a loud sigh and a huge eye roll. "You're like the only one who doesn't, you know."

She knew, all right. Her face warmed, and she pressed her lips together. "Why don't you come over this weekend? You haven't spent the night in awhile."

"Better idea." Andrea grabbed both of Cassie's hands, grinning widely. "Ask your mom if you can spend the night on Friday! We'll go to Lokomotion!"

Lokomotion was a nearby adventure park, with motor cars and miniature golf, laser tag, bumper boats, and lots of arcade games. Cassie had never been, though her family drove by it every Sunday on the way to church. She'd always wanted to go. "Yeah! That sounds great. I'll ask her."

"Perfect. Now let me put some lipstick on you."

☙ ❧

"Adam and I are back together," Amity announced at lunch. Nobody reacted. Cassie knew they'd all been expecting it. "Aren't you guys happy for me?"

"Why do we care?" Maureen said. "You'll just break up again in a few weeks."

Amity gasped, and Cara sent Maureen a nasty look.

"Of course we're happy for you, hon," Cara said to Amity. "We're just not surprised. We knew he'd want you back."

Amity looked pacified. She picked up her pizza and took a huge bite. "Oh, and something else!" she said, chewing quickly and then swallowing. "I decided to get baptized. So you guys are all invited on Sunday."

"Wow, that's great!" Janice said.

"What church do you go to?" Cassie asked. She'd never heard Amity talk about church and hadn't even realized she was religious.

"We all go to the same church," Amity said, inclining her head toward the girls at the table. "The big one across the street. Where do you go?"

"I go to church in Fayetteville," Cassie said.

"You should come to our church, Cassie," Maureen said.

"Yeah!" Amity said. "At least come for my baptism."

"Sure," Cassie said. "I'd love to. What time Sunday?"

"Six o'clock. Call me and I'll tell you where to go."

"Okay. And sometime you can all come to my church."

"That sounds like fun," Cara said. "I love going to new churches."

Cassie could just imagine herself walking into church with her friends around her. Maybe even Tyler would notice her.

The thought jolted her. Riley was the one with the crush on Tyler, not Cassie.

⊙~⚹~⊙

"Please, Mom? Andrea really wants me to spend the night. She said we can go to Lokomotion!" Cassie needled her mom after dinner while the two of them cleaned the kitchen. "I haven't spent the night at her house in like months!"

"I don't want anyone gone this weekend. It's as simple as that."

"But why?" Cassie scraped pieces of chicken and rice into the dog's food bowl. "Isn't it easier on you when we're gone?"

"Tell you what. Why don't you invite Andrea to spend the night here? Then you can have a sleepover, and I'll be satisfied you're home."

"Will you take us to Lokomotion?"

"No."

So much for that. But having Andrea over was better than nothing. "Okay. I'll ask her."

Cassie waited until she was done with the dishes before

plopping down on her bed and pulling out the phone.

Andrea answered on the first ring. "Hi, Cassie!"

"Hey." Cassie lay back on the unicorn bedspread and stared at the white popcorn ceiling. "My mom said I can't spend the night."

"Oh, no," Andrea said with a sigh. "That's too bad."

"Yeah," Cassie said. "But she said you can come over here!"

Andrea didn't say anything for a moment. Then she said, "That's so sweet of her. I don't think it will work for this weekend, though. Maybe next time."

Cassie wasn't that surprised, but the disappointment sprang up in her chest strong enough to make her want to cry. Why did it feel like they were constantly functioning on different schedules? "Okay. Thanks for the invite, at least."

"Yeah."

Cassie hung onto the phone a moment longer, trying to think of something witty or funny to say. She knew the other girls talked to each other on the phone for hours at a time, but the only thing coming to Cassie's mind was her history test in the morning, and she knew Andrea didn't want to talk about that.

"Well," Andrea said, breaking the silence, "I better go. I'll see you tomorrow."

"Yeah. Bye," Cassie said, and hung up. No wonder no one wanted to hang out with her. She wasn't very exciting.

Returning to the kitchen, Cassie put her phone on the counter and rested her chin on her arm. "Andrea can't come."

"Well, try another friend. Who's that other one you're always talking about? Charity? Amnesty?"

"Amity."

"Maybe she wants to come."

Cassie thought about it. Amity had invited her to her baptism. And she was very friendly with Cassie these days. Inviting someone new made her heart start up a nervous rhythm. But maybe it was time she quit relying solely on

Andrea for companionship. "Okay. Yeah. I'll try her."

Cassie had Amity's number programmed into her phone, but she'd never used it. She sat on her bed and stared at it, giving herself a pep talk. They were friends. She could do this. It wasn't scary. Taking a deep breath, she pressed Amity's number.

"Hello?" Amity said, her voice that tone of cautious curiosity.

"Hello, Amity? It's Cassie."

"Oh, hi, Cassie," Amity said, and then she launched into a rambling monologue about how her annoying sister was trying to get past her legs into the closet and Amity wouldn't let her.

It was fascinating, but mostly because Amity could talk about nothing for minutes at a time.

"Wow," Cassie said when she finally finished. "Did she get what she wanted?"

"Probably. Heifer can't fit into my clothes, anyway."

Did she just call her sister a cow? Mrs. Jones would ground Cassie for a week if she did that. Cassie cleared her throat.

"Amity, I was wondering if you want to spend the night this Friday."

"Really? At your house?"

"Yeah." Amity sounded excited, interested, at least, and that made Cassie hopeful. She hoped they'd have something to talk about if it was just the two of them. Usually she had Andrea to direct conversation.

"Sounds fun! I'll ask my mom, okay? I'll tell you in school tomorrow."

"Sure." She wanted an answer now, but she could wait one more day.

"Argh! Get off me!" Amity's voice screeched loudly in the phone, and another girl's voice hollered just as loudly. "Sorry, Cass, gotta go!"

Amity hung up without another word, but Cassie gave a

little laugh. It seemed like Amity thought of her as a friend.

☙❦❧

Cassie jerked the brush through her straight brown hair before school, glaring at herself in the mirror. Hair that never did anything right, a face that looked too young, and a body that curved in all the wrong places. She lifted her shirt and pinched the skin around her belly.

And boobs. Why didn't she have any yet? She was almost fourteen. Amity, Andrea, Cara, even Riley had enough cleavage to fill out a bikini. Cassie turned sideways and examined her reflection. Flat as a washing board. Flat as a sidewalk. She knew boys with bigger boobs than she had.

Her eyes landed on the roll of toilet paper beside the sink. Her fingers snatched the end of it, unrolling until she had a good wad. Then she stuffed it into her bra.

It was a little lumpy, but not bad. Except now she was lopsided. Cassie grabbed another handful and stuffed the other side.

Crapola, now she was uneven! A few more pieces here . . . there . . . done.

So much better! Cassie threw another shirt on over the top so the lumpiness wasn't so obvious. If she didn't hurry, she'd miss the bus, and she certainly didn't want to explain to her mom why.

She waited in the school bathroom for her friends to arrive, hoping they wouldn't notice the added depth to her chest. Andrea came in first, and she gave Cassie a hug before turning to the mirror. Cara and Amity followed. Cassie grabbed Amity and tugged her over to the side.

"Did you ask your mom? Can you spend the night tomorrow?"

"Oh yeah," Amity said, her friendly smile fading slightly. "Yeah, sorry. I can't do it this Friday. My mom said no." Her eyes swished to a corner of the bathroom and then focused on Cassie again. "But I'll see you at my baptism, right?"

"Of course." Cassie forced a smile. "I'll be there."

She picked up her books and hugged them to her chest, feeling the toilet paper squish against her skin. For once her mom had given her permission to have someone spend the night, but so far she'd been shot down. She exited the bathroom, frustrated. She couldn't waste this opportunity.

She'd just have to ask Riley.

CHAPTER TWENTY-FOUR
Too Much Stuffing

Riley was only too happy to spend the night, and on Friday the Joneses and Riley went out to dinner.

"How does Western Sizzlin' sound?" Mrs. Jones asked her husband as they drove the twisty country roads toward the bigger town.

"Sounds great," he said.

"I'm really not that hungry," Cassie protested for the hundredth time. The steak restaurant with an all-you-can-eat buffet would not be good for her meal plan. "You could have just left me and Riley at home. We can make something."

"I like Western Sizzlin'," Riley said, totally not catching on to Cassie's angst. "I'd rather eat there."

Cassie pinched her arm and tried to communicate with her eyes, but Riley only frowned at her.

"Ouch," she muttered. "Why'd you do that?"

Cassie crossed her arms over her chest with a huff and stared out the window.

Everyone ordered the buffet line at the restaurant, and Cassie relaxed a little. The buffet had a huge salad bar. She could eat that and avoid the heavy, fatty foods.

"Can Riley and I sit by ourselves?" she asked her mom.

Mrs. Jones hesitated, then nodded. "Yes, but I want to be able to see you."

"No problem." Cassie grabbed Riley's arm and dragged her over to a booth. She smiled, feeling much more in control of the situation. "Yay! Now it's just us."

"I'm so glad you asked me over," Riley said. "I was getting bored at home."

Cassie gave her arm a squeeze. "I'm glad you came." She didn't mention how Riley had been third choice. "Let's get some food."

Cassie stuck to the fresh veggie portion of the salad bar, but Riley attacked the mashed potatoes and macaroni and cheese and pastas. Cassie tried not to stare at the food on her friend's plate when they sat down again.

"All you're having is salad?" Riley asked.

Cassie shrugged like it was no big deal, even though her stomach yelled at her to steal Riley's plate. "I'm really into vegetables right now."

"I got broccoli too. I just put cheese on it. See?" Riley pointed out the broccoli covered in gooey yellow sauce.

"That's good," Cassie said. It looked delicious. She stabbed her lettuce and tomatoes and shoved it in her mouth.

"Do you even have dressing on that?"

Cassie didn't answer. She was too busy trying to gag down her dry salad.

Riley gave her a sympathetic look. "I'll get you some salad dressing."

Before Cassie could stop her, she got up and went to the salad bar. When Riley returned, she had two little plastic cups of salad dressing with her. "I brought you Ranch and Thousand Island. I wasn't sure which one you'd want."

Neither, Cassie wanted to say. But she couldn't be rude. "Thanks, Riley. I'll take the Thousand Island."

"That's my dad's favorite," Riley said. She watched as Cassie poured the dressing on her salad and then resumed eating.

Cassie had to admit, the salad tasted much better this way. She ate it all, and even scraped her plate for the last bits.

"I'm getting dessert," Riley said, jumping up for the third time. "Want some?"

"I'll pass," Cassie said.

Riley returned with two plates covered in little cheesecakes and cookies. "Want one?"

Was this a conspiracy to bring her down? Cassie's hand rose as if of its own accord. "Just one." She held the little square in her hand and sniffed it, then took a nibble. The soft creamy texture melted on her tongue, and she closed her eyes, relishing the sweet lemon flavor. Her next nibble was a little bigger, and then the bite was gone. Going down her throat and settling into her stomach, joining the lettuce and tomatoes and salad dressing.

"So," Riley said, lowering her voice and leaning closer. "I couldn't help noticing that your boobs got bigger." Her eyes darted to Cassie's chest, and she bobbed her head.

The heat rushed to Cassie's cheeks. "You can tell?" She'd tried to be so subtle.

"What did you do, stuff your bra?"

"Yes." Cassie reached a hand to her chest and felt the poky toilet paper. "Is it obvious?"

Riley lifted one shoulder. "It's not like so bad. But maybe you should just get a padded bra or something. Your boobs look a little lumpy right now."

Cassie wilted with embarrassment, and then she giggled. "Lumpy boobs."

"Not exactly what you're going for," Riley said, and they both giggled.

The family finished eating and headed back out to the blue van parked in front.

"Oh, I'm so stuffed," Emily, Cassie's younger sister, said. She held her belly in her hands and groaned.

"Me, too," Riley said. She joined Cassie in the very back of the van. "I ate way too much."

"I feel like there's a rock in my stomach," Cassie agreed.

"But you didn't eat very much," Riley said.

Mrs. Jones' head pivoted toward them from the front of the car. "What?"

Cassie waved a hand at Riley from behind the middle row, shushing her. "She means I didn't eat very much dessert. Even though Riley said it was really good."

Mrs. Jones faced front again, and Cassie leaned her head on the seat in front of them so her mom couldn't see her. "Be quiet," she mouthed to Riley.

Riley nodded, though she looked puzzled.

Emily, Riley, and Cassie went to their shared bedroom at the back of the house as soon as they got home.

"What's going on?" Riley asked Cassie when Emily went to the bathroom.

Cassie rolled her eyes. "No idea. My mom's suddenly become freakish about what I eat. So I have to pretend like I'm eating lots of food."

"Why?"

"I don't know. She wants me to get fat or something. Speaking of." Cassie pressed her hands to her stomach and shook her head. "I feel huge. I've got to do some exercises."

"Why?"

If Riley asked that again, Cassie was going to blow a gasket. Didn't she understand? "To stay skinny, of course!" She lay down on the floor and put her hands behind her head. "I'm going to do some sit-ups. Want to join me?"

Riley lay beside her, still uncertain. "How many?"

"Maybe a hundred?"

At around twenty, Riley sat up. "I can't do anymore."

"Okay," Cassie gasped out between counts.

Riley watched her. "Do you do this every day?"

"No." Cassie's abs screamed in pain as she neared a

hundred. "Just sometimes." Crapola. This was hard. Breathe. Move. Breathe. "Takes a lot . . . of work."

She finally finished, and Cassie jumped to her feet. "I'm going to run up and down the stairs a few times. Want to come?"

"No." Riley moved over to the desk and opened a notebook. "I'll just wait for you to come back."

"Suit yourself," Cassie said.

○⁓⁓⁓

Riley ended up staying Saturday night, too, and the girls lay in bed talking well after midnight.

"Do you like anyone at church?" Riley asked.

"No," Cassie said. Tyler's blue eyes and teasing grin popped into her head. "But I know you do."

"Yeah. Tyler."

"Do you think he likes you?"

"Maybe. He's always nice to me."

"That's a start. He used to be a jerk." Cassie wished there were more boys at church. The rest were all younger than her. If she didn't have Riley, she wouldn't have any friends there.

"But you'll get to meet more boys soon," Riley said, a note of envy in her voice. "When you turn fourteen."

"Yeah," Cassie said. "I'll get to go to the church dances." The dances were open to kids all across the region, which meant there would be boys there from Fayetteville and Rogers and Bentonville, even Tulsa and Missouri. But there was a catch: no one younger than fourteen could go.

And Cassie's birthday was only two months away. Riley had to wait until the summer.

"Maybe you'll meet someone."

"Maybe." Cassie tried to picture the boy of her dreams in her mind's eye, but she had no idea what he looked like. The faceless image wisped away like a cloud on a windy day. "I guess we'll see."

They sat with each other in church, just a few pews back

from Tyler and his brother Jason. Riley couldn't seem to peel her eyes from the back of Tyler's head, which made Cassie giggle. Even worse, though, she found herself staring at him as well. And one time, when he glanced over his shoulder, he caught her. He gave her a grin. Cassie ducked her head, the blood rushing to her face with a fury.

Tyler walked over to their pew after the sermon. "Funny to see you two sitting together."

"We're always together," Riley said, looping an arm through Cassie's. "She's my best friend."

"I have lots of best friends," Cassie said. Andrea was definitely one of them. Maybe even Amity.

Tyler started past them, then turned around and said over his shoulder, "Aren't you coming to Sunday School?"

Cassie shrugged, pulling her arm free. Riley leaned in close and hissed, "He's being nice again!"

"I know," Cassie hissed back, a little irritated. Tyler didn't actually like Riley—did he?

Why did that bother her?

⊙⋎⚘⋏⊙

"Hurry, Mom, we're going to be late!"

It was already a quarter to six, and the Joneses weren't anywhere near Amity's church. Cassie checked the text message Amity had sent her half an hour ago.

Everyone's in the dressing room by the font. Just go there when you get here.

Dressing room? Font? Cassie had no idea where any of those things were. She got more anxious with each passing second. She couldn't miss this.

"There's the church," Mrs. Jones said, pulling the van into the parking lot. "I'll just drop you off and find a parking spot."

"Drop me off?" Cassie sputtered. She craned her head back, taking in the church that was bigger than her junior high. "I've never been here before! I won't know where to go!"

"Just ask someone," Mrs. Jones said snippishly. She came to

a halting stop at the curb.

Cassie glanced at the clock. Five till. Yeah, she didn't have any other option. It was do this or miss it. Heaving a sigh of exasperation, she threw open the door and ran outside, shivering a little at the cooler air. But she didn't stop for her jacket. There was no time.

She yanked open the first sent of double doors and burst into a giant foyer. More doors stood in front of her and large corridors went either direction away from the foyer, with a ramp leading up to a balcony. Cassie came to a complete stop. Where was she supposed to be?

A man walked by heading for one of the corridors, and she stepped in front of him. "Excuse me. Where's the font?"

"Font?" he asked, crinkling his brow at her.

"Yes." She hopped around impatiently. "My friend's getting baptized and I'm about to miss it."

"Oh! This way." He turned around and headed for the ramp.

Cassie ran along behind him, so grateful for his help.

He opened a set of doors at the top and led her down a hallway. Cassie looked over the railing and saw the chapel below, four times the size of the one at her church. Three aisles separated the rows of chairs, situated more like an amphitheater than any church she'd been in.

"There." He pointed to what looked like a stage set into the middle of the wall.

Except now that Cassie looked closely, she could see people in white standing on the stage. That was the font!

"Just go down this hallway, and you'll get there."

"Thanks," Cassie gasped out. She went as fast as she dared without running. That was Amity! Amity was already in the water, standing next to a man also in white clothing!

Cassie came around the corner and nearly tumbled into the pool of water. "Amity!" she whispered, waving.

Amity looked at her with wide eyes, and someone grabbed Cassie's arm, pulling her back.

"You're about to walk into the font with her," Janice said, stifling a laugh. She smiled at Cassie, and Cassie filed into place with the rest of their friends, relieved to have found them.

The man with Amity said a few words and then dunked her under the water, similar to how baptisms were done in Cassie's church. Except here everyone clapped, so Cassie did too, delighted and thrilled for her friend to have made this step in her life.

Amity's mom waited by the font, and she wrapped Amity up in a robe, then gave her a hug. "Come on. Back to the dressing room."

Cassie followed the other girls as they went down the hall and into another room. The counter had curling irons, blow dryers, and brushes, probably for people to use after being baptized.

"You barely made it," Maureen said to Cassie. She plugged in a curling iron.

"I thought you were going to walk into the font with me, Cassie," Amity said from behind one of the changing stalls. That brought laughter from all the girls.

"Congratulations, Amity," Cassie said. "I'm glad I got to see it."

"Why don't you ever curl your hair?" Maureen plucked at one of Cassie's straight, dark strands. "It would be so pretty."

Cassie shrugged. "I try. It won't curl."

Cara picked up the curling iron and wrapped a strand of Cassie's hair around it. She held it for ten seconds, then released it. The strand relaxed against Cassie's chest, as straight as before.

"Nope. Won't curl," Cara said, bouncing the strand in her hand.

Cassie laughed. "Told you."

Amity came out of the stall, her hair bound in a towel but her clothes dry, and the girls all took a turn hugging her.

"Why didn't you come to Lokomotion with us on Friday, Cassie?" Maureen asked.

A hush came over the girls, and all eyes turned to Maureen. Cassie wasn't sure how, but she got the impression Maureen wasn't supposed to have said anything.

"What?" Maureen said with a shrug.

"I couldn't come," Cassie said, her voice sounding strangely small to her ears. "My mom said no."

"Oh. So Andrea invited you?"

"Yes."

Maureen turned to Andrea. "So when Cassie couldn't spend the night, you invited Amity instead?"

Cassie looked at Amity, who hadn't taken her eyes from Maureen. "You stayed the night at Andrea's on Friday?" Was that what Amity meant when she said she couldn't stay at Cassie's house?

"Yeah," Amity said, dragging her gaze away from Maureen. "It was kind of a last-minute thing."

Cassie glanced around at her friends. Everyone else avoided looking at her. Amity must have told them how Cassie invited her over but she decided to go to Andrea's instead. The burn crept up behind her eyes, but Cassie pushed it down. She wouldn't look like a baby in front of them. "Cool. Hope you guys had fun."

"What did you do?" Maureen said, as if she just couldn't let it drop.

"Riley came over," Cassie said.

Maureen nodded knowingly. "It's a good thing you have her for your best friend."

The message came through loud and clear: Cassie wasn't one of their best friends. Cassie didn't want to stand there any longer with them. "Glad I could come, Amity. See you guys later." She walked out, biting her lip and choking back the tears before her mother could see them.

CHAPTER TWENTY-FIVE
Shown Up

That night Cassie dug through her mom's bathroom cupboard until she found the plastic hot roller holder. Her mom had put these in Cassie's hair when she was in fifth grade, and even though they'd had to use lots of hair spray, it had worked. Why wouldn't it now?

"You just plug this in here," Mrs. Jones said, showing Cassie the cord on the contraption. "Let it get hot for at least twenty minutes. Then you wrap your hair. You really need two of these because you don't want to put a lot of hair on each one, but I only have this one."

"It's fine," Cassie said, watching in the mirror as her mom showed her how to wrap the strands around the rollers.

"Then let it sit in your hair until it cools. That could be like half an hour. If you take it out when it's still warm, the curl won't set. Only after you remove them do you want to hair spray it."

"So I'll have to wake up an hour early to do this."

"Yes."

Cassie exhaled and nodded. "Okay."

When her alarm went off at five in the morning, Cassie didn't hesitate. She rolled out of bed and plugged in the cord to the hot rollers, then set her phone for twenty minutes. She plopped back into bed and waited.

An hour later she stood in front of the mirror, carefully pulling her fingers through the thick curls. She didn't recall ever seeing so much volume and body in her hair, and the softness framed her face, making her look older and thinner. She grabbed the hair spray, showering the curls with long-lasting hold. She wore a maroon shirt and her smallest pair of jeans, which still tried to shimmy off her hips.

Emily came in to brush her teeth, groggy and blurry eyed. "Wow, Cassie," she said around her toothbrush, "you look so pretty."

"Thanks," Cassie said. She opened up her makeup drawer, grateful her mom let her wear it now, and put a silvery eyeshadow all over her eyelids, following that up with mascara. The only lipstick she had was a dark red, but after she put it on, she wiped it back off. It didn't look good.

She fluffed her hair one last time. She was ready.

Cassie didn't stay in the bathroom before school waiting for the other girls to arrive. Instead she stood by her locker, thumbing through a textbook and pretending to be thoroughly uninterested in everything around her.

"Cassie?" Nicole and Jimmy arrived holding hands, but Nicole couldn't take her eyes off Cassie. "You look like a rock star!"

Cassie blinked. "Do I? Oh, thanks."

Jimmy's gaze followed her even when Nicole started to walk away, and she yanked his hand until he faced front again. Cassie hid a smile.

"Oh, my gosh." Andrea skidded to a halt in front of Cassie's locker. "What did you do?" She stepped up to Cassie and fluffed the hair. "You look beautiful! Why weren't you in the bathroom? Come on, let's show everyone!"

Cassie resisted Andrea's pull on her arm, still wounded

from the previous evening. "I'll see them later. I've got things to do right now."

"Like what, study?" Andrea gave the book a scornful look.

Cassie didn't budge. She spotted Emmett and waved. "Emmett!"

Seeing her, he swiveled from his locker. His face lit up, and he came over.

With him, he brought Miles.

I'm a rock star, Cassie told herself. She smiled brightly at both of them. "Hi, guys! How was your weekend?"

"Great," Emmett said. "We didn't see you at Lokomotion."

Cassie ground her teeth together, and she cursed her mom for not letting her go. "Yeah, I was busy." She met Miles' gaze and winked. To her utter surprise, he blushed.

The warning bell rang, and she pushed away from her locker. "I guess I better get to class. I'll see you guys!"

"Cassie." Andrea caught up to her, staring at her like she didn't know her. "You really look great."

The resentment bubbled up in Cassie's chest, but she bit it back. *You notice me now*, she thought.

Andrea was still talking. "I'm really sorry about Friday. I didn't know you'd invited Amity to spend the night. I never would have asked her."

Liar! Cassie knew it without a doubt. But she just gave Andrea a cool smile. "It's no biggie. I had a great weekend. I spent a lot of it with Tyler."

"Who's Tyler?"

"Just a boy from church. He goes to Central."

"Is he cute? Are you going out?"

The feeling that surged through Cassie was strangely powerful. "Oh, no, we're just good friends. He's so sweet. He does have the deepest blue eyes."

Andrea stayed right with her all the way into Mr. Adams' class. She tried to say something else, but Cassie hushed her as Mr. Adams called the class to order. Then Andrea whispered,

"I want to come with you sometime and meet Tyler."

Cassie shrugged without looking at her. "Sure. Anytime." She said it with a bored tone, like she couldn't care less.

Good thing Andrea couldn't see the victory dance going on in her head.

Throughout the entire morning and all the way to lunch, Cassie's classmates stopped to compliment her. Boys she didn't even know said hi to her. Girls moved their seats a little bit closer to whisper to her.

Was this what it was to be popular?

She stopped at the bathroom before going to the cafeteria and frowned when she saw how the curls had fallen. No longer thick spirals around her face, they'd descended into gradual waves, falling around her shoulders. She shoved them up with her hands, but they didn't stay. Next time she'd bring hair spray to school.

She played it cool when she sat down next to Andrea and just gave little smiles when the other girls fawned over her. Anger still simmered in her chest. What did they say about her when she wasn't there? *Poor little Cassie. She thinks she's one of us. Cassie isn't here. Don't tell her.*

The anger grew every time she considered it.

Amity kept trying to talk to Andrea, tried to tease her and joke with her, but Andrea just wanted to know more about Tyler.

"There's nothing more to tell," Cassie whispered back, quite truthfully. "And I don't want anyone else to know, so be quiet."

Andrea nodded, shooting Amity an annoyed look and scooting closer.

"So I know it didn't work out for last weekend," Andrea said as they walked back to the lockers after lunch. She gripped Cassie's arm as if unwilling to let her get away. "But how about this weekend? You can spend the night. Bring some money, we'll go to the movies. Oh, but don't tell Amity. She'll want to come, and I don't want her there."

Was it that simple? A new look, and everyone wanted to be her friend? "Sure," Cassie said.

After Andrea walked away, she wondered how many times a similar conversation had taken place between Andrea and Amity, but with Cassie being the one left out.

~~~

It started to snow on the way home from children's choir Thursday evening.

"Maybe they'll cancel school tomorrow!" Cassie said, excited. Since snow wasn't a common thing in Arkansas, anything more than an inch usually shut down the whole city.

"Don't get your hopes up," Mrs. Jones said. "It's not sticking."

Barely had she spoken when the car slid sideways, nearly barreling off the road.

"What was that?" Cassie asked, shooting her mom an alarmed look.

"Well, maybe it's sticking more than I thought," Mrs. Jones murmured. She drove very slowly the rest of the way home.

By the time they'd finished dinner, half an inch of whiteness coated everything outside. Annette and Scott ran from window to window cheering, and Cassie refrained only because she was too mature for such antics.

It's snowing! she texted Andrea.

I know! came the reply. Maybe we won't have school!

Yay! But then Cassie thought of something. What about spending the night?

Oh, we can still do that!

Just as Cassie and Emily turned out their bedroom light and settled down for bed, a knock came on the door. Mr. Jones poked his head in.

"Wanted to let you girls know you can turn off your alarms. School's been canceled for tomorrow."

Now Cassie cheered, forgetting she was supposed to be the mature one. Emily ran to the window and looked outside to the hill behind the house.

"It's like several inches!"

Cassie joined her. "That's awesome!"

"If you want you can stay up and watch a movie," Mr. Jones said, a mischievous glint in his eyes. "Just don't wake the younger ones."

He didn't have to suggest it twice. Cassie and Emily shot out of bed and hurried downstairs to watch a movie.

───※───

"Are you still going to come over?" Andrea asked Cassie on the phone.

"I hope so," Cassie said. It was Friday morning, and no more snow had fallen. Little more than an inch clung to the ground. "My mom said the roads should be clear this afternoon."

"Oh, good. Call me when you're coming, then."

Cassie peered out the back window, spotting her younger brother and sister gathering up what snow they could and chucking tiny balls at each other. "I will."

Shutting her phone and feeling as giddy as a kid, Cassie pulled on her tennis shoes, a jacket, and a pair of gloves. Then she ran outside to join her siblings in the snowball fight.

"Let's make a fort!" Emily said.

"There's not enough snow," Cassie said. "Especially the way you guys have been throwing it."

"We'll get what's left!" Scott said.

He and Annette ran off to gather whatever they could, and Cassie shrugged. She could play along.

After twenty minutes, they'd scraped most of the snow off every rock and piece of dirt and grass in the yard, but the snow they had was only the size of a misshapen basketball.

"Not much of a fort," Cassie said. Her toes curled inward inside her shoes, feeling like chunks of ice attached to her feet.

Her fingers burned with the cold, melted snow dampening her gloves.

"I think we should call it good and go in," Emily said.

"Yeah," Annette said. She cupped her gloves to her face, only the little blip of her pink nose poking out.

"Definitely. I'm done." Cassie started up the wooden deck stairs, and her siblings clomped behind her, the stairs shaking with each step upward.

"Who wants hot chocolate?" Cassie said. She put a pot of water on to boil, feeling extremely jovial and excited. She took off her wet gloves and held her hands over the water, waiting for the steam to warm her.

"Me, me!" The other three gathered around her.

"Get the mugs and hot chocolate."

"Do we have any marshmallows?" Scott opened the cupboard and began searching.

"We have cream." Emily pulled it out of the fridge.

Cassie grinned as she poured the boiling water into each mug, already filled with the hot cocoa powder. "Stir it first, then I'll give you cream if you want some."

"I found ice cream," Annette said, pulling a tub of mint chocolate chip out of the freezer.

Oo, that sounded good. Cassie stirred her hot chocolate along with her siblings, then helped each of them decide on the topping they wanted.

She went for the ice cream.

But as wonderful as it tasted, the horrible feeling that she'd consumed too much food settled over her, pressing down on her shoulders like a heavy weight.

"Time to exercise," she announced. "Who wants to run the stairs with me?"

They looked at her like she was crazy.

"I will," Annette said.

Cassie favored her youngest sister with a smile. "Up and down twenty times. Come on, let's go!"

CHAPTER TWENTY-SIX
Finding Light

After lunch, Mrs. Jones decided the snow had melted enough to take Cassie into town.

"It probably helps that we scooped most of it up into a snow ball," Cassie said as they drove down the hill and around the pastures toward Springdale.

Mrs. Jones laughed. "You kids were creative."

"Well, you know." Cassie shrugged. "We have to make the most if it when it happens. We don't see snow very often."

"Better than in Texas. Maybe once in the whole seven years we saw snow."

Texas was further and further from Cassie's mind these days. She remembered how much she'd hated Arkansas when they moved here. All she'd wanted to do was go back to Texas. Home, she'd thought.

Now she couldn't imagine leaving.

She remembered the conversation with her dad about maybe moving back, and her heart constricted with fear. She didn't want to go back.

"You made it!" Andrea greeted Cassie with a large, enthusiastic hug. "I'm so glad!"

"I'll pick you up tomorrow," Mrs. Jones said.

As soon as she left, Andrea turned to Cassie. "I was thinking about tomorrow. Maybe I could spend the night and then go to church with you?"

"Hey, that would be awesome!" Cassie could just imagine what the kids at church would think if they saw Cassie with Andrea.

"We have to get ready for the movies." Andrea went down the hall to her room, and Cassie followed. "We can't look like we stayed at home all day. What did you do today, anyway?"

"Played in the snow." Cassie stared into Andrea's closet with her. "You?"

"I just watched TV and talked on the phone. Playing in the snow's not fun by yourself."

Probably true. Cassie hadn't really thought about how boring it might be to not have any siblings.

"Here." Andrea pulled out a white button up sweater. "Try this on. It will go good with your jeans." She fingered Cassie's straight hair. "We can try and curl it again too."

"I think it only works with the hot rollers," Cassie said. "And they take forever."

Andrea sifted through the shirts and found a long sleeved blue one for herself. "We have to look nice. There will be boys there."

Something tightened in Cassie's gut. "What boys?"

"Connor, Michael, Adam, you know, a few from school."

"Miles?" She was afraid to ask.

Andrea paused. "I didn't invite him. We can, though."

"That's all right." Probably better. If he were there, Cassie would get super nervous. "Wait. Did you say Adam?"

"Yeah. Why?"

"Isn't he Amity's boyfriend?"

"I'm not sure." Andrea shrugged. "Maybe they broke up." Then she smiled and leaned closer. "I think Connor might ask me out."

Connor had been on Cassie's soccer team a few years ago

and was a total jerk. "You still like him?"

"What, you don't?" Andrea looked shocked.

"He's mean."

"He won't be mean to you. Not if he's my boyfriend."

That didn't inspire confidence in Cassie. "Is the movie theater even going to be open?"

"Yeah, my mom already called and checked. They're running."

"What movie are we going to see?"

"I don't know. What do you want to see?"

Cassie had no idea. She just hoped it wouldn't be one that her mom wouldn't approve of.

After dinner, Mrs. Wall drove them to the movie theater. Andrea and Cassie got out and shivered in the cold, but they didn't have long to wait before a group of boys came over and joined them.

"Hi, Andrea," Connor said, slipping his arm around her and hugging her to his side.

"Where's Amity?" Adam asked, shoving his hands into his jeans.

"She'll be here later," Andrea said.

Cassie turned to her, surprised. "Amity's coming?"

"Of course." Andrea waved her off.

"But I thought you said you didn't want her to know about this."

"I changed my mind."

That made perfect sense. Not. Did Andrea intentionally create drama?

"They've started selling tickets!" Connor said, moving forward. The movie theater doors opened, and the small crowd rushed in.

Andrea kept looking toward the doors. "Have your money, Cassie?"

"Yes." Cassie fumbled with her pocket and got it out.

"Where's Amity?" Andrea muttered, pulling out her phone

and sending off a text.

The movie started, and Andrea shelved her phone into her purse. "I guess they won't make it."

"They?" Cassie asked.

"Yeah. Amity and Maureen."

So much for just Cassie and Andrea. "That's too bad."

⊙~✵~⊙

Cassie stayed with Andrea for several hours on Saturday, but all Andrea wanted to do was watch TV. Cassie hated to admit she was rather relieved when her mom showed up.

"Oh! Ask her if I can spend the night," Andrea said, following Cassie to the door.

"Can Andrea spend the night tonight?" Cassie asked her mom as they put her overnight bag in the trunk. "She wants to come to church with us tomorrow."

Mrs. Jones looked at Andrea, who rested her chin on Cassie's shoulder and shot her a big grin.

"Not this Sunday," Mrs. Jones said. "But that would be nice some other time."

Andrea pulled away and gave Cassie a hug. "Thanks for coming." Leaning closer, she whispered, "Say hi to Tyler for me."

"Will do," Cassie said, her face flaming.

"You've got a meeting at church tonight anyway," Mrs. Jones said as they drove back home. "Andrea wouldn't like it."

"Why? Is it boring?"

"Probably. It's all about remembering who you are, being moral and honest, and helping in your community."

"Andrea would like all that."

Mrs. Jones gave Cassie a dubious look and didn't say anything else.

The youth meeting was at the church in Rogers, so Mrs. Jones drove Cassie out there after dinner. Cassie wore a dress and had no sooner stepped out of the car then someone screamed, "Cassandra!"

She turned around in time to see a small black-haired girl run straight into her, nearly knocking her over with her enthusiasm.

"Hi," Cassie said, though she had no clue who she was talking to.

"I hoped you'd be here!" The girl took a step back and smiled brightly.

Only then did Cassie recognize her, and only just. "Elise?" she gasped out.

She and Elise had met at church camp two summers before. Except back then, Elise was blond, the straight strands running down her back. Now her hair was jet black and hung to her shoulders. Thick eyeliner and black lipstick adorned her face.

"Wow, you look—different," Cassie said.

"You look gorgeous." Elise swung her hand out, pushing Cassie away, and gave her a once-over before whistling. "I always thought you were pretty but that's an understatement now!"

Cassie's face warmed under the praise. She couldn't take her eyes off Elise and felt strangely shy. How could this be the same girl she'd bonded with that summer?

"Let's go in and sit down. I'll introduce you to some people." Elise wrapped an arm around Cassie and winked at her.

Cassie let her pull her into the chapel. But she'd only taken two steps when someone said, "Cassie!"

Cassie swiveled another direction and saw Ana Julia, the quiet, pretty girl from last summer. Her heart leaped in relief, and she pulled away from Elise to hug Ana Julia. "Ana! You're here!"

"You too!" Ana beamed at her.

She hadn't changed. If anything, she seemed even sweeter than before, her face radiant as she smiled.

"Sit with us," Ana Julia said, motioning to the empty spot next to her.

Elise stood a few pews up, body half tilted in an impatient stance.

"Just a minute," Cassie said. She returned to Elise and said apologetically, "I'm going to sit with Ana Julia. Want to join us?"

Elise's eyes swept over Ana Julia and those next to her. "That's okay. I'll talk to you after."

"Sounds good." Cassie let out a little breath, glad Elise hadn't been irritated. Then she returned to Ana Julia, who gave her hand a squeeze as she sat down.

The discussion was as her mom predicted: how to be examples in their community and stand for the right, how to be honest and moral in a society where lying had become second nature, and how to find joy in life. Cassie absorbed every word, feeling her spirit lift lighter and lighter. She believed what was taught, and she sensed that if she could just keep this light with her all the time, she wouldn't worry so much about who her friends were or how her clothes fit or what she ate.

But it wasn't that easy to keep the light with her.

The meeting ended, and the kids gathered around the kitchen for cookies and punch.

Ana Julia hugged Cassie again. "I'm so happy to see you. You look wonderful."

"You too," Cassie said, her heart swelling. "I wish you lived closer."

Elise came over and took Cassie's hand, holding it in her own. "I can't believe it's been so long since I've seen you. Give me your number again, I lost it. You've got to call me. We'll hang out."

"Yeah, sure." Cassie retrieved her phone and gave Elise her number, then programmed her own with Elise's.

"Thanks, beautiful." Elise leaned over and pressed a kiss to her cheek. "I have to go, but we'll talk soon!" She waved and walked out.

"How do you know her?" Ana Julia asked.

"Camp a few years ago," Cassie said, a little piece inside of her twisting mournfully. "I didn't have any friends, and Elise was there for me. She made sure I participated in the activities and didn't feel left out. She was so sweet."

"I guess now it's time for you to be there for her."

Cassie nodded. "Yes. I guess so."

☙❦❧

On Monday, the teachers handed out report cards for the fall semester. Cassie held her breath, but when she looked at each one, it was the same: an A, the highest score she could get.

"Don't forget," Ms. Talo said as everyone gathered to leave for lunch after fourth hour, "your Type III projects are due in two weeks. You should have them almost completed by now."

Ms. Talo had mentioned the Type III project the week before, and Cassie struggled now to remember what it stood for. It had to be real-world based and solve a problem. It had to create a product or a service. And it had to be created for a real-world audience.

"What are you doing for yours?" Cassie asked Nicole as they walked toward the lunch room.

"Making a video, of course," Nicole said with a smile. "But this time I'm going to an animal shelter. I'm going to film a commercial of the animals to try and raise awareness, maybe even get donations."

That sounded like a fun project. Why hadn't Cassie thought of that?

"What are you doing?"

"I have no idea," Cassie admitted. "I'll think of something."

"What grades are you guys getting?" Maureen asked at lunch, making a face as she snapped open her can of soda. "I don't think any of my teachers like me. I got all Bs so far.

That's Bs. BS. Get it?" She laughed, and Cara giggled.

Amity just sniffed and poked at her French fries, her face twisted into a sad expression.

"What's wrong, Amity?" Janice asked.

"Nothing, nothing," Amity said, one finger going up to wipe her eyes. She turned to Andrea and whispered something.

"What is it, hon?" Cara asked, leaning over the table to look at Amity. "Did something happen with Adam?"

Amity sighed and shook her head. "I'm fine. It's nothing really."

Cassie glanced at Janice, who gave an eye roll and went back to her sandwich. Andrea patted Amity's arm. But no matter how they pried, Amity wouldn't tell.

Cassie didn't give much thought to Amity until the next day, when once again Amity acted all weepy and put out in the bathroom before school.

"What's wrong, Amity?" Cassie asked.

If she thought she'd have more luck than the other girls, she was mistaken.

"Nothing, nothing, I'm fine," Amity said.

Then Andrea walked in, and the two of them put their heads together and whispered.

Cara came in next, humming to herself. She gave Cassie a big smile. "Hello, Miss Cassie!" she said.

"Hi, Cara," Cassie said, returning her smile. The more Cassie got to know Cara, the more she liked her. Easily the prettiest of all of them, she only spoke when there was something to say, and every time she spoke to Cassie, it made her feel special.

Cara's eyes darted to Andrea and Amity in the corner. Cara stepped closer to Cassie and whispered, "I think Amity just wants attention. Don't worry about her."

Cassie nodded, though she wasn't sure.

"What's wrong with Amity?" Cassie asked Andrea as they

walked to first hour.

"I can't tell you," Andrea said. "It's a secret."

Cassie remembered what Cara had said and shrugged. "It's probably no big deal anyway."

"I can't believe you said that!" Andrea gasped, pressing her hands to her chest.

"Is it?" Cassie raised her eyebrows and stopped walking. She lifted her chin. "Can't be that important, or she'd want the rest of us to know."

Andrea pursed her lips together. "She doesn't want anyone to worry."

Cassie snorted. "Right. That's why she's crying in front of all of us."

"If you must know." Andrea heaved a sigh, then grabbed Cassie's arm and pulled her behind the stairs as if someone might spy on them. "Amity's got cancer." She drew back and stared at Cassie, waiting for a reaction.

Cassie blinked. She hadn't expected that. She literally felt her blood run cold. "What?" Now she felt lousy and horrible for not being more concerned. "What kind? Is it fatal? Is she going to die?"

Andrea nodded somberly. "It's very bad. And she probably will die. But she doesn't want everyone to know so we can enjoy our friendship while she's still with us."

"Still with us?" Cassie burst into tears.

"Shh, shh." Andrea hugged her. "Now don't say anything, okay? Amity doesn't want you to be sad for her."

In spite of what Andrea said about not worrying and acting normal, Cassie could not get Amity's sickness out of her mind. The guilt clenched at her chest, to think she'd laughed and thought there was nothing wrong. She watched Amity with worried eyes the next day before school and at lunch, wishing they were better friends so she could talk to her about it.

Amity, at least, seemed to have come to grips with her illness. She laughed and flirted with the boys at lunch, almost as if everything were normal.

Cassie had to focus at voice lessons. Ms. Malcolm had given her another new song, and Cassie was excited to show off how much she'd practiced.

"You memorized both of them, Cassie!" Ms. Malcolm said, giving her a pleased smile as she rested her hands on the piano keys. "Fantastic job! You'll be ready for our recital in the spring for sure!"

Cassie smiled. "I really liked both of those songs. I felt like they were written for me."

"Them and many others." Ms. Malcolm dug around in her bag. "Let's see what else we have. Some day, Cassie, you're going to make me famous."

It was a compliment of the highest order, and it thrilled Cassie that her voice teacher thought so highly of her.

CHAPTER TWENTY-SEVEN
Conspiracy

By Thursday Amity acted like such her normal self that Cassie had a hard time believing she could be sick.

"Is she just so used to the idea?" she asked Andrea in first hour.

"I guess so," Andrea said, fixing her hair barrette and keeping her eyes on her reflection.

"I'm going to ask her," Cassie said.

"No, don't!" Andrea spun to Cassie and grabbed her arm. "It will really upset her! She'll be so angry at me for telling!"

Cassie scanned Andrea's face, the wide blue eyes, and she got that feeling, the one she was starting to recognize: Andrea was lying. But she couldn't flat out accuse her of it. And what if she was wrong? So she just nodded and said, "Okay." But she made up her mind to ask Amity at lunch.

Oddly enough, Andrea wedged herself between Cassie and Amity at the lunch table and kept up a steady stream of conversation, not allowing the two of them to talk at all.

Andrew, Michael, and Connor walked by, grinning and bobbing their heads at the girls.

"Is he still your boyfriend?" Cassie asked, keeping her eyes on Connor.

"Sort of. I think so," Andrea said. "We haven't talked since he asked me out last week, but we haven't broken up."

Some boyfriend. If that was dating, Cassie decided she'd hold out a little longer.

Andrew picked up a piece of paper and chucked it at their table. "Looks like you girls dropped some trash."

Cassie had been friends with Andrew a few years ago when they were in choir together. She hadn't really spoken to him since they started junior high, but like all the other boys, he'd gotten taller, his face thinner, and his hair more stylish. She wondered if he still sang.

"Are you calling us trash?" Cara picked up one of her French fries and threw it at him.

Except she missed. She hit the vice-principal right as he walked past the boys.

Everyone froze. Cassie covered her mouth with her hands, and Andrea bit down on her lower lip.

"Who threw this?" The vice-principal picked up the French fry between his forefinger and his thumb and held it out for all to see, a glower on his face.

It took a brief moment, but then Cara cleared her throat and stood up. "I did, sir."

He looked at her, and the glower vanished. "You did, huh?"

"Yes."

"Well, you know there are rules about throwing food in the cafeteria. So make sure you don't do it again."

"Yes, sir."

He turned around and left the cafeteria.

"What?" Janice hissed, leaning toward Cara and speaking loud enough for all to hear. "He totally just let you get away with it!"

"Shh." Cara waved her hand, her whole face flushed pink. "Let's just get out of here before he changes his mind."

Cassie couldn't believe it either. Looked like the teachers also adored Cara.

"I know it might feel like it's a long time away," Ms. Vanderwood said, her ever-present smile across her face as she spoke to the choir students in her class, "but our trip to New York is in five short months!"

Five short months. Cassie rolled her eyes along with everyone else in class. There wasn't anything short about five months.

"I promised your parents that we'd raise money to help with the costs. So here's our first fundraiser!" She pulled out a stack of fliers and tapped them on the piano. "Selling magazines!"

Chris, a seventh-grade redheaded boy, snorted. "Is that a joke? No one buys magazines anymore."

A girl laughed, and Cassie struggled to keep a straight face. Her parents faced this same problem with their paper route. Every month the numbers were lower and lower because more people decided to do electronic news instead of a real paper.

Ms. Vanderwood was not perturbed. "Hopefully you'll find someone, Chris, because this will help you get to New York."

Cassie needed all the help she could get. She accepted the flier handed to her.

"Make a list of all the people you can talk to. Neighbors, teachers, friends from church. And make sure you tell them this is for your trip to New York! That means something to people!"

Cassie bobbed her head in tune with Ms. Vanderwood's words. She didn't have a lot of free time, but she could ask people when she went places. She would do her best. Although the thought of trying to fit one more thing on her plate made her head ache.

Her headache didn't go away when she got home, either.

"Cassie, I need you to set the table for dinner," Mrs. Jones said.

"Oh, Mom," Cassie said, her eyes feeling sticky and dry. "I'm super tired. I just want to go to bed."

Wrong thing to say. She watched her mom's face get hard and stern. "You'll sit and eat with us."

Not this again. Almost every night now her mom watched her like a hawk, forcing her to eat more food than she wanted to. She'd taken to doing lots of exercises before bed to compensate.

She couldn't do it tonight.

"I have a super big headache. Like really."

"I don't believe you."

Now she was a liar, too? "I'm not lying!" Big tears formed behind her tired eyes and made their way down her face. "I'll sit here but I'm not eating!"

"You will eat, Cassandra!"

"I won't!" Sobbing now, shaking with anger, Cassie jerked out a chair and sat down at the table.

Emily set the table around her, shooting nervous, concerned glances her way. The rest of the family sat down, and Mrs. Jones served chicken and rice to the family, one of their go-to dishes.

"Eat, Cassie," she murmured, passing the food to her.

"No."

Her mom set the rice down in front of her and stared at her. "You'll stay here all night until you do."

Part of Cassie thought to herself, *how hard can this be? Take a bite and be done*. But the other part gritted its teeth and dug its heels in. No way was she giving in. "Fine."

Everyone resumed eating. Cassie shoved her plate into the middle of the table and rested her head on her arms. Her thick, swollen eyes closed.

Someone shook her shoulder, and Cassie jerked upright, blinking in surprise. No one else was at the table.

"Cassie."

Cassie turned her head to see her mom leaning toward her.

"Cassie, you're burning up. I'm sorry. I didn't believe you really didn't feel well. Go rest."

"Okay," Cassie said. She got up and stumbled to her room, collapsing on her bed before she had the chance to realize she'd won that battle.

Her headache was worse in the morning. And now her throat hurt, a deep painful ache that made it hard to swallow. She stood in the bathroom, gurgling hot water and leaning her body against the sink because standing by herself was too hard.

"I don't think you should go to school today," Emily said beside her, grabbing her own toothbrush.

Cassie spit out the water and hovered over the sink. "I can't miss. I have a test in English."

"You always have a test."

"That's junior high for you." She forced herself to stand long enough to get dressed and then collapsed on the bed, breathing heavily.

"I'm going to tell Mom you're sick."

"No. No." Cassie heaved herself up. "I'm going to school."

Somehow she got pants and a sweater on and dragged herself out the door. It was freezing again. Cassie put on a hat and a jacket and still shook while they stood at the bus stop. She got on and slid into the spot next to Jeremy but didn't greet him. While he chattered away at her, she leaned her head against the window and shivered.

She skipped the bathroom routine and sat in front of her locker, resting.

"Cassie!" Andrea spotted Cassie in the hallway and she ran over. "I've been looking all over for you. I have to talk to you." She paused. "You have big shadows under your eyes. Why weren't you in the bathroom?"

"I'm tired," Cassie said. "I just wanted to sit." She didn't budge from where she leaned against her locker.

"You look cadiving." Andrea extended a hand, and Cassie

took it, allowing her to pull her to her feet. "Are you sick?"

"I think I might be," Cassie said. She sneezed, bringing her elbow up to her nose to catch it. Three times.

"Maybe you stay over there," Andrea said, putting distance between them.

"Thanks," Cassie grumbled. "What did you want to talk to me about?"

"Oh!" Andrea faced Cassie and offered a wide smile. "Amity got her test results back yesterday. She doesn't have cancer! She's totally fine!"

Andrea's words managed to penetrate past the fog in Cassie's head. "What test results? She didn't have the results yet? Why did you say she had cancer?"

Andrea waved her hands back and forth in front of her body. "She thought she did, but it was a false alarm! Isn't it wonderful?"

"So great," Cassie said, even while her doubts went into full sprouting mode. "We should congratulate her, right? Tell her how happy we are for her."

"No! No, I mean, because she doesn't want to make a big deal out of it. I was just telling you so you could leave her alone about it. And not bring it up." That wide smile was back.

"Okay," Cassie said, quite certain she was lying. But why? What benefit did she get from making something like that up?

"Are you all right, Cassie?" Mr. Adams asked when the girls walked into his math class.

"Actually my head really hurts," she said, wincing as she pressed a hand to it. "Do you have any Tylenol?"

He studied her a moment, then said, "You know I'm not allowed to give medicine to students." He leaned closer and whispered, "But if you were to find some in my bag when I wasn't looking, you could take it."

Cassie gave him a tight smile. While he lectured the seventh graders, Cassie found his black leather bag and fished around for the pill bottle. She sighed in relief when she found it, grateful for his confidence in her.

CHAPTER TWENTY-EIGHT
For the Love

Cassie sneezed her way through all her morning classes, her headache only slightly diminished by Mr. Adams' Tylenol. Her teachers gave her wary looks as if they were afraid they might catch whatever she had. Which, to be perfectly honest, they might.

"Are you sick, Cassie?" Janice asked at lunch.

Cassie put her head in her hands and mumbled.

"She doesn't feel so well," Andrea said, sitting across from them.

"You should probably go home," Amity said. She stole a handful of Cara's fries, and Cara batted at her. "Just call your mom."

"I might," Cassie said. She'd made it through her English test the hour before, and that was why she'd come. Then again, the school day was half over.

"Hey, you guys," Maureen said, her eyes lighting up. "I saw this car on the way to school this morning. It was sweet! All black and convertible."

"A convertible?" Amity tossed her hair. "I thought you wanted a pickup."

"I love a big truck," Maureen sighed.

"I get the truck," Cara said. "I already picked one out. Big and red."

"Country girls," Amity sniffed. "I'm getting a red Porsche. Rides sleek and low."

"Like you?" Maureen snorted.

Amity elbowed her and the others laughed, except Cassie, who didn't get the joke and didn't feel like laughing.

"What about Cassie?" Maureen said, turning her attention to her.

Cassie sighed inwardly. She hated it when Maureen focused on her. Somehow she always became the butt of the joke.

"Something reasonable," Janice said. "A four-door car."

"A station wagon," Amity said. "Like my grandma used to drive."

"Her family can't afford a car," Maureen said. "She'll have to drive a bike and put extra seats on it!"

They all busted up laughing, even Cara, who usually tried not to laugh when Maureen made fun of Cassie.

Cassie didn't say anything. Her head hurt too much to defend herself.

"Yeah, but you know what, Cassie's going to be the prettiest of us all," Cara said. She probably felt bad for laughing.

"It's true," Janice said. "We all wish we had your tan skin, Cassie."

"And you're so skinny," Amity added.

"I'm fat," Cara said. She puffed out her cheeks and stuck her belly out.

Cassie burst out laughing. She couldn't help it. "You couldn't be fat if you tried."

"I want to be as skinny as you." Cara reversed the direction of her air and sucked her cheeks in.

"Me too," Andrea said. She did the same.

"Why?" Janice said. "Cassie doesn't eat. Why would anyone want to be that skinny?"

"I eat," Cassie protested. "My mom makes me. Every

night."

"Well, she better," Amity said, whacking her on the thigh. "You'll waste away into nothing otherwise. And then what would we do?"

"Find someone else to make fun of," Cassie muttered.

Maureen choked on her soda, and then she laughed so hard she snorted it across the table. "I can't believe you said that!"

"What did she say?" Andrea demanded.

Cassie looked at Maureen, and Maureen grinned. "I'm not telling. But you wouldn't believe it came out of sweet little Cassie's mouth."

Cassie gave a tiny smile. Maybe she just needed to lighten up.

Cassie went straight to bed when she got off the bus. She slept all evening and all night, and when she woke up, she could barely even groan, her throat hurt so bad. A glance around showed it was daylight already. No one else was in her room, not even Emily. Cassie wanted to ask where her sister was, but her head felt full of cotton, and she didn't have the strength to call out. When was the last time she'd eaten? She couldn't remember. She closed her eyes and went back to sleep.

She woke up again when her mom bumped her bed.

"Mom?" she murmured.

"Hi, Cassie. I wasn't trying to wake you, just fix your blanket." Mrs. Jones sat down on the edge of the bed, leaving some space between her and Cassie. "Can I get you something? A bowl of soup? Water?"

Cassie nodded, looking at her mom through hooded eyes. "Which one?"

"Both." Her lips felt dry and cracked. "And chapstick."

"Sure, sweetie."

Mrs. Jones came back in a few minutes later with a bowl of soup. She helped Cassie sit up so she could take spoonfuls of the chicken noodle soup from the bowl.

"I'm sorry I was so hard on you the other night," she said. "I didn't know you were sick."

"I didn't know, either," Cassie said. "I just knew I had a headache."

Neither of them said anything, and Cassie sensed words behind her mother's silence, questions, concerns. But she didn't voice them, and Cassie wondered what held her back.

Cassie finished the soup and lay back down. "Thanks, Mom. I'll just rest a bit more."

Cassie slept for days. The weather was nice enough on Saturday that the whole family went caving without Cassie at Devil's Den, the national park less than an hour away. Cassie wasn't even envious. She used the time to sleep and rest and sleep.

Her friends kept calling her, texting her, wanting to make sure she was okay, and that made Cassie feel all happy inside. Only Cara never called or texted, but Cassie didn't expect her to. Their friendship was a little bit different.

Cassie stayed home all day Sunday also, but since Riley called her later and gave her a play by play of everything Tyler did at church, she didn't feel like she missed anything.

"And there's a big dance coming up next month," Riley said. "Right after your birthday. You'll be able to go."

"You will soon." Cassie was secretly glad to get to go before Riley, though. She wanted to see what it was like by herself.

"Will you be in school tomorrow?"

"Hopefully. My throat doesn't hurt anymore. I'm still tired, but I'm doing all right."

"Okay. I'll let you go and I'll see you tomorrow."

"Thanks," Cassie said. "See you tomorrow."

Though she didn't have a lot of energy, Cassie dragged herself from bed on Monday and got ready for school. She didn't feel sick anymore, just a bit drained, probably from eating nothing but crackers and soup for days.

She stepped into the school bathroom and applied concealer to her eyes, not wanting Andrea to tell her she looked dead again.

"Hey, you're back!" Amity came in first and surprised Cassie by giving her a hug. "We missed you!"

Andrea came in behind her. "You're healthy now, right?"

"Rude!" Amity smacked her on the back of the head.

"Just joking." Andrea smiled at Cassie.

"You're okay!" Cara came in next, also giving Cassie a hug. "You got to eat more, hon! You're wasting away!"

"I was sick," Cassie said. It was a real reason, at least.

Amity hooked her arm through hers and walked with her to the locker hall. "You brought money today, right?"

"I've got my lunch money," Cassie said. "Why?"

"Because this week is your chance to order a flower for your Valentine." Amity winked at her. "You know who."

"My Valentine?" Cassie sputtered. "What?"

"It's something StuCo is doing," Cara said, appearing beside them. StuCo stood for Student Council, and though several of the girls had run, only Cara was on it. "We're raising money by delivering flowers on Valentine's Day. You pick the flower and who you want it delivered to, and we deliver them on Valentine's Day. It can even be anonymous."

Flowers. Valentine's Day. A shiver went down Cassie's spine. Would anyone send flowers to her? "When is Valentine's Day?"

"Friday," both girls said at the same time.

"Where do I order?"

"In the cafeteria. You can do it during lunch."

"There's also a dance after school," Amity said. "You should come."

"Uh-huh," Cassie said, though she didn't want to. She wanted to try a church dance first. "Maybe next month."

Cassie didn't go sit immediately with her friends when lunch time came around. Instead she found the table against the wall where ninth-grade StuCo members were taking orders.

"You want to order some Valentines?" the girl behind the table said. Her dark hair was pulled into a ponytail, and she smacked her gum with each word. They weren't allowed to have gum, but maybe she, like Cara, could get away with things others couldn't.

"Yes," Cassie said. She pulled out her wallet. "How much are they?"

"Two dollars each. Just fill out this paper with who you want it to go to and we'll deliver them."

Two dollars each. Cassie let out a careful breath and filled out the forms. One for each of her friends. Maureen. Andrea. Cara. Janice. Riley. Amity.

And the last one. Her heart beat faster in anticipation, and she fought the urge to hide her paper from the girl. Not like that girl cared. She wrote, very carefully, *Miles Hansen*.

The girl collected all of the cards from her. "That's fourteen dollars."

Cassie glanced around and slid the cash over, feeling like she was doing a covert drug deal.

"Did you put who it was from?"

"No," Cassie said. "They're anonymous."

"Okay, thank you!"

Cassie nodded and slipped away, her heart pounding so hard in her chest that she pressed her hand to it. Now she just had to wait a few more days to see if anyone would send her one. Hope and anticipation fired up in her heart. Someone somewhere had to have a crush on her.

※

Cassie remembered to take her fundraiser information to voice lessons and church on Wednesday. It was the first time she'd had the chance to sell any magazines, and she couldn't believe she actually sold a few. She suspected the only reason she did was because people felt sorry for her.

On Thursday Ms. Vanderwood asked for the forms back, and Cassie brought her envelope up with everyone else, glad she wasn't turning it in empty.

"Good job, everyone," Ms. Vanderwood said. "This will get us a long way on our journey to New York. Pull out your binders!"

Time to sing. Being here felt more and more like a drudgery. If it weren't for the trip to New York, Cassie might actually quit.

They were halfway through dinner at home when Ms. Vanderwood called, asking to speak to Cassie.

"Yes?" Cassie asked, taking the phone into the living room. "This is Cassie."

"Cassie, I got your envelope, but something seems to be missing."

"What is it?"

"You didn't forget something, maybe?"

Cassie frowned. How could she? It was just an envelope stuffed with order forms and money. "No."

"There was no money in your envelope, Cassie."

No money? That wasn't even possible. "Are you sure? Did you check in the order forms?"

"I'm sure, Cassie. I checked everywhere."

"I know it was there. I don't know what happened." Cassie squeezed her eyes shut, trying not to panic. Where could the money be?

"Did it fall out in your car, maybe?"

"I don't know. I'll check. I'll call you later." Cassie hung up the phone and slipped on a pair of shoes.

"What's going on?" Mrs. Jones asked, watching her. "Where are you going?"

"There was no money in my fundraising envelope," Cassie said, breathless. "I have to check the car." She ran out the door without another word, pausing just long enough to grab a flashlight.

    Nothing. There was nothing in the car. She searched under the seats, by the windows, behind the seats. No money had fallen out. Cassie sat back on her heels and fought tears. She'd have to pay the difference. Ms. Malcolm, the people from church, they paid money for a magazine subscription, and someone had to make sure that happened.

CHAPTER TWENTY-NINE
Great Expectations

"Did you find it?" Mrs. Jones asked when Cassie came in.

"No." She returned to the table, out of breath, her face hot. "I don't know where it went. I had all of it last night, I know I did!"

"Okay. We'll find it. Let me put away dinner and we'll search the house." Mrs. Jones stood up and began gathering dishes.

"What about that money you were counting earlier, Scott?" Annette said. "Where did you get it?"

Cassie's head turned toward her younger brother. Annette was only seven, but she was sharp as a tack. If she spotted something unusual, she didn't hesitate to say so.

"What money?" Scott grumbled, his face pinking.

Cassie leaped at him. "You took it!"

"Scott?" Mr. Jones said, his tone full of warning.

"I don't know what you're talking about."

"Do I need to check your room?" Mrs. Jones stood with her hands on her hips, and Cassie was certain the murderous look in her eye matched Cassie's.

Scott slinked lower in his chair and shrugged his shoulders.

"Fine. But if I find it, you're grounded from TV for a

month."

With a loud sigh, Scott threw himself from the table and went to his room. Mrs. Jones followed, with Cassie right behind.

"Here." Scott pulled a pile of checks and cash from the top dresser drawer.

"I can't believe you took this!" Cassie exclaimed, jerking the bills out of his hand.

"It's not yours," he said.

"It's definitely not yours!"

"Cassie, you've got your money. Call Ms. Vanderwood. I'll deal with Scott."

Cassie relented and backed into the hallway. Mrs. Jones closed the door. Cassie hurried away to call her music teacher, glad that at least the money had been found.

Cassie's eyes flew open on Friday morning.

Valentine's Day.

This was the day, the day she would find out if anyone liked her.

She woke early and set the hot rollers again. It had been weeks since she'd last curled her hair, but today was a special occasion. She wanted to look her best.

She stared at her reflection while she wrapped each hair piece around the roller. Should she have put her name on Miles' flower? If he knew it was from her, what would his reaction be?

She couldn't take the chance that it would be negative. She couldn't lose his friendship.

What if he recognized her handwriting?

She staggered under the thought, dropping a roller on the floor. She ducked down, searching for it, burning her fingers when she found it. He wouldn't recognize it. They had never exchanged notes or anything like that. It would just be a random girl's handwriting. She consoled herself with those thoughts and finished doing her hair. She put her makeup on while the rollers set, and by the time she pulled them off, she was dressed and ready for school.

With an hour to kill.

It had been a long time since she'd worked on her book. She pulled up the latest draft she'd printed for Ms. Talo but never given her. Every time she read through it, she found something else wrong, and she wanted it to be perfect when she sent it to the publisher. The writer's conference was in a few weeks. She had to be ready for it.

She took the printed manuscript into the kitchen and drew up short.

There, in every child's spot, was a little heart-shaped box. Cassie knew within it would be little chocolates.

Her mother did this every year. Somehow Cassie had forgotten. She stared at her box for a long time before walking into the living room and sitting on the couch. She had to be stronger than that.

The other kids woke up and ate their chocolate for breakfast, but Cassie just sat on the couch. Her nerves got tighter with each passing second. Soon she'd be at school. Soon they'd deliver the flowers. Would she get one?

The first thing she did when she got to school was hurry to the bathroom to check on her hair. As expected, it had already started to go flat, but this time Cassie was prepared. She pulled out her tiny hair spray bottle and misted her hair all over.

"Happy Valentine's Day," Andrea said, coming into the bathroom. "Love your hair!"

"Yours too." Cassie fluffed Andrea's curls. "Hot rollers?"

"Yep."

"Hey, guys!" Amity came in. "You should have told me you were going to curl your hair! I would have too!"

"Happy Valentine's Day!" Cara was right on her heels. She smiled and air-kissed each one of them and placed a chocolate heart in their hands. "Love ya. And you. And you. Love ya." She air-kissed Cassie last. "You eat this chocolate, you hear?"

Cassie smiled and nodded.

Amity stepped up to the mirror and brushed mascara on her eyelashes. "I've decided to break up with Adam."

"Again?" Cara said.

Amity shrugged. "He's too immature. It's time to move on."

"But certainly not today," Cassie said. "It's Valentine's Day."

"Better today than have him think we're okay."

Cassie totally disagreed. But what did she know? She'd never had a boyfriend.

"I'll go find him now," Amity said. She walked out of the bathroom.

"Is she really going to break up with him?" Cassie asked Andrea, dumbfounded.

Andrea shrugged. "I guess so."

The warning bell rang, and the girls wandered out of the bathroom, heading for their lockers. Cassie had just put away her books when she spotted Amity, standing next to Cara and Andrea and sobbing. Closing her locker, she walked over to join them.

"What is it?" she asked. Had Adam broken up with Amity first? Why would she care?

Amity just shook her head and cried. Cassie's eyes darted to the objects in Amity's hands: a small stuffed teddy bear and a box of chocolates.

Cara rubbed Amity's back and crooned. "It's okay. You couldn't have known." She met Cassie's eyes and said, "After Amity broke up with Adam he gave her a Valentine's Day gift." She nodded at the teddy bear.

"I didn't know!" Amity cried. "He's s-s-so sweet! I have to go back out with him!"

Cassie pressed her lips together. "Sorry, Amity," she said, but really she was trying not to laugh. *Next time don't break up with someone on Valentine's Day*, she wanted to say.

She kept the sentiment to herself.

☙ ❀ ❧

Andrea was moody all through first hour. The two girls sat in the hall grading papers, and Cassie tried to joke with her, even threw erasers at her, but Andrea just sighed and and looked sad.

"What is it?" Cassie finally asked. "It's Valentine's Day. You should be all happy."

Andrea shrugged. "There's not much to be happy about."

Cassie chucked another eraser at her. "You're one to talk! You have a boyfriend."

"Yeah, he's not going to give me stuffed animals and chocolate."

Ah, that's what this boiled down to. Andrea was jealous of Amity.

"Maybe he'll send you a flower." Cassie smirked.

Andrea rolled her eyes. "The flowers are stupid. No one's going to send me any."

Cassie pressed her lips together and returned to grading the papers. She hoped Andrea didn't really feel that way. Was that what the other girls thought too?

Andrea heaved a loud sigh. Then another. And a third. Cassie finally lifted her head.

"What?"

"It's just . . ." Andrea kept her eyes down and played with the edge of her shirt. "Cara said she might be moving to another school."

This was news to Cassie. "When did she say this?"

"She told me this morning. But she said not to tell anyone."

Instantly Cassie's suspicion-meter went to red alert. Whenever Andrea said not to tell anyone, she was usually lying. "What school?"

"Shiloh."

Shiloh was the private school across the street from their

own. "Why?"

"Her parents think she'll have better friends there."

Cassie furrowed her brow. The details gave credence to Andrea's claims. "Well, I hope she doesn't." She turned back to grading the math tests, trying to imagine their group without Cara. Cara was the glue that held them together through their spats and drama, with her calm, peace-maker nature.

Andrea let out a little sniffle, then another.

"It'll be okay, Andrea," Cassie said, putting the pen down. "Maybe she won't go. Sometimes it's just talk."

"It's not that," Andrea said, shaking her head. She sniffed again.

"There's something else?"

Andrea nodded. "But I can't tell you."

This was getting irritating. "Then don't." Cassie returned to grading.

"I'm sick," Andrea blurted. "I've got Toxic Shock Syndrome and I might die."

Cassie's jaw dropped. "The tampon disease?"

"Yes. I have more tests next week to find out for sure."

Cassie knew absolutely nothing about this illness. But just a few days ago Andrea had told her Amity was dying, and she turned out to not be. She didn't want to seem insensitive, but Andrea wasn't the most trustworthy person.

The thought made her feel guilty. She patted Andrea's arm. "Hopefully it will be okay."

⁂

"Type IIIs are due on Friday!" Ms. Talo said as the fourth hour bell rang and dismissed everyone for lunch. "You have one week!"

Cassie groaned inwardly. It was becoming a chorus. Every day when classes ended, Ms. Talo sang it out.

As if that would somehow make it happen.

"When do I have time to do a stupid project?" Cassie

grumbled. She hadn't even started it.

Other kids were just as busy as her, though, and they managed to get it done. She knew she would get no leniency.

Cassie struggled to keep silent at lunch as her friends wondered if they would receive Valentine's. She wanted their flowers to be a surprise. And Cassie could only hope she would also get one.

As the delivery time approached, she got more and more anxious. Her friends would receive their flowers, and they should feel loved, special.

And Miles. How would he feel?

Would it be totally obvious Cassie had sent them? Maybe she should have sent one to herself.

Sixth hour started, and the teacher began the lecture. But she was interrupted a few minutes later when the door opened.

"I've got Valentines!" the older student said, stepping into the room with a handful of flowers.

Cassie sat up straighter, anticipation surging through her veins. But as the student called out names, Cassie's was not one of them. She sank back into her seat, a lump forming in her throat.

The student turned to the teacher. "We've got more. So I'll be back."

Cassie sat up again. It wasn't over.

The anxiety kept up all through class as student after student received a flower. Her head pulsed feverishly every time the flower delivery arrived. But finally the girl said with a cheery wave, "That's all. Happy Valentine's Day!" And she turned around and walked out.

Cassie stole a quick glance around. Half of the students had received several flowers, and a few only one. But only a handful had received none, like Cassie.

She slinked lower in her seat, wishing she could disappear. Wishing she'd stayed home from school. What on earth had made her think she was pretty? Special? Nobody else thought so.

    The tears stung her eyes. Valentine's Day was a bust. Nobody loved her.

Episode 5: Red Flags

CHAPTER THIRTY
Worst Holiday Ever

Cassandra Jones hated Valentine's Day.

That's what she decided as she sat in seventh hour choir, the only girl out of all her friends who hadn't received a flower. Cassie shoved all her emotions deep into her chest, not about to show to the other giggly girls how alone and sad she felt. She ignored Maureen's attempts to talk and pretended like she didn't see the flower under her chair. When choir ended, she tried to escape to the bus unseen, but people kept stopping her in the hall to tell her she looked nice or wish her a happy Valentine's Day. Cassie gritted her teeth, trying not to notice the flowers in her peers' hands, and nodded.

She hated this day.

Cara and Andrea stood by Cassie's locker, both of them with three flowers in their hands. The lump in Cassie's throat hardened to a rock, and she feared she would cry. She tried to evade them to get to her locker, but Cara turned around, her light brown eyes landing on Cassie.

"Oh, Cassie! I know this one's from you." She smiled and brandished a white carnation. "I recognized your handwriting. Thank you, sweetie!"

Cassie just nodded, making the backpack-to-locker switch quickly. "I've got to go."

"You're not coming to the dance?" Andrea asked. Andrea was Cassie's best friend, and this morning she'd told Cassie she had a rare sickness and was going to die. But the flowers must have cheered her up, because she seemed fine now. If she'd even been telling the truth.

"Don't think so," Cassie said. "Bye, guys."

Cara joined her, following her to the end of the lockers. "Are you okay?"

"Yes." Cassie nodded. "I'm good."

Cara's eyes flicked over her face. "Call me, okay?"

"Sure."

It was only when Cassie got on the bus that she allowed herself to cry. Unwanted and unloved.

By the time Cassie got home, her feelings of self-pity and loathing had changed to confusion and resentment. She locked herself in her room and called Cara.

No one answered. Cara's chirpy voice came on, requesting her to leave a message, but Cassie didn't feel like it. She hung up the phone and stared at the ceiling.

No more wallowing in misery. Cassie left her room and found her mom in the laundry room.

"You didn't eat your chocolates," Mrs. Jones said, giving her a hug. "Happy Valentine's Day."

Cassie had forgotten about the box of chocolates her mom left her on the table. "Not so much," Cassie grumbled.

"Why not?" Mrs. Jones drew back to study her. "Something happen?"

The tears roared behind her eyes, pooling and overflowing. "No. I just don't have anyone."

"You're only thirteen, sweetie. The time will come when you'll have a boyfriend."

Crapola, there they went. Slipping and sliding, the tears cascaded down her face. "I don't need a boyfriend, Mom. I just want my friends to appreciate me." And she told the whole flower story, how she bought a flower for all of her friends and not a single person bought one for her.

Mrs. Jones hugged her tightly. "Honey, you have one of the kindest souls I've ever seen. Your capacity to give is bigger than theirs. So you might feel a little empty sometimes, but it's one of your biggest gifts. Other people just don't have it, no matter how hard they try."

In a way, that made sense, though it didn't really make her feel better. "Can you take me to Cara's house?"

"What for?"

"She told me to call her but she's not answering. So I thought I'd just go over." As far as proximity, even though she lived a good ten minutes away, Cara was a closer neighbor than her other friends.

"Okay. Give me a few minutes to get dinner going and I'll drive you out there."

"Thanks, Mom." Cassie threw her arms around her mom on impulse.

"You can return the favor in two weeks when I have jaw surgery. I'll need you to help out."

"Jaw surgery?" Cassie pulled away, furrowing her brow. "Why?"

"I should have gotten braces as a kid and never did. So now we have to fix it." Mrs. Jones smiled, revealing her misaligned teeth. Cassie hadn't really paid attention before.

"Is it safe?"

"Perfectly. I just won't be able to eat."

That didn't sound so bad. Cassie shoved the thought about food away.

Cassie's heart lifted on the drive out to Cara's house. Maybe she could even convince Cara to come over and spend the night, and the two of them could bond. Of all the girls, Cassie sensed a depth and sincerity to Cara, but it was hard to connect with her because she was so shy.

She remembered how she'd judged Cara in elementary school because she was beautiful and quiet and all the guys liked her. Cassie had assumed Cara was a snotty person. It shamed her now to have thought that.

Mrs. Jones pulled to a stop in front of Cara's home. All the lights were on.

"Be right back," Cassie said, tumbling from the car. She ran up the walkway and rang the doorbell.

The door opened, and Cara stood there, dressed in a sparkly black top and tight jeans, her hair curled and in a high ponytail. "Cassie!" she exclaimed. She pulled the door wider and ushered her into the house. "Did you decide to go to the dance? Want to ride with us?"

The dance. Cassie had completely forgotten.

Us?

She looked over Cara's shoulder and saw Maureen standing in the kitchen, slicing up pizza.

"Hi, Cassie!" Maureen called.

Cassie heaved a sigh. So much for inviting Cara over. She couldn't even talk to her privately because Maureen was there.

"What's wrong?" Cara asked, touching her arm.

Cassie's lip trembled, and she burst into tears. She threw her arms around Cara and sobbed.

Cara gave a little cry of surprise. "What is it? What's wrong?"

How could Cassie tell her she hated Valentine's Day and felt unloved? She couldn't. So she said, "Andrea told me she's dying and you're switching schools and I feel like everything's falling apart."

"Oh, hon." Cara pulled back. She grabbed a tissue from a box on the counter and dabbed at Cassie's face. "I'm not switching. Why would she say that?"

"Who said that?" Maureen asked, joining them. "Andrea? Andrea's a liar. She can't help herself."

Cassie blinked at them in surprise. "Does everyone know this?"

"I'm not going anywhere," Cara said.

"You're not switching schools?"

"No way," Cara said with a laugh. "I'm on StuCo here."

Cassie took a deep breath. "And Andrea isn't dying?"

Now Cara looked sympathetic. "She's not going to die. She's just dramatic. Lots of people get skin cancer."

"My dad had it," Maureen said helpfully.

"It's totally curable," Cara said.

Cassie looked back and forth between the two of them. Skin cancer. Curable.

But Andrea had told Cassie she had Toxic Shock Syndrome.

"Thank you. I feel much better," she said, though in reality, she wasn't sure what she thought of her best friend now.

"You sure you don't want to come to the dance with us?" Cara asked. "There's lots of room in the car."

"I'm good." Cassie found her hand and gave it a squeeze.

Cara smiled and squeezed back. "I'll see you Monday, then."

On Monday, Cassie found something else to occupy her mind besides her flaky friendship with Andrea. Several of her teachers brought applications to free, government-sponsored summer camps, and Cassie wanted to go to all of them. In history she filled out the application for a camp on the Holocaust, and in English she filled out one for a creative arts camp.

"For this one you'll have to send it samples of your art," Ms. Talo said when Cassie brought the completed application to her desk. "A video of a monologue and singing for the performance part, or if you want the writing part, a sample of your writing."

"I can do that," Cassie said, thinking of the book she'd finished typing up. She was also a decent singer and actress. Both sounded fun.

Ms. Talo once again reminded the class that their Type III projects were due on Friday, and Cassie realized she'd run out of time. She needed to decide what she was doing and get it done.

Mrs. Jones bought some poster board for her, and Cassie sat and brainstormed at the kitchen table, trying to figure out what on earth to do it on.

No ideas came to her.

"Am I working the store tomorrow, Daddy?" she asked Mr. Jones before bed. She worked at her dad's soccer store a couple times a week.

"I'm planning on you."

"Can you bring my poster board? I have a big project due on Friday."

"Sure, I'll take it there. Anything else you need?"

If only she knew what she was doing her project on, she'd have an answer. "Not so far."

By the time she got to the soccer store on Tuesday, she had an idea. She could do a presentation on her book. It was a real life project with a real life problem. She needed to find a publisher, but first she had to get through all her revisions.

She sat in the stockroom of the store, outlining in light pencil on the poster board how she would show the real life applications of her book. She also had to show how it would appeal to the general public.

The bell jangled as a customer came in, and Mr. Jones began talking, showing off the new goods coming in for the start of soccer season. Cassie focused on her work and tuned out the conversation.

The door jingled again, and this time Mr. Jones called, "Cassie! Come help, please!"

She dropped her pencil with a frustrated sigh. Just when she was getting something done.

The traffic didn't stop, either, which left her father happy and Cassie irritated.

"Soccer season starts up in a week," Mr. Jones said. "For once people are coming to us."

"That's really nice," she said. And then her mind went back to the poster board in the stockroom and how much she still needed to get done.

A little before five, her dad closed the store so he could take her to choir.

"Oh no!" Cassie exclaimed as they pulled into the art center, "I forgot my poster!"

"That's all right," Mr. Jones said. "I'll bring it home with me tonight."

"You can't forget," Cassie said, alarm still firing through her chest. "I need to finish it."

"I won't forget."

⁌⁌⁌

Mr. Jones did forget. He forgot again on Wednesday, which meant Cassie would have to get the poster from the store when she worked there on Thursday.

She tried not to panic Thursday morning as she got ready for school. She only had that night to get her Type III done.

Fourth hour English class was a flutter with whispers and students commiserating together.

"Is yours done?" Leigh Ann asked Cassie.

"No." Cassie shook her head. "I barely even started. I'm kind of freaking out."

"Yeah, me too."

Ms. Talo called them to order, though it took a few minutes for them to calm down.

"It sounds like," she said, giving them all stern looks, "you guys did not budget your time correctly."

Cassie lowered her eyes. That would be about right.

"I'm going to give you an extension. You have all weekend to finish your Type IIIs. But that's it. If you don't bring it in on Monday, you get an automatic F."

Cassie exhaled a huge sigh of relief. She could do that. She pulled out her notebook and wrote "interviews" across the top. She could spend tomorrow getting classmates' reactions to her book and include that in her project.

By Saturday evening, she wasn't quite done. She taped several drafts of her book to the poster board and included a binder with her plan of action to reach out to different publishers. She didn't have her classmates' responses to her book typed up yet.

Cassie set her alarm for early Monday morning so she could finish. Typing up the interviewed responses took longer than she expected, and suddenly Emily was yelling down the stairs that they needed to go.

"Crapola, Crapola, Crapola," Cassie muttered, rolling up the poster board and shoving the papers into her backpack. She'd have to borrow glue and tape at the office and put it all together.

Her hand went to her face and she froze. She was still wearing her glasses! She gritted her teeth. No time to put in contacts now. She'd just have to be in glasses today.

She ran straight to the office from the bus.

"A little behind on your homework?" the receptionist said, carrying a steaming mug over to her desk. She watched Cassie tear off pieces of tape and place visual aids on the poster board.

None of your business, Cassie thought. "Yep." She shoved her glasses up on her nose, hating that she'd had to wear them.

She didn't even want to bump into her friends, but of course Amity and Maureen were standing at her locker. Amity laughed when she saw Cassie.

"What happened to you? Did you get glasses?"

"Cassie's always had glasses," Maureen said. "You just didn't know her then."

"I wear contacts," Cassie said, irritated. "And who cares? If I wore glasses would you not be my friend?"

"Sheesh, someone's grumpy. I was just kidding around," Amity said.

Cassie considered apologizing but decided not to. They

were rude to her all the time.

Besides, she was totally stressing this project.

☙❦❧

The nervous energy hung like an electric cloud over the English class when Cassie walked in. She put her poster board along the wall with the others and waited her turn. She scanned the projects and furrowed her brow. She hadn't added any color or eye-catching design to her board, but many others had. Already she felt inferior.

Her name was called third. "Cassie, come on up and tell us about yours," Ms. Talo said.

Exhaling, Cassie wiped her palms on her pants and picked up her poster board. "I did my Type III on the book I wrote last year. It's applicable to real life because people like to read books. And the problem I'm attempting to solve is making the book into a final draft so I can get a publisher. Finally, it's accessible to all people as fiction." She launched into the explanation of her project, certain everyone in the class would think her lazy for using a book she'd written the year before.

"Excellent job, Cassie," Ms. Talo said. "This book of yours will probably consume many more years of your life before you're done with it, but that's how these giant projects go." She checked her clipboard. "Jimmy, you're up."

Cassie deposited her board with the finished projects and returned to her seat. It was a boring Type III, and she hadn't even presented it well.

"You're moody today," Maureen said in choir. "You wouldn't smile or joke with anyone at lunch."

"I didn't get a lot of sleep," Cassie replied as Maureen elbowed her in the ribs over and over again. "Quit it."

"Just trying to get you to smile." Maureen widened her mouth, showing all her teeth as her lips curved upward. "See?"

"Yeah, you look goofy." Cassie gave her a light shove, and Maureen pretended to topple over.

"And everyone thinks you're the nice one."

That did make Cassie laugh. "Are you going to set them straight?"

"They won't believe me." Maureen grinned. "Here." She reached into her purse and pulled out a half-eaten chocolate muffin, stuffed back in the original wrapper. "This will make you feel better."

Cassie's mouth watered at the sight. "I can't eat that."

"Sure you can." Maureen shook it at her. "It's a muffin. They're healthy."

Were they? Cassie relented, taking the chocolaty confection.

CHAPTER THIRTY-ONE
Considering Promises

"Guess what!" Amity said at lunch. "Adam and I got back together!"

Cassie hid her face behind a cup of water. Was this going to be the most important gossip of their eighth grade year—if Amity and Adam were together or not?

"Hey, Cassie," Janice said, sitting down next to her, "I heard something today, and I wanted to ask you about it."

"What?" Cassie asked, swiveling to face her.

Janice lowered her voice. "Was there a boy that used to live at your house?"

"Yes." This wasn't a secret. "Elek. He lived with us last year for, I don't know, maybe a month. Why?"

"That's what Riley said in civics class."

"Why?" Cassie repeated. Where was this going? "He wasn't my boyfriend or anything."

"No, I didn't think that," Janice said. But she seemed awfully reluctant to say whatever it was she did think. "It got brought up in class that a boy was arrested for stealing a car and nearly killing someone. And Riley said he used to live with your family."

Cassie gasped, a cold chill running through her veins. "It

couldn't have been Elek. He's kind and considerate and honest. He would never do that."

Janice nodded, looking worried. "Maybe it wasn't him. I thought you should know, though. In case you hear something."

Cassie swallowed hard, feeling sick inside. During the weeks that Elek lived with her family, he'd been like an older brother. He'd watched out for her and talked with her and helped her with her chores. Even before then, he'd always been friendly at church and when he came in to the soccer store.

It had to have been someone else.

Her parents didn't mention anything about Elek at dinner, and Cassie relaxed. If anything had happened to him, his mother would have called.

"I have my writer's conference tomorrow," Cassie said, beaming at her mom. "I'm going to bring my draft with me in case they have publishers there. This could be my ticket!"

"I'm so happy for you," Mrs. Jones said. "And it's time to start thinking about who you want at your birthday party."

Right! Fourteen was quickly approaching. "Amity and Andrea," she said without hesitation.

"No Riley?"

Cassie rolled her eyes. "Not this year."

⁂

Cassie got up early to curl her hair for her field trip. It was such a lengthy endeavor, but so worth it. She couldn't wait to meet other kid writers like herself.

She hummed a little as she stood in front of the bathroom mirror at school, holding her makeup compact and brushing eyeshadow and blush on her face. She had to make sure she looked good today.

She snagged Amity and Andrea as soon as they came in the bathroom. Luckily, they were the first ones there.

"My birthday's this Friday," she said. "I want you both to

come."

"Oo, I can't wait!" Amity said.

"Wouldn't miss it," Andrea agreed.

Cassie tried not to dwell on how Andrea missed last year's birthday.

"Is Riley coming?" Amity asked in a slightly snotty voice.

"Good grief, no," Cassie said, annoyed. "Why would she?"

"I don't know, Maureen said she's your best friend."

Cassie threw her arms up. "Like Maureen would know! You guys are my best friends."

Amity smiled. "Aw. You're so sweet."

Janice came into the bathroom, scanning their faces until she saw Cassie. "Cassie," she said, "you've got to see this." She grabbed Cassie's arm and hauled her into a corner.

"What? What is it?" Janice didn't usually act so dramatic and urgent.

"Here," Janice whispered, uncurling a newspaper clipping and pressing it into Cassie's hand.

As soon as Cassie started to read it, her blood went cold. She gripped the paper so tight it trembled, and she had to read twice to fully process the words.

Elek Mellas, 18, Springdale resident, was arrested Monday evening for grand theft auto and attempted homicide. Being held on bail for . . .

The words blurred before Cassie's eyes, and she took a staggering breath. It was Elek. It really was. He was in jail. The makeup compact slipped from her hand and shattered on the floor. She took another shaky breath and then began to sob.

"What is it? What happened?"

Amity and Andrea descended on Cassie like vultures for a feast. Cassie leaned her head into Janice, who held her while answering their questions.

"She just found out a friend of hers is in jail. She's sad."

That part was obvious. The other girls made noises of

sympathy and consolation.

The bell rang and Cassie straightened. She needed to pull herself together; she had a conference to go to. Even though she felt all torn up inside, she knew she couldn't waste this opportunity.

"Thanks for letting me know," Cassie said quietly. She threw her broken compact in the trash and went to her locker.

"Oo, pretty!" Cara said, walking past her and tugging on her hair. Her smile dropped when she saw Cassie's face.

"What is it?" she said. And then she wrapped Cassie up in a hug. "It's okay. It'll be fine, whatever it is."

Cassie wiped her eyes again. "Yeah. I know. Thanks." Her smile wobbled, but she kept it in place. She couldn't be crying like this all day.

⚘

Ms. Talo's expression morphed from excitement to concern when Cassie walked into the English classroom.

"Cassie, are you okay? Are you still coming to the conference?"

Cassie bobbed her head, clutching her binder with the manuscript beneath her arm. "I am. I just got some bad news this morning and I'm a little . . ." Her voice faltered. "I'm dealing with it."

Ms. Talo stepped up to her and put her hands on her shoulders. "It seems like bad things always happen when we're in the middle of something wonderful. Put it out of your head for the day and focus on the conference. When you get home, you can think about it again."

Good advice, even if easier said than done. Cassie took a deep, cleansing breath and closed her eyes. When she opened them again, she was ready.

Two ninth graders rode with Cassie and Ms. Talo to the conference, which was being held at a retreat center in Fayetteville.

"What do you write?" the ninth grade boy asked her. "Poetry?"

"I like poetry," Cassie said, "but I love writing stories. I brought my book with me." She patted the folder in her lap.

"Book?" he asked. "Like a collection of your stories?"

"One story. It's about three hundred pages."

The girl gasped and leaned forward to see Cassie better. "You wrote a real book?"

Cassie nodded, a little shy. "What about you guys? What do you write?"

"I write poetry," the girl said. "I brought my collection."

"Comics," the boy said. "I like to draw as much as I like to write."

"Wow, that's cool," Cassie said. "If I ever need an artist, I know who to contact."

He laughed and leaned back in his seat.

The first meeting was in a big room, and kids gathered from all the local schools, maybe thirty or forty kids total. A woman got up and spoke to them about listening to their muses and finding their creative talent, but Cassie didn't pay her too much mind. She had no problem listening to her muse. It was getting her muse to shut up that was harder.

She glanced around at the adults in the room. Which ones were publishers? Editors? They were who she needed to talk to. Her fingers caressed the colorful binder, thick with her finished manuscript. It was time to give life to this baby.

The woman broke them into groups and sent them to what she called "Break out session one."

Cassie followed her instructions and went to the third room on the right. Unlike the big room, which had been full of chairs, this one had rows of skinny tables. She sat down behind one.

"Hi, kids!" a peppy woman said, walking to the front of the room. "So you like to write?"

Cassie joined in the excited cheer.

"I know! That's why you're here! And you probably want to get published someday!"

Yes. That's what Cassie wanted.

"Let me tell you all about drafting your short story, because that's going to be your ticket in." She pointed at all of them as she spoke. "Before you can submit your story to a magazine, you need to write it. And it has to be phenomenal."

She launched into the elements of writing a short story, and Cassie let her pencil drop. She exhaled in disappointment. She didn't want to be published in a magazine, and she didn't want to write short stories. She'd written a novel. She wanted to find a book publisher.

The next two sessions were also a disappointment for Cassie, who didn't want to learn the elements of a plot or how to create great characters. They broke for lunch, and she hoped the next one, which was a critique session, would be better.

A man in a sweater vest with a pink tie led this group.

"This is where you'll see how well your peers respond to your writing," he said. "Hopefully you all brought a sample?" He looked around the oval table, and heads bobbed.

Cassie had brought more than a sample. She had the whole book here, if anyone wanted to read it.

"Then let's go around the table. Read as much as you want, though I'll cut you off if you go past ten minutes. And then everyone can give feedback. Remember, critical feedback points out what is wrong without tearing it down. We want to encourage each other to improve."

Cassie contributed to the session, complimenting and giving suggestions. When it was finally her turn, she took an excited breath and then plunged in, reading the first chapter. Nothing too exciting happened in this chapter; it was where she introduced the four friends and gave a bit of history on how they met, what their personalities were like. There was a tiny hint of the criminal element and some tension among the friends, just enough, she hoped, to entice the reader to want to find out more. She finished reading and set the pages down, waiting to see what they would say.

"Is this a completed book?" the teacher asked.

"Yes."

"Very nice. Kids, what do you think?"

"I really liked the way you described the characters," a girl said. "I could see them in my head."

"And the foreshadowing. I knew something bad was coming," a boy commented.

"I want to know what happens next."

Cassie beamed as the feedback came in, all of it positive.

"Sounds like you have all the great makings of a fiction writer," the teacher said. "Keep it up, and I'm sure we'll see your name in the future."

Cassie's heart swelled with pride. But she still wasn't sure how to get published.

As the next kid read his piece, someone tapped Cassie's arm. She swiveled enough to see the girl next to her handing her a note. Cassie took it, raising an eyebrow curiously. She opened it up.

Hi! I really liked your writing style and think your story is great. Can I read more? We can keep in touch.

Cassie pursed her lips to keep her smile hidden. Her first fan mail.

At home during dinner Cassie told her family all about the conference.

"And I didn't find a publisher," she concluded with a sigh, "but I got a brochure that lists different publishers on it. I have to submit a query letter first."

"What's a query letter?" Emily asked.

Cassie shrugged. "I'm not sure. I might have to call them and ask."

The phone rang, and Mrs. Jones turned around to grab it. "Hello? Oh, hi! No, it's so good to hear from you, we've been so worried!"

She looked at her husband and whispered, "It's Elek."

Cassie stiffened, all of the emotions from the morning rushing back to her. Her parents knew about Elek, then. How long had they known? She tried to discern the conversation from her mom's side, but Mrs. Jones took the phone into the laundry room and closed the door. A moment later she came out and hung up the phone, then sat down as if nothing had happened.

"Well?" Cassie said. "What news?"

Her mom blinked at her in surprise, then looked down. "Stay after dinner and we'll talk."

Cassie waited while everyone finished eating, then helped clear the table to get them out a little faster.

"Now tell me what's going on with Elek."

Her parents exchanged looks.

"You might want to sit down, Cassie," Mrs. Jones said.

Cassie sat. "I already know he was arrested. I know what he did."

"You do? How?"

"Someone brought me a newspaper clipping at school."

"Oh," Mrs. Jones said softly. "Well, that was Elek. He's in

jail. He's very sorry about what he did and doesn't even know why he did it."

"Is it true? Did he really threaten someone with a gun?"

"Yes."

"Where did he get it?"

"An excellent question, and I don't have the answer. I do know he's in a lot of trouble."

The tears stung Cassie's eyes again. "He ruined his future."

Her mom took her hand and squeezed her fingers. "He's closed some doors and put himself on a different path than he was on. But hopefully it's not ruined."

That was looking at things positively. But Cassie's heart ached for Elek. Some things could not be undone.

CHAPTER THIRTY-TWO
Birthday Blues

"Cassie, are you ready to go?" Mrs. Jones called from her bedroom.

"Almost!" Cassie yelled back. She had voice lessons in half an hour and church after that, but right now she had the telephone in her hand, her heart beating a mile a minute as she tried to find the courage to make this phone call.

Just do it, she told herself, and she dialed the number.

"Raspberry Publishing."

"Hi." Cassie took a deep breath, trying to still the flutter in her heart. "I got a brochure about your publishing company from a writer's conference I went to. I have a book I want to send in."

"Okay. We have a standard set of steps you need to go through first. Did the brochure have instructions?"

"Yes." Cassie nodded. "It said first I need to submit a query letter. What is that?"

"Do you know what a query is?"

Cassie furrowed her brow. A query was a question. But that didn't fit in the context of a letter. "No."

The woman's voice grew more superior. "As a writer, a dictionary is your best friend. If you don't know what something is, you should look it up."

"Okay," Cassie said, embarrassed now and feeling chastised. "Want me to get one?"

"No, I'll tell you. A query is a question."

Yes, she knew that. Cassie pressed her lips together to keep from getting irritated. "How does that fit in a letter?"

"Your letter is going to be a question for the publisher. Asking if we want to look at your book. So you tell us something about it, make it sound enticing, and send us the letter."

"Okay," Cassie said. This woman clearly thought she was an idiot. "Thanks." She hung up the phone. "Time to make my query letter."

⁂

Ms. Malcolm presented Cassie with a trophy at voice lessons.

"You were my number one student last month," she said. "You learned all your songs and had the best results on the pitch tests."

"Really?" Cassie exclaimed. She held the trophy tenderly. Her first one.

"You become a better singer every day. Just keep practicing. Oh." Ms. Malcolm reached into her bag and pulled out a chocolate bar. "Happy birthday."

Cassie beamed. Her birthday was Friday. She was almost fourteen.

"Grandma wants you to come over to her apartment for your birthday," Mrs. Jones said as she drove Cassie to church. "But since your party is on Friday, I thought we could go over tomorrow."

"I don't really want to see Grandma," Cassie said. Her dad's mom lived nearby in Fayetteville, at the old-people home. But Grandma wasn't very nice, and Cassie didn't like to be around her.

"She loves you, Cassie. It's not her fault she's the way she is."

"I know," Cassie grumbled. Grandma had a stroke decades earlier that changed the synapses in her brain, trapping her in perpetual adolescence. And she was mean, like the girls in the movies who tried to make people feel bad.

"We'll just go for dinner. But I need you to act happy, Cassie. You've been so sad lately."

"Just because of Elek," Cassie said. "It really troubles me that he would do that."

"I know, sweetie. But remember, being sad and depressed is the opposite of light. And if you don't have light, you can't help other people."

Cassie thought on those words all the way to church. If being light and happy would help other people, she would try to be lighter and happier.

Riley stood in the hallway just inside the church doors, her arms crossed over her chest, a hard frown on her face.

"Riley," Cassie said, slowing down to step beside her. "What's wrong?"

"I need to talk to you," Riley said. She grabbed Cassie's arm and dragged her around the corner to the bathroom.

"What is it?" Cassie asked, shaking free. She didn't like this habit people had of pulling her off to corners for secret talks.

"Amity told me she's going to your house on Friday for your birthday."

"Amity told you?" Cassie crinkled her nose. "Since when do you and Amity talk?"

"I guess since she wanted to make sure I knew." Riley's eyes glistened, and her nose pinkened. "I thought I was your best friend."

Not since the fifth grade. "Riley, I have a lot of best friends. And my mom said I could only have two people over."

"So you picked Amity Stafford over me?"

Cassie put her hands on Riley's shoulders, trying to console her. "Amity's new here. I thought it would be nice for her to be invited to my party."

"Whatever." Riley jerked away. "Andrea dumped you like a hot potato last year, and now that she's talking to you, you're all over her like a lost puppy."

"I am not!" Cassie's face warmed, anger fueling up inside her. "She's my friend, and she happens to like me."

"Well, don't call me if she doesn't show up."

"I certainly won't," Cassie snapped, "since you're the only person I know who does that."

Riley's eyes narrowed, giving her face a pinched look. She turned and marched out of the bathroom, though her attempt to slam the door fell short as it slid slowly back into place.

Cassie sighed, immediately feeling guilty for fighting. It wasn't even true. Last year Andrea *had* ditched Cassie.

☙✦❧

Elek's mom called that evening.

Cassie answered the phone and took it to Mrs. Jones. "It's for you," she said, handing her the cordless. Then she returned to the kitchen and sat there, tapping her nails on the table.

What was being said? What more had happened with Elek?

Jumping up, she ran downstairs to the other phone in the basement. She picked it up and turned it on very quietly, hoping no one would hear her.

" . . . never did anything like this before," his mom said, tears clogging her already heavily accented voice. "Has he called you?"

"He did call us," Mrs. Jones said, her voice soothing. "We talked to him yesterday."

"What did he say? What happened?"

"Just that he's sorry. He's not sure why he did it."

"Maybe drugs, maybe he was high. Not like him. He's always been so good."

Except he'd been having trouble with his friends. Cassie remembered that was the reason Elek moved in with them in the first place. His mom had been worried about the influences around him.

"We have no money. Can't get a lawyer for him."

"The state will get him a lawyer. Don't worry. He'll be taken care of."

"But he's guilty." She sobbed, her anguish evident through the phone line. "Who will protect him?"

Cassie slowly slid the phone back into place, hot tears stinging her face. What a horrible situation Elek had gotten himself into.

"I'm going to see Elek at the jail after church on Sunday," Mrs. Jones told Cassie as they cleared the table after dinner. "Do you want to come?"

"To the jail?" The thought terrified her.

"That's where he is."

Cassie didn't want to go to the jail. All kinds of crazies were there. But she wanted to see Elek, she wanted to support him and show him she still cared. "Okay. I'll come."

"We'll have to go straight from church. Visiting hours don't last very long."

"Okay."

⚜

Mrs. Jones picked Cassie up from school so Amity and Andrea could ride home with her for the birthday party on Friday.

"You were like, the queen today, Cassie," Amity said, bouncing around in the backseat. The three girls sat in the very back of the van, where they could talk without being overheard. "I think everyone talked to you."

"It was pretty cool," Cassie admitted. Her name had been called over the morning announcements, and almost everyone she saw said happy birthday to her.

"So." Amity pulled out her phone and scrolled through the numbers. "It's time we called Miles."

"No way." Cassie slapped the phone out of Amity's hand.

Amity gave her an impish look. "Andrea's going to back me

this time. Right, Andrea?"

"Yep," Andrea said, looking up from a text message.

Cassie panicked as Amity pressed a name on her phone. "No, Amity, don't!"

Amity put one finger in her ear and spoke into the phone. "Hi, is Miles there? This is Amity."

Cassie made another desperate lunge for the phone. "That was so last year, Amity. I don't like him anymore." She shot a pleading look toward Andrea, but Andrea wasn't even watching.

"Hi, Miles, how are you? Great!" Amity put one hand and a leg in front of her, fielding off Cassie's attacks. "Did you say happy birthday to Cassie today? No? Well, I'm going to her house, I'll tell her for you. No problem." She smiled. "You know she likes you, right?"

Cassie gasped. The fight went out of her as she pressed her hands to her chest. She wanted to yell, to scream that it wasn't true, but she couldn't. Her mom would hear, Miles would hear—and it was true. "As a friend. Just as a friend," she yelped.

"Do you like her?"

Cassie clapped her hands over her ears, wishing it would stop.

"Sure. That's fair. Well, have a good weekend, Miles. We'll see you Monday." She hung up the phone and gave Cassie a sympathetic smile. "He doesn't like you."

"Amity, you jerk!" Cassie slapped her forearm hard, but Amity didn't seem to notice.

"He said you're sweet and pretty and a good friend. But just a friend."

Cassie sucked in deep breaths, humiliated and rejected. Amity slid closer and put an arm around her.

"He used to like you, but you took too long. People move on."

"Me, too." Cassie shoved Amity off her. "I don't like him

anymore either."

On the other side, Andrea gave a little laugh. "I think you made Cassie mad, Amity."

"Understatement," Cassie huffed, pulling her knees up and crossing her arms over her chest. She should have invited Riley.

"You're not really mad, are you?" Amity asked when they got back to Cassie's house.

"I'm furious," Cassie said. But she could feel the anger fading already.

"It's good to know, isn't it?" Amity said. She and Andrea followed Cassie into her room and dumped their things on the bed. "At least you're not left wondering if he likes you now."

"I told you I don't like him anymore," Cassie said. "It's hardly relevant."

"What does relevant mean?" Amity murmured to Andrea.

"Beats me," Andrea said.

"Speak English, Cassie," Amity said, laughing and throwing a pillow at her.

Mrs. Jones came to the doorway. "How does Mexican sound for dinner?"

"Great!" Amity said, perking right up. "I love nachos!"

Mrs. Jones let the girls sit by themselves at the restaurant, and Amity quickly ordered nachos and a quesadilla. Andrea glanced sideways at Cassie before ordering an enchilada with extra cheese sauce.

"It's your birthday, Cassie," Andrea said. "One night won't hurt you."

Cassie liked the thought. "I'll have a chimichanga."

The waiter nodded. "Okay, thank you."

Amity leaned forward and bobbed her head toward the waiter after he left. "He's kind of cute."

"Too old," Cassie said. "He has to be at least seventeen."

"I didn't know you like Mexicans," Andrea said.

"I like them all," Amity said with a wink.

They fell silent, and then the waiter returned with their food. Cassie inhaled, her appetite less than it had been ten minutes ago.

CHAPTER THIRTY-THREE
Fortunate Events

Cassie found Riley before the sermon started on Sunday.

"I'm sorry we argued," she said. "I feel really bad about it. I can't invite everyone I want, and I didn't think you and Amity would have a good time together."

"Did you have a good time with Amity?" Riley asked.

"Yes," Cassie lied. "We had fun. But you can come over another weekend and we can have a second birthday party."

"I don't want to be mad anymore either."

"Then let's not be."

"Okay." Riley cracked a smile. "I'm not mad."

"Me neither."

"Well, happy birthday." Riley sighed. "You get to go to Sunday School with the older kids now. Tyler's in there."

"I'll watch him for you."

They both laughed, and Cassie said, "I'm much more excited for the dance this Saturday than staring at the back of Tyler's head."

"I'm so envious." Riley stuck out her lower lip. "You have to tell me everything, especially if there are cute boys."

"You know I will," Cassie promised.

Their mothers beckoned them to come sit down, and the

girls separated.

Cassie felt a little nervous to go to the other Sunday School class, but the teacher welcomed her when she came in and made her feel at ease. She looked for an empty spot and saw one next to Sue. She went and sat down, giving Sue a smile even though the girls weren't friends.

Sue bobbed her head in greeting, then turned and spoke to Michelle the whole time. Not once did she glance at Cassie or talk to her.

None of the other kids did, either, not even Tyler, who sat by his brother Jason, and they had their own quiet conversation.

Cassie swallowed hard. Just a few more months until Riley turned fourteen, and then Cassie wouldn't be alone.

༺ ༻

"Ready, Cassie?" Mrs. Jones said after church.

They had come in two separate vehicles so Cassie and her mom could go to the jail while the other kids went home.

"I guess so." Cassie clutched her scriptures to her chest and climbed into the car beside her mother. "You think anyone else will be there in a dress?"

"Oh, I'm sure. Lots of people go to church before visiting loved ones in jail."

"What time are visiting hours?"

"Until five o'clock today. We don't want to miss it."

The jail was only a few miles down the road, and by the time they parked and got to the visitor's entrance, it was only a little after one.

A long line had already formed outside a window with thick glass. Cassie evaluated the other people in the line and stood closer to her mother. A man with shoulder-length greasy hair and chains connecting his vest to his billowy black pants rested with one arm against the brick wall interior. There was no smoking inside, but somehow the scent lingered in the air. A skinny woman with long hair and sores on her face stood stock-still in line, hands clasped together and eyes glazed as she stared at the window. A much larger woman bumped up next to the man beside her, so close he was able to slide his hand in her back pocket without moving more than an inch.

Another woman got in line behind Cassie, reeking as if she hadn't bathed in a month. It took all Cassie's willpower not to plug her nose.

The line inched forward until it was their turn at the window. A man in a uniform behind the glass told them to write down their names and who they were visiting, and then sit down and wait their turn.

"Only two visitors at a time," he told them.

"There's only the two of us," Mrs. Jones said.

Cassie followed her mom to one of the hard, yellow chairs. She felt conspicuous with nothing in her hands.

The time slipped by ever so slowly. She had nothing to read, nothing to do but sit and stare at the people. She watched the doors leading out of the lobby open and a guard step out to call the next name. One man holding a hardback book stepped up with a teenage boy, and the guard frisked him. Then he took the book and turned it upside down, shaking all the pages. Finally he removed a utility knife from his belt and cut the cover right off the book. The guard dumped it in the trash and gave the book back to the man.

"Why did he do that?" Cassie murmured to her mom.

"The book could be used as a weapon if someone's determined enough."

There were probably a number of such determined people in this place. Cassie leaned her head on her mom's shoulder and closed her eyes, trying to wish the time away.

"How long has it been?" she murmured after what felt like an eternity.

"Almost three hours," Mrs. Jones whispered. "Should be our turn soon."

But it wasn't. When the stinky woman who had come in behind them got called, Mrs. Jones stood up. "I'm just going to check what's taking so long."

She came back a minute later, looking more riled up than a hornet's nest. "Let's go."

"What?" Cassie stood, blinking in confusion, and followed her mom out of the jail. She inhaled a deep gulp of air, never noticing before that it could have flavor. The air tasted sweet. "Aren't we going to see Elek?"

"Apparently there's a new rule: Only two visitors per day."

"But we're only two people.

"Yes. But Elek's mom visited him this morning."

"Well, why didn't they say something?" Cassie exclaimed. "One of us could have gone in!"

"Because they don't care about the visitors. They threw our sign in sheet away when they realized we couldn't both go in and didn't bother to tell us."

Cassie might have cried if she wasn't as angry as her mom. "They made us wait four hours for nothing?"

"That's exactly right."

The disappointment settled in Cassie's chest like a lead weight. Not only had they wasted the day, but she hadn't even gotten to see Elek.

⚜

The phone rang Monday evening as Cassie sat working on homework. She answered it absently. "Hello?"

"Hello, I'm looking for Cassandra Jones. Is she there?"

Cassie straightened up. Usually people calling the landline wanted her parents. "Yes, this is Cassandra."

"Cassandra, I'm calling from Raspberry Publications. We received your query letter last week for your book, *Walk Beside Me*?"

"Yes," Cassie said, an anxious, sick feeling rising in her throat.

"We'd like to request the entire manuscript. Can you mail it to us?"

She pressed her hand to her chest. "Yes. I sure can." Somehow she spoke without shaking or sounding too excited. "What's the address?" She jotted down what the woman said, then hung up the phone. "Yes!" she shouted, throwing her arms up in the air.

"What is it?" Emily asked, poking her head out of their bedroom.

Cassie turned around and ran to her mom's room, then banged on the door.

"Come in," Mrs. Jones said.

Cassie pushed open the door and found her mom on the far side of the bed, cutting out strips of paper. "They asked for my book! They want to read the whole thing!"

"Cassie, that's great!" Mrs. Jones jumped up and hugged her. "Really good. Congrats, honey!"

Cassie couldn't wait to tell everyone at school.

※

Cassie knew Amity and Andrea and Maureen wouldn't care about her book. They might even make fun of her.

But Nicole would care, and Emmett, and Leigh Ann. She hunted them down in the locker hall.

"Guess what!" she said, grabbing Nicole's arm just as she started to take Jimmy's hand. "There's a publisher that wants my book!"

"What? No way!" Nicole said.

"Hey, that's great," Jimmy said. "Are they going to publish it?"

"Oh, no," Cassie said, embarrassed she'd given the wrong impression. "They just want to read it. But isn't it cool?"

"You're so cool," Nicole said. "I can't wait to have you sign the book for me when it gets published."

Had Nicole just said she was cool? Cassie shook it off even as the praise went to her head. "You'll definitely get a copy."

"Get a copy of what?"

Cassie turned around at the sound of Emmett's voice, her face already breaking into a smile. "My book! A publisher—wants—" She faltered.

Emmett wasn't alone. Next to him stood Miles, and suddenly, Cassie couldn't breathe. And not in a good way. Her mind flashed back to the conversation Amity had with him just a few days ago, and the person standing in front of her felt like the enemy.

"I've got to go," she said, pushing past them both and walking the other direction as fast as she could without running.

Thanks to Amity, Miles knew Cassie liked him. And Cassie knew for certain that he didn't like her.

⁂

Riley was more excited for Cassie to go to the dance on Saturday than Cassie. Riley texted her nonstop, reminding Cassie that she wanted all the details.

Cassie, on the other hand, found a family of butterflies had decided to take flight in her stomach.

"Your first dance," Mrs. Jones said when Cassie came into the kitchen. She held Cassie out at arm's length and smiled at her. "Are you ready?"

"Yes." Cassie had curled her hair and wore a pink shirt with a black skirt. A matching pink ribbon adorned her dark locks. She bounced around anxiously. "What if no one asks me to dance?"

"Oh, they will. These church boys are bred to be polite."

The dance was all the way at the Rogers building, half an hour away. Mrs. Jones dropped Cassie off, and she walked toward the building conspicuously, hoping she would see someone she knew very soon so she wouldn't have to be by herself.

Kids were flooding the building from every door. Cassie wandered into the gym and marveled at its transformation. The lights were dimmed, streamers strung across the ceiling, a long table set up against the wall and covered in food. A few chairs were set up, but mostly it was empty. Cassie found an empty spot and stood there, pretending she wasn't nervous and feeling out of place.

"Well, Cassandra Jones."

A giggle had her turning her head to the left. There stood Elise, still with her black hair and black eyeliner, giving Cassie a happy smile.

This new Elise intimidated her, but she was still a familiar face. Cassie smiled and peeled away from the wall.

"Hey."

Elise grabbed her in a big hug and rocked her like a baby. "You're finally old enough to come! I've been waiting for you! Come on. You need to meet the guys before it starts." She took Cassie's hand and pulled her from boy cluster to boy cluster, introducing her with a flirtatious tilt of her head and a breathy laugh.

Then the music started, and Elise slipped her hand away. "You're on your own now. Have fun!" She gave a little wave and melted into the crowd.

Before Cassie could panic or make her way back to the wall, the tall boy in front of her said, "Want to dance?"

She spun back to him. "Um, yes. Sure." She didn't know how to dance! Why hadn't she thought of that before she came?

It turned out to be very easy. He placed a hand on her waist and took her other hand, then proceeded to walk with her in a wobbly circle while the slow song played.

This wasn't how Cassie imagined dancing, but it was nice. When the song finished, he thanked her and moved away just as another guy came in and asked. She lost track of their names, even their faces, and she laughed so much that by the end of the night she'd lost her voice.

"I've never seen you here. Are you new?" a boy with reddish blond hair asked.

"No," Cassie whispered, the best she could with her vanishing voice. "I just turned fourteen."

"No way!" He raised both brows. "I thought you were sixteen, at least."

Cassie smiled. "You're the first. Everyone always thinks I'm younger."

"Well, you're very pretty," he said, and Cassie didn't know what to say to that.

Then the song ended and she danced with another, then another.

When the lights turned on and the dance ended, Cassie fluttered to the door to watch for her mom, a blissful happiness drifting around her.

"How was it?" Mrs. Jones asked as Cassie closed the van door. "Did you have fun?"

"So much fun," Cassie whispered. "I lost my voice." She beckoned to her throat. "I danced six times!" She held up her fingers in case her mom couldn't hear. She smiled and leaned her head against the headrest. She'd never felt so beautiful and couldn't wait for the next dance.

CHAPTER THIRTY-FOUR
Desperate Measures

"I have one more song for you to learn before the spring recital," Ms. Malcolm said, peering at Cassie over the rim of her reading glasses.

"One more?" Cassie swallowed. She'd already learned three, and she worried she'd get up to sing and get them mixed up. She still got nervous, no matter how many times she performed in front of people.

"Yes. Your voice is maturing and you're grasping the more difficult pieces quite well. I want to show you off."

When she put it that way . . . Cassie straightened her shoulders. "Okay. I can do it."

Mrs. Jones picked Cassie up after lessons and drove her to church for the usual Wednesday night activities. They passed the mall on the way there, and Cassie said, "Can we go shopping? I'd really like to get a new dress for the spring recital."

Her mom hesitated, and Cassie held her breath. Her parents had struggled financially for the past year, and it was highly possible a new dress simply wasn't in the budget. But then she nodded.

"That would be fun. How about Friday after school? I'll pick you up."

"Sure!" Cassie could hardly believe her mom had agreed.

Friday, Cassie waited out front of the building with the other car riders. She saw Miles and Andrew but stayed away from them, instead standing with Amity and Andrea even though she wasn't interested in whatever video they were watching on Amity's phone.

Anything to avoid Miles. They hadn't spoken since last month when Amity told him about Cassie's secret crush, which obviously wasn't so secret any more. A few times she'd seen him walking toward her as if he was going to talk to her, but Cassie always moved away before he could. She couldn't bear the embarrassment of having him tell her to her face that she was a sweet girl and a nice friend but nothing else.

"There's my mom," Amity said, putting away her phone. "Bye, guys!"

With nobody else to talk to, Andrea turned her attention to Cassie. "Why is your mom picking you up again?"

"We're going shopping."

"Oh yeah! For what?"

"I need a dress for my spring recital."

"Oo, fun! Send me pictures."

The familiar blue van pulled up to the curb. "I will," Cassie said. She didn't glance back at Miles or Andrew to see if they had noticed her. She gave Andrea a side hug and walked to the car.

"How are your friends?" Mrs. Jones asked, waving at Andrea as they pulled away.

"Fine, I think."

"Wasn't that Miles Hansen out there?"

"We're not friends," Cassie said.

"Oh."

That one little word left too much room for interpretation, so Cassie quickly changed the subject. "Where are we going shopping?"

"I thought we'd go to the mall, if that's okay?"

"Perfect!"

Mrs. Jones chuckled. "I didn't know you like clothes shopping. Usually when we go to the mall, you just want to go to the bookstore."

"I have to branch out sometimes," Cassie said, her face warming.

"It'll be fun. We'll find you a dress, then we can go out to dinner, just the two of us." Mrs. Jones smiled at her.

They stopped at the high-end department store at the front of the mall, which surprised Cassie.

"Can we afford this?"

"Of course." Her mom gave her a serious look. "Just don't buy the most expensive dress you find."

Cassie laughed.

The spring fashion was all on display, and Cassie found several floral, knee-length dresses with flaring skirts. She loved the style.

"Grab a few, let's try some on," her mom said.

Cassie did, and then she hesitated as they walked to the dressing room with her selections in her arms.

"Are you going to come in with me?" she asked.

"Don't I always?"

"Well, you don't have to."

"You don't want me to?" There was no mistaking the hurt that flashed through her mom's eyes.

"I guess it's fine," Cassie said, embarrassed they were having this conversation. "Just . . . don't look, okay?"

Now her mom laughed. "Is this a modesty thing? I'm your mom, Cassie. I've seen it all."

That statement did nothing to ease her embarrassment.

Once in the dressing room, Cassie's fingers lingered on the hem of her shirt, reluctant to pull it off. She undid her jeans but didn't remove them either.

"I'll close my eyes. How's that?" Mrs. Jones said.

"Okay," Cassie said. She waited until her mom's eyes were closed tight, and then she yanked the shirt over her head. Holding her breath, she grabbed the dress off the hanger and dropped it over her shoulders before letting out an exhale.

"You can look now," she said.

Mrs. Jones quirked her lip upward as if fighting a smile. Then her eyes softened. "It's beautiful. What do you think?"

Cassie flattened down the soft cottony material, looking toward her feet and examining her belly. "It doesn't make me look fat?"

"Nothing could. You're too skinny."

Cassie turned sideways to study her reflection. She gave a little sigh and pushed up on her bra. A few weeks earlier she'd padded it with toilet paper, but she never could smooth out the lumps, so she'd quit doing it. "I don't have any boobs."

"Well, honey, they're made out of fat, and there's none on you."

Cassie tilted her head and considered that. She hadn't put much stock in her mom saying she was too skinny. But she was as flat-chested as a seven-year-old. Was it possible there was a connection? "Maybe I'm just a late bloomer."

"Maybe," her mom said in an unconvinced tone.

She looked again at the dress, at the extra fabric around her chest, made to support the budding breasts of a teenage girl. "Could we look at bras while we're here?"

Mrs. Jones looked at her, and Cassie was pretty sure from the twinkle in her eye that she knew exactly what Cassie wanted. "We could."

When they left the mall three hours later, Cassie felt pleased with her purchases. She had even eaten everything her mom ordered for dinner—in exchange for one very special item.

A padded bra.

But by the time she got home, the pleased feeling had traveled into her belly to join her dinner and morphed into a pointed rock.

Mrs. Jones wanted Cassie to show off her dress to her father, and Cassie held it up, keeping a big smile. Then, finally, her mom released her, and Cassie fled to her room.

She crouched over the toilet, taking deep breaths to calm her racing heart, her hands trembling where they gripped the porcelain bowl.

Something's wrong with me.

The thought hadn't occurred to her before. She just wanted to be beautiful and popular. Being thin seemed like the sure way to do it, and it had worked, to some extent. Andrea had quit being her friend last year, but when Cassie lost weight, they became friends again.

If she gained it back, would she lose Andrea? Amity? Cara?

Janice would be her friend. She always had been. And even Riley hadn't seemed to notice if Cassie was fat or thin.

The small lumps of chocolate cake she'd managed to evict from her stomach floated in the toilet like clumps of pudding. She closed her eyes, then shut the lid and leaned her head on it.

Dieting was one thing. Making herself throw up was something else. There was no pretending this was normal. This made her feel worse than eating too much. She felt ashamed.

Cassie flushed the toilet and stood up, gargling water before drying her hands. She wouldn't do this again. She wasn't that messed up.

⁍⸺✦⸺⁌

"I made myself throw up on Friday," Cassie confessed to Andrea during first hour. Once again they had the hallway to themselves while they graded papers.

"You did?" Andrea's blue eyes went wide. "How?"

Cassie waved her off. "Doesn't matter. I don't want to do it again." Unbidden, the tears welled up. "It hurt. And it doesn't make me feel good."

Andrea remained quiet for a moment, marking a paper and

putting it into one pile before doing another. "Why did you do it?"

"Because I ate some chocolate cake and felt really gross."

"What are you going to do?"

Cassie shook her head. "I don't know, but I can't do that again."

"Do you think you should see a doctor?" Andrea said the words slowly, almost as if she were measuring their weight.

Cassie looked at Andrea. She'd gotten used to Andrea's casual friendship, the laughter and fun, but one thing she hadn't felt was that Andrea actually cared for her. "I think I'm okay. I just need to control my eating."

"You're still having your period, right?"

Funny Andrea should ask that. Cassie couldn't remember the last time she'd had it. She shrugged. "It's not always regular."

Andrea put another graded paper on the pile. "I heard that Tylenol is an appetite suppressant. You could try taking some before lunch."

Mr. Adams kept Tylenol in his school bag, and he trusted Cassie enough to let her take some when she needed it. She felt a little guilty, taking advantage of that trust, but she had to see if it would work. "Okay."

"My mom also has laxatives at home. I could bring you some. Then if you do eat too much, you don't have to throw it up."

"That might be a better option," Cassie agreed.

"I'll bring you some tomorrow."

"Thanks," Cassie said. But instead of feeling relieved, the knot in her chest tightened. She'd just sucked someone else into her evil plan when what she needed was someone to suck her out.

⁂

"You're really quiet."

Cassie looked over at Riley Wednesday evening at church

and forced a smile. The two girls were alone in the chapel, skipping the first aid class going on in the gym. Riley had asked to talk, and Cassie had agreed.

"I have a big recital on Saturday, and I'm thinking about my songs," Cassie said. "I have to sing four."

"Is that why you've looked nervous all week?"

"Yeah." That wasn't it, really. Cassie hadn't been able to stop thinking about her missed periods since Andrea brought it up. And her mom saying she didn't have breasts because there wasn't enough fat on her. That, plus the making herself throw up, and she'd spent every waking moment wondering if she should get medical help.

She hadn't made herself throw up again, at least. Andrea had given her some laxatives, but Cassie hadn't used them either.

"I tried to talk to you in choir but you ignored me."

"No, I didn't," Cassie said, getting defensive. "I just didn't see you."

"Because you were too busy talking to Maureen."

They'd had this conversation before, and Cassie brushed back her irritation at Riley's insecurity. "She just wanted to know what's wrong with me."

"So she noticed?"

"I guess everyone has." Cassie sighed.

"You haven't been as happy as you usually are. Are you sure it's just your music thing?"

Cassie looked down at her hands and then over at Riley. "If I tell you, you can't tell anyone else."

Riley's face went white. "What is it, Cassie?"

"You promise?"

Riley nodded, concern on her face.

Cassie took a deep breath and exhaled. Why was this so hard to say? "I made myself throw up."

Riley scrunched her nose together, and the tip turned pink. "Why would you do that?" she asked, an unexpected tremor in her voice.

"I don't know. I have a problem with food."

"That's serious, Cassie," Riley whispered.

"I know." Cassie's head bobbed. "I know. I'm trying to stop."

"Please stop." Riley took her hand. "I promised I wouldn't tell, but if you don't stop, I will."

Cassie realized with surprise that this was the reaction she'd hoped Andrea would have. She wanted someone to help her. "Okay. I'll stop."

"I'm going to check up on you," Riley warned.

"That's fine." Cassie wiped at unexpected tears. "Thanks."

"My mom's been planning what session I'm going to at Camp Splendor this summer," Riley said, her eyes on Cassie's face. "Want to go together?"

"Yes." Cassie nodded. "That sounds like fun."

Riley gave a brief smile. "I promise I'll be nice this time."

Cassie laughed, a weepy sound through her tears. "Even better."

CHAPTER THIRTY-FIVE
Grasping for Attention

Ms. Malcolm wanted all of the performers to be at the community center an hour before the recital started so she could get them placed and organized. Mr. Jones drove Emily and Cassie to the large performance hall, Emily for her piano pieces and Cassie for singing.

"Which entrance is it?" he asked.

"I don't know." Cassie smoothed her beautiful floral dress and hoped her curls hadn't fallen flat. "Just drop us off, we'll find it."

"Okay. Your mom and I will be back with everyone else in an hour."

Emily climbed out behind Cassie, her light brown hair done in similar curls. But she wasn't allowed to wear makeup yet. Cassie, on the other hand, had put on lipstick and eyeshadow and mascara. The way her padded bra looked under the new dress made Cassie feel eighteen and sophisticated. They waved to their father and headed for the entrance.

Inside they drew up short. Some kind of convention was going on, with the halls crowded by clusters of vendors displaying soaps and lotions, all attempting to squirt something in the hands of those who walked by.

"Which way to the recital?" Emily asked, holding her sheet music in her hand.

"I don't know. Let's go this way." Cassie led the way between the vendors, her low heels clacking on the porcelain floor.

The hallway came to a T, and Cassie went left.

"Now where are we?" Emily asked.

"Like I know?" Cassie said, getting annoyed. It looked like a cafeteria. Cassie spotted a door to the right and went for it. It opened up to a flight of stairs going down.

"That can't be the right way," Emily said. "I didn't even know this place had a basement."

"Well, now you do." Cassie clattered down the stairs.

"You really think Ms. Malcolm is going to be down there?"

Cassie had no idea, but she wasn't going to say that. Her heart fluttered with mild panic, and she knew she just had to keep moving. "We'll find her."

There was a door at the bottom of the stairs, and Cassie pushed it open.

"This isn't it," Emily stated behind her.

Somehow, they had found their way into a laundry room. Several sets of washers and dryers churned, the fresh scent of detergent filling the room like a thick fog.

"Let's go back." Cassie grabbed the door handle and pulled. It didn't budge. She tried again and released it.

"I think it locked behind us."

"Well, that's just great!" Emily exclaimed. "We're going to miss our recital and Ms. Malcolm will kill us!"

"Calm down," Cassie muttered, and she walked forward past the machinery. "We'll find a way out of here."

"Use your cell phone to call Mom," Emily demanded. "Tell her we're lost."

Cassie hated to give in to her sister's demands, but the panic was going postal on her. She dug around in her purse while they walked, fishing out the phone. As soon as she opened it, she groaned. "No signal."

"Just keep walking. We'll find someone."

The maze of hallways continued, but Cassie thought she detected the scent of food. "This way."

Emily followed, grumbling, but what else was she going to do?

They turned a corner, and to Cassie's relief, they were in a kitchen. Several workers scurried about in white jackets and hairnets, stirring pots and banging dishes.

The girls only stood there about ten seconds before someone spotted them. The man yelped in surprise.

"What are you doing here?" he asked.

"We're lost," Cassie said. "We got down here and can't get back up. We have a recital to go to."

"Then you want the performance hall." He looked at them like they were crazy, or like maybe he thought they'd intentionally come down here. "I'll show you."

"Thank you," Cassie said with immense relief. She ignored the glare Emily gave her.

Ms. Malcolm gave them both the evil eye when they walked into the room.

"I said to be here half an hour ago."

"Sorry," Emily said. "Cassie got us lost."

Cassie glared at her sister but said nothing. Never mind that they'd arrived half an hour ago. They'd just been hanging out downstairs.

She could still smell the scent of food on her clothes.

☙ ❦ ❧

Cassie worried she wouldn't be able to get her nerves under control after that rough entrance, but her first song was only scratchy in the beginning. By the second song, she was on perfect pitch, and she saw how Ms. Malcolm beamed at her from the piano. Cassie sat down in between pieces to listen to the songs of the other students, both piano and voice. Twice more she got up to sing, but each time, she sang it flawlessly.

Finally the recital ended, and Ms. Malcolm stepped to the microphone, her gold ballroom gown glittering under the heavy lights.

"I want to thank you all for coming tonight," she said. "For supporting your children as they master music and prepare to become prominent musicians. And now it's time to give out the trophies and medals for the students' achievements this past year."

Cassie's eyes went to the table behind the microphone, covered with dozens of sparkling trophies and medals dangling off the edge.

"For best new soloist—Michelle Hanks!"

She clapped politely for the blond girl about her age. She recognized her from the children's choir, but they sang different parts, so Cassie never talked to her.

"Best new pianist—Darren Phipps!"

Cassie tuned out the awards she knew she wasn't eligible for.

"Most improved—Cassandra Jones!"

Most improved? Was that a backhanded compliment? Everyone clapped, and Cassie stood up to claim her award, smiling hard so no one would see her annoyance. She sat down again. This was what she'd worked for all year? She looked down at the six-inch gold trophy of a girl holding a music note.

"Best pitch recognition—Cassandra Jones!"

Cassie's head shot up in surprise. Arching an eyebrow, she made her way to the stage again. This time she accepted a medal on a rainbow ribbon. Her lip quirked upward in a half smile, and she studied it as she made her way back to her chair. That wasn't so bad.

She examined her two awards and clapped enthusiastically as the other names were called. Emily won one in piano, as well.

"And the highest award of the year, the most accomplished

overall musician—Cassandra Jones."

Cassie gasped. No way. She'd actually won three awards? And the best one of all? Pleasure warmed her face, and she couldn't hide the giant grin that spread from ear to ear. She made her way to the front and accepted the trophy, twice as big as her other one, with a gem-encrusted treble clef on a square base. It was beautiful, and she knew she glowed as she hugged Ms. Malcolm.

"Keep up the hard work," Ms. Malcolm whispered in her ear. "You earned it. Keep going."

Cassie returned to her seat, body hot with pride. It didn't matter if Ms. Vanderwood didn't appreciate her musical abilities. Ms. Malcolm was the expert.

Riley found Cassie as she was leaving her locker Monday morning. "How did the weekend go?"

"Great," Cassie said, surprised to see Riley. They rarely bumped into each other at school, outside of choir. "I won a few awards at my recital. How was yours?" Cassie pushed open the doors leading to the math wing, and Riley followed.

"That's not what I mean," Riley said. She lowered her voice and whispered, "I mean with the eating."

"Oh." Cassie let out a loud exhale. "I'm trying, okay? I ate dinner every night. And I didn't make myself throw up."

"Good." Riley gave her a fierce look. "You better be honest with me."

"I will," Cassie promised. She continued on to Teacher Helper, checking the halls for Andrea.

Mr. Adams sent Cassie to staple a packet together for his afternoon science classes, and Andrea slipped in right before the bell rang.

Cassie took one look at her pink nose and splotchy face and knew something was wrong. She gathered up the packets, stuck the stapler in Andrea's hand, and pulled her into the hall.

"What's wrong?" Cassie whispered, sliding onto the linoleum beside her as she continued stapling papers.

"My dad made pancakes for breakfast," Andrea said. "And I tried not to eat them. But I ate four. Four of them!"

That was a lot. But Cassie didn't say that. "I'm sure just one time won't hurt you."

"But it's not just once! We had donuts for breakfast yesterday and I ate three!"

Cassie's stomach turned over at the thought. She couldn't imagine eating one donut, let alone three. "Well, just decide you're going to eat healthier from here on out."

Andrea's eyes flicked over Cassie's face, intent in their probing. "Can you teach me how to throw up?"

Cassie sucked in a breath, shocked at the request. "I don't do that."

"But you know how. I know you do."

Cassie swallowed hard and then shook her head. "Don't do it, Andrea. It's not normal."

Andrea's hand snaked out and grabbed Cassie's arm. "Teach me. If you're my friend, you'll teach me."

Cassie met Andrea's gaze, flattered that Andrea would ask her, scared of losing her friendship if she said no. But even more, Cassie knew she could never forgive herself if she got Andrea started on a dangerous habit. "I can't."

Andrea pulled her hand back and folded her arms across her chest, an angry scowl on her face. "Some best friend you are."

"I *am* your best friend," Cassie said, pleading with Andrea to understand. "That's why I won't do it."

They passed the rest of the hour in silence, Cassie's heart hurting because she wasn't sure how to help her friend.

Andrea intercepted Cassie at her locker before lunch. "Do you still have those laxatives I gave you?"

"Yes," Cassie said, hesitant. "I never used them."

"Give them to me."

Cassie pulled out the packet of powder from the back of her locker and passed it over to Andrea, as covertly as a drug deal.

"Be careful," she warned.

Andrea gave her a haughty look. "I've always supported you. Helped you."

"You have," Cassie answered, feeling guilty for not being as supportive. "I just don't want you to get hurt."

Andrea threw her hair over her shoulder and continued to the cafeteria. Cassie lagged behind, wondering what was going down.

By the time Cassie sat at the table with their friends, Andrea had a tall plastic cup full of water and was adding the powder. Cassie sat down across from her, watching as she stirred it with a spoon.

"Where did you get the cup?" she asked.

"Cafeteria lady," Andrea answered without looking up. The mixture took on an orange hue, the contents spinning around and around the clear cup.

"What is that?" Amity asked, looking over.

Cassie unwrapped the apple she'd brought, already sliced. "A vitamin C drink," Cassie said, automatically covering for Andrea.

"Oh." Amity started to return to her sandwich, but Andrea said, "It's a diet drink."

Immediately Amity swiveled back to her. "Andrea! Not this again! Why are you taking a diet drink?"

"Because I'm fat," Andrea replied, taking a huge swig of the orange mixture.

"No, you're not, and I'm tired of hearing you say that!" Amity whacked Andrea's leg.

"I'll stop when I'm skinny."

Cassie watched the interchange with interest. She'd given Andrea the perfect cover. But instead of using it, Andrea had fueled the discussion, giving Amity a reason to overreact.

Andrea held onto her plastic cup with both hands, loudly calling Amity off, as Cara and Maureen also got involved, telling Andrea how she didn't need that and was beautiful already.

All of this could have been avoided. But somehow Cassie didn't think Andrea wanted to avoid it.

⁂

"Cassie, an envelope came in the mail for you," Mrs. Jones said, greeting the children when they walked in the door from the bus.

"For me?" Cassie's curiosity immediately piqued. She didn't get mail very often.

"It's on the table."

Intrigued, Cassie made her way to the kitchen. A thick manila envelope sat on the table. Cassie picked it up, her heart rate increasing as she realized it felt like pages inside. Pages of paper. She read the return address: Raspberry Publications.

Cassie gasped. They'd sent her manuscript back! Was this a good thing or a bad thing?

With shaking fingers, she undid the clasp at the back and pulled out the papers. The first one slid off the top and glided to the table.

It was on official letterhead. Cassie picked it up.

Dear Cassandra,

Thank you so much for sending in your manuscript. We read it with interest and believe you have a lot of talent for such a young girl. With that in mind, I have a few recommendations for things you can do to improve your manuscript.

The letter went on to list everything the editor had thought wrong with her book, and Cassie's eyes burned with humiliation. She reached the end.

After you make these changes, we invite you to submit your manuscript again. Best of luck to you, and continue to write and improve your skill!

Sincerely,

Edward Hill
Acquisitions Editor

Cassie's heart started beating again, a flicker of hope igniting in her chest. So it wasn't a flat out rejection. They hadn't hated her book.

This could even be a positive thing. If she fixed what the editor didn't like, he'd want her book for sure.

Buoyed up by her self-pep-talk, Cassie hurried downstairs to the computer so she could make changes.

Mrs. Jones came down and found Cassie at the computer. "Do you remember the schedule for this week after I have my jaw surgery?"

Cassie looked up from the computer, furrowing her brow in confusion. "Jaw surgery?"

Mrs. Jones gave a huff of impatience. "We've been talking about this for days. I'm really going to rely on you. You have to help out with your dad and the other kids."

"Right." Cassie slowly nodded her head, some of the memory coming back. "When is it?"

"Tomorrow. I'll be gone when you kids get home from school, but your dad will bring me home before dinner. I bought some eggs and tomato soup. Can you make dinner?"

"Tomorrow?" Cassie echoed. Her eyes flickered back to the computer screen, still half focused on her editorial changes.

"Yes." Her mom pressed a hand to her forehead and heaved a sigh. "I need you to step up for the next few days. I won't be able to do anything."

"I will."

"Okay." Mrs. Jones started to walk away, and then she glanced down at the letter beside the computer. "What are you doing?"

Cassie grinned and held up the sheet of paper. "I got a letter back from the publisher! They want me to change a few things and then resubmit!"

Mrs. Jones gasped. "Cassie! That's so wonderful!"

"I know!" Cassie fidgeted in her seat with excitement. "I might actually get published soon!"

CHAPTER THIRTY-SIX
Burglar

Cassie forgot about the jaw surgery until she got home from school and her mom wasn't there. But as if knowing that might happen, her mom had left her a long list of things to do—for the rest of the week.

"Hey, guys," Cassie said, scanning the paper while addressing her siblings, "Mom and Daddy will be home in a few hours. Let's get everything cleaned up, okay? Scott, you do the dishes. Emily, you fold the laundry. Annette, empty the trash and set the table. I'll make dinner."

"You have the easy part," Emily said. She'd been a lot more argumentative lately, something Mrs. Jones blamed on the fact that she was almost thirteen.

"I don't care," Cassie said. "Mom told me to make dinner, but if you want to, fine. I'll do the laundry." Cassie put the paper down and headed for the laundry room.

"I didn't say I wouldn't do it," Emily grumbled, shoving past Cassie.

Whatever. Cassie shrugged and started on the tomato soup. She made a few grilled cheese sandwiches to go with it, though she knew her mom wouldn't be able to eat solids.

She helped Annette set the table, and she had just finished

when a car rumbled into the driveway.

Annette ran to the dining room and peeked out the window. "They're home!" she announced.

Cassie stayed back while the younger kids ran to the door to greet their parents. Mr. Jones shepherded Mrs. Jones in, one hand on her elbow, helping her take cautious steps to the couch. Cassie tried to act nonchalant, but her heart squeezed when she saw her mom's swollen and bruised face.

"How are you feeling?" she asked, joining the rest of the family at the couch. Her father puffed up a few pillows and laid them under Mrs. Jones' head.

Mrs. Jones gestured to her face and grimaced. "Can' talk," she said without opening her mouth, the words coming out pinched and flat. "M'okay."

"Are you hungry? Can you eat some soup?"

Her mom held up her finger and her thumb, keeping a tiny distance between them.

"I'll get you some." Cassie hurried to the kitchen to get her mom a bowl, trying to think what else she could do for her. Jello! Maybe her mom could eat some Jello.

"Thank you, Cassie," Mr. Jones said when she returned. "I'll sit with your mom and help her eat. Go ahead and eat with the others."

"Cass," Mrs. Jones said, snatching Cassie's arm. "T'morrow."

Cassie stared at her, waiting for more, but Mrs. Jones let go and mimed writing on her palm.

Oh! The paper with instructions. She jumped up and grabbed it, then returned to her mom.

Mrs. Jones pointed to the words by *Thursday* and handed it back to Cassie.

"I already read it," Cassie said. "I'm riding the bus home with Emma." Emma was a grade younger. She was in choir with Cassie, but that was all Cassie knew of her. "She'll take me to choir."

Mrs. Jones nodded and relaxed.

"And how will I get home?"

"I'll pick you up," Mr. Jones said. "As soon as I've closed up the store. So I might be a few minutes late."

"Sure. No problem."

"Go eat," her mom ground out.

Cassie returned to the kitchen. She put some water on to boil first so she could make Jello, then she ate with everyone else.

☙ ❦ ❧

"Did you guys hear?"

Cara burst into the bathroom Thursday morning, all excited. She pushed her blond hair away from her face, brown eyes glittering.

"Hear what?" Amity asked. She waited while Andrea piled blush all over her cheeks.

Cassie stood stock still in front of the mirror except for the wand of mascara in her hand. She widened her eyes and swept the brush over her eyelashes.

"A dance. It was just decided last night, but we're going to have a dance tomorrow here at school!"

"That's not much notice," Amity said.

"How much notice do you need?" Cara returned. "Either you can come or you can't."

"I'll be there," Andrea said.

Cara turned to Cassie. "Cassie? You never come. Can you come tomorrow?"

Cassie put the mascara away, studying the black case while she twisted it closed. She'd never gone before, but now that she'd gone to a church dance, she felt like maybe she would enjoy a school one. "I'll see if I can."

The warning bell rang, and the girls packed up their makeup. Amity stopped in the hallway to giggle with a few boys, and Cassie fell into step next to Andrea.

"Do you think I could ride with you to the dance

tomorrow?" she asked.

"Sure. You can spend the night if you want."

The quick answer surprised Cassie. "Okay, great. I'll call you tonight to make sure."

"Just bring your stuff to school and ride home with me. It'll be fine. Oh." Andrea paused. "Don't say anything to Amity or Maureen."

"Why?" Cassie looked at Andrea, studying her.

"Because I haven't asked yet. Just to be sure."

Cassie had the sneaking suspicion there was more to it than that.

By lunchtime all anyone talked about was the dance. The vice-principal announced it during second hour, and kids began to make plans to attend. Amity still complained about it being last minute.

"I'll need to go shopping. I don't have anything to wear."

"It's not a formal affair, Amity," Cara said with an eye roll. She opened her carton of chocolate milk. "No ball gowns required."

Amity swiveled to Andrea. "You'll have to come over and help me decide what to wear."

Andrea picked at the pizza she'd grabbed from the lunch line. "We'll see," she said in a surly voice. She took a bite of her pizza and put it down, mopping at the greasy pepperonis with her napkin.

"No, seriously," Amity said. "Come over after school. That way we can make sure we don't wear the same thing."

Would Andrea say something about Cassie spending the night?

But Andrea said, "I don't have to do anything, Amity. Maybe if I'm not busy." She took a few more bites of her pizza and scowled at Amity.

Andrea lingered at the table after the bell rang, tearing her remaining pizza into pieces. Cassie stood but didn't leave.

"How come you didn't tell Amity about me spending the

night?" Cassie asked.

"I didn't want to. Besides, she might invite herself. She does that all the time."

"Are you mad at her?"

Andrea heaved a sigh. "She's so annoying sometimes. Follows me around and can't do her own thing."

Did Andrea say the same thing about Cassie?

They walked out together, but Andrea stopped at the bathroom. "I'll see you later," she said.

"I'll call you tonight," Cassie said. She waved and walked to her class.

Cassie didn't see any of her friends until before seventh hour, when Maureen launched herself at Cassie as she opened her locker.

"Cassie!" She grasped her arm and shook her. "Where've you been? We've been looking for you in between every class period!"

"I've been in class," Cassie said, confused by the sudden concern for her whereabouts. "I took my books with me so I didn't need to come to my locker."

Amity crashed into Maureen's side, her eyes red-rimmed. Cara and Janice ran up beside her.

Cassie took in the girls' faces, Maureen's crazed expression. "What's wrong?"

"Andrea," Amity said without preamble. "She had an asthma attack. They took her to the hospital."

"What?" Cassie gasped out. Alarm and horror flashed through her. "Is she okay? What happened?"

"She's okay," Cara said. "I've been texting my mom, and she's talking to Mrs. Wall. They're taking her home soon."

"She tried to make herself throw up," Amity blurted. Her greenish-brown eyes glared at Cassie. "Right after lunch. It triggered the attack."

"Why would she do that?"

"Because you do," Amity said. "She was copying you."

The accusation was heavy in Amity's voice, and the guilt sliced through Cassie, even though she hadn't done anything. "I don't do that!"

"It's not your fault, Cassie," Cara said.

Cassie shook her head, tears stinging behind her eyes. "She shouldn't have done that!" The tears escaped, rolling down her face. What if Andrea was seriously hurt? Was Cassie to blame?

"Did you teach her how?" Janice asked, her voice urgent.

"No! She asked me to, but I said no! I don't do that, you guys, I don't!"

Janice put an arm around Cassie's shoulders and hugged her. "She's okay. No one blames you."

Cassie caught Amity's eye right before Amity whirled away. Some people blamed her.

⸺⸻※⸻⸺

Cassie had a difficult time concentrating in choir. She fumbled along through the songs, her nose running, her voice wobbly. At least Maureen hadn't been accusatory.

"Are you going to the dance tomorrow?" Maureen asked as choir let out and they walked toward the buses.

"Maybe," Cassie said. If Andrea was okay, anyway.

As if reading her mind, Maureen said, "Andrea did this for attention. She probably didn't even have an asthma attack."

"I didn't know she has asthma."

"She's got everything," Maureen said, going to her bus.

"What's wrong?" Riley asked, catching up to Cassie. "You look like you've seen a ghost."

"I'm fine,'" Cassie said. Which was the truth.

"You're not doing that thing again, are you?"

"No," Cassie snapped with more vehemence than she'd intended. Riley happened to hit on a sore spot. "No," she said, calmer this time. "Everything's fine."

Riley didn't question her again. They got on the same bus, but neither of them said anything. Cassie pulled out her phone and scanned through her text messages, pretending to be occupied. She sent a text to Andrea, asking if she was okay, and then another text to Cara to see if she had any updates. Then she dropped her phone in her backpack and stared out the window.

"Well, I'll see you later," Riley said, getting off at the elementary school to catch her bus.

"Yeah," Cassie said.

She pushed Andrea from her mind as she rehearsed the day's schedule. She'd ride the bus to Emma's house, and they'd ride to the choir practice together. She hoped there'd be time to use the bathroom because she really had to pee. Cassie settled into her seat and pulled out a book, losing herself in the fictional drama.

Twenty minutes later she glanced up as they approached Emma's stop. She looked around for Emma and frowned when she didn't see her. Was she not on the bus?

The bus pulled to a stop, and Cassie clambered to the front.

"You sure you're getting off here?" Rhonda the bus driver asked, blinking her heavily lined eyes. "Emma's not on today."

Where was Emma? But Cassie swallowed back her trepidation and nodded. "Yes."

"Okay."

The doors opened, and Cassie stepped out. She started up the long driveway to Emma's house without another look at the bus, but she heard its engine roar as it pulled away.

The sun beat down mercilessly, a reminder that May fast approached, and with it the hot days of summer. Cassie wiped sweat from her brow and took deep breaths as she climbed the steep driveway. She stepped into the tree cover. They formed an effective barrier over the driveway, casting it into shade. Cassie switched her binder to the other hip, her eyes on the brick house at the end, noting there were no cars in the driveway. A knot formed in her stomach. She climbed the rock-laden porch steps and rang the doorbell.

No answer. No sounds came from inside.

Cassie tried again, but she wasn't surprised when there was still nothing.

What now? She didn't have Emma's number. And she didn't want to bother her mom. She'd just have to wait. She sat down on the steps and cupped her chin in her hands. But now her bladder was complaining, and she squeezed her legs together. How long would she have to sit here?

Maybe the door was unlocked.

She told herself not to go inside; it wasn't her house. But Cassie really, really needed to pee. Standing up, she tried the knob.

Locked.

But there was another door connected to the garage. Less sure of herself than ever, Cassie stepped over and turned the handle.

Unlocked!

She tiptoed through the empty garage and into the house, listening as her footsteps creaked on the wooden floor.

"Hello?" she called. "Anyone here?"

No response came, and Cassie closed the door behind her. The lights were off, but she made out a living room to her right with leather chairs and a fireplace. To her left was a kitchen with dark cabinets and a dark counter.

She wandered down a hallway and breathed a sigh of relief when she found a bathroom.

Once she'd taken care of that immediate need, she stepped into the kitchen and hesitated. She was very thirsty. Emma wouldn't care if she got a drink, would she? Feeling like an intruder, Cassie opened the cupboards, looking for a glass.

Instead, she found snacks.

Her stomach rumbled as she stared at the rice cakes and crackers. She extended her hand, fingers arching until they touched the plastic packaging. She hauled it down and pulled one out, sniffing it and inhaling.

Just one. She'd eat just one.

Maybe two.

By the time she'd finished three, her thirst had grown so she couldn't ignore it. Turning away from the snacks, she resumed her search for a glass, finding one in the third cabinet. Then she got water from the spigot on the fridge. She sipped it and glanced around at the calendar taped to the wall, the fliers stuck on the fridge with magnets.

Had she gotten her dates mixed up? Was she supposed to be somewhere else? Cassie put the glass down and went to her backpack, fishing around until she found her phone.

Just as she pulled it out, the doorbell rang.

Cassie froze. This wasn't her house. She wasn't even supposed to be in it! She couldn't answer the door.

But what if it was the police? What if someone saw her come in and thought she was a burglar?

The doorbell rang again, and Cassie remained hunched over her backpack, frozen with uncertainty. And then a voice called out, "Cassandra Jones? Are you in there?"

It was a man's voice. Cassie closed her eyes, her heart in her throat. They'd come to arrest her. But she couldn't hide; they knew she was here. Grim-faced and willing to face her fate, Cassie shouldered her backpack, grabbed her binder, and opened the front door.

An older man stood there in a T-shirt and shorts, no police uniform in sight. Caught off guard, Cassie cocked her head. "Yes?"

He smiled, the wrinkle lines around his eyes crinkling. "Are you Cassandra?"

"Yes."

"I'm Emma's neighbor. Her mom called me and asked me to come over here to see if you were here."

"Oh!" Cassie wilted in relief. "Where is she? Is she on her way?"

"Well." He chuckled. "Funny thing, that. Apparently she told your dad she'd just pick you and Emma up from school. When you weren't there, she realized you must have ridden the bus. Can you call someone to come get you?"

Dad! Cassie groaned inwardly. He must have forgotten to tell her. Or maybe he just forgot completely. "Yeah, I'll call my dad."

"Want me to stay with you until he gets here?"

"No, it's okay." Cassie let herself out of the house and sat on the porch steps. "I'll just sit here until he comes."

Cassie passed the time waiting for her father by texting her friends, especially Andrea, to see if she was okay. She heard back from Cara and Riley but no one else.

Mr. Jones closed the store early and came to get Cassie, but even so, it took almost an hour before he got to Emma's house. She stood when her father's car approached, her emotions vacillating between relief and embarrassment and anger.

"I missed choir," she said, climbing into the car. "How could you forget to tell me?"

"I'm sorry," he said, not meeting her eyes as he turned the car around and started back down the massive driveway. "I've been a bit busy scheduling things."

Cassie wasn't ready to let it go. "I just sat here for like an hour and a half!"

"I'm sorry," he repeated. "What more do you want me to say? Your mom will be able to take you next week. It's just one time."

Cassie crossed her arms over her chest and let out a huff. She could hardly wait for her mom to be better.

Andrea still hadn't texted back, so Cassie called her when she got home.

"Hello?" Andrea answered, surprising Cassie by sounding as perky and cheerful as ever.

"Andrea!" she cried. "Are you okay? I've been so worried about you!"

"I'm fine," Andrea said. "So you heard what happened?"

"Yes!" Cassie fairly trembled with indignation. "How could you do something like that? I told you not to."

"It didn't work, anyway," Andrea said with a sigh.

Cassie pressed her lips together, wishing she had something she could say to convince Andrea not to do this. But she understood the feeling. It was only the past few weeks that Cassie had stopped thinking of food as the enemy.

"Anyway," Andrea said, perky again, "you're spending the night tomorrow, right?"

"You remembered," Cassie said.

"Of course. But you didn't tell anyone, did you?"

"Nope."

"Great. Bring your things to school but don't let anyone see. I'll help you find something to wear to the dance."

A flicker of anticipation burned in Cassie's chest as the reality of a dance descended upon her. She'd enjoyed the church one so much. This had to be even more fun. "Can't wait!"

A school dance and a sleepover at Andrea's house. Maybe this was it. She'd finally be one of the popular girls.

Episode 6: Someone Special

CHAPTER THIRTY-SEVEN
Dance Off

Sleepover at Andrea's house. Her first school dance.

Cassandra Jones tapped her toes anxiously against the linoleum in fourth hour, her sleeping gear stuffed in her locker. The more time she spent with Andrea, the closer she got to being a part of the exclusive in-crowd. And Andrea had been excited this morning, telling her they'd do makeovers, warning her not to let anyone else know. The sleepover was a secret.

The day was halfway over. Just a few hours to go.

Ms. Talo, Cassie's English teacher, dropped two envelopes on Cassie's desk.

"What are these?" Cassie asked, picking one up.

"Congratulations, Cassie." Ms. Talo winked and walked away.

Cassie cocked her head, her heart rate quickening in anticipation. What was this? Could it be related to her book somehow? She'd written a book the year before and recently submitted it to a publisher. She glanced around to make sure none of her classmates were watching, and then she slipped her finger beneath the flap and opened it. She unfolded the paper inside.

Dear Cassandra Jones,

Congratulations! You have been selected to attend the Fine Arts Camp in Mena, Arkansas.

The letter went on to list the dates and supplies she would need.

Cassie pressed a hand to her mouth, surprised and delighted. The summer camps! Cassie had forgotten all about her application to the art camp, where she'd sent in a writing sample and recorded a monologue and song. She'd been accepted into the writing portion of the camp, which had been her first choice. It also stated that if she changed her mind and decided to do theater, they could make a spot for her there as well.

She opened the other letter now, already anticipating what it would be. The Holocaust camp listed her as an alternate in case someone else dropped out.

She shrugged it off. She'd gotten into the one she wanted. She bounced in her chair, suddenly more excited for summer than ever before.

⁂

"What did you decide about the dance, Cassie?" Cara asked when Cassie sat across from her at the lunch table.

"Oh, yeah," Cassie said. "I'm going." Thanks to Andrea, but she couldn't say that. For some reason Andrea wanted her to keep their sleepover a secret.

"Really?" Maureen looked at her, arching one eyebrow above her light brown eyes. "Your mom's letting you?"

"Yes," Cassie said, a bit defensive. "Why not? She let me go to a church dance last month."

For some reason, Maureen and Amity both burst out laughing.

"A church dance!" Maureen chortled. "Did everyone wear hats and suspenders?"

"We're not Amish," Cassie said.

"I bet they weren't allowed to hold hands!" Amity hooted.

"Can I walk in front of you and pretend we're dancing?"

Maureen said, imitating a boy with her voice low.

The two girls laughed like they thought they were hilarious, but Cassie felt only irritation. She rolled her eyes.

"I bet it was fun," Janice said, leaning closer so Cassie could hear. "I'd like to come some time."

"It was fun," Cassie said, her face warming. "And I'd love for you to come next time. We have another one in May."

"Really? Do you do them often?"

"Almost every month."

Janice looked impressed, and Cassie felt a bit better.

⁂

"Do you want to ride to the dance together?" Maureen asked in choir while Ms. Berry did sectionals with the altos. "You can ride my bus home with me."

Cassie looked up from her sheet music. "Why?" Maureen never invited her to do anything. Mostly she didn't talk to Cassie unless she was teasing her.

"I don't want to go by myself."

"I thought you always go with Cara."

"She's staying after school to help with StuCo."

That explained the invitation. Cassie turned back to her sheet music. "I'm riding over with Andrea." She could say that, couldn't she? Andrea had said not to tell about the sleepover. Cassie hadn't.

"Oh." Maureen shrugged. "I'll see if I can go with Amity, then."

"Sounds good." Cassie didn't say anything else. Maureen's mockery at lunch still bothered her.

"Maybe after the dance I could spend the night."

Cassie lifted her eyes again. "With Amity?"

"With you."

Cassie furrowed her brow. This conversation was getting weird. "I don't think that would work out." Since Cassie was going home with Andrea, anyway.

"You never know. Ask your mom and tell me at the dance."

"Sure." Cassie wanted to laugh at the irony. A week ago she would have loved an invite from Maureen. Right now it only annoyed her.

After school she evaded Maureen and pulled her sleeping gear from her locker.

Andrea joined her and helped her stuff it in her backpack. "That way no one asks questions. You're just going with me to the dance," she said.

Mrs. Wall was already at the curb when they walked out, so Andrea and Cassie just waved goodbye to Amity and climbed into the car.

"Did you see Amity's face?" Andrea said, laughing from the passenger seat as she turned to looked at Cassie. "She was so jealous she wasn't coming!"

"Why are you mad at Amity?" Mrs. Wall asked.

"Just girl stuff, Mom," Andrea said. She faced forward again, but not before Cassie saw the pleased smile on her face.

But when Amity called an hour before the dance and asked Mrs. Wall for a ride, Mrs. Wall said yes.

"Mom," Andrea said. "I don't want to ride with her."

"It's just the five-minute drive to the dance. And Maureen is with her. You don't have to talk to Amity."

Andrea sighed and huffed and dragged Cassie back to her room.

"Come on," she said. "Let's get ready for the dance."

Andrea did her best to curl Cassie's hair, though only the ends retained any of the styling. She put Cassie in a white, sleeveless button-up shirt, and Cassie turned in the mirror from left to right to admire her tanned, skinny shoulders contrasting with the pale color.

Andrea fluffed her own hair, which had taken perfectly to the curl and softened her face as the strands fell around her cheeks. Dark mascara framed her blue eyes, and Cassie tried not to feel envious. She'd never be as pretty as her friend.

"Ready?" Andrea said, turning to her with a smile. She

grabbed some red lipstick and ran it over Cassie's lips.

"Ready," Cassie said, catching a glimpse of her reflection again. She looked fourteen for sure.

"Let's go then."

Andrea sat in the back with Cassie. When they stopped at Amity's house, she rolled down the window and told Amity to sit up front. Maureen climbed into the back with the two of them.

"You look really pretty, Cassie," Maureen said.

"Thanks." Cassie looked down at her dark hair, longer than her shoulder blades and twisting slightly at the ends. Then she looked at Maureen, who had pulled her long wavy hair into a braid over her shoulder. "You too."

Andrea didn't say anything, but every time Amity spoke, she made ugly faces and mimicked her words.

The basketball gym had been decorated for the dance. The lights were down low and kids milled about inside and around the concession stand. They paid their money to get into the dance, and then Amity was off, prancing into a group of boys, throwing her chest out and giggling. Cassie clung to the walls as the music played, peppy pop music with a fast beat.

"How does anyone dance to this?" she asked Andrea.

"Easy. Everyone knows the dances. See?" Even as she said it, a country song came on, and all of the girls pulled away from the boys and formed rows, then cheered and whooped as they moved to a choreography Cassie had never seen before. Andrea peeled away from the wall and joined them.

"I don't know it," Cassie said to Maureen, feeling stupid. "Where did everyone learn the dance?"

Maureen shrugged. "Online videos. It's pretty much everywhere."

Which meant, of course, that Cassie hadn't seen it. She didn't have time to get online and peruse music videos. Nor, to be honest, did she care to.

A slow song came on. Finally, something she could dance to. Cassie straightened up, wondering which of her classmates would come over and ask her to dance.

But the floor cleared, and only a few couples wandered out to dance. A full minute into the song, Cassie leaned back against the wall.

Nobody was going to ask her to dance.

Not only that, but the couples out there held each other in bear hugs, every part of their bodies touching. She understood Amity's mockery earlier. That kind of dancing definitely didn't happen at church.

Andrea came back over, her face flushed. "So fun! Why aren't you dancing, Cassie?"

"No one asked me."

"Well, then ask them!"

Yeah, right.

Two fast songs followed the slow song, but Andrea stayed with Cassie this time. When another slow song came on, a boy Cassie didn't know came over to them.

"Hi," he said to Andrea. "Want to be my girlfriend?"

Maureen and Cassie both looked at Andrea, waiting for her response. Technically she was still going out with Connor Lane, though she hadn't mentioned him in weeks.

"Sure," Andrea said. She took his hand and went out to dance.

Jealousy rippled through Cassie. She watched the two of them out there, holding hands and swaying to the music. Why weren't guys interested in her?

Four songs and no dances later, Cassie said to Maureen, "I'm going into the hallway." The loud thumping music and strobe lights were giving her a headache.

"I'll follow you. Maybe Cara's working the concessions. I didn't see her in here."

They wandered out of the dark gym and into the fully lit corridor.

"Hey!" Maureen said. "Did you ask your mom if I can spend the night?"

Of course Cassie hadn't. She was staying at Andrea's. "Well," she said, having no choice but to fib, "she just had jaw surgery this week. She's not been feeling so great. I have to do a lot around the house to help her."

"I can help too! Sometimes my mom gets headaches. I know how to take care of someone."

Crapola. This wouldn't be so easy to get out of.

"Call your house," Maureen urged. "Just ask."

Not sure what else to do, Cassie pulled her phone out of her pocket. She turned away from Maureen and pressed the button for home.

No one answered. She breathed a sigh of relief and turned back. "My mom must be sleeping. She didn't pick up."

"We can try later. Let's look for Cara at the concession stand."

Sure enough, their friend was there, her blond hair pulled up on her head in a ponytail, emphasizing her high cheek bones.

"Hey!" Cara greeted. "My shift's almost over, and then I can go dance. How's it going?"

"Awesome!" Maureen said.

Super boring. But Cassie kept quiet. Apparently this was normal.

"Are you having fun, Cassie?" Cara asked, looking directly at her.

"Sure," Cassie lied. She wished Andrea had left her at home. She was in the middle of a great book. "But you guys need to come to a church dance with me next time. They're so much fun."

"We'll see you in there soon," Maureen said to Cara, taking Cassie's arm and pulling her away.

"I don't want to go back in," Cassie said, resisting as Maureen headed for the gym.

"Why?" Maureen let her go.

"No one's dancing except couples. I don't have a boyfriend." Cassie leaned against the wall again.

Maureen joined her. "You will someday."

"Maybe." She couldn't imagine a boy being interested in her.

"My dad saw you in one of my pictures. He said you're the prettiest one of all of us."

Cassie laughed.

"No, seriously."

Cassie peered at Maureen, trying to make sense of her. Usually Maureen was all practical jokes and sarcastic humor. But sometimes, she was nice, almost tender. Confusing.

Maureen gestured at her phone. "Try your mom again."

Cassie groaned inwardly. Why couldn't Maureen just drop this? Cassie hauled her phone back out.

This time her dad answered.

"Hello?" his low voice said into the phone.

Cassie pressed the volume button way down, hoping Maureen hadn't heard. She kept silent.

"Hello, Cassie?" he said again. "Is everything okay?"

She didn't say a word. If she stayed very quiet, he'd think she'd butt-dialed him.

"I'm going to hang up. But text me if something's wrong."

He hung up, and Cassie put her phone away, her heart beating very hard. "No answer again," she said.

Maureen looked disappointed. "Oh well. Maybe next weekend."

"Yeah, maybe," Cassie echoed.

She was grateful when the dance ended, and she and Andrea made it back for the clandestine sleepover. She didn't know why, but she felt guilty for keeping it a secret from them. Why did the girls have to hide things?

CHAPTER THIRTY-EIGHT
Divisions and Splits

The morning announcements came on during first hour on Monday. Cassie paid them no mind, concentrating on a homework assignment that was due in third hour. Next to her in the hallway, Andrea had her phone out and was snapping selfies.

"And just a reminder," the formal voice said over the loudspeaker, "cheerleading tryouts are this Saturday. Any person desiring to try out needs to fill out a waiver and drop it off at the counselor's office before Friday. There will be practices after school every day this week."

Andrea dropped her phone. "Oh no," she gasped.

"What?" Cassie asked, looking up from her textbook.

"I forgot to tell my mom! I've got to stay for all the practices."

"You're trying out?" Cassie should have known. Last year, Cassie's friends Riley and Farrah had tried out, though neither had made it.

"Of course! Amity and I practice every time we're at my house."

"Oh, well, good luck," Cassie said, not meaning it at all. She didn't want her to make the squad. She just knew it would be the end of their friendship.

But apparently she was the only one who felt that way. It was all the girls talked about at lunch.

"So Maureen and Cara are coming to my house to practice," Amity said. "What about you, Andrea?"

"I can't today," she said. She had gotten over her "thing" with Amity, even though Amity never even realized she was mad at her. "My mom said I can stay for the practice after school but then I have to go home. But tomorrow everyone can come to my house."

Cara shook her head, taking a swig of her chocolate milk before speaking. "I can't tomorrow."

Cassie nibbled on her stick of cheese, watching all of them figure out their schedules. Already she felt left out.

"Am I the only one not trying out?" Janice asked, twirling a strand of her dark brown hair around her finger.

"Are you, Cassie?" Amity asked, focusing hazel eyes on her.

"No," Cassie said.

"Why not?"

"I don't want to."

"Me neither," Janice said. "Dancing's not my thing. I never even did Pep Squad, so I can't try out."

"Same," Cassie said, feeling a new kinship for Janice.

"Yeah, but," Amity said, "won't you two feel kind of awkward when the rest of us are cheerleaders and you're not?"

There was that. With any luck, none of her friends would make it.

※

"You look good," Riley said to Cassie in church Wednesday.

The girls had just finished a devotional and were outside doing some relays. The weather had cooled slightly but still had the lazy warmth of spring to it. The trees held pink and white flowers instead of leaves, the grass bright green with new life.

"Thanks," Cassie said. She sat down at a picnic table, catching her breath. Sprints were easier than running, but still not her favorite thing. "I've been eating more."

"That's great. How are you feeling about it?"

"It's fine."

"Your skin has better color to it."

"Yeah, well, that's because the sun's out again and I'm getting a tan." She still hadn't gotten her period back, though. Should she be worried about that? She hoped it wasn't going to be a permanent issue.

"Hi, Cassie. Riley." The table dipped slightly as Tyler sat down across from the girls.

Cassie gave him a furtive look. Did he know Riley had a huge crush on him? Was that why he always came over and said hello?

"Aren't you girls going to play?" he said, nodding at the other teens now throwing a football across the field. "Flag football. Come on."

"So you can yell at me when I miss the ball?" Cassie said. She'd never forgiven him for yelling at her when they played basketball together two years earlier.

"What?" He blinked his light blue eyes at her.

Apparently he didn't remember.

"Nothing." Cassie stood, not liking the way her body grew hot under his gaze. "I'm gonna get a drink of water. You can stay here, Riley."

She thought Riley would want to take advantage of the moment with Tyler, but instead she jumped up. "I'll go with you."

As soon as they were out of earshot, Cassie whispered, "Didn't you want to stay with him?"

Riley shrugged. "I never know what to say when you're not there."

They stepped into the air-conditioned church building, and Cassie gave a little shiver as the chilled air blew across the sweat on her forehead. She waited while Riley bent over the water fountain, then took her turn.

"Cassie?"

Both girls turned to see Sister Mecham coming down the hall.

"Oh, good, I was hoping to see you," she said.

"Yes?" Cassie hadn't really spoken to the church leader since last summer, when she'd been the camp director.

"You babysit, right?"

Cassie nodded.

"I'm looking for someone to babysit for me over the summer for three weeks. You won't stay the night, of course—well, except sometimes—but I've got a temporary job and need someone to watch my kids. Since you have three younger brothers and sisters, I thought you'd feel comfortable doing so."

"Sure, I'd love to!" Cassie said, already imagining the money she'd earn. "I just need to know the dates. I have lots going on this summer." The trip to New York, art camp, Girls Club camp with Riley . . .

"Thanks, Cassie!" Sister Mecham gave a big smile. "I'll talk to your mom and get the details ironed out."

After she walked away, Riley elbowed her. "Lucky! I want a babysitting job."

"Yeah, well." Cassie elbowed her back. "You only have one younger brother to put up with."

"But I put up with you," Riley returned. Then she took off running.

"Ha ha!" Cassie called after her.

⚜

"We are just weeks away from our trip to New York!" Ms. Vanderwood beamed at each of her choir students, wringing her fingers together in eager anticipation. "Please turn in your letters of recommendations!"

Cassie removed the letters she'd collected from church

members and teachers. She wasn't supposed to read them, but of course she had. They all praised her work ethic and integrity, stating she'd be an excellent candidate for the choir trip.

Though Cassie suspected it didn't matter. The children's choir was taking a trip to New York in June to sing at Carnegie Hall. Cassie had raised most of her money through fundraising, but she, unlike the other kids, wouldn't be singing. The performance was on Sunday, and Cassie's family strictly observed the Sabbath, which meant she couldn't sing with the choir. She didn't quite know what she'd do instead, but it didn't really matter. Getting to go to New York was enough.

"Great!" Ms. Vanderwood put all the letters into a file box. "Next week we also have our school performances, just like last year. Let's file into the auditorium and run through the acts."

Two days of nothing but singing. Cassie enjoyed these performances for elementary kids from nearby schools, but she tired of them very quickly. It was so much work to dance around with a giant smile.

She found her spot on the risers and launched into her performance face, making exaggerated facial expressions and giving emotional cues to the imaginary audience, just as her voice teacher, Ms. Malcolm, had taught her. When she glanced around, though, she noticed she was the only one with any sort of expression. The other students stood still and stoically, faces placid and mouths barely moving as they sang the notes.

Cassie straightened and sang with more confidence. She was a performer. She'd spent the past few years being coached and trained by various musical teachers and conductors for onstage productions.

The practice finally ended. Cassie approached Ms. Vanderwood at the conductor's stand as she put music folders back into the plastic tub she hauled around.

"Ms. Vanderwood," Cassie said.

The woman looked up and gave Cassie a smile. "Oh, hi, Cassandra. What is it?"

"I just noticed a lot of people aren't acting on the risers. Is that what we're supposed to be doing?"

"Oh, I'm glad you brought that up." She put the lid on the bin and pulled it upright so it rested on two little wheels beneath it. "I need you to tone it down up there. This is a choir, not a solo act. You're calling too much attention to yourself."

Cassie worked hard to keep her mouth closed. She nodded. Ms. Vanderwood had always complimented her before on her gestures and facial expressions, using her as an example. But now she didn't want her to be noticed. And last year Ms. Vanderwood had bumped Cassie from first soprano to second soprano.

Somehow she must have fallen out of favor with her music director.

As the school week wore on, tensions mounted, and the girls became more and more anxious. The school seemed taken over by hopeful cheerleaders, doing routines in the hallways, stretching out in the aisles.

"I'm so nervous," Amity blubbered on Friday, downing a Diet Coke. "This is like one of the most important things of my life."

Cassie snickered, but nobody noticed.

"I've been practicing so hard," Andrea said. "I know the routine by heart."

"My splits aren't as good as Amity's," Maureen said. "I just know she's going to make it."

"Amity, you're really good," Cara said. "You all are. You're going to do fine."

Cara alone looked calm, eating her pepperoni pizza as if nothing were amiss.

"Are you nervous?" Cassie asked her.

Cara winked at her. "I feel great. I'm super prepared."

Amity and Andrea exchanged glances, then Amity gave Cara a bright smile.

"I'm sure you'll do great tomorrow, also!" she said.

When Cara stood up to throw her trash away, Amity erupted into conversation.

"Cara's the worst one out there. She doesn't have the rhythm right, and she can't even lift her legs very high."

"I know," Maureen said. "I hate to get her hopes up, but she doesn't have what it takes."

"She hasn't even practiced as much as we have," Andrea piped up.

They settled back into a hushed silence as Cara returned. But Cara didn't seem to notice. The bell rang to end lunch, and Cara said, "If I don't see you before then, see you guys tomorrow!"

"Good luck," Cassie said again, standing up. "Call me as soon as the results are in."

꧁꧂

Cassie spent Saturday morning worrying about cheerleading almost as much as if she were trying out. Half of her was afraid her friends wouldn't make it, and she already knew how crushed they'd be. The other half of her feared they would make it and wondered what would happen to their friendship.

She knew the results were being posted at three. When no one called her, she called Andrea. Andrea didn't answer, so Cassie tried Maureen.

"Hi, Cassie," Maureen said.

"Well?" Cassie asked. "Do you know?"

"I just checked the list," she said. "I have the results."

"And?" Cassie asked, holding her breath.

"None of us made it. Except Cara." Maureen didn't sound sad so much as she sounded angry.

"Oh!" Cassie arched an eyebrow. "Cara made it? She must have done really well."

"Not really. The judges just picked her because she's got blond hair. Hey, I've got to go. I'll talk to you later."

That didn't make sense. Intrigued, Cassie tried Amity next. Amity, unlike Maureen, was sobbing.

"I didn't make it!" she said. "I knew the dance better than most of those girls, my high kicks were the best, and I didn't make it!"

"I'm so sorry," Cassie said, actually feeling bad for her.

"But Cara did!" Amity continued. "She didn't even finish the dance! She forgot the routine and just stood there with a smile. She still made it!"

"Really?"

"Yes! It's so unfair!"

Cassie consoled her the best she could before calling Cara.

"Cassie," Cara said. "Hi."

"Hi, Cara," Cassie said. "Congrats! I heard you made cheerleading!"

"Thanks," Cara said. "I think you're the only person who's happy for me. I knew it would be this way if one of us made it but the others didn't."

"Did the tryout go well?"

"Well, I actually messed up a few times. But when you mess up, my mom told me to just smile and pretend like nothing's wrong, so that's what I did. I guess it worked!"

The stories all corroborated the same thing. Now Cassie wished she'd seen the tryouts.

"It won't be as much fun without the other girls," Cara went on. "But I guess I'll just have to make new friends."

Uh-oh. That familiar knot returned to Cassie's stomach. This was what she'd feared: a drifting apart. "I'm sure it will be fine," she said, for Cara's sake as well as hers.

She'd barely hung up when Janice called. Cassie didn't usually spend so much time on the phone, but she answered immediately. "Hello?"

"I guess you heard?" Janice said.

"Yeah, Cara made it. Awesome, huh?"

"I don't think she should have. Amity said she had a horrible tryout."

"I think they should be happy for her and support her. Maybe they're just jealous."

"They're not, Cassie. I saw Cara practice. She wasn't good at all."

Cassie furrowed her brow. "Then how did she make it?"

"She's pretty. She has the perfect cheerleader body. That's how." Even Janice sounded mad.

"Do you think it's bad she made it?" Cassie asked.

"She's going to change now. She'll spend more time with the cheerleaders and act the way they do. She won't want to be our friend for long."

"I worry about that, too," Cassie admitted. "But maybe she won't."

"Oh, she will. You'll see."

Cassie hung up the phone, and she couldn't help feeling like Janice was right.

CHAPTER THIRTY-NINE
Glances and Blushes

"Yearbooks arrived today!" Cara popped over to the lunch table, her cheeks flushed with excitement. She carried several hardcover books under her arm and dropped them in the center of the table. "Most people won't get theirs until tomorrow," she said. "But since I'm on the yearbook staff, I got yours today!"

Almost as if by mutual agreement, none of the girls had acted angry with Cara for making cheerleading. But when the current cheerleaders crowded around Cara at the lockers, Cassie knew the resentment on her friends' faces was mirrored on hers. At least Cara turned down their offer to eat lunch with them.

"Oh, great!" Amity squealed. She picked up the first book. "This one's Maureen's. Andrea. Cassie."

Cassie accepted her book with a smile. They all flipped through, laughing at pictures, searching for themselves.

Cassie paused on her school photo and frowned. She looked like a little girl, nine or ten years old, not thirteen, as she had been. She glanced around at her beautiful friends and doubted she would ever fit. She picked up her cup to take a drink and realized she only had ice left. Cassie stood and scanned the water fountains, looking for the one with no line.

"Cassie!" Maureen shouted loudly. "Your fly's undone!"

Everyone at the table craned their necks to look at her. Cassie's eyes shot down to her pants, and sure enough, the zipper was down. Her face warmed and she sat back down, cursing Maureen as raucous laughter filled her ears.

"Only Cassie!" Amity cried, laughing so hard she was wiping her eyes.

Cassie blinked hard, afraid she might cry. "Thanks, Maureen. You could have told me quietly."

Cara gave her a sympathetic smile. "It's happened to all of us before."

Amity jerked haltingly to her feet, then mimed looking down at her pants. "Oh!" she cried, throwing her arms wide. "My fly's undone!"

"Holy crap," Maureen said, imitating Cassie's voice. "Everyone will see my granny underwear!"

"Stop, guys," Cassie said, trying to keep calm. "It's not that funny!" She banged her cup on the table, and the ice flew out like a frozen fountain, scattering across the tabletop and making them shriek louder.

"Sorry, sorry, you're just too much," Amity said, shoulders still shaking. "Come on, it's all in good fun." She put an arm around Cassie's shoulder. "Where's your yearbook? I want to sign it."

"Here, sign mine." Janice had a pen out already and handed her yearbook to Amity.

"Here, Cassie, do mine," Andrea said.

Everyone had forgotten about the fly incident, and Cassie let out a slow breath, glad they'd moved on. But her heart still hammered and her face was hot with embarrassment. And even though she felt stupid, her friends really didn't mean anything by it.

Why did they constantly make her the butt of their jokes, though? Sometimes she didn't even like them.

She tapped the pen to her lips and focused on Andrea's yearbook in front of her. She and Andrea had been best friends for a year, and then not for a year, and now they were almost like best friends. Cassie loved her dearly, but she also had a wary regard for her, understanding a side to Andrea she hadn't known before.

"Also," Cara said, "they're accepting applications for ninth grade StuCo. Just stop by the yearbook office to pick one up."

"I'm not running," Amity said with a snort. "Too much work."

Cassie had run rather unsuccessfully in seventh grade. But things had changed this year. She was in a cool group. She looked different. She might even consider herself popular.

"Well, I'm running again, of course," Cara said.

"I'll run," Janice said. "I want to be more involved."

"Yeah, why not?" Andrea shrugged. "I didn't make it last time, but I'll try again."

"Me too," Cassie said, surprising even herself. "I'll run."

"We can plan our campaigns together," Janice said, her face flushed with excitement.

The lunch bell rang before Cassie had started writing in Andrea's yearbook. She stood up, tucking the book under her arm. "I'll have to finish this later, Andrea, and get it back to you."

"That's okay," Andrea said, still bent over Cassie's book. "I'm not done either. I'll get it to you after school."

Cassie kept her message superficial, highlighting the fun they'd had and thanking Andrea for introducing her to a new group of friends. She left out all the negative emotions, all the hurt feelings.

Maureen handed Cassie her yearbook in choir.

"Andrea gave this to me to give to you. I signed it also. I hope that's okay."

"Of course!" Cassie beamed at her and accepted the book. "I want all my friends to sign it."

"Sign mine, too," Maureen said, handing it over.

"Okay." Cassie put it in her lap, then flipped through her yearbook until she found Maureen's message, then read it discretely, surprised to find it saying how much she appreciated Cassie's friendship and cheerful smile.

"My church dance is tomorrow," Cassie said, looking up at Maureen. "Want to come?"

Maureen's eyes widened. "Yeah! I'd love to."

※

Cassie hit the print button on the computer screen and settled back, watching as the printer spit out page after page of her finished manuscript. It had taken weeks, but she finally had it edited and proofed the way the editor had requested.

"Are you ready, Cassie?" Mrs. Jones appeared in the office doorway, purse on her arm and keys in hand.

"Almost." Cassie looked down at the simple gray dress with a brown belt she wore. The dance was later that night, but Cassie had a youth activity at church first. "We can stop at the post office on the way there, right?"

"As long as we leave now."

Cassie stuffed the manuscript into the thick envelope she already had prepared. "I'm ready."

"You look really nice," her mom said as they drove into town before heading toward Rogers. "Are you excited for the dance?"

"Very." A little nervous, too. Maureen and Amity and Andrea were all coming, riding with Andrea and meeting Cassie at the chapel before the dance started. "The school dance was so boring, I talked this one up to my friends. What if it's not that great?"

"Your friends will love it." Her mom gave her a grin. "They'll have a blast."

Cassie opened the mirror on the visor and sighed at herself. She'd clipped her dark hair at the hairline, getting it out of her face. The rest of it fell in straight sheets to her shoulders, plain as ever. She pulled red lipstick out of her purse and dabbed some on her lips. Her face had filled out slightly since she was eating more, and she tried to be at peace with this. Even her period had come back.

The trip to the post office went as quickly as Cassie had hoped, and thirty minutes later her mom pulled into the Rogers chapel.

"I'll pick you and your friends up after the dance. Call me if you have any issues."

"Okay," Cassie said, exhaling and smoothing her dress as she climbed out of the car. "Bye."

Inside, the youth were being divided into groups for scripture study and challenges. Cassie wandered about, waiting to be put in a group, when someone shouted, "Cassandra!"

She barely turned her head before a small person barreled into her, throwing her arms around Cassie's neck and pressing a kiss to her cheek.

"You're here. I'm so glad!"

Cassie took a step back and recognized Elise. The new Elise, with her dyed black hair and black-ringed eyes and black lipstick. "Hi," Cassie said, giving her a smile and trying not to show how much this new person intimidated her.

"Let's get out of here," Elise said, taking her hand and tugging her toward the exit.

"I just got here," Cassie said, resisting.

"We can come back for the dance," Elise said.

Cassie still didn't move, and Elise gave a huff.

"I have a friend who lives just down the street. She said she might come to this, but she's not here. Just walk with me over to her house."

Cassie relented. "Okay," she said, allowing Elise to tug her out the door.

The evening sun beat down on them, and Cassie hummed as she walked along the sidewalk with Elise. Elise didn't let go of her hand.

"It's such a beautiful day," Cassie said.

"I know, I love the sunshine." Elise sighed, tipping her face toward the sun and squinting her blue eyes. She turned back and smiled at Cassie, revealing a little of the girl Cassie used to know.

Cassie squeezed Elise's fingers. "Are you all right? You seem different."

"Oh, I'm great." Elise turned down a street, pulling Cassie along. "We're almost there."

The single-story brick house sat in the middle of a street of nearly identical houses. Elise let herself in, calling out, "Hello? April?"

The entryway was dark, with a kitchen leading to the right and a TV blaring over the fireplace.

"In here," a voice called from the kitchen.

Cassie lingered behind, following Elise but not too closely. The house smelled musty and a little rotten, and she didn't feel comfortable. Elise stopped at the kitchen table and leaned against it. Cassie paused in the doorway.

April stood at the counter, messing with the drawers. She was a larger girl with a silver nose ring and pink streaks in her shoulder-length blond hair. She wore a flannel over her white T-shirt and cut-off shorts. "Who's that?" she asked, bobbing her head at Cassie.

Elise turned toward her. "This is my friend, Cassie."

April studied Cassie with narrowed eyes. "Is she cool?"

"Yeah, she's cool."

Cool. A warm finger of pride brushed away some of Cassie's misgivings. No one had called her cool before.

"Cool," April repeated.

Cassie waited for Elise to say something about church, but she didn't. And then April pulled a carton of cigarettes out of the drawer. She tapped it in her palm, releasing a few of the slender sticks.

"Smoke?" she asked, offering one to Cassie.

"No," Cassie said, so startled she didn't even hesitate. "I don't smoke."

April stuck one in her mouth and eyed Elise. "You said she's cool?"

"Yeah, she's cool, but she doesn't smoke," Elise said, a note of agitation entering her voice. "So?"

April shrugged. She fished a lighter from the drawer and lit her cigarette. "So. Nothing."

She held the pack out toward Elise. Cassie held her breath. If Elise started smoking, she was afraid she'd cry. She didn't want to know.

Elise shook her head. "Nah."

April exhaled, blowing a puff of smoke into the small kitchen. Cassie added that odor to the others in the house.

No one spoke. Cassie crossed her arms over her chest and shifted, wishing she was still at the chapel. Or even outside, feeling the clean, warm sunshine on her face.

"Well," Elise said, finally pushing away from the table, "I guess we'll go."

April waved. "Kay. We'll see you."

"Bye."

Cassie didn't say bye. She shouldn't have come.

She took in a deep breath the moment they stepped outside. She held it, tasting the freshness before releasing it.

"Sorry about that," Elise said. "I didn't know she'd be smoking."

"Okay," Cassie said, because she didn't know what else to say. She'd spent enough time around Andrea to recognize a lie.

Andrea called Cassie's cell phone five minutes before the dance started.

"We're here," she said. "Out front. My mom won't leave until she sees you."

"I'll be right there."

No one had questioned Cassie about her absence earlier. She was trusted as a girl who made the right decisions, and the guilt pricked her conscience. She knew she shouldn't have left the chapel, but she'd gone anyway.

She put it all from her head and tried to focus on the upcoming dance. She stepped outside and smiled brightly when she saw Maureen, Amity, and Andrea standing around Mrs. Wall's car.

"You guys made it!" she squealed, excitement chasing away any of the earlier gloom. She hugged Andrea. "I love your dress!"

"Thanks." Andrea wore a flower-printed dress with fluttery sleeves. It came almost to her knee. She turned around to the car. "See, Mom? Here's Cassie. You can go now."

Mrs. Wall wasn't quite ready. "Cassie," she called.

Cassie ducked her head and looked into the car.

"Your mom's really okay with bringing everyone home?"

"Absolutely," Cassie said, nodding vigorously. "Yeah, it's totally fine."

"Okay, then." Mrs. Wall still looked uncertain. "Go in, then. Have fun."

"You can go," Andrea said, making a shooing motion with her fingers.

"I'll go once I see you safely inside," Mrs. Wall returned.

Andrea made a face and looped her arm through Amity's. "Let's get inside."

The dance had started, the halls and corridors emptying of kids. Music played in the gym, and Cassie led the way to the doors. She turned around to see her friends still lingering in the hall.

"Come on," she said, gesturing. "Let's go in."

"I don't want to," Maureen said. "This is going to be super lame."

"You came all the way here to stand in the hallway?" Cassie

said, getting annoyed. Maureen had sounded excited yesterday. Now it was lame?

"No," Andrea said, pushing away from the wall. "We may as well go in."

"Thank you," Cassie breathed, holding the door for her and going in after her. Maureen and Amity could stay out here.

It took a moment for Cassie's eyes to adjust to the dark, but when they did, she was not disappointed. Already dozens of kids danced together in the middle of the floor.

A boy stepped over to Andrea and held out his hand. "Want to dance?"

She looked at Cassie, slightly bewildered, and Cassie nodded.

"Go!"

"Sure." Andrea took his hand, and he led her onto the floor.

A tall boy with a head of crazy blond hair stepped up to Cassie. "How about you? Dance?"

She glanced behind her to see Maureen and Amity had come into the gym. She turned back to him. "Yes."

He spun her out onto the dance floor, immediately weaving her into fancy dance moves that she had no hope of copying. Cassie burst out laughing, and he did too. She didn't stop laughing the whole dance.

"What's your name?" he asked when it finished, during the brief pause before the next song started.

"Cassie. You?"

"I'm Andy."

"Nice to meet you," Cassie said, her face warming as she studied him more. The wild blond curls were kind of cute.

"Can you do something for me, Cassie?" he said.

"Sure," she replied, curious what he would want.

"I brought my friend Josh today. It's his first time, and he doesn't know anyone. Will you dance with him?" He pointed to a boy in a plaid shirt and beige pants, standing against the wall with a cup of punch in his hands.

Cassie shrugged, a little disappointed Andy didn't need something for himself. "That's fine. Do I have to ask him?"

"Nah. Come on over, I'll work it out for you." Andy gestured Cassie forward, and she followed him to the wall just as another song began.

"Hey, Josh," Andy said.

Josh looked up and gave a toss of his head, sending the strands of his straight blond hair back behind his face. "Hey, Andy," he said with an easy smile. His eyes were a light blue behind round glasses frames.

"This is Cassie," Andy said, bringing her forward. "I brought her here to dance with you."

It was hard to say for sure in the darkened room, but it seemed as though the pale skin on Josh's cheeks flushed pink. "Thanks," he said, though he didn't sound so grateful.

"So go dance," Andy said. "The song's halfway over."

Cassie waited. Josh held out his hand, looking unsure of himself.

"Want to dance?" he asked.

"Of course," Cassie said, giving him what she hoped was an encouraging smile.

Josh's fingers closed around her hand, and he pulled her onto the center of the floor. His hand clasped hers tightly while the other hand went to her waist. "Is this how it works?"

"Almost." Cassie rearranged his fingers so they threaded hers, then rested her hand on his shoulder. "Now we're good."

His muscles were tense beneath her hand, and she tried to think of conversation to help him be less nervous. "This is your first dance?"

"Yes. Ever. Well, except at school, but it's different."

"Oh, yes." Cassie laughed, remembering her own school dance experience. "Nobody actually dances."

He laughed with her, his shoulders relaxing. He had nice eyes, Cassie decided.

"How many dances have you been to?" he asked.

"This is only my second. But I loved my first one so much, I couldn't wait for this one. I even brought all my friends. Hey!" She brightened as she thought of something. "It's their first time too. You should ask them to dance! They are just as nervous as you are!"

"Yeah, okay." He looked much more at ease now, and his hand swayed hers in time to the music as he moved with her around the dance floor.

"Where are you from?" Cassie asked. "I haven't seen you before."

"No, I don't live here. I go to school with Andy. In Tahlequah."

"Tahlequah?" Cassie echoed, unfamiliar with the location.

"It's in Oklahoma. About two hours from here."

"Ah." She nodded. "I'm from Springdale. About thirty minutes from here."

She parodied his words, and he grinned at her.

The song finished, and Cassie dropped her hand. "Thanks for the dance, Josh."

"Thank you."

She started to turn away, and then he grabbed her arm, spinning her back.

"Cassie!"

"What?" she asked, lifting an eyebrow in surprise.

He dropped her hand, and this time there was no mistaking the blush on his face. "I just thought since we only got half a dance, we could do one more?"

"Sure, of course." Cassie returned to the dancing position.

Josh's hand closed around hers, his gaze focused on her so intensely that she felt like she should look away. But she didn't.

The song started, and Josh moved her in tune to the music. Cassie stole a glance at the wall and saw that Maureen, at least, was dancing with Andy. And there was Andrea, dancing with Tyler. Only Amity hadn't moved.

"What grade are you in?" he asked.

"Eighth grade," she said.

"Eighth!" he exclaimed. "How old are you?"

Cassie couldn't tell what he meant by that tone. "I'm fourteen. You?"

"Um, well." His eyes darted to the corner and then back to her. "I'm afraid to tell you."

"Why?"

"You might think I'm too old."

Too old for what? But Cassie just gave him a bewildered look. "I won't."

"Promise?"

"Yes."

"I'm sixteen." He looked apprehensive as he said it, his eyebrows raised above his wire frames.

Sixteen! The two-year difference between them meant the world. "So you can drive?"

He bobbed his head. "I have a license, yeah."

She thought of something else. "What grade are you in?"

"Tenth grade."

"You're in high school!"

He nodded again. "See? That's why I didn't tell you."

"Well, that's silly." She waved him off. "It's not like it makes a difference."

"Really?"

"Really." So she'd never talked to anyone that much older than her. It didn't mean she couldn't.

The song ended, and Cassie stepped back. Amity, Andrea, and Maureen all stood by the wall again. Cassie frowned. "Will you ask my friends to dance now?" She pointed them out. "They came with me. They're not usually nervous, but here they seem to be."

"I get that. I'm not usually nervous either. But this is a different kind of dance." He took her hand again. "Lead the way."

Cassie pulled him over to her friends and put on a big smile. "Hey guys! Are you dancing?"

"Yeah, we've all danced, except Amity," Maureen said.

Amity, the perpetual flirt. Why wasn't she dancing? Cassie frowned at her and thrust Josh her direction. "I want you guys to meet my friend Josh."

"Hi, Josh," Amity said, her eyes flickering to life as she looked him over.

"Want to dance?" he asked her, letting go of Cassie's hand to extend it toward Amity.

"Yes." She uncrossed her arms and pushed off the wall, sending an undecipherable look toward Andrea.

Maureen moved closer to Cassie. "Do you like him?"

"Who?"

"Josh!"

"Oh." Cassie looked back at the blond boy leading Amity across the dance floor. "Yeah, he's nice."

"He was holding your hand, Cassie."

"Oh, it wasn't like that!" Cassie laughed. "I was bringing him over to you guys to meet him."

Both girls stared at Josh and Amity as they danced, Amity laughing, tossing her wavy brown locks over her shoulder. Cassie sighed. What guy would ever choose Cassie over Amity?

"I've met the famous Tyler now," Andrea said behind them. "Super hot."

"He is," Cassie said, surprising herself.

The song ended, and Josh and Amity returned to the girls.

"Cassie?" he said, holding out his hand.

"Sure," she said, accepting.

CHAPTER FORTY
Popularity Calls

Cassie made sure Josh danced with both Maureen and Andrea, but he came back to dance with her in between each one.

"I hope you don't mind that I like to dance with you," he said during the fourth dance.

"No, of course not," she said. "We all want to dance."

"Yeah, but I only want to dance with you."

Cassie started to laugh, but then she realized his eyes were quite serious behind the wire-framed glasses. "You do?"

"You're the prettiest girl I've ever met."

Cassie stared at him in disbelief.

He squeezed her hand. "Sorry. Was that too bold?"

"No, no," she said, shaking her head and trying to wrap her mind around that. He thought she was pretty? The prettiest?

He let her go when the song ended, but he said, "I'm really glad I came tonight. Or I might not have met you."

"Same," Cassie said with a smile, flattered by all the attention.

Cassie gave a little sigh of contentment when she returned to the wall.

"I think I like him," Amity said as Josh took Andrea for

another dance.

"Who?" Cassie asked. She looked around the room, but she hadn't been paying attention to who Amity danced with.

"Josh," Amity said. "He's fine. Super blue eyes and kind of scholarly with those glasses. Plus he's in high school."

Maureen arched an eyebrow at Cassie, but Andy came over and claimed Maureen for a dance just as Tyler's brother Jason asked Cassie to dance.

"How's the dance going for you?" Jason asked. Unlike his younger brother, Jason had never been anything but kind to Cassie. He was a bit quieter than Tyler, taller and more serious, but always friendly and considerate.

"So much fun," Cassie said. "I love these dances."

"Yeah," Jason said. "It's a good way to get to know other people. Like that guy there." He nodded at Josh and gave Cassie a little smirk. "He seems to have enjoyed meeting you."

"He's been very nice to me and my friends," Cassie said.

"Uh-huh." Jason gave her a wink as if they were in on a secret together.

Cassie wasn't surprised when the song ended and she spotted Josh making his way toward her. But before he got to her, Amity intercepted him, taking his hand and pulling him onto the dance floor.

A wave of annoyance at Amity's brazenness washed over Cassie. She shrugged it off, pressing her lips together in a firm line and going back to the wall. It was just how things went. Guys always liked Amity more.

Cassie watched Amity and Josh for a moment before deciding to grab another cup of punch. She stepped toward the dance floor in time to hear her name.

"Cassie!"

She looked up and saw Amity beckoning her over.

"What is it?" Cassie asked, stepping to her and Josh.

Amity still clutched his hand in hers. She released it now and pulled Cassie over to stand in front of him. "Here, you guys dance. I need a drink."

Cassie watched her duck out of the gym, mildly concerned. "Is she okay?"

"I think so." Josh's fingers closed over hers, and his easy grin shoved away her worries. "She just said she was thirsty and I should dance with you." He leaned closer and whispered in her ear, "I'm glad, though. I'd rather be with you."

◦~·~◦

"I got Andy's phone number," Maureen said breathlessly as the girls piled into Mrs. Jones' car after the dance. "Do you think he'll text?"

"Tyler said he can't wait to see me at the next dance," Andrea said. "It was so much fun, Cassie! Thanks for inviting us!"

Only Amity was quiet, so Cassie nudged her. "Did you have fun?"

"Yeah," she said. "Yeah, it was great. Did you get Josh's number?"

"Who's Josh?" Mrs. Jones asked, a note of intrigue in her voice.

"Just a boy I met," Cassie said.

"And you got his number?"

"Uh-huh," Cassie confirmed, face warming.

"Did he get yours?"

"Yes." Cassie waited for the rest of the twenty questions, but Mrs. Jones must have decided to hold off—for now.

Amity and Andrea were dropped off first at Andrea's house, and then they continued out of town toward Maureen's house.

"So you know what was wrong with Amity?" Maureen said, leaning closer to Cassie, who sat beside her in the middle seat.

"No," Cassie said, who had noticed Amity was being quiet but hadn't realized something was wrong. "What was it?"

"Well, you know how she said she liked Josh, right? And

then she went off and danced with him."

Like she owned him. Cassie nodded, remembering the spurt of silly jealousy she'd felt.

"While she danced with him, all he could talk about was you. She got so sick of hearing it that she ended the dance early and told you to dance with him."

"Oh!" Cassie gasped. So that was what had happened! "I had no idea!"

Maureen nodded, her eyes glittering. "She was really upset. Guys don't usually turn her down."

And for Cassie! She couldn't even believe it. "That's crazy!"

"He really likes you," Maureen whispered before settling back in her chair.

Josh called Cassie on Sunday, and while Cassie normally struggled to make small talk on the phone, somehow he kept the conversation going for an hour. By the time it ended she knew he was the youngest of three boys, liked to hunt, enjoyed a good barbecue, and couldn't wait to see her again.

And then he said the words that blew her away.

"Can I be your boyfriend?" he asked.

Cassie had spent the past year daydreaming about a certain boy asking her those words, both dreading and hoping it would happen. She could hardly believe it now. It wasn't Miles doing the asking—but she knew for a fact that he didn't like her. So why not Josh?

"Um, wow," Cassie said, buying time. "I didn't expect that."

"You didn't? I thought you knew how much I like you."

"Well, okay, then," Cassie said. "Sure."

She waited to feel something. A sense of euphoria, of triumph, the heat of sudden love and passion. But nothing happened. If anything, she felt a little let down.

"Yes!" he said, clearly feeling all the sensations Cassie was not. "When can I see you again?"

"I don't know." Tahlequah was two hours away, after all.

"The next dance?"

"I can drive, you know. I'll come up and see you on a Saturday. We can hang out this summer."

An anxious knot formed in her stomach. This suddenly felt real. He had a car, and she was his girlfriend, and he expected things from her.

Like kissing.

The anxious knot doubled up, and Cassie feared she'd be sick.

"Listen, I've got to go," she said. "I'll call you later, okay?"

"Sure, beautiful," he crowed. "Talk to you soon."

Cassie's hand shook as she ended the call. Then, unable to keep it to herself, she called Andrea.

By Monday, half the school knew Cassie had a high school boyfriend. Girls cornered her in the hall and asked questions, wanted to know what he looked like, how they'd met. Cassie's initial reluctance was rapidly replaced by pride, as if she'd accomplished something by landing an older boy. Even her friends treated her with a certain cool factor they never had before.

"Cassie, I need to make sure I'm in science with you next year," Amity said at lunch. "Who are you taking?"

They'd all been given schedule sheets in first hour, and they were supposed to fill them out with their first and second choices of classes for ninth grade.

"Make sure you put choir down," Maureen said, tapping the spot for seventh hour. "We'll be in there together."

"I'm trying out again," Janice said. "Hopefully I'll be with you guys next year."

"Me, too," Amity said.

Cassie nodded. "I hope you get in this time."

By the time lunch was over, she'd signed up for science with Andrea and Amity, Spanish with Andrea, history with Janice and Andrea, and math with Cara, Andrea, and Amity.

"Don't forget," Cara said as the bell rang and they all stood up to leave, "StuCo votes are next week."

Cassie hadn't forgotten, and she felt more confident than ever. Now that she had a boyfriend, she was sure to make it.

⊙~⋅❀⋅~⊙

"Cassie." Andrea grabbed Cassie's arm the moment she stepped into the bathroom Tuesday morning. "You won't believe what Amity said."

Cassie glanced around the bathroom. Neither Cara nor Amity had arrived yet. "What?"

Andrea lowered her voice. "She's telling everyone that Josh liked her before you and he'll eventually go back to his first love."

"What?" Cassie gasped out. She wasn't disillusioned enough to think she was in love with Josh, but he was her boyfriend. Amity had no right to make Cassie look bad that way.

"Don't worry," Andrea said, squeezing her arm. "I told her off. Everyone knows it's not true."

"Hey, guys!" As if summoned by an invisible force, Amity herself walked into the bathroom. She smiled, flashing white teeth as she tossed her light brown hair over her shoulder. "I couldn't sleep last night, I kept remembering how much fun we had at the dance." She let out a long sigh. "Josh and Andy were so sweet, weren't they? Making sure we had someone to dance with. I wrote Josh a letter last night. I just need his address so I can mail it. That's okay, right, Cassie?" She focused on Cassie now, her eyes slightly narrowed, though Cassie couldn't tell if it was a sincere question or a challenge.

This was her chance. She sensed Andrea behind her, waiting with bated breath for the drama.

But Cassie couldn't bring herself to confront her. Instead she shrugged. "Yeah, it's fine. I'm not worried. Josh is crazy about me." That was as bold as she got.

"That's great," Amity said, her smile tightening.

Watching her friend examine her reflection, Cassie decided she would conveniently forget to give her the address.

But by lunchtime, Cassie realized she didn't need to worry about Amity. When Amity mentioned Josh's name for the third time, Cara laid into her.

"You need to stop talking about Cassie's boyfriend that way," she said, her tone uncharacteristically harsh. "We know you like every guy you see. Have some respect for your friends."

That silenced Amity.

"The Lokomotion lock-in is this Friday," Janice said. "Who's going?"

"What's the lock-in?" Cassie asked, happy for the subject change.

"Oh, it's put on by our church," Janice said. "We spend all night there. You can do laser tag, bumper boats, miniature golf, go-karts, but you can't fall asleep!"

"Sounds like fun! Can anyone go?"

"We're all going," Amity said.

"You want to come, Cassie?" Janice said. "We'll get you a ticket."

"Yes!" Cassie smiled. She was finally a part of this group. "I would love to."

Josh called again that night. Cassie told him about the day, about Amity's actions, and Josh reacted angrily.

"Amity? Who's Amity? I don't even remember her. She's nothing beside you. Sorry, not trying to be mean, but your friends aren't even pretty. I only danced with them to be nice."

The flattery warmed her heart, and Cassie leaned toward the phone, wondering if she might be developing feelings for him after all. "Really?"

"You don't even know, do you? You're beautiful. I couldn't believe it when Andy brought you over."

Cassie laughed. "You're pretty cute, too. You have nice eyes."

"You said you're going to a lock-in on Friday?"

"Yes."

"Will there be boys there?"

"Hmm." Cassie hadn't asked considered that. "Pretty sure."

"You're not going to like another guy, are you?"

"What? No way." She laughed again. She hadn't really noticed any boys since Miles.

"Promise? You tell them you have a boyfriend."

"I promise."

Cassie hung up, delighted by the fact that a boy adored her so much.

Cassie had never experienced popularity like she did now.

She missed two days of school for the field trip performances with her choir. When she got home, she fielded calls from all her friends. Amity wanted to know if she might have a chance with Andy. Andrea wanted to complain about Amity. And Maureen pretended to be Josh, dropping her pitch and trying to sound like a boy, which only made Cassie laugh harder.

Friday was the end of school assembly, even though they still had two weeks left. Cassie wore a dress to school, as was required for the choir concert.

She spotted Maureen at her locker before school started, dressed in a red blouse and jeans. Cassie grabbed her arm.

"Maureen! You're not wearing a dress!"

Maureen frowned at the blue and black print dress Cassie wore. "Why should I be?"

"The choir concert! It's required!"

Maureen's eyes went wide, and she let out a little gasp. "I forgot!"

Cassie checked the time on the clock by the lockers. "Call your mom!"

Maureen already had her phone out. "Mom? I need a dress. For the school assembly. It's in like ten minutes! Yes. Hurry!"

She hung up, her cheeks flushed. "She's coming."

"Great."

The warning bell rang, and Cassie turned to head to class.

"Cassie! Wait with me."

Cassie faced Maureen. "Okay. Let's tell the office so we don't get marked absent."

The halls emptied as the students disappeared into classrooms. Cassie stood with Maureen at the school entrance, waiting anxiously for the appearance of Maureen's mom. The announcements came on, and then the classes were dismissed to the gymnasium for the assembly. Cassie took a deep breath, hopping nervously from foot to foot.

"We're going to miss the performance," she murmured.

"No, we won't!" Maureen snapped. But she looked just as agitated.

Finally her mom's car appeared, and Maureen threw the doors open. "Come on!"

The two girls raced down the sidewalk, and Maureen accepted the skirt from her mom. "Thanks!" she said, already turning around.

But Cassie spotted another car and frowned, squinting her eyes in recognition. "Daddy?"

The door to the little sports car opened, and Mr. Jones climbed out. "Hi, Cassie."

Maureen stopped and stared at him also.

"What are you doing here?" Cassie asked.

"The school called me and told me to be here."

"Why would they do that?" The school hadn't done that before.

"I don't know." Mr. Jones shrugged. "Let's go in."

Maureen pressed her hand to her mouth. She tugged Cassie's hand and whispered, "You're going to win an award!"

"What?" Cassie whispered back.

"Yes! That's why the school called him!"

Could it be? Cassie tried not to get her hopes up, but the

thought excited her.

Maureen changed into her skirt quickly and the girls ran to the gymnasium, arriving just in time for the choir performance. Ms. Berry gave them the evil eye, but they both managed to catch their breath enough to sing.

Afterward, Cassie spotted her dad on the bleachers and climbed up to join him, Maureen following her.

"Oh, I'm sure you won something!" she breathed, clutching Cassie's hands and squeezing them.

Cassie watched as all of the teachers stepped up to the microphone and named their students of the year. When Ms. Talo stepped up, Cassie's heart rate quickened. Surely if any teacher was going to award her, it would be her English teacher. Ms. Talo always praised her and recognized her hard work, especially where her book was concerned.

"Erica Reeder," Ms. Talo said, and Cassie sank back with a sigh. That had been her best chance.

"I'm not going to win anything," she told Maureen.

But Maureen did not let go of her hand. She squeezed harder and held her breath with each teacher that went to the mic. Cassie bit her lip.

Mr. Adams stepped forward. Cassie and Andrea were student helpers in his seventh grade math class, and he taught her science class. He did tend to show Cassie more leniency than other students. Maybe—

"Cassandra Jones," his deep voice boomed into the microphone.

Maureen squealed and threw her hands up, releasing Cassie. Which was just as well, since Cassie had to walk down the bleachers and across the gym floor, her face burning with embarrassment and pride as the whole student body looked on. She shook Mr. Adams' hand, accepted her certificate, and returned to the bleachers.

"I told you," Maureen said, beaming as proudly as if she'd won herself.

CHAPTER FORTY-ONE
Free Pass

Right before the assembly ended, the principal stepped up to the microphone and reminded them about the in-school basketball game.

"All students wishing to stay and watch the game can pay a dollar. The rest will return to their classes."

Cassie hugged her dad and said goodbye, then stood to go to class.

"Where are you going?" Maureen said, standing as well. "Cara and Amity are sitting over there." She pointed to the other side of the bleachers.

"To class," Cassie said. "I hate sports."

"Oh, no you don't." Maureen grabbed her arm. "You're staying for this."

Cassie couldn't imagine anything more boring than watching a bunch of boys throw around a ball. "I didn't bring any money."

Maureen hauled a dollar from her purse and slapped it into Cassie's hand. "Now you've got money."

She had no choice. Swallowing a sigh, she handed over her dollar to the collecting teacher and climbed the bleachers again, settling in beside Amity and Cara.

"Cassie, hey!" Amity said, scooting over and bumping her shoulder.

"Hey."

Someone poked Cassie in the back. "Hey, Cassie."

The boy voice made her turn around. She widened her eyes when she saw Miles, Emmett, Will, and Andrew.

"Hi, guys," she said uncertainly.

They all smiled and waved at her, and Cassie wondered which one had poked her. She couldn't help glancing at Miles before looking away, her face burning as she remembered the last time they'd talked.

"Is that your yearbook?" Emmett asked, nodding at her unzipped backpack.

"Yes."

"Can I sign it?"

"Sure." Cassie handed it over, a bit baffled. Her eyes went to Miles again before darting away.

Maureen leaned close to her and whispered in her ear, "I heard Miles likes you."

"He doesn't," Cassie whispered back. "We asked him."

"Months ago. Things change."

Cassie didn't believe Maureen, not for a second. She sat stiffly as the game began and pretended to be interested. But she just wasn't. Opening her backpack, she pulled out a book.

"No, you don't!" Amity whacked her shoulder. "You didn't come here to read!" She took the book and smacked Cassie's leg with it.

But I want to read, Cassie thought.

"Yay!" Amity cheered as one of the teams scored. She grabbed Cassie's hands. "Clap!"

Cassie clapped.

"Now stomp your feet and yell!"

Cassie giggled, feeling silly as she did as instructed.

To her surprise, she found herself enjoying the game. She forgot about her book and cheered alongside Amity, who grinned at her every time she did.

The game ended, and they all stood to go back to class.

"Here, Cassie," Will said, offering her yearbook to her. "I hope you don't mind, I signed it too."

"Sure, that's fine," Cassie said, again marveling. Will hadn't spoken to her since sixth grade, when he asked Cassie to be his girlfriend and she turned him down. He'd spread ugly rumors about her, and they hadn't talked since.

The boys headed down in front of the girls, and Cassie opened her yearbook. Her hand fluttered to her mouth, and she froze.

It wasn't just Will and Emmett who signed her yearbook, but Miles also. And beneath the half a page of handwriting, he'd written his name with a heart beside it.

⁂

"Cassie, who are you riding home with?" Amity asked at lunch.

Cassie shrugged. Tonight was the lock-in at Lokomotion. "I don't know. Who's got room for me?"

"You can ride with me," Amity said.

"Or me," Maureen said.

"I already told my mom you were coming with me," Andrea said, her tone bossy. "She told your mom, also."

"I guess I'm going with Andrea."

Maureen frowned. "I already asked my dad. He said he'd pick us up when it's over and bring you to my house." Maureen's parents were divorced, with her mom living out in the country close to Cassie and her dad in town near the other girls.

"Sure," Cassie said, trying not to show how pleased she was by the attention. "I'll ride with Andrea tonight and you tomorrow."

Even with that settled, Cassie made sure to find Andrea quickly after school in case her friend forgot. She didn't want to be stranded.

"Are you ready?" Andrea said, giving Cassie a big smile as they got into Mrs. Wall's car.

"Yes!" Cassie shifted her weight in the seat. "Have you done this before? Is it hard to stay awake?"

"Oh, yeah, we all did it last year, and it's *so* hard." Andrea rolled her eyes to emphasize how hard it was.

One more adventure they'd all had without Cassie. It might have taken nine months, but she finally felt like they accepted her, included her.

"Now," Andrea said after dinner as she plugged in her curling irons, "time to make ourselves pretty."

"There's no hope for me," Cassie said, flicking a strand of nearly black hair and staring at her reflection. Dark, almond-shaped eyes peered back at her.

"Yeah, whatever," Andrea scoffed. She grabbed Cassie's shoulders and turned her, scrutinizing her. "You could do with a change, though. I know!" Her eyes lit up. "Let's cut bangs!"

Amity had recently cut giant bangs that looked like claws on her forehead. Cassie wrinkled her nose. "I don't think that's a good idea."

"Not like Amity's!" Andrea said, laughing. "Just a few hairs. Like this."

Before Cassie could protest, Andrea snagged a handful of hair and snipped it off. Cassie gasped as the strands floated past her nose.

"Look, look!" Andrea pressed her cheek next to Cassie's and rotated her to see in the mirror.

The effect of such a simple change was immediate. Cassie's eyes appeared even larger and more luminous directly beneath the locks of hair. "Wow."

"Let's curl them."

"I like them the way they are," Cassie said, eyeing the hot metal barrel as Andrea approached her.

"They'll look better this way."

More like claws, Cassie thought. But she held still as Andrea wrapped the hair around the rod and turned inward.

"Ouch!" Cassie reared back as something hot seared her forehead. The hair unraveled from the curling iron, frizzy and haywire from the attempt.

"Oh, I'm so sorry!" Andrea cried. "Did I burn you?"

Cassie lifted the bangs and winced at the exposed flesh on her forehead. "Yes."

"It's okay." Andrea pushed the bangs back down. "This will cover it." She pulled out a bottle of hair spray, and Cassie cried out as the stinging drops hit her face.

"Shh, shh! There, you can't even tell."

Cassie looked again at her reflection. She could still see, thought it wasn't so obvious. And the bangs looked nice.

Andrea and Cassie immediately began looking for the other girls when they got to Lokomotion, but Amity found them first. She ran over to them.

"Andrea, Cass—whoa!" She pulled up short when she saw them, her eyes locking on Cassie's. "Wow! I love the bangs!"

"Thanks," Cassie said, a little sheepishly.

"Guess what, guess what!" Amity said, grabbing Cassie's arm and jumping up and down. "Janice and I both made Unison! We'll be in choir with you and Maureen next year!"

"That's great!" Cassie said, joining her in her enthusiastic movement.

"Come on. Everyone's over here. We're doing laser tag first." Amity led them over to Maureen, Cara, and Janice.

"I love your hair," Janice said. "Did you cut bangs?"

"Andrea did," Cassie said. "She did a good job. She just burned my forehead a little." Cassie laughed and lifted her bangs to show off the burn.

"Ouch," Janice said. "But yeah, pretty good."

Cassie was awful at laser tag. Her score was so bad it was humiliating, and she gladly abandoned the game for the go-karts outside.

"Stay in your lane on the track," the guy said as he helped them into their cars. "Don't run into other cars or we'll take you out."

Cassie gripped the steering wheel and stared down the roadway. How hard could it be? She'd never driven a car before, but everyone else was managing just fine.

The timer buzzed, and she pressed her foot into the gas pedal. The car lurched forward and nearly stopped before Cassie rammed her foot into it again. Then it jerked before taking off down the track.

Too fast. She gasped and let go, forgetting to turn her wheel. The car slammed into the side of the track.

"Not good," Cassie murmured, turning her wheel and managing to hit the gas at the same time.

The car swiveled back into its lane just as another car roared past, and Cassie collided with it.

"Watch it!" the kid driving yelled.

"Sorry!" Cassie yelled back. Her heart pounded harder, and sweat beaded on her forehead. She'd expected this to be easier.

She breathed a sigh of relief when she got back to the track. But as she went around the next curve, she turned the wheel too hard and rammed into another car.

"Hey!" the guy in charge shouted. "Stop hitting the other cars!"

"I'm not trying to!" Cassie cried. She maneuvered her car away and eased onto her gas pedal, slowly moving down the track.

There was another car in front of her, and it was going slower than she was. She turned the wheel to go around it just as the car came to a halt.

"Why are you stopping?" Cassie exclaimed, unable to hit her brake fast enough. Her head whipped forward as she slammed into the rear of the other vehicle.

"That's it, you're off the track!" The guy was out there now, and he gestured with his thumb back to the line. "Out!"

Really? She'd been kicked out? Her face hot, Cassie tried to keep her head high as everyone in line watched her walk of shame off the track.

Maureen and Amity were waiting.

"What happened?" Maureen asked.

"Did you seriously get kicked out?" Amity peered at Cassie. "You're more of a rebel than I thought."

⊙〜⋇〜⊙

Cassie did bumper boats next, and then miniature golfing, and then she sat down in a chair and struggled to stay awake. By the time the event ended at seven in the morning, she was never so happy to leave somewhere.

She and Maureen fell asleep almost the moment they got to Maureen's dad's house. They woke up around three in the afternoon, and Maureen kept up a steady chatter as Mr. Hemming drove Cassie home.

"Did you have fun?" Mrs. Jones asked from the dining room when Cassie stepped inside.

"Yes," Cassie said. She didn't mention the go-kart incident.

"Good." Her mom picked up a pile of envelopes and tapped them on the table. "I have some news—about Elek."

Cassie froze, one hand running through her hair. Elek was only a few years older than her, but he'd been arrested two months earlier for stealing a car and threatening a girl. "And?" She barely opened her mouth to ask, afraid of what the answer would be.

"He has a court hearing next month. Do you want to come?"

"Is that like a trial?" Cassie whispered. Her heart squeezed at the idea. People would judge him. People who didn't know anything about him.

"Kind of. But with only a judge. No jury."

"And I can come?" She thought she would cry.

"If you want to. It won't be easy for you to hear. It's right after your choir gets back from New York."

She nodded, blinking hard. She knew what would happen to Elek, and she knew this might be her last chance to see him. She wanted to be there, no matter how difficult it was.

"I thought so." Mrs. Jones smiled and rattled the envelopes again. "This letter came for you."

A letter! Cassie brightened instantly and plucked it from her mom's fingers. It wasn't a big envelope like the one the publisher sent. So who could it be from? "Who sent it?"

Her mom gave her a mischievous smile. "I don't know."

Cassie narrowed her eyes and flipped it over, scanning the return address. "Josh! Josh wrote me!" She ran to the room she shared with Emily and closed the door before opening the letter.

Hey beautiful! Josh began. He went on to detail his day and how happy he was now that she was his girlfriend, and how he couldn't wait to see her again. The hand-written letter rambled on for four pages, and he gushed over her and told her he was totally in love with her. He included a picture of himself and asked her to call him.

Glowing with the compliments and the knowledge that someone besides her mom thought she was beautiful, Cassie called him.

"Hey!" he exclaimed. "I'm so glad to hear from you. I missed you so much. Did you miss me?"

Cassie hadn't really thought about him that much. She'd been having fun with her friends. But she sensed it wouldn't be polite to say so. "Yeah. I missed you."

"Did any boys hit on you at your lock-in?"

She laughed at the idea. "No. Of course not."

"Good. I thought about you all weekend. I worried you'd find someone else."

"Nope." Cassie sat down in a chair and played with her toes. Should she feel something when she talked to him? Excitement? Desire to see him?

"You're not that kind of girl, are you? You're loyal."

He said it with such fondness in his voice. Cassie considered the question. Was she loyal? Loyal to Josh? She had no reason not to be.

Even if Miles had signed her yearbook with a heart.

"Yep. I'm loyal," she said.

"Let's plan a barbecue for when school gets out. Andy and I will come up, we can spend the day with you."

Cassie straightened, imagining how Amity and Maureen would take that news. "Can I invite my friends?"

"Sure. Maybe we'll bring up a few other guys."

Cassie closed her eyes, imagining how pleased the girls would be. She'd be the most important person if she pulled this off. "Oh, I can't wait!"

"Great. I love you."

Cassie nearly choked. Josh had said it in the letter several times, but reading the words hadn't affected her the way hearing them did. She gave a weak laugh.

"Don't you love me?" he said into the silence.

"We're still getting to know each other," she said. "Let's do one thing at a time."

"Okay," he said, sounding a little disappointed. "You're right. Talk to you later, Cassie."

Cassie took Josh's picture to school the next day. All the girls wanted to see, and they looked at Cassie with gazes of admiration and something like envy. Cassie felt it. She reveled in it.

"He's cute," one girl said. "How did you get a guy so cute?"

The question bordered on offensive, but Cassie shrugged it off. "I guess he just likes me."

When she told Amity and Andrea about the barbecue before first hour, it was all anyone wanted to talk about. Except Janice, who seemed a little put out.

"Josh wrote me a long letter," Cassie said. She hesitated,

then blurted, "He says he loves me."

She half expected her friends to echo her sentiments of reluctance, but instead they squealed and hugged her and jumped up and down.

"How romantic!" Amity said.

"Did you bring the letter?" Maureen asked.

Cassie nodded and pulled all four pages from her binder. She had no say in the matter as her friends took it from her and read it together. The bell finally rang, and Cassie collected the letter before heading to class.

Her mind whirled as pieces clicked into place. Something about having a boyfriend, about someone else seeing her as desirable, made her more so to everyone else.

"Cassie, I need to talk to you," Andrea said before lunch, finding Cassie at her locker and hauling her down the hall.

"What is it?" Cassie said, freeing herself and frowning at Andrea.

"Janice said you were saying things about me behind my back," Andrea said.

"What?" Cassie exclaimed, her mouth dropping open.

"She said you said I'm bad at cutting hair. And it's not the first time you've said things about me."

Cassie couldn't believe it. She vaguely remembered a conversation with Janice where she mentioned Andrea had cut her bangs, but she hadn't said anything negative, had she? She straightened her shoulders. "I only said that you cut my hair and I burned my forehead. Janice is lying." Cassie had never said such bold words against one of her friends, but anger moved her.

"Why would she lie?" Andrea asked.

Cassie shrugged, scrambling fast for a reason. "I don't know. Maybe she's mad that everyone's excited about Josh and Andy? She didn't even get to meet them at the dance."

The answer seemed to satisfy Andrea, who nodded. "She did seem a little annoyed this morning."

"Yep. That's what I mean."

"Okay." Andrea hooked her arm through Cassie's. "I believe you. She's just jealous or something. Let's go to lunch."

Cassie couldn't help seeking Janice out at the lunch table. She saw Janice look their way, take in the way Andrea and Cassie walked in arm and arm. They sat together across from Janice, but Cassie made sure to turn her shoulder to Janice. Cassie pointedly ignored her, laughing and talking with Amity and Maureen and Cara, making plans for the big barbecue with Josh and Andy over the summer.

If that was a hurt expression on Janice's face, Cassie ignored it.

CHAPTER FORTY-TWO
Casting Lots

On Tuesday Cara helped them put up their posters for the StuCo campaign. Cassie followed Andrea, putting her poster up next to hers and not saying a word to Janice, who trailed along behind looking miserable.

"This is a good spot," Cara said, stopping by the cafeteria.

Several posters already cluttered the wall space, but Cara moved them over to make room. She used yellow stuff to get hers to stick, then Andrea and Cassie added theirs.

"Meet me at the bathrooms next," Cara said, walking away.

"My poster won't fit," Janice said. "Can you guys scoot yours over a little more?"

Cassie looked at Andrea and rolled her eyes.

Andrea just shrugged. "You can move them if you want." She started down the hall after Cara, and Cassie followed without hesitation.

"Cassie," Janice said. "Can I talk to you?"

Andrea glanced over her shoulder but didn't stop. Cassie told herself to keep walking, but her heart squeezed with sympathy. She faced Janice, crossing her arms over her chest and trying to look mad.

"What?"

"I'm sorry," Janice said, blinking, her brown eyes bright. "I know why you're mad at me, and I don't know why I said that."

Cassie could've said something nasty, something about how Janice was just jealous because she'd never had a boyfriend, but Cassie wasn't actually angry anymore. "I thought you were the one person who didn't talk about people behind their backs. Now I know you're just like everyone else."

"You're right. I honestly don't know why I did. I promise, I'll never do something like that again." Janice's nose had gotten pinker, and at any moment it looked like she might cry.

"I forgive you," Cassie said, not wanting to see the other girl burst into tears.

"I'm so sorry. Really, I am."

"Forget it," Cassie said. "It was stupid, wasn't it? Not even something to make a big deal about." She meant it, too.

Janice nodded. "I hate the stupid drama. I'm going to stay out of it from now on."

Cassie exhaled as well, relieved not to be in the middle of a disagreement anymore.

⁓⁓※⁓⁓

As Friday and voting day drew nearer, Cassie and Andrea campaigned together, handing out little fliers and sticks of gum with their names taped to the wrapper. Kids smiled at Cassie and called her by name, and she just knew this was her year. She'd finally achieved the social status she'd always wanted.

The voting took place during fourth hour, and at lunch everyone talked about who they voted for.

"You guys, of course," Maureen said.

Amity elbowed Cassie. "Did you vote for Miles?"

The heat crept up Cassie's face, and she forced herself not to react. "Of course. He's my friend."

"I hear he wants to be more than that," Maureen said.

Cassie hadn't told her friends about the heart in her

yearbook. Nor could she tell them how often she'd reread his friendly message and dissected every word, from, "so glad I met you in fifth grade" to "watch out for paper airplanes," looking for hidden meanings. "I don't think so. Besides, I have a boyfriend."

"You almost sound like you regret that," Cara said, giggling.

"What?" Cassie straightened and attempted to look indignant. "No way! I—" *love Josh.* The words died before they left her lips. She didn't love him, and she didn't want to cheapen the word by using it frivolously. "Josh is awesome. I can't wait to see him again!"

"You can like more than one guy," Amity said, taking a bite out of her chicken sandwich without looking at any of them.

That brought laughter and more ribbing from the girls at the table, but a knot of anticipation had formed in Cassie's stomach. She couldn't eat, not when she had to wait until seventh hour to hear the results of the voting.

"Want to come over after school today, Cassie?" Amity asked, jarring Cassie out of her suffocating thoughts.

She caught her breath, and then remembered to act chill when she said, "Sure. I'll text my mom and make sure it's okay."

Cassie tapped her foot impatiently all through her sixth hour social studies class, anxiously awaiting the announcements to turn on and give her an update.

When the intercom buzzed on, her teacher stopped speaking, a bored expression on her face.

"Good afternoon, Cougars!" a girly voice said. "We're so excited to announce for you your student body representatives for next year! We'll start with the ninth graders."

Cassie tuned her out, one foot bouncing restlessly on the linoleum flooring.

"And now for the eighth graders! First the boys."

She bobbed her head when she heard Miles' name, which

was no surprise. Her heart squeezed with anticipation. She clenched her fingers together and bit her lip.

"For the girls, we have Iris Waters, Cara Barnes, Melanie Jacobs, Melissa Farms, and Janice Seidelbacher."

What? Cassie let out all her air in a whoosh, unbelieving. Janice made it but not her? How was this even possible? Janice was slightly overweight and didn't even have a boyfriend! Cassie's hands trembled and her eyes stung. She concentrated hard to keep control of her emotions.

At least Andrea hadn't made it either. She didn't feel quite so alone.

But still, Janice? She practiced smiling, knowing she would have to pretend to be happy for her friends when she saw them again.

"You can spend the night if you want," Amity said as Mrs. Stafford drove them to Amity's house after school.

Cassie peered at Amity, sitting beside her in the back of the car. "Really? I'll ask my mom."

"Yeah. We can go swimming. I have a pool."

"You do?"

"Yes," Mrs. Stafford said from the front. "We have a challenge every summer to see who can get the best tan. I hang out at the pool all summer long, and then Amity comes along in the last week and gets the darkest. Happens every time."

"Cassie would win, though," Amity said. "She's already got such dark skin."

Cassie lifted an arm and studied her skin color, darker than Amity's but still rather pasty. "I get a lot darker in the summer."

"Do you have Native American ancestry, Cassie?" Mrs. Stafford asked.

Cassie got asked this question a lot. "I'm not too sure." She vaguely recalled her mom saying they had Latino blood from somewhere.

"Maureen does," Amity said. "You should find out. Maybe it's the same tribe."

Cassie considered Maureen with her long light brown hair and light eyes. It was hard to imagine her as Native American.

They stepped into the one-level rambler, going through a side door, past the kitchen and music room to a hallway with the other rooms.

"Here's my room," Amity said. She dumped her bag on the bed, and Cassie did the same. "Are you sad you didn't make StuCo?"

Cassie wrinkled her nose. She'd hoped Amity wouldn't bring it up. "It's fine."

"I voted for you. I thought for sure you'd make it."

"Me too," Cassie admitted. "I was surprised Janice made it."

"Everyone likes her, though. She's nice and friendly."

"Aren't I?" Cassie said, feeling wounded.

"Well, yes," Amity said, bobbing her head. "But you used to be really quiet, you know? No one knew who you were. But now we do," she added quickly. "You'll probably make it next year."

She supposed that made sense. But she'd had enough. She wasn't trying again next year.

"Let's get a snack," Amity said, and Cassie followed her back into the kitchen.

"You're eating again, right?" Amity said, pulling a jar of pickles from the fridge.

"Yes," Cassie said, her face burning slightly. "I have been for awhile."

Amity made a meat and pickle sandwich, then handed it to Cassie. "You got really skinny. Like, too skinny."

"I didn't know anyone noticed," Cassie said, accepting the sandwich. She sat at the table and waited for Amity to join her.

"You didn't talk about it and we weren't sure how to help."

The conversation made Cassie think of something, and she

had to speak up. "I didn't teach Andrea how to make herself throw up. She asked me, but I told her no."

Amity sat across from her and took a bite of her sandwich. She gave a shrug. "It's fine. Andrea's weird sometimes, you know? I don't think we're best friends anymore."

Cassie studied Amity and felt a kinship for her she never had before. "I know the feeling. I thought at the beginning of the year that Andrea and I were becoming best friends again, but she's not honest with me. I don't really have a best friend, I guess." Again. As always. Cassie resisted a sigh.

"But you have close friends." Amity got up and poured them both a glass of milk. "That's something, right? You have us."

"Yes. I guess I have five close friends instead of one best friend."

Amity lifted her glass and held it toward Cassie. "To friendship."

Cassie bumped the glass with her own. "Friendship."

Cassie's eyes flew open Tuesday morning. For the first time that she could remember, she was excited to go to school.

Because it was the last day of eighth grade.

She smiled at her reflection while she brushed her teeth. She brushed on some blush and mascara, having become competent enough with make-up to do it herself.

"Who's taking my class again next year?" Ms. Talo asked in fourth-hour English. "All of you, I hope?"

Most hands lifted, including Cassie's.

"Good. Today I want you to pull out a piece of paper and write down all the things you accomplished this year. Give yourself a good pat on the back."

Cassie obliged, tapping her pen on the paper and considering eighth grade. The year had been pretty amazing. She'd finished her book and sent it to a publisher. She was in the select choir. She had a group of good friends, including

Andrea. She had a boyfriend. In a few weeks, her choir was going to New York. And next year, she'd be a ninth grader.

She hummed a little as she detailed her past successes. Next year could only be better.

The table buzzed with anticipatory gossip and summer plans when she sat down at lunch.

"Who's coming to my house today?" Cara asked.

"I can't," Cassie said. "I have another choir practice."

"Always singing, always at choir," Maureen said.

"We're going to New York in two weeks," Cassie said. "We have a lot to prepare for."

"That's so cool," Janice said. She'd been super nice and loyal to Cassie since their disagreement. "I wish I could sing as well as you, Cassie."

"She's dedicated," Cara said. "Whatever Cassie wants to accomplish, she will."

Cassie opened her juice box and kept her eyes on the straw, hoping no one saw how she beamed under the praise. "Oh, hey," she said, lifting her eyes as she remembered. "This Friday is the barbecue. You're all coming, right?"

"Absolutely!" Amity exclaimed. "To see Andy again!"

"And not hit on Josh," Cassie said with a glower.

Amity crossed her heart with her hands. "Of course not."

"I can't wait to meet him," Janice said.

"I'm not sure I'll be there," Cara said. "I'll try, though."

"You have to come!" Cassie exclaimed. "You haven't met him yet!"

"Yeah, or Andy," Amity said.

"You should invite Tyler," Andrea said nonchalantly.

"Andy's enough," Maureen said. "He's so cute."

Cara laughed. "Looks like this is a party I can't miss."

None of the teachers seemed to want to have class any more than the kids did. Mr. Adams let the students write on the board and eat candy all during fifth hour, and Cassie didn't want to go to choir. They wouldn't be doing anything, anyway. She approached his desk right before the bell rang.

"Can I get a note for me and Andrea for seventh hour? And we can just hang out in here?"

"Didn't you spend enough time with her already today?" he asked, eyes twinkling above his gray mustache.

Cassie shrugged. "It's about to be summer and I won't see her every day."

He pulled out a pad of paper and tore off two sheets for her. "Sure."

Cassie looked at the paper. It was a generic, typed message that said, "Please excuse _____ to _____ room for _____." Mr. Adams hadn't filled in the name of the student, just his name and the reason, for end-of-year clean up.

Cassie smiled. She wrote her name in pencil, and then she put Maureen's name on the other. Ms. Berry accepted the notes, and then Cassie carefully erased Maureen's name and wrote Andrea's.

. Together they went and got Andrea, using the same note again, and when that worked, they collected Amity and Cara. The five girls returned to Mr. Adams room, intoxicated with their rebellious ways, giggling and goofing off.

"Shouldn't we go get Janice?" Cara asked. She seated herself at a desk and pulled out a deck of cards from her purse. It was like a magical purse, full of crayons and playing cards and who knew what else.

"You can," Cassie said, sitting down next to Andrea and Amity, watching as they scrolled through photos on their phone. "But you're going to see her after school, right?"

"No. She's not coming over."

Cassie shrugged. "I guess we'll just see her Friday." It felt empowering, in an odd way, to not involve Janice. Like it boosted Cassie onto a level above her.

The other girls didn't even glance up from their activities. If they noticed, they thought nothing of it.

The conversation took a definite turn for the silly as they squealed over pictures and beat each other at cards. And Cassie reveled in her success, imagining how much more important she'd be after this weekend's barbecue.

And maybe, just maybe, she'd get her first kiss.

Available in spring 2019!

Southwest Cougars Year 3: Age 14